W9-BHG-424

PRAISE FOR MEG TILLY AND HER NOVELS

"Tense plotting. . . . A strong installment that hopefully portends more."
—*Booklist*

"This warmhearted romantic comedy delivers a feisty heroine, a sexy hero, and some very chilling suspense—all done with a fresh edge."
—*New York Times* bestselling author Jayne Ann Krentz

"*Solace Island* sparkles with the winning combination of mystery and romance sprinkled with humor and a very sexy hero. What's not to love?"
—*New York Times* bestselling author Mariah Stewart

"Fast-paced and fun, great reading entertainment."
—*New York Times* bestselling author Kat Martin

"With steady pacing and engaging storytelling, Flynn [Tilly] effortlessly blends mystery and romance in a contemporary style that makes this story stand out. This sexy, heartfelt romance is sure to delight readers everywhere."
—RT Book Reviews

"[A] fetching debut . . . a satisfying romance in a cozy, small-town setting."
—*Library Journal* (starred review)

THE
RUNAWAY
HEIRESS

MEG TILLY

JOVE
New York

A JOVE BOOK
Published by Berkley
An imprint of Penguin Random House LLC
penguinrandomhouse.com

Copyright © 2021 by Meg Tilly
Excerpt from *Solace Island* copyright © 2017 by Sara Flynn;
copyright © 2018 by Meg Tilly
Penguin Random House supports copyright. Copyright fuels creativity, encourages
diverse voices, promotes free speech, and creates a vibrant culture. Thank you for buying
an authorized edition of this book and for complying with copyright laws by not
reproducing, scanning, or distributing any part of it in any form without permission.
You are supporting writers and allowing Penguin Random House to continue to
publish books for every reader.

A JOVE BOOK, BERKLEY, and the BERKLEY & B colophon are registered
trademarks of Penguin Random House LLC.

ISBN: 9780593201084

First Edition: July 2021

Printed in the United States of America
1   3   5   7   9   10   8   6   4   2

Book design by George Towne

This is a work of fiction. Names, characters, places, and incidents either are the product
of the author's imagination or are used fictitiously, and any resemblance to actual persons,
living or dead, business establishments, events, or locales is entirely coincidental.

If you purchased this book without a cover, you should be aware that this book is stolen
property. It was reported as "unsold and destroyed" to the publisher, and neither the author
nor the publisher has received any payment for this "stripped book."

To Peggy Feury

June 20, 1924–November 20, 1985
You taught me how to dive into a
character's skin and inhabit their life.
The sharing of your knowledge fundamentally
changed the way I walked in the world,
shifted how I viewed my own actions and words
as well as those of others.
Much love and gratitude always.

PROLOGUE

SARAH SLIPPED OUT THE BACK DOOR OF ROOKIE'S Sports Grill, squinting in the bright sunshine. She rolled her shoulders, more habit than necessity. When she had started the job two weeks ago, by the end of her eight-hour shift, her arms, hands, and shoulders had been shaking with fatigue. *It's remarkable, really, how quickly one can adjust to anything.* And on the heels of that thought, her mind flipped to Kevin and the trapped, suffocating feeling that always accompanied thoughts of him, which caused bile to rise in her throat. Her hand reached out, searching for something solid to hold on to. Her other hand, by habit, rose instinctively to cradle her abdomen before she realized what she was doing and forced it to her side. That loss, in particular, the hollow emptiness almost knocked her to her knees. *Stay in the now,* she ordered herself in an attempt to force back the memories and nightmares that had been visiting her with increasing ferocity. *Be in your body. Where are you now? In the alley behind Rookie's. What do you feel?* Sarah exhaled slowly. What did she feel? *Scared. Scared shitless.*

Not living in the past. Live in the now. Right now. The side of the building under her palm was warm from the sun. Slightly rough, the once white paint, peeling. The front of her jeans were damp and sticky from the mug of root beer a kid in booth three had bowled over. Sarah had managed to snag the thick glass mug on its descent. No easy feat as she'd been taking orders two tables over. Applause had ensued. "I'd say"—Della had called from her post behind the bar—"that you just performed the waitressing equivalent of the triple-Lutz!" Sarah felt her face flush with the memory. Had been doing so well keeping her head down, not drawing attention to herself, and suddenly all eyes had been on her. She had calmed the crying kid with a promise of a free refill, then hurried back to the kitchen, worried about the attention, but grateful, too, that she didn't have to get the vacuum out in the middle of the lunch rush to deal with broken shards of glass.

The screen door swung open. Della came out into the alley. "Hey there," Della said. She fished a half-smoked joint out of the pocket of her faded plaid shirt and lit up. "I thought you'd be long gone. You forget something?" Della was planning to work a double shift again. Brutal hours, but she didn't have a choice. The bank was threatening foreclosure on her house.

"No. I was just daydreaming." Sarah pushed away from the building.

Della nodded, took a long toke, then tipped the joint toward Sarah. "Want a hit?"

Sarah shook her head. "Thanks for the offer though." Even though she didn't smoke, she was touched by the generosity of the gesture. "See you tomorrow," Sarah called over her shoulder as she headed past the sour-smelling dumpster.

"Yup." Della leaned her bony hip against the building, took another long toke, shut her eyes, and tipped her face up to capture the late-afternoon sun. As Sarah turned left out of the back alley onto E. Knoxville street, she could see Della, eyes still shut, exhaling a long, slow stream of smoke into the air.

Sarah walked on. A gray pickup truck rumbled by, but other than that, it was pretty quiet out. It generally was in the little town of Brimfield, Illinois. That was one of the reasons Sarah had decided to stop there. It was a small, sleepy town off the beaten track, and the last place on Earth Kevin would look for her. She crossed her fingers, knowing the act wouldn't dissuade him from attempting to track her down, but it offered comfort nevertheless.

She was sticky, with a stain down her front, and she smelled of root beer. However, she wasn't going to be deterred from her plan. She would slip into the post office on the way to her room at Ma Green's boardinghouse. Hopefully, the promised separation agreement documents from her mom and dad's old attorney and family friend, Phillip Clarke, had arrived. Sarah would then take them to the public library, get them signed, notarized, and mailed back before the post office closed for the night. Once the separation agreement was signed and notarized, the clock would start ticking. And in a year from today she would be free. Free. Kevin would no longer have power over her. Legal or otherwise.

So why was she feeling so jumpy? The taste in her mouth, slightly bitter, acidic. Her gut felt queasy. Perhaps the mayonnaise on the chicken sandwich she had eaten at lunch break was off? *You've got to stop obsessing like this,* she told herself sternly, even though her pulse was racing. *You're probably having an anxiety attack. Kevin's four states away. Most likely he's at the precinct, steamrolling over some unlucky soul.* Sarah turned onto N. Galena Avenue, shaking her arms to try to dispel the tension, and that's when she saw him.

Kevin. Close-cropped hair. Built like a tank. Brutal sledgehammer fists. He was leaning idly against his car, eyes trained on the post office door. A lit cigarette dangled from his fingers.

Kevin. She scrambled backward, desperate to get out of view. *How did he find me?* In her haste, she'd forgotten about the brick pharmacy steps and was airborne for a second before hitting the ground hard. *Phillip must have told Kevin where I am.* Sarah stumbled to her feet, her eyes hot, feeling as if her last tenuous thread to her beloved parents had just been severed. *How could he have betrayed their trust like that? Betrayed mine?* She turned, sudden hot tears streaming down her face as she ran. Ran as fast as she could, her heart pounding loud in her ears, the copper taste of blood in her mouth.

Della was heading into the diner when Sarah burst into the alley, wild-eyed, desperate, jelly-kneed with fear. "Help me," Sarah croaked, her voice barely a whisper. "Please. I need a ride."

1

IT WAS WEDNESDAY, MARCH 10, AND THE SECOND Sarah exited the bare-bones bathroom of the dilapidated motel off Highway 5, she knew she had screwed up royally. "Jade?" she called, knowing it was useless, because it was clear Jade had split. The front door was ajar, and an early-morning breeze whipped into the room, causing the droplets of water from the shower to chill on her skin. She wrapped the towel tighter around her as she crossed the room and closed and locked the door. Small good it would do now. Sarah's legs were feeling wobbly, so she went to the bed and sat. Charlie, her ancient calico cat, hopped onto her lap and started purring. The tenderness of his warm, furry comfort made her want to weep. She didn't. It was a luxury Sarah couldn't afford. She needed to take stock, regroup, and figure out what to do next.

Thank God she had brought her purse into the bathroom with her. Otherwise, her car out front would probably be gone too. The room had been tossed. The thin mattress of the bed had been pushed off the box spring, and the yellow manila envelope that contained Sarah's stash of cash was gone. *How did Jade know where it was?* Sarah had waited until Jade had gone into the bathroom the night before to slip it under her side of the mattress. She figured it would be safer underneath her while she slept than in her purse. The girl must have cracked the bathroom door open and watched, laughing to herself.

Sarah exhaled, shook her head. She should have known better.

Strange how one small random act of kindness could produce such a lousy outcome. As Sarah sat there, her hand on Charlie's vibrating body, her mind was flooded with "if onlys." If only she *hadn't* gotten off that exit ramp to grab a bite at that coffee shop just outside of Portland, Oregon. If only she *had* said yes to that extra cup of coffee. If only it *hadn't* been raining. If only she *had* parked on the other side of the parking lot.

But she hadn't.

Sarah *had* stopped at that particular coffee shop. She had refused the coffee. It had been raining when she had exited the coffee shop, her head tucked into her jacket collar in a feeble attempt to ward off the torrents of rain thundering down. And as she turned left toward her car, she saw in the shadows, out of the corner of her eye, a desperate young woman tugging on the arm of a burly trucker. "Please, Mister, wanna give me a ride?" The man was leering down at her, and Sarah could tell he had nothing but smut on his mind. Sarah had told herself, *Keep walking; not your problem,* but as Sarah passed, she noticed how young the girl was. Too young to be at a truck stop by herself, in the pouring rain, talking to strange men. Couldn't be more than fifteen, sixteen max. Why was she on the road? What was *she* running from?

That was her misstep. She had seen the ghost of herself rather than the young woman for who she was. Sarah's first instinct was correct. Jade was trouble. Sarah should have kept walking, but instead, the girl ended up riding shotgun, filling the interior of Sarah's car with the smell of unwashed body, malodourous BO, and Wrigley's spearmint gum. And

Sarah found herself headed to Santa Monica, California, because Jade had said her folks lived there.

"No good deed . . ." Sarah murmured to herself. "You're such a patsy." She closed her eyes for a moment, gathering herself. Then she opened her purse, took out her wallet, and rifled through the contents. *Great* . . . She had to shut her eyes again, exhaling slowly. Once she'd dropped Jade off, Sarah had planned to head back toward Northern California to find another sleepy town off the beaten track that she could disappear into. That was no longer an option. She was in LA, and that's where she would have to stay, with only half a tank of gas, a cat, and $136 to her name.

2

MICK TALFORD SAT AT THE BACK OF THE THEATER feeling slightly numb as the final credits for *Retribution* rolled. The usually stuffy and sedate crowd at the Directors Academy were on their feet, stamping and cheering, whistles piercing the air. Holy shit. Another hit. He felt a light tap on his shoulder. Turned. A young woman from the studio's publicity department whispered discreetly in his ear, "If you'd follow me, sir." He staggered to his feet, feeling slightly dazed. How the hell did he keep churning out these hits? And the next thought was, how long before it all crashes down? Because it would. This was Hollywood after all. Nothing they liked better than kingmaking, raising some poor schmuck up, and then, once he felt invincible, the bloodletting and public disemboweling would begin.

Mick followed the publicist in her gray suit, who murmured into her mouthpiece, "I've got Talford. Heading your way." They ducked through the thick velvet curtain at the back. A male publicist was waiting by a door with a big grin on his face. "Fantastic movie, sir. Great job!" He saluted Mick as he opened the door, then stood at attention, his skinny chest puffed out as if Mick were a five-star general. Mick nodded his thanks as they hurried by, his mouth dry. He hated the aftermath of movie screenings, having to go on a stage, try to sound intelligent, answer idiotic questions. The door closed behind them, and for a split second he was tempted to stay there, in that dark corridor that would lead to the backstage of the theater. Better yet, he glanced at the red glowing emergency exit sign. He could sneak out now, go to Musso and Frank Grill, sit in a booth in the back, have a glass of wine, slather their delicious sourdough bread with butter, and dig into a chicken pot pie.

Mick trailed his fingertips along the metal push bar on the door as they passed the exit, longing to run.

"Watch your step here, Mr. Talford," the fresh-faced publicist said helpfully. As if he were a doddering old man. He didn't blame her. Lately, the weight of his thirty-eight years seemed to lie heavier than usual around his shoulders. Mick ascended the stairs and stepped into the wings, where his producer, Paul Peterson, was waiting for him. "Heeeeeey, my man," Peterson drawled. He did a weird sort of shimmy, jutting out his lower jaw as if he'd grown up rough, was a guy-from-the-hood. Nothing could be further from the truth. He was a middle-aged man who had grown up in a goddamned mansion in Bel Air. Peterson yanked Mick into a bear hug, thumped him on the back. "You did it again! Knocked it out of the park! What did I tell you? We got a hit! A monsterfucking hit! Listen to them out there. They love us! They're gonna come back to see this movie again and again and tell all their friends. And we're gonna get even richer!" Peterson chortled gleefully, rubbing his hands together. "Best thing I ever did was hooking my wagon to you. You're a fucking genius. A money-making machine, and I love it. Love being rich, rich, rich!" Peterson was right. The two of them had made money by the truckload, with more rolling in every day. "Listen to that," Peterson said, cupping a hand around his ear. "Music to my ears." The audience hadn't quieted down as they usually did once the lights went up. If anything, the noise level had grown since Mick had exited his seat. Had gotten louder and louder as the crowd continued to roar their approval. It should have exhilarated him, but no. All Mick felt was slightly depressed as he watched Peterson dance around backstage like a gleeful, bald-headed elf high-fiving anyone within arm's distance.

The president of the Academy was onstage, introducing them now.

"After this," Peterson said, puffing his chest proudly, "we, my friend, are going to do some serious partying." He opened his arms expansively, as if he were riding in the lead car of a ticker-tape parade. "And not to worry, I've set up everything! One hundred percent paid for! The entire tab is on me!"

Partying was the last thing Mick was in the mood for, but Peterson was so happy, looked so pleased with himself, that Mick slapped an answering smile on his face. "Sounds great."

"Great?" Peterson squeaked, eyes bulging. "Are you kidding? What I have planned is going to blow your socks off!" Peterson leaned in with a grin and wiggled his bushy eyebrows. "Literally . . ."

Mick stifled a groan, hoping he had read Peterson's innuendo incorrectly. A slight headache was taking up residence behind his eyes. He was contemplating the relief of begging off with the weight of guilt he would feel for raining on Peterson's parade.

"And now, the moment you have been waiting for . . . Mick Talford and his producer, Paul Peterson." The Academy president gestured to the wings, where they were waiting.

"It's showtime," Peterson said, slinging a sweaty arm companionably around Mick's shoulders. "Let's go do the old razzle-dazzle, my friend."

Mick took a breath, as if about to plunge into an ice-cold pond, donned the bad-boy Mick Talford swagger and attitude that felt like an ill-fitting suit, and then strode out into the bright lights and onto the stage.

3

"RACHEL . . ." THE WOMAN AT THE EMPLOYMENT agency glanced down at the form on her clipboard. "Jones?"

Sarah got to her feet. "Yes," she said. "That would be me."

"I'm Ellen Davis. This way, please."

Sarah followed the woman into her office, mouth dry.

Ms. Davis flipped to the next page on her clipboard. Sarah could see over her shoulder that the woman was now reading the fake CV and reference letters Sarah had typed and printed at the public library that morning.

"Have a seat." Ms. Davis gestured to a chair in front of her desk as she rounded it and sat down.

As Sarah sat, she surreptitiously slid her palms down along her thighs so the black dress pants could erase the slight dampness before clasping her hands in her lap.

The woman flipped to the last page, scanned it, then placed the clipboard on the desk in front of her. "Everything seems in order," she said. "Your scores on the technical skills test were quite impressive. I don't foresee a problem getting you placed. What sort of hours are you interested in working?"

"I'm pretty flexible. And it doesn't have to be office work. Basically, I'll take whatever job you have available."

"Nights? Weekends? Long hours okay?"

"Sure."

"Huh . . . Interesting. Actually—" Ms. Davis's fingers rapped a quick staccato on the desk as if she were playing descending scales on the piano.

"But I'm not interested in stripping or escort work or anything like that," Sarah hastily added. This was Hollywood after all. Best to make sure the woman hadn't gotten the wrong idea.

Ms. Davis didn't look up, her fingers flying over her keyboard. "Of course. Not to worry. We don't handle that kind of 'work placement.'" Then she swiveled slightly in her chair, eyes narrowing as she leaned forward, focused on her computer screen. "Ah! Here we go." A huff of air that could have been laughter escaped her lips. "Well . . . it's worth a try," she murmured. "Lord knows, he's burned his way through all my other options." Her birdlike gaze moved away from the screen to settle on Sarah's face, taking in the dark-rimmed glasses. Luckily, the woman's perusal didn't linger on the mousy brown hair Sarah had re-dyed in the bathroom sink of the motel room last night.

Sarah looked back, keeping her expression a blank, calm canvas, a polite smile on her face, determined not to let her nerves peek through.

"Plain. Practical. No-nonsense. Might be just what the doctor ordered." Ms. Davis nodded as her gaze traveled down the conservative cream blouse Sarah had steamed in the shower. She took in the black slacks, the sensible black pumps; then her gaze slid back up to Sarah's face. "This position requires gumption, backbone, plenty of grit. No running for the hills just because the client has a few rough edges."

"No, ma'am." Sarah forced her hands to lie still in her lap. "I understand."

The woman's fingers rapped on the desk again. "Most of the specifications fit." Her unblinking eyes narrowed to a laser-like focus. Suddenly she shrugged and then relaxed in her chair. "The job pays twenty-four dollars an hour. It's live-in. Is that a problem?"

A problem? A heaven-sent gift from God was more like it. Sarah's mind flashed to handing over her last hundred-dollar bill to pay for the motel last night. The eleven o'clock checkout meant returning to the motel after her visit to the library and packing all her belongings in the trunk of her car. She would have preferred for Charlie to have the run of the motel room, as he was not a fan of car travel. It wasn't ideal, but she'd had to leave him in the car with the windows cracked open during this interview, yowling in his carrier bag as if he were being murdered. Didn't have enough to cover another night, $56.95 to her name. "Live-in is fine. Preferable, actually."

"Wonderful. When can you start?"

Sarah released the breath she'd been holding. "Whenever," she said, as if she wasn't in dire financial straits and planning on sleeping in her car tonight. "I could start today if you like?"

"Even better." Ms. Davis scribbled something on a slip of paper. "Here's the name and address. Mick Talford. Hopefully, Rachel, you'll last longer than the previous assistants I've sent."

Rachel? For a split second Sarah's mind blanked. *Oh yes! Rachel.*

"I'll do my best." Sarah smiled in a reassuring manner even though her heart had skipped a beat.

Ms. Davis stood, rounded the desk, and handed the paper to Sarah. "The client is a talented director. Good luck," she said, shaking Sarah's hand. "You'll need it."

4

MICK DUMPED TWO ADVIL INTO HIS HAND, SWAL-
lowed them dry. Leaned against the bathroom counter and
stared into the mirror. He looked like shit. All work and no
play. Hell, he couldn't even remember what "play" was anymore. He could hear the sounds of Peterson's party through
the closed door. So many people, overflowing his living
room, his kitchen, the gardens, swarming the place like
cockroaches. The bacchanalian revels had been going strong
for seventeen hours, and no one was showing any signs of
leaving. When people got tired, they'd sleep on the spot, or
stumble into one of his spare bedrooms, or pass out on a
chair, a sofa, or one of the loungers by the pool. A few had
been sprawled out on the lawn until the early-morning sprin-
klers had awoken them. Luckily, his bedroom was vacant.
When the partying hordes had arrived, he'd taken the pre-
caution and locked his bedroom, both from the hall and the
door leading in from the garden. He hadn't done that the first
time Peterson and his mob of sycophants had taken over his
house. He'd ended up needing to purchase a new bed and
bedding. Mick glanced at the clock. Three thirty p.m. Mick

had hoped against hope that when morning arrived everyone would disperse, but they hadn't. As long as Peterson's store of booze and gigantic serving bowl of cocaine remained, Mick would have an impossible time clearing his house of unwanted guests. Couldn't throw them out, as he had a reputation to maintain. The "Wildman," the "rebel from the wrong side of the tracks, who burned bright and lived hard." It was exhausting keeping up the facade.

He heard his bedroom door open. The high-pitched sound of inebriated giggling. Shit. Had forgotten to relock the bedroom door behind him. He scrubbed his hands across his face.

"Yoo-hoo . . . Where are you, Mick?" More giggles.

"We playing hide-and-seek?"

Damn. Clearly there was more than one woman needing removal from his sanctuary. Great. If Mick had to guess, it was probably a couple of the hookers Peterson had sicced on him the moment the Mercedes van spewed the gaggle of working girls onto his driveway.

He straightened, exhaled, and exited the bathroom.

"Hey! Here's the man of the hour," squealed a peroxide blonde who was wearing a sheer tank top, a skintight, aqua leather mini, and clear platform shoes with a goldfish swimming inside. "What luck! And me, all hot and bothered and ready to party." She flung herself onto his bed. Her braless double-Ds remained pointing skyward, a clear indication that a surgeon was responsible for her bountiful breasts. She struck a pose that would have had any normal red-blooded man's tool leaping to attention. What she didn't realize was that type of porn star sexuality always worked as a highly efficient cock-blocker for Mick. The blonde shifted her body, her long legs rubbing against each other like a cat in heat, before she let them spread, as she licked her pouty lower lip.

Ah. The old no-undies maneuver. He glanced away.

Her redheaded companion trailed her hand along the top of Mick's dresser. "We're no-limitations kind of gals," purred the redhead. "If you know what I mean." She was being flirtatious, but he could see the hard edges and bitterness lurking behind her smile. Her years were well masked but starting to show. He hoped she had saved, had a backup plan. So many working girls squandered whatever they earned, as if investing or saving the cash would affix the memory of the earning into their psyche.

"Thank you, ladies, but I'm going to have to decline your kind offer."

"Why? What's the problem?" The blonde sat up, her eyes slightly unfocused from booze or drugs. "I can cure limp dick like nobody's business."

"Nothing to be embarrassed about. Seriously. It's no big deal for pros like us," the redhead chimed in, sashaying toward him, her hips undulating, sliding her arms around his neck like a noose. "See, we've been watching ever since we got here. You haven't hooked up with anyone yet. Peterson's worried. And when Peterson's not pleased, the bonuses are less hefty. So . . ."

Mick disengaged her arms from his neck, holding his breath to avoid breathing in the smell of heavy perfume, lipstick, and sweat. "Again. Thank you for your generous offer." He stepped back. "However, I'm going to have to ask you ladies to vacate my bedroom. There are plenty of people who would appreciate your talents. I suggest you—"

The redhead's eyes narrowed. "Be that way. We were prepared to play nice, Mick, but you've screwed the pooch now." She lifted her fingers to her mouth and emitted an earsplitting whistle. The door burst open. Peterson marched into the room in his birthday suit, holding a purloined sunflower from Mick's garden over his head like a baton twirler at the head of a parade. Mick shut his eyes, wishing he could eradicate the image of Pete's tiny mushroom-sized dick bobbing around. No luck. Peterson bopped him on the head with the sunflower, as if he were a king dubbing a knight, and the gang of naked, dripping-wet revelers that had swarmed into the room grabbed Mick and hoisted him over their shoulders like a human sacrifice. They carted Mick out of his bedroom, through the hall, into the living room, and through the double doors, straight into the garden and heading for the pool.

"Peterson," Mick growled through clenched teeth. "This is not funny. If you value your life, you will—"

"It's for your own good, Mick, my man. You've lost your joie de vivre." Peterson was red-faced and roaring with laughter. "Off with his clothes!" At first Mick attempted to free himself, but the drunken, grinning lunatics were crowding in close, clutching at him, pinning him, ripping at his shirt, his pants. Mick made an executive decision. It wasn't worth injuring anybody and enduring a lawsuit. Out of the corner of his eye, he could see Peterson proudly overseeing. Waving that damned sunflower as if he were conducting a symphony at Carnegie Hall. "Into the pool! Into the pool! It's time for a celebratory swim!" Peterson sang.

"Peterson. Don't even—" Mick was hoisted in the air. "For Chrissake—the water in the pool looks like a fucking swamp—"

"Aaaand . . . a one . . . two . . . three!" Mick felt the hands release their grasp on his ankles and wrists. As he soared through the air, he sucked in oxygen and braced himself for the smack when his body made contact with the surface of the sludgy green-tinged water. Down, down he sank. Then, once submerged, it was almost peaceful. The water muted the noise above him. He could see more bodies hit the water. Lack of apparel seemed to be the common theme. For a moment, he wished he had gills so he could stay in the relative quiet, swim around on the bottom of the pool until everyone went home.

When he finally surfaced, climbed out of the pool, and shook the water from his eyes, the crowd had moved on to new entertainments. A threesome was taking place in the lower garden and apparently welcomed an audience. He glanced around for his clothes. Found them scattered like water lilies on the pool's surface, sinking slowly downward. He would gather them later. Mick sloshed along the Spanish tiles around the pool's edge to the bathhouse, water streaming down his body. He wasn't too hopeful, but it was worth a try. Yep. The stack of towels that had filled the bathhouse linen cupboard when he'd purchased the place had been depleted. When or by whom? He had no idea. Mick sighed.

A couple ensconced on a lounge chair glanced over as Mick strode by. "Hey, Mick," the guy said, giving him a thumbs-up. "Loved *Retribution*, and this party is fire." The guy's girlfriend had multiple body piercings and a tattoo sleeve. Her gaze trailed the expanse of Mick's naked body. "Yeah," she cooed, her eyes turning sultry. "Real fine . . ." Making it clear that if Mick crooked his little finger, she'd come running.

There was a time when a party like this would have rocked Mick's boat. Women looking him over would have caused his chest to swell just a little and his ego to expand. Not anymore. Weirdly, it made him feel a deep-seated melancholy, a sense of isolation, as if people with a moral compass were a myth. Decency and human kindness were a fairy tale made up as a bedtime story to lull innocent gullible children into thinking the world was a good and wonderful place.

He entered from the garden through the kitchen door. *Ding dong . . . Ding dong . . .* The doorbell was ringing. *Ding dong . . .* Nobody was answering it. *Ding dong . . . Ding dong . . .*

He strode down the hall and pulled the door open. "If you're here for Peterson, he's out back in the garden." Mick stepped aside to let her pass.

However, the prim Mary Poppins creature that was perched on the doorstep just blinked at him. Her mousy brown hair was scraped severely back from her face and corralled in a tight knot at the back of her head. Thick-framed glasses stood in stark relief against the creamy paleness of her complexion. Her eyes, wide behind the charcoal frames. She had surprisingly long, lush lashes. Her uniform, for that was all one could call it, was boring. Conservative. Black slacks, neat cream blouse, sensible footwear. Must be one of those evangelical types banging on doors trying to save the world and selling unsuspecting fools a promise of heaven. Either that or it was a costume and she'd been hired to strip. "The Peterson party is out back," he repeated.

Her gaze slid downward, then abruptly jerked up to lock on to his eyes. A flush rose upward from her neck, suffusing her face with color.

Not a stripper. The blush made that obvious. She must be there to try to convert him. Belatedly, he realized he was sans apparel. He felt the corners of his mouth twitch upward. How many times had he been deep in the work only to be disturbed by some uninvited do-gooder trying to help him find salvation, or someone fundraising, or political canvassing. Didn't matter how often, or politely, he would inform them he was not interested. Every month or so someone else would ring his doorbell. *This will teach 'em to knock willy-nilly, uninvited, on a stranger's door.* He nonchalantly stretched and leaned against the doorframe as if he always strode around nude. It was difficult, but he managed to suppress his laughter. *Wish I'd thought of this sooner. Maybe answering the door naked will get me put on a do-not-disturb list.*

5

HE WAS NAKED. THE MAN—WHO SUPPOSEDLY WAS her new employer—had answered the door unshaven, stark naked, dripping wet, and hung like a bull. Not that the size of his appendage had any bearing on the matter. *Why the hell did you look down?* Sarah squeezed her eyes shut, could feel the heat in her face. She had two choices. She could turn around, get in her car, and start the long drive down Mulholland Drive with the desperate hope that she could land another position before night fell. Or she could take this job, which would mean a place for her and Charlie to sleep and hot water. That would mean putting up with this jerk for a week or two while she replenished her cash stores. Whereas sleeping in her car, who knew what sort of assholes she'd run into? Lord knew, she seemed to have a talent for running into more than her fair share.

Sarah took a second to center herself, unclenched her fists, then opened her eyes. "Mick Talford, I presume?" she said, smiling blandly, keeping her gaze and her chin up. "I'm Rachel Jones from the Windham Employment Agency, your new assistant."

He blinked, the cocky grin vanishing from his face. "My assistant?" He scowled. Music and the sound of the party were blasting past him, spilling through the doorway to envelop her like a hot desert wind.

"I was told this was a live-in position." She could smell the fragrance wafting up from the huge vase of white trumpet lilies that was sitting on the front doorstep. As she'd approached the mansion, she had noticed flowers with the small envelope with *Mick Talford* scrawled in gold cursive nestled among the blooms. Before ringing the doorbell, Sarah had bent over and inhaled deeply, savoring their scent as she let memories of a happier time wash over her. Her mother had always placed a vase of fresh lilies in the entryway. At the thought of her mother, the longing and loss stiffened Sarah's spine. "If you would please direct me to my quarters so I can settle in? Once you've made yourself presentable, I'd be happy to meet with you and discuss what my duties will be."

"I'm sorry. The agency made a mistake. I requested a male." His voice was flat. Dismissive. As if life were always that easy. As if he were choosing between a pair of shoes. He started to shut the door. She should have let him, the chauvinist pig. No one in their right mind would want to work for this dickhead. But instead of letting logic have its way, anger had her jamming her body into the doorway. Making it impossible for him to close the door, unless he was prepared to knock her off her feet. "Well, too bad." She reached out and snagged her suitcase in case the madman decided to pitch it into the flora and fauna. "You got me."

"It's not up for discussion. This is a bachelor's residence. I'm not going to pussyfoot around my own home to avoid offending your 'womanly sensibilities.' Furthermore"—he slid his gaze down her body and then back up again, the expression on his face one of distaste, as if he'd found her lacking—"quite honestly, I don't need the distraction."

Sarah's hand itched to fly out and smack that condescending look off his face.

"Hey, Mick?" A redheaded woman poked her head out of a doorway down the hall. "You enjoy your dip?"

A platinum-blonde head appeared over the redhead's shoulder. "You're all wet, and we're lonely." The blonde made a moue with her mouth.

"Look, Mr. Talford," Sarah said, using the tone of someone speaking to a not-very-bright five-year-old. "There's Tweedledee and Tweedledum. Female, from the looks of it." She smiled at him brightly. "So, that makes mincemeat of your paltry objection to anyone of the female persuasion gracing these hallowed halls."

The weary air of boredom vanished from his face. His gaze narrowed at the challenge in her voice. She thought she saw a flash of something in his eyes, maybe laughter? Too fleeting to know, because it was gone and he was leaping into the air, his head thrown back as he roared, teeth bared, causing Sarah to jump slightly. *What the hell? Who does that?* she thought, more than a little annoyed that he had managed to startle her. But apparently, he wasn't finished with his little display. When Talford's feet hit the ground, he started pounding them on the floor as if he were a Samoan readying himself for battle. His fists thumped hard against his bare chest, as if it were a drum. The man was still roaring. Of course. She rolled her eyes and kept a slightly bored expression pasted on her face. Although, with his wild mane of wet hair, he did look rather impressive in a messed-up way. Sort of like a lion daring the sun to rise. His penis thwacking from side to side.

Sarah felt an unexpected urge to laugh bubbling up, but she stuffed it down. Didn't want him to think she was condoning this type of disreputable behavior. She had a feeling he was hoping she would shriek in maidenly vapors and scamper to her car as if the demons of hell were snapping at her heels. The two women's heads in the doorway had vanished fast enough.

"Yeah. I get it," Sarah said, keeping her voice dry as unbuttered toast. "You've got a penis. Eek." She threw up her hands, then dropped them, and leaned in as if divulging a confidential secret. "Hate to break it to you, buddy, but so does forty-nine point two percent of the population."

Instead of getting pissed off at her smart mouth, the contrary man grinned at her as if she had pleased him mightily. Laughter sparkled like flecks of gold in his amber eyes. Jerk. She straightened and took a firm grip on the handle of her suitcase. "Now, if you would please direct me to my room, it would be much appreciated."

6

"I'M SORRY. HER FACE DOESN'T RING A BELL." THE woman, Zelia Thompson-Conaghan, gathered the photos of Sarah that he had given her, slipped them into the eight-by-ten manila envelope, and handed the packet back to him. "Wish I could be more help." It was only then that she looked at him. The expression on her face was pleasant, but she didn't fool him. Not one bit.

"That's interesting," Kevin Hawkins replied, keeping a tight rein on his temper, because unfortunately, the woman's husband, Gabriel Conaghan, had chosen to sit in on the interview. The man was a very well-known crime fiction author and had friends in high places. It wouldn't be wise to piss him off. "You see, the nurse I interviewed at the hospital was certain that the woman you knew as Mary Browning—who was in your employ for several years— was the exact same woman in these pictures." He removed the photo he'd taken of Sarah on the beach, smiling at the camera, back when they were happy, back before he knew she was a lying, two-faced bitch.

He trailed his finger along her face in the photograph,

across her throat, which he'd occasionally wrap his hands around, to remind her who was in charge, to watch the fear rise in her eyes. Sometimes he'd leave it at that, back off with a laugh. But when the occasion warranted more extreme measures, he would tighten his grip around her long, slender throat tighter and tighter until she lost consciousness.

He turned the photo to face the owner of Art Expressions Gallery. He purposefully held the photo a little too close to Zelia Thompson-Conaghan, moving his energy into her force field, causing her to take a half step back.

"I'm sorry," the woman repeated firmly, crossing her arms, chin lifting defiantly. "I can see how at first glance someone could make that mistake, but the woman in this photo has sleek, straight blond hair. My employee had frizzy, light brown." Something in the woman's tone had caused her husband to cross the room and stand beside her. "You mentioned this woman you are seeking—"

"My wife."

"Yes. Your wife. She had beautiful blue eyes. I'm sorry to be the bearer of disappointing news, but Mary's eyes were brown."

"Brown?"

She nodded. "Yes, a nondescript brown really. Nothing special. You mentioned your wife was five eight? Even in heels, Mary was shorter than me. I doubt she was more than five three, five four tops."

Stupid bitch. Clearly it was time to lean a little harder. "Then why"—he thrust his face into hers—"did you state in the missing person report you filed with the Solace Island Police that she was five seven to five eight and her eyes were blue?"

"Back off, asshole." Gabriel Conaghan was in front of the gallery owner now, grim, determined. So much for not pissing him off. Oh well, in for a penny.

Kevin knocked the man's hand from his chest. "You mean Lieutenant of the New York Police Department, 19th precinct." His eyes were now locked with the man's, but he could hear the woman's sharp intake of breath. "And I would suggest you don't lay hands on me again or I will have you arrested for assaulting a police officer so fast you won't know what hit you." He paused for a second to make sure his point was taken. "Now," he said, shifting his weight to his left leg so the woman was back in his line of vision. He was pleased to see that her body had stiffened and the color had drained from her face. "Why don't we start again?"

7

"I DID IT!" SARAH SAID, DISENGAGING HER DISGRUN-
tled cat from his carrier and giving him a celebratory hug.
"I brazened my way past that madman director and got us
a place to stay. And, oh my, what a place. Can you believe
this?" She turned Charlie's body so he was facing outward
and could take in the glorious accommodations of their
residence above the garage. "It's not just a room, Charlie.
It's an entire apartment. See, we've got a little living room
slash dining room area, and through here a cozy kitchen
looking out over the garden. Now, I bet you're thinking
that's it, but you'd be wrong, my furry friend. It just could
be that that conniving little ingrate, Jade, unwittingly did us
a favor, because behind door number one is . . . this lovely
large bedroom with en suite!" She couldn't help but do a
couple of happy dance steps. "You know, this Mick guy
could be Beelzebub, Charlie, so what? I'm not scared. Been
harassed by the best. Hell, that madman on Solace Island
could give the devil himself a few lessons, and my ex was
certainly no walk in the park." She snuggled Charlie in
close, giving him a gentle scratch behind the ears. "You've

never met Kevin." She suppressed a shiver. "Let's keep it that way."

She longed to sink onto the bed, stretch out, see if it was as comfortable as it looked, with its plump abundance of fluffy pillows and soft duvet. An afternoon nap would be divine.

Ah well. The daydream was almost as satisfying as actually getting to indulge.

"However," she told Charlie, "just because I have to work, there's no reason you can't enjoy the creature comforts in my stead." She plopped her cat on the gorgeous duvet. He glared at her indignantly, stalked to the side of the bed, leaped down, and strode out the bedroom door, tail lashing.

"Okay, you aren't sleepy. That's your prerogative." She followed him into the living room, where he was winding his body around the fabric grocery bag that contained the last of his food. Tight finances had forced Sarah to switch to dry kibble while they were on the road. Charlie was not pleased. Had refused food for the first two days, but finally hunger had gotten the best of him.

She took out his bowls, got him water and a small handful of food. While he scarfed it down, she filled his litter box, placed it in the bathroom beside the pedestal sink. Then she washed her hands and face. As she was smoothing her hair, her burner phone pinged. She glanced at the screen. "The big boss man wants to see me," she informed Charlie. "Wish me luck." She slipped out the front door and locked it behind her.

In the last hour, a steady stream of people had spilled out of the main residence and tumbled into their cars. Based on the noise level, the almost manic laughter, and the unsteady gaits, many had no business being behind the wheel of a motor vehicle. Hopefully, there were designated drivers in their midst.

As she headed down the stairs at the side of the building, she noticed that the circular drive and the long driveway leading to the road was relatively empty now. When she had driven up earlier, it had been packed cheek to jowl with high-priced vehicles. As she stepped onto the driveway, a solitary holdout, a silver Jaguar convertible, roared to life. She recognized Mr. Talford's playmates, the redhead and the blonde, who had both squeezed into the front passenger's seat. They apparently had forgotten all about Talford. Seemed to be enamored with the diminutive, round-bellied, bald man behind the wheel. The car's tires squealed as it tore down the drive, the breeze making the women's hair flow behind them like in a cheesy shampoo commercial. The vehicle screeched to a halt a few moments later to wait for the automatic gates to swing open. Clearly the astronomical prices at the gas pump weren't a concern for this trio. Once the gates were open, the car sped through and disappeared from sight.

Sarah crossed the circular drive, climbed the two low steps to stand once again at the front door. She closed her eyes, took a deep, calming breath, centering herself for what lay ahead.

"Come on in. Door's unlocked," Beelzebub's voice crackled over the intercom speaker, making her jump. "Nervous much?" His disembodied voice sounded faintly amused. Sarah set her shoulders, glanced up, and saw the discreet camera overhead, trained on the doorstep. "Yep. That's right. You're on *Candid Camera*." She was tempted to give him the finger but managed, just barely, to restrain herself.

8

AFTER MICK HAD SENT THE LAST OF THE REVELERS on their way, he'd opened all the windows and the patio doors, windmilling his arms in an attempt to disperse the smell of booze, drugs, and most importantly, the suffocating cling of the working girls' perfume. Didn't matter what perfume they used. Vanilla. Floral. Musk. To him, all hookers smelled the same. Smelled of home and claustrophobia. Made him feel sweaty, as if he might suddenly wake and find himself trapped in that old life again.

The place had been called Frank's Chicken Ranch. When Mick was six, his grandpa turned up his toes, and his grandma Flo renamed it the Desert Rose Ranch. She'd sprung for a giant disco ball and some new carpet in the parlor. Drove into town and went wild at Michaels. Bought a shitload of vases, a glue gun, bedazzled the hell out of them. Stuck the vases all over the place, stuffed full of various arrangements of plastic flowers and greenery. Then she typed a new menu of services, the new prices reflecting the "upgrade in decor." Didn't matter how many vases his grandma wanted to bedazzle, the place would always be a bunch of double-wide trailers hoisted up on a concrete foundation out in the middle of the dusty Nevada desert.

Mick's mom, Judy, had been gone more often than not. But when times were tough, she'd come scratching on the back door, needing food and a place to stay. She wasn't a hooker, per se, but she wasn't averse to spreading her legs if money was low. She had no idea who Mick's father was. Or if she did, she wasn't talking.

Mick tugged his mind back to the present. It was a waste of time and energy to wallow in the past. Running around dirty-faced and barefoot among the tumbleweeds attempting to avoid rattlesnakes of both the reptilian and human kind, with a constant hunger residing in his belly. That was a distant memory. A dream. He was grown now. Mick Talford. Auteur filmmaker, a creative force to be reckoned with and rich beyond his wildest dreams. The mere act of sitting behind his mahogany desk in his wood-paneled study made him feel better, back in control. He was dressed. Thank God. Peterson and Co. had been flushed out of his abode. He would now be able to properly focus and send the mock Mennonite on her merry way. Once that was accomplished, he was going to take a long, hot shower, go to bed, and sink into deep, blessed slumber.

He heard the front door open and shut, her footsteps, hesitant, in the hall. An unexpected feeling of anticipation coursed through him, a heightening of his senses. Weird. Must be lack of sleep muddling his thoughts.

"Mr. Talford?"

"In here," he called, settling back into his chair. She appeared in the doorway. He gestured toward the chair in front of his desk. "Have a seat."

She sat. The sunshine caused her to squint slightly behind the thick frames of her glasses and highlighted the smooth, creamy luminescence of her skin.

"Right," he said briskly, pulling his focus back to the business at hand. "Remind me your name? I was a trifle preoccupied when you first showed up."

There was a barely discernible hesitation before she opened her lush, unadorned lips. "Rachel Jones," she said.

His bullshit detector pinged, but about what? The director in him was slightly intrigued, but he shoved it aside. The hesitation was likely caused by her memory of him standing in the doorway stark naked. If not, what did he care? His objective wasn't to understand the inner workings of her mind. He wanted this woman to make the sensible decision and recuse herself from working for him with no pesky bleating about sexual discrimination. A simple "we were incompatible" verbal agreement would suffice. They would shake hands, and she'd trot back to the employment agency and find another job.

"So, you want to work for me. Why?" Mick had the sense he had seen her before. Was she a wannabe actress? Had she auditioned for him?

"I need the job." The timbre of her voice surprised him. She gave off a cool, contained "look, but don't touch vibe." Prim. Classy. Her vocabulary and manner were that of an intellectual elite. And then there was that voice—husky, almost raw-sounding—that conjured forth images of hot sex, silk sheets, good whiskey, with a drizzle of honey. He hadn't paid attention to her voice before, had been distracted. But now? He could bathe in it. Yeah, with that voice, that face and killer bod, she had to be an actress. Kudos to her. It was a pretty novel ploy to get his attention. Dressing up like a librarian, applying to be his assistant. "I don't see what is so funny about my desire for work." There was a bite to her voice. He could see her back stiffen.

"I didn't say it was funny."

"You laughed."

"Barely." Might as well call her on it. "You an actress?"

"God no," she said with distain, as if he'd asked if she worked weekends walking the Strip. Huh. So, she wasn't an actress. A reporter, perhaps. Trying to get the inside scoop? She was glaring at him, which somehow made him feel rather happy. She wasn't the kowtowing sort. He wouldn't get "Yes, Mr. Talford. No, Mr. Talford. Whatever you say,

Mr. Talford" from her. Which had gotten pretty damned boring.

"A reporter, then. Who do you work for?"

"No. One. That's why. I'm here," she said pointedly.

He leaned back in his chair, looked at her for a long moment. "You can cut the bullshit," he said, breaking the silence. "I'm not buying it. I've seen you before." He tapped his forefinger to his temple. "I'm absolute crap with names, but I never forget a face."

She leaned forward, pretty little teeth bared, opened her mouth as if about to spit some insult out.

"Yes," he drawled, hoping he could nudge whatever acidic comment was hovering on the precipice of her lips to tip over into his waiting hands. She was entertaining in a Meyer lemon way. He didn't want to drink a cup of the juice, but biting into a wedge could be rather refreshing. However, he'd overplayed his hand, because instead of gracing him with some tart rejoinder, she snapped her mouth shut. Closed her eyes briefly. When she reopened them, all irritation had been erased from her face. Her fists had unclenched and were now resting peacefully in her lap. "You were about to say?" he inquired, hoping against hope.

NICE TRY, BUDDY BOY, SARAH THOUGHT, *BUT I'M not going to bite.* "Not important." She smiled blandly at him. "For the record, I've never met you." *Actually, never heard of you before this morning. So sorry if that hurts* your *delicate sensibilities, but there you have it.* It pleased her to toss his phrase back at him, even if it was only in her mind. "I'm not an actress or a reporter looking for a scoop," she continued, as if she possessed a placid, peaceful disposition. "The only thing I want from you is a paycheck. To be fairly compensated for the hours I put in. Now, if you would please tell me what my duties will be, I can get started."

"As I stated when you arrived on my doorstep, I want a male assistant."

Well, that's too damn bad. Welcome to the twenty-first century. "You can't not hire me on the basis of my sex, at least not in the great state of California," she informed him sweetly. If he did, that would be classified as sexual discrimination. Which she was sure was a can of worms he'd rather not open. The expression on his face was hilarious. She could see him grinding his teeth. *That's right. Think of the negative publicity.* Sarah beamed at him in a helpful sort of manner. "So, I think it's best if we set gender aside. I am a highly qualified assistant. On a good day, I can type one hundred words per minute. I am well versed in Excel, financial software, bookkeeping, accounts receivable, and—"

"Look. The employment agency must not have represented the scope of what is required of you. Yes, the skills you mentioned are needed for this post. However, I write whenever the muse strikes. Sometimes an idea or the solution to whatever project I'm working on drops into my brain—maybe it's a more effective way to shoot a scene or a dialogue change. The muse doesn't care if it's two a.m. Often I am most creative in the wee hours of the morn. Which means you would be required to drag yourself out of bed, come to the main house, and take notes. Without complaining or bellyaching about how late it is or how tired you are, because frankly, I won't give a damn."

Sarah almost laughed out loud. The man had no idea of the kind of shit she'd had to put up with for the last seven years of her life. Hell, forget about going back that far. One month ago she had been kidnapped and was trapped on a yacht with a psychopathic serial killer who was convinced she was his long-lost dead sister. *Oh yeah, and he was an "artiste," who incorporated his victims' blood into his paintings, and I was to be a part of his next masterpiece. So don't try to scare me off with your talk of "the muse." Typing notes at two a.m. is a frikkin' walk in the park.* "Understood," she said, as harmless as old dishwater. "I can do that."

"I'm not finished." Rather than looking pleased that she was willing to work at his beck and call, he seemed irritated. "I would want those notes typed up, printed, and put on a USB drive before you returned to bed. These would be placed on the entryway table by the front door so I could bring them into work."

"Fine. Not a problem."

The arrogant bastard held up a tanned well-shaped finger. He had nice hands—she'd give him that. "But that's not all," he continued. "Seeing as how I already have an extremely well-qualified executive secretary at my office who handles the bulk of my paperwork and scheduling, the position I am presently filling requires more than secretarial skills. Did the Windham Employment Agency mention that? I thought not. What I need is a *'personal* assistant.'"

Sarah's breath caught in her throat. Images flashed through her mind, her on all fours taking it from behind, her dropping to her knees, unzipping his fly, wrapping her mouth around his cock. *He did say he'd require you to come over in the middle of the night. Was that a feeler he sent out to see how far you'd be willing to go?* Sarah might have been on the run for four years, but that didn't mean she'd been living in a bubble. She had access to magazines and the Internet, which were awash with stories of how corrupt and perverted Hollywood was. *Stay calm. Don't panic. Use your words.* "And what exactly does being a 'personal assistant' entail?"

A FEW YEARS AGO, MICK MIGHT HAVE FOUND THE wary expression in her startlingly blue eyes hilarious. Now it made him want to punch something—a wall, or the person who'd made her expect the worst from men. "No," he said pointedly. "Not that. I have no need or desire to be serviced by my employees. What kind of animal do you think I am?"

She opened her mouth, then shut it. Clearly, she couldn't refute the erroneous conclusion she had leaped to. This woman, with all her preconceived ideas and uptight judgments, was never going to work out. He felt a flare of anger, tired of constantly being painted by an old paintbrush. "Get your mind out of the gutter, Ms. Jones. No. As depraved as Hollywood is, if someone is employed by me—or another reputable person with any semblance of morals—a personal assistant does not assist in *all* personal needs. It's a glorified term for a gofer."

"A gofer?"

"That's right. On top of the office skills that are required day and night as a personal assistant, if your employer says jump, you say, 'How high?' I really can't see you voluntarily agreeing to that."

"You have no idea how high I can or cannot jump. Try me." She smiled at him blandly, her head slightly tilted, one elegant eyebrow arched upward. She was pretending to be subservient, passive, but he could feel the defiance in her simmering just under the skin. Stubbornness, too. However, it was her hands that did him in. There was something heartbreaking about how tightly they were gripped together in her lap.

"Fine," he said, surprising himself. "We'll give it a go. One week. Then we'll reassess."

She exhaled. "Thank you." A flash of vulnerability streaked across her face.

Damn. He wished he hadn't noticed. "Save your thanks. I'm not some bleeding-heart do-gooder. If you screw up, I will fire you so fast your head will spin." He rose to his feet. "You'd do well to remember that."

"Would you like me to start now?"

"No. God no. I just emptied my goddamned house. Start Monday. After I leave for work.

"And just so we're clear, what I require from you, in addition to office skills, is a well-run household. I don't want to have to think about plumbers, roofing repairs, when my dry cleaning is ready for pickup and where. I want to come home to food in the fridge, the garbage taken out, a clean house, clean clothes, and fresh linens. What I don't want is someone looking over my shoulder, making holier-than-thou judgments, or disapproving of my lifestyle choices. Got it?"

"Yes, sir," she said, rising to her feet as well. He had the feeling she was mocking him behind that inscrutable mask she was wearing.

"Mick," he barked. "You can call me Mick."

"All right"—she hesitated briefly—"Mick." And God help him, he liked the sound of his name on her lips.

9

MONDAY MORNING MR. HIGH-AND-MIGHTY HOPPED into his sleek, jet-black Porsche 911 Turbo S, which looked like something the devil would drive. What surprised Sarah was that Mick departed at dawn. He gunned the motor so it sounded like a ravenous beast calling her from the comfort of bed to crack the curtain open and peek out the window. "Oh my, you must be some kind of hotshot," she murmured with a tinge of sarcasm. Nevertheless, she watched as his vehicle roared down the driveway, tires leaving a trail of burnt rubber, his engine popping exuberantly, as he disappeared from view. "Off to terrorize the rest of mankind, no doubt," Sarah muttered as she let the curtain fall and then staggered bleary-eyed to the bathroom to take a shower. She got dressed, put a small handful of cat food on a saucer and fresh water in Charlie's bowl, then headed to the big house ready to work. It had been lovely to have the weekend for her and Charlie to settle in. Such a luxury, not to be on the road, on the run, to sleep uninterrupted, to take a bath, have a cup of tea. Simple pleasures.

She rescued the abandoned lilies on the front step, carried them into the kitchen, and snipped off the ends of their stems. She emptied the old water into the sink and refilled the vase, ripped open the little plastic packet of flower food, and sprinkled it in for good measure. Then she carried the vase of flowers to the entryway and placed them on the mirrored entry armoire, which needed dusting. She glanced around and wrinkled her nose. Dusting was the least of it. There were half-spent liquor bottles, takeout containers, partially emptied pizza boxes. Even with the window wide open, the smell of stale booze and musty air permeated the place. As with his office, there was an inordinate amount of crumpled balls of paper and Post-its scribbled on and discarded or made into paper airplanes that littered the living room. There was an especially heavy profusion surrounding the metal wastepaper basket, which was full to overflowing. She could see dust bunnies congregating in the corners of the rooms and under the furniture. A vacuuming would help, but a thorough carpet cleaning would be even better. She felt momentarily overwhelmed by the sheer volume of housework that needed doing in the entry and living room alone. She found a roll of large garbage bags under the kitchen sink and returned to the living room. "Eww . . ." Someone had thrown up behind the sofa. She stared at the mess a little bit longer, then straightened her spine, shoved her squeamishness aside, cleaned up the vomit, then turned her focus toward making inroads with the rest of the mess.

Since Sarah was already on a garbage run, she made the rounds through the remainder of the house. By the time she was done, there were two bags stuffed full of garbage, another of recyclable paper, and a final one of empty booze bottles. She lugged it all to the back door off the kitchen, turned the dead bolt, so the door couldn't swing shut and lock her out. She found a plethora of garbage cans in a shed off the garage and deposited the contents of her garbage bags in their proper containers.

She swung by her apartment and checked on Charlie, who was sleeping contentedly on her bed, then returned to the house. Sarah found the cleaning supplies in a cupboard in the utility room, rolled up her sleeves, turned the stereo on, music blasting, and set to work.

IT WAS A LITTLE AFTER EIGHT P.M. BY THE TIME MICK returned home. He and the cast had just wrapped a grueling all-day press extravaganza. Round robins in the morning, then the ten-minute one-on-one TV interviews. Answering the same damn questions over and over. Exhausting. His voice was ragged from all the nonstop talking, and tomorrow—God help him—it was rinse-and-repeat. He parked, shut off the engine, and exited his vehicle. First thing he was going to do was pour himself two fingers of good whiskey. Maybe he'd crash in front of the TV, watch something mindless, then go to bed.

The moment he approached his house, he could feel the difference. The porch light had been turned on. Usually, when he came home after dark, he'd fumble around a bit before his key found the lock. He couldn't park in the garage. The battery in his opener had bit the dust while he was in the throes of post-production for *Retribution*, and he hadn't had a spare minute to purchase a new one. As he exited his car and walked toward the front door, he could see light spilling from under the closed curtains in the apartment above the garage. She was up there. In a way, it made him feel less alone and yet more aware of how lonely he was at the same time.

He unlocked the door and stepped inside, and it was as if some sort of magical spell had been woven over the place. The bone-deep weariness seemed to be draining out of him and some unfamiliar sensation taking its place. A large vase of long-stemmed white flowers graced the entryway. The floors and furniture gleamed, and the air smelled clean and fresh, with a faint hint of lemon. For a moment, he was tempted to turn around, jump back in his car, and drive far and fast to outrun the cautious hope that maybe, finally, he'd have a home instead of the pigsty it had become. Why had he allowed the place to get so bad? Yes, he was busy and hadn't noticed as the slow slide into disreputable took root. *Why didn't you ask Lois to hire a cleaning service months ago?* And on the heels of that thought came another. *Is it because deep down, a cesspit is all you feel you're worth?* The thought resonated throughout him like a clarion bell, and in that moment Mick made a vow. Once he scared Rachel off, he would have Lois set up somebody to come in and clean.

Mick shut the door softly behind him and continued into the living room. Not only was it spotless, but it felt welcoming, too. Homey. Reminded him of how it had looked when he'd first purchased the place six months ago. Fully furnished, right down to the dessert cutlery and rolls of thick toilet paper in the johns. He'd bought the property in an all-cash deal. Had moved out of his suite at the Chateau Marmont and into the house two weeks later. Paid an arm and a leg for all the little personal flourishes. Didn't care if the previous owners had spent a lifetime accumulating the various decorative pieces. If one paid enough, anything was for sale, and he'd wanted a home with a sense of history. A place that looked like what he'd imagined home was while growing up. But it hadn't worked out. Didn't matter how often or long he washed, or how successful he became, the dirt and dissipation had been bred into his bones. In a matter of six months, the place had looked like a larger version of the series of tacked-together semi-wides that he, his grandma, and the twelve women who worked at Desert Rose Ranch had called home.

He rotated slowly, taking in the room. The garbage was gone. Obviously. He should have done it himself before he'd left for work that morning. He felt his face heat up. Was glad he was alone. He continued his perusal. The layer of dust that had coated everything had been eradicated. Everything gleamed. The cushions on the sofas had been fluffed, enticing one to sit down. On the steel and wooden coffee table, she'd put more flowers in a low round vase. This arrangement was more informal, a tumble of greenery and flowers clearly pilfered from his garden, which warmed

the room and added color and light. On the side table, in a
delicate china dish, rested the old-fashioned lemon drops
that had been opened and lying on the kitchen counter.
He'd removed them from a giant gift basket that Columbia
had sent over last week, along with a note and a script that
they were hoping he'd take a look at.

The kitchen. Suddenly it felt of the utmost importance
that he get to the kitchen as quickly as possible. Who knew
what magic Ms. Rachel Jones had wrought there? Maybe
there was a pie.

As a boy, he used to slip into the school library at the end
of the day and head straight for the P section. Then, when
no one was looking, he'd slide one of Peggy Parrish's Amelia Bedelia books inside his sweatshirt, and out he'd saunter,
no one the wiser. He'd hop on the school bus, glare at anyone who attempted to sit next to him, scare them off, his
secret warming against his skin. He'd loved those books,
even though Amelia Bedelia was a girl. Amelia seemed like
a perfectly normal person, but she was always goofing up,
making mistakes, and yet her wondrous apple pie at the end
always solved her every problem. Once a mouthful of that
delicious pie was popped into their mouths, Mr. and Mrs.
Rogers forgave all her mess-ups. Amelia didn't know how
normal people saw and did things. Maybe she had grown up
in a brothel, too.

His mouth was watering by the time he pushed open
the swinging doors. Should have known disappointment
awaited him. Should have known better than to start building castles in the sky, because, yes, the kitchen was spotless, but there was no tasty treat on the counter. Maybe she
tucked something delicious in the fridge? He moved to the
refrigerator and opened it. Empty shelves of gleaming glass
and chrome stared back at him mockingly. And suddenly
he was back on the school playground again. Shane Endi-
cott had grabbed Mick's brown paper lunch bag and was
dangling it in his big meaty hand over Mick's head. Didn't
matter how high Mick jumped, he couldn't reach it. All the
kids jostling, gathered around, laughing their stupid heads

off. "And what do we have today?" Shane would call out every time. And like a call-and-response, the other kids, with their fancy lunches stuffed with Hostess Twinkies and barbecue potato chips, would shout, "Peanut butter sand-wiches!" as they fell about laughing.

"Goddammit." Mick slammed the fridge door shut. He could feel the heat rising up his neck and ears. "What the hell am I supposed to eat?"

10

SARAH LAY ON THE SOFA. HER STOMACH GROWLED hungrily, but she was reluctant to move. It would be different if a feast awaited her, but she was carefully rationing the remainder of the peanut butter Ritz crackers and carrots. Had three of her crackers this morning with half a withered carrot. Would have three more and the other half of the carrot tonight. She had to make her food last until she got paid. Charlie had gobbled his kibble the second it hit the bowl and was now in a happy stupor. He'd wedged the lower half of his body between her arm and her body, and the upper half of his torso was draped across her chest. He kneaded her softly, purring up a storm while he nuzzled his face against her neck. Charlie had ignored her when she'd returned to the apartment. Pretended he could care less whether she came or went. But after he was fed and she'd flopped on the sofa, he'd jumped up, snuggled in, the day's abandonment forgiven.

She'd heard his royal highness's car arrive a few minutes ago. Found she was holding her breath slightly, hoping he'd like what she had done. She'd worked like a dog. Would be aching tomorrow, for sure, but it had been worth it. There was something satisfying about making his home shine. She'd felt almost as if the house were thanking her. She yawned, rolled her shoulders to release some of the tension. Charlie was not amused. Stopped purring, gave a little warning growl, unsheathing his claws to hold her in place.

Boom . . . boom . . . boom! Someone knocked on the door, startling the two of them. Charlie's claws went from partially extended to clamping on. "Ouch, Charlie!" Sarah disengaged his sharp nails and dumped him unceremoniously onto the floor.

Boom . . . boom . . . boom . . .

"Hold your horses," Sarah muttered, rising to her feet. "What do you want to bet," she said to Charlie as she crossed to the door, "that he's not here to thank me most graciously for the work I've done?" She swung the door open. Mick was standing on the landing, surrounded by darkness. There was an angry, wounded look in his eyes, like a wild creature caught in the leg trap. "Yes?"

"Where's my food?" he demanded indignantly.

"Your what?"

"You heard me." He set his jaw, as if daring her to take a shot.

Okay. So, she was officially working for a paranoid madman. She exhaled slowly. "I didn't steal your food. I cleaned your fridge, but the shelves were already empty. Perhaps your friends cleared out your fridge before they left."

"I didn't accuse you of stealing my food." He shook his hands in the air as if he wished he could wrap them around her neck in frustration, a faint hint of color rising along the ridge of his chiseled cheekbone. "*This* is why I requested a male assistant. Aren't so damned emotional. All I did is ask a civil question—"

"Civil? You banged on my door at"—she glanced at the clock on the stove—"eight twenty-four p.m.—"

"I *didn't* accuse you of stealing anything," he roared. "I said, 'There's no food in my fridge.'" He smacked one hand against the other for emphasis. "When we had our meeting,

I specifically said I wanted 'food in the fridge.' And I came home to nada."

"I hate to break it to you," she replied calmly. "But if you want *food in your fridge*, you've got to *leave cash with your gofer.*" There was a time when the sound of a raised voice would have caused her to crumple, but the last few years had toughened her up. Sarah Rainsford would be a punching bag, emotional or otherwise, for *no* man ever again.

"Good God, woman." He threw his hands in the air. "This is not some sophisticated ploy to rip you off. Buy the damn food, bring me the receipt, and I'll reimburse you."

"I'm sorry," she replied. "That's not possible. If you require me to purchase something, I'll need you to pay for it up front." Unfortunately, her stomach chose that moment to growl like a ravening beast.

His eyes narrowed. She made herself meet his gaze, stand tall, and not fidget.

"You're broke."

She felt her face flush, tried to push the feeling of shame back down deep into her gut, where the inner goblins resided. "I don't know what you're talking about."

"Don't bullshit a bullshitter, lady." She opened her mouth to protest. "Can it. That East Coast hoi polloi accent won't work with me. You're dead broke." He stated it as fact. "Makes total sense. Only reason a classy act like you would be willing to work for someone like me. Must be pretty hard up to accept a position, room and board in the home of a well-known hell-raiser."

"Shut up." Her voice snapped out like the crack of a whip.

Remarkably, he did.

They stared at each other in silence, the sound of the tree frogs deafening in the stillness.

"Besides," she said, needing to break the silence and lessen the acute embarrassment she was feeling. "When exactly would I have had the time to accomplish this mystery grocery shop, let alone cook? Huh? I was on my hands and knees scrubbing your kitchen floor until fifteen minutes ago. You live like a pig." *Shit.* She regretted the words the second they left her lips. Her breath caught in her chest as she waited for the axe to fall. Would he kick her out tonight? Or would he let her leave in the morning?

To her surprise, he didn't bellow "You're fired." Just shrugged like he could care less. However, that tinge of color had returned to stain his cheekbones, the tips of his ears. "And yet here you are, ready and willing to live in the sty." The words were harsh, but there was no heat in the delivery. Sarah could see in his dark eyes something that looked almost like regret. "Besides, nobody asked you to scrub my floors."

"That's what you said you wanted. A clean house, fresh sheets, et cetera, et cetera."

"Good Lord, woman, use your brain. I didn't hire you to scrub my toilets. You are to take shorthand and type when I need you to. In your downtime, I want you to organize my home, make it run smoothly. Hire a cleaner. Keep an eye on the gardeners. Make sure they're doing whatever it is they're supposed to do. Handle the details. So I'm not ashamed to entertain in my home. Have you looked at my pool? The damn water is green. It's disgusting. Figure out why. Have somebody fix it."

"Algae," she murmured. Suddenly tired. So tired. Her parents had had a swimming pool at their beach home in the Hamptons. Sparkling blue water. That first summer after she and Kevin married, she'd joined her parents as she always did to escape the heat and humidity of New York. She used to like swimming. Until one summer's day, her parents were attending the neighbor's beach party, four houses down. Sarah had stayed back because Kevin was driving out from the city to spend the weekend. She had been doing laps in the pool and hadn't heard his car arrive. He'd been pissed off she hadn't greeted him properly, that was until he discovered a new game he enjoyed. He had shoved her under the water, pinned her there, and watched the show. Then he'd dragged her to the surface by her hair, only for a second before shoving her under again. Over and over, each time keeping her under for longer. Add to that Norman Rockwell memory, the impromptu "dip" in the freezing Pacific Ocean three weeks ago off Solace Island, when she'd had to smash the window and leap from her captor's yacht. On the upside, she had deprived him of the exquisite pleasure of orchestrating her long, torturous death. Something she took great satisfaction in. However, two unpleasant aquatic memories seemed to have ruined any pleasure she could derive from large bodies of water. Even small ones were now an issue. Used to be there was nothing she liked better than a hot bath to wind up the day. No more. It was a shower or nothing.

"It's what?"

For a second she couldn't remember what they had been talking about. Oh yes. The pool. Green water. "Algae." She leaned against the doorframe, hoping to get a grip on the sick, nauseous feeling that always arose when her mind touched on Kevin. "I'll get someone on it tomorrow. But again, you'll have to leave cash for me to pay them."

He reached out, startling her. "It's okay." He released her elbow immediately, backed up slowly, hands up. "I was just steadying you. You got pale. You all right?"

"I'm fine, thank you," she said, tugging her mind away from the past, settling into the now. Her stupid stomach rumbled again. Louder this time.

"What have you eaten today?" His gaze was too intent, looking for clues, cracks past the mask to the person inside.

"None of your business." Her throat felt constricted.

"Have you eaten today?" Acting like it was a casual question, but it didn't fool her.

"Again." Working to keep her expression calm. "None. Of your. Business."

He took another step back. He was now leaning against the metal hand railings that encased the small landing outside her door. He nodded. Shoved his hands into his jeans pockets. Seemed deep in thought. She could hear a few coins jiggling. She used to have spare cash lying around in her previous life. A huge old-fashioned metal milk bucket by the fireplace that she'd picked up at an antique store back home had been full of her spare change. It always amazed her how fast it accumulated. What she wouldn't give to have access to that milk bucket now.

"Well," he said, voice brusque. "Since you messed up and failed to stock my fridge—"

She felt her hackles rise but kept her mouth shut. Pointless to argue. Would just prolong the time before he returned to his house and she could lie down again. "I am now forced to leave the comfort of my home and go out for dinner. At this late hour, it would be impossible to find a dinner companion. Since I can't tolerate eating in a restaurant alone, you'll have to come with me."

He wanted her to what? "I beg your pardon?"

"It's okay," he said, with an annoying smirk. "I forgive you. A rookie mistake. Tomorrow, though, I'd like to return home to a full fridge." Irritating man. "Yeah . . . yeah . . . I know. Gotta leave cash. My, you're such a miserly sort. I expect you'll be wanting me to pay your hourly rate to accompany me to dinner?" He shook his head and rolled his eyes as if she was the one who suggested it.

"I said no such th—"

"Fine." He threw up his hands. "You drive a hard bargain, Ms. Jones. Well, what are you waiting for? Go get your coat."

"Coat?"

"Sweater, jacket, whatever it is you wear at night to keep the chill at bay—" His gaze jerked downward. "What the hell is that?"

Charlie poked his head around her legs to check things out.

"My cat." Sarah had hoped to keep Charlie out of sight. "He's really well trained." He wasn't. "Won't claw the furniture or anything." Except when he felt like it. "Hope you don't mind."

"I hate cats."

"I'll keep him in the apartment. You'll never know he's here."

"We'll discuss it over dinner. Let's go. Lock up the beast. I'm starving."

11

MICK SHUT HIS MENU AND LEANED BACK, SLUNG HIS arms along the back of the leather-clad corner booth at The Palm. He glanced at Rachel, who was sitting stiffly opposite him. She hadn't said a word on the ride over. Hadn't cracked open a menu either. Stubborn. He crooked his fingers, and the waiter approached the table.

"Yes, Mr. Talford." The waiter's pad and pen were at the ready. "You've made a decision?" The waiter turned to Rachel. "What can I get you?"

"I'll just have some water, please. I'm not hun—"

"Like hell you will. I'm not about to stuff my face with you looking on." He glanced at the waiter's name tag. "Tom, bring us a couple of four-pound lobsters, some of that three-cheese potatoes—"

"I can't eat a . . ." Rachel's eyes looked huge in her face.

"You don't like lobster?"

"Of course I do. Who doesn't? It's just—four pounds? Seriously?"

"They only do big at this restaurant. If you can't finish your food, we'll bring it home. Cold lobster makes a good snack. Actually, make 'em five pounders. I'm ravenous. Hey." Mick rubbed his hands together gleefully. "I got a great idea. Let's do surf and turf. Bring us a rib eye, too. We can split it. How do you like it cooked? Medium work for you?" She just stared at him as if he'd lost his mind, which pleased him enormously. "Great. Medium it is. And a couple of your fancy sauces, too, green peppercorn, béarnaise, et cetera."

"Mick. Seriously—"

"Fine." Mick sighed like they were an old married couple and she was nagging him. "We'll get some vegetables. Give us some creamed spinach, asparagus, and one of your chop-chop salads." He spread his arms wide. "Anything else, my dear?"

"I'm not 'your dear'—or your anything else, for that matter."

"Wow. Impressive," Mick said. "Very difficult to speak through clenched teeth, but you managed admirably. And I hate to niggle about pesky little details, but you are my personal assistant."

"Insufferable," Rachel muttered, but he could see the hint of a reluctant smile lurking behind the clamped-together lips.

"Cocktails? Wine?" the waiter cut in smoothly.

"Yeah." Mick snapped his fingers. "Thanks, Tom. Almost forgot. We'll have a bottle of Amarone. Unless my companion would prefer white, or a cocktail?"

"I don't drink alcohol, but thank you for the offer," she said. "Mineral water with a little lime would be great."

"Do you still want the bottle of Amarone, sir?" the waiter asked.

"Nah. Do you sell it by the glass?"

"Of course, Mr. Talford. I'll put your order in and get your drinks right away."

The waiter left. Mick watched Rachel glide her fingers lightly over the silverware, as if memorizing the pattern. Then she moved her utensils to their appropriate spots, carefully unfolded her napkin and placed it on her lap.

There was a feeling of sacred ritual to her movements, a dreaminess that caused a softening on her face, a slight inner smile curving the corners of her lips.

"Do you abstain for religious reasons?"

"Pardon?"

"You said you don't drink. That a God thing?"

"No." The smile disappeared, leaving only the constant tinge of sadness in her eyes.

He should leave it be. "You ever tasted an alcoholic beverage?" So much for changing the subject. It was his damned curiosity—his strength and his kryptonite. "Or do you just reject the concept out of hand?"

"Of course not." She looked at him, her expression inscrutable. Then she lifted her chin, her steady gaze unapologetic. "I've found alcohol doesn't agree with me. I don't like the taste."

"Are you an alcoholic?"

"No." She smoothed the napkin in her lap. "I just don't like the way booze makes me feel."

"You don't like being out of control."

"Who does?" She lifted a shoulder nonchalantly, but he could sense something beyond what she was saying.

"I do," he replied. "Sometimes it's fun to let loose, go wild, swing from the rafters, whether it be booze, hot sex, fast cars. I also find at the end of the day a drink or two can help soften the edges, make the world a more palatable place."

"And I've found I need the sharp edges clearly visible and delineated so I can see where they are. I'd prefer not to cut myself on them and bleed out on the floor." She said it like a joke, but he could feel the truth shimmering behind the statement.

"Ah . . ." he murmured. "How old were you when you quit?"

"Twenty."

"Not even legal."

"Legal enough." A flicker of something flitted across her

face, and then it was gone. "And I hate to break it to you, but from the copious amounts of empty bottles that were scattered around your house, I'd say you indulge in more than a drink or two."

If she was expecting him to be offended, she was sorely mistaken, because he was enjoying the hell out of her tart rejoinders. Made him feel seen, human, with foibles and flaws, instead of this God-like persona that his box office successes had created. He didn't know why people seemed to flock to his movies when there were so many films out there that were better crafted, more deserving. Mick had spent the last nine years on a wild roller-coaster ride that only seemed to climb higher and higher. Felt as if he couldn't breathe sometimes, his breath held shallow in his chest, because he knew the safety bar was defective.

"It wasn't just me who drank all of that. As you can probably ascertain, I've got a lot of . . . friends." The devil in him made him lean on the word slightly, and sure enough, color rose in her face. Never mind that he was lying. He didn't have a lot of friends. Not true ones. Hangers-on and sycophants—those were the sorts of "friends" that tumbled in and out of his house, drank all his booze, ate whatever food was in his fridge.

The waiter walked by with a basket of garlic cheese toast, momentarily capturing Rachel's gaze like a catnip toy dangling on a string, before she yanked her eyes back and focused on the linen tablecloth in front of her. He could see her throat constrict as she swallowed hard. The fumes of delicious food were probably wreaking havoc on her salivary glands. And he was filled with a perverse sense of satisfaction that he'd crafted a way for her to accept his invitation to dinner with her pride intact. Not hungry, my ass.

SARAH FORCED HERSELF TO EAT SLOWLY, TO SAVOR, even though she could have happily planted her face into her food and not lifted it until the plate was licked clean. She placed a juicy, butter-doused chunk of lobster into her mouth. An involuntary moan escaped from her lips.

"I know." Mick grinned happily as he plopped some creamed spinach onto his plate. "It's good, huh?"

"It's delicious," she said, and then cleared her throat because her voice had come out in that low, husky cadence that happened only with delicious food or mind-blowing sex. "I'm glad you wanted company." That was better. Her voice sounded almost normal, not like she was on the fringe of a food-induced orgasm. She carved another piece of lobster, squeezing lemon over it, and dunked it in the butter. "They have a . . ." *What the hell? Shut up, girl.* She stuffed the bite of lobster in her mouth and chewed.

"They have a what?" Mick said, of course, because nothing seemed to get by the bastard. He was cutting into the rib eye, but she could see him watching her through his disgustingly long lashes. It was criminal that such lush, thick lashes were wasted on a man.

"A comfortable decor," she said with a smile, heart thumping because for a second she had relaxed her guard.

"That's not what you were going to say." A slight smile on his face, eyes gleaming like he was so damned smart. He was right, of course. She'd been thinking about summers as a child spent at their beach house in East Hampton. Saturday was the staffs' day off, and so at the end of the day—sun-kissed and tiny particles of sand still clinging between her toes no matter how much she rinsed off— Sarah would climb into the back seat of the Rolls-Royce, the cream-colored leather upholstery smooth and slippery against her sundress. The car was her dad's baby. He had spent hours on the weekends polishing its deep-blue exterior or tinkering under the hood of the 1973 Corniche coupé. Her mom and dad would ride in front, relaxed and carefree in their summer linens and tans. They'd go to The Palm in the Hamptons. It was tradition.

"Sure, it was," she lied. "I like the wooden beams and

the comfy booths. Would you pass the cheesy potatoes, please?"

He leaned forward, propped his head on his hand, elbow on the table, a hint of laughter in his eyes.

"Potatoes?" she said, brazening it out, polite inquiry on her face.

He sat back, slapped his thigh with a hoot of laughter that had people's heads turning toward their table. "You are something," he said, shaking his head. He sounded almost admiring, which didn't make sense. "Balls the size of cantaloupes."

"Wow. Thanks. In your menial vocabulary, I presume that is considered a compliment?" she said, reaching across the table and snagging the potatoes. That comment yanked another laugh from him. She felt good. Felt seen. Didn't know how he'd managed to do it. The majority of the population never looked past the mask she presented. She plopped some of the potatoes on her plate, strands of melted cheese trailing from the spoon, the scent of their greasy goodness making her mouth water.

"I'll bet," he said, toying with his wineglass, watching her over the rim, "you come from one of those stuffy old families." He grinned. "Probably can trace your ancestors back to the first *Mayflower*."

Pretty much. Getting too close to the truth. Time to change the subject. She popped a forkful of the potatoes in her mouth. "Umm . . . these potatoes are so tasty. Sheer heaven."

"Glad you approve," he said, taking a mouthful of wine, holding it on his tongue for a second, then tipping his head back for the swallow. There was something about the way he savored the flavor of the wine that made heat pool low in her abdomen. And for a split second she had the oddest desire to slide along the leather banquette, cradle his face between her hands, and taste the remnants of wine from his lips.

"That." He leaned forward. "There." His hand had risen

as if to pull the thought from her mind. "What were you just thinking?"

"Seriously?"

"I want to know. I'm curious."

"Oh well," she said, returning her attention to her plate. "As my employer, you have a claim on my time. Not my thoughts."

12

THE ROAR OF A LUXURY SPORTS CAR YANKED SARAH from sleep, disoriented, her heart pounding. *Kevin* was the first thought that dropped into her sleep-soaked brain. The engine sound was similar to the Maserati GranTurismo he had pressured her into putting on her black American Express card the day after they returned from Vegas. "A wedding gift," he'd said. "After all, that rock you are wearing didn't come cheap."

However, as the bedroom slowly came into focus, Sarah remembered where she was, and the nausea and panic gradually began to subside. She lay back down on the sinfully comfortable bed and inhaled long and deep. She was safe for the time being, had a full belly of food and a place to stay. She would savor that blessing. Charlie resettled, draping his furry body over her shoulder, tucking his head into the nook of her neck, his paws gently kneading and then releasing the shoulder of her pajamas as his body vibrated with a rumbling purr. "Don't get too comfy," she told him, stroking him softly. "I'd love to stay here with you, but there is work to be done. A three-minute cuddle is all you get, and then I'm off." It was amazing how much heat one little cat could generate. She let three minutes slip into four, then five. Finally she made her move, reluctantly disengaged Charlie's sleepy body, mindful of claws, then padded into the bathroom. Catching sight of herself in the mirror made her chuckle. She had the satisfied look of someone who'd just indulged in a week of fabulous, mind-blowing sex. Apparently, an obscenely delicious dinner had a similar effect.

After she finished her morning ablutions, she got dressed, ate a quick breakfast consisting of the leftover chop-chop salad and cheesy toast. She'd really wanted to chow down on some of the protein components, but she needed to be pragmatic. The salad had dressing on it and was already rather wilted. It needed to be consumed first. She put some food and fresh water out for Charlie, then headed to the big house, the specter of her ex lingering in her psyche like a persistent low-grade toothache.

KEVIN WAS IN HIS MASERATI, ATTEMPTING TO GET out of the damn JFK airport parking lot when his cell phone rang. Some dipshit was holding up the exit line, hadn't pre-paid, probably a woman. He glanced at his dashboard. Phillip Clarke. The lawyer handling Sarah's parents' estate. He cracked his neck to release tension, then hit answer. "Hello, Phillip. Thanks for returning my call."

"Mr. Hawkins." The lawyer's dry, crackly voice came over the speakerphone. He had met the elderly bureaucrat at the wedding reception. The Rainsfords' family lawyer appeared frail, as if a strong wind could send him flying. Unfortunately, age hadn't dimmed the man's razor-sharp intellect.

"I wanted to keep you up to date with regards to the search for Sarah. I'm able to confirm that it was indeed a photo of her splashed across the *Washington Post* and the *New York Times*. She was tangled up in the Tristin Guillory mess on Solace Island. He held her captive." He and Sarah would need to have a little talk about that. If she'd allowed that privileged prick to bang her, she was dead, inheritance be damned.

There was a pause on the other end of the line, as if it were a bad connection and there was a slight delay before the full connotation of his words landed.

"So, you found her?" the lawyer finally said, his voice void of any inflection. Kevin would have preferred to deliver the news in person. Would have been easier to read Clarke, but meetings with the old man had to be scheduled weeks in advance. Clarke always canceled at the last minute due to some bogus "emergency," and the rescheduling dance would start all over again. "Is Sarah with you now?"

"No. Unfortunately, by the time I had arrived on the Gulf island, she was gone. However, I spoke with several of the nurses at the hospital, the police, the woman at Art Expressions Gallery, where she worked—"

"And they confirmed that this Mary Browning was indeed Sarah?" Clarke cut in. "I'm surprised. The news clipping you showed me didn't look anything like her."

Whether it actually was Sarah or not, it was vital that Phillip Clarke believed it was. If Kevin wasn't able to produce proof positive that Sarah was alive, then in a couple more years the $385 million tied up in the Rainsford estate would be going into a fucking charitable trust. As in accordance with Sarah's parents' wills, said trust would be run by none other than the sneaky little dipshit Phillip Clarke Esq. Well, Kevin was no dummy. He'd had access to a calculator. He'd done the math. The setup fee, along with the "fiduciary services and asset management" fee, was over a cool $5 million for the first year. It would then "drop" to a mere $3,080,000 annual fee, which would rise in conjunction with the increased value of the investments. Yeah. He had the old man's number. Had a couple of other theories about the corrupt old bastard he was checking into as well. The lawyer could pretend he was above it all, but the kind of payday and power that came from overseeing the Rainsford estate was a hell of a motivation to declare Sarah Audrey Rainsford Hawkins dead.

At least in the limbo land Kevin was trapped in now, he had access to the joint checking account with $35,000 arriving from Sarah's trust like clockwork at the end of every month. Life would be even sweeter once Sarah was back under his control. He wouldn't have to settle for the scraps. All that beautiful money would be his. A four percent rate of return on $385 million would net him $15,400,000 year in and year out. Of course, Kevin would have to keep a closer watch on Sarah now that he knew she was a runner. Wouldn't allow her the multitude of freedoms she'd enjoyed before. He would keep her at arm's reach at all times, even if it meant shackling her to the basement wall.

"Oh, it's Sarah, all right," he told the lawyer. "One hundred percent. She dyed her hair a dishwater brown and slapped on a pair of glasses."

"Which would beg the question why?"

"Why what?" Kevin replied, smooth as an ice-cold slug of Grey Goose, but he knew what was being inferred. He inched his car forward, his mouth bitter with memories. The Rainsfords hadn't thought he was good enough to marry their darling, shit-don't-stink daughter, and it was clear Phillip Clarke shared their narrow-minded opinion. When Sarah refused to give him up, her parents arranged for her to meet with Phillip to draw up a prenup. Stupid bitch.

Well, Kevin had shown them who was in charge. Instead of taking Sarah to Central Park for the promised picnic, he'd driven the two of them to the airport for a "surprise getaway to Vegas, baby." He'd crossed all the t's and dotted his i's. Had prearranged a spa day for her. While she was getting pampered, he'd snagged her driver's license, cased the casino until he found a stripper who was similar in looks, height, and weight. Took a little bit of convincing and a thousand bucks, but it was totally worth it. An hour and a half later, he and "Destiny" exited the courthouse with a marriage license tucked in his back pocket. "Don't forget," the Clark County clerk had said as she handed over the document. "This license is only valid for use within the

State of Nevada and must be used within a year from the date of issue."

"Won't be a problem, ma'am," he'd replied. "Me and my little honey are planning on tying the knot tonight." He'd given Destiny a big old kiss and slap on the ass for good measure, and then they'd strolled out of the office hand in hand. All that playacting had made the two of them horny, so she'd thrown in a BJ on the ride back to the hotel for good measure.

When Sarah had returned to their hotel room, dazed and massaged to a mellow complacency, he led her downstairs, a docile lamb to the slaughterhouse of sin. They downed a couple of green-apple martinis at the bar while watching the topless dancers prance around on the stage. It was especially fun sitting beside his wife-to-be watching "Destiny" drive the patrons wild, knowing she had serviced him a mere hour before. It had been Sarah's first foray to a strip bar. Apparently, it wasn't her cup of tea. Said it made her sad. Insisted on leaving before the set was over. She was hungry, wanted dinner, but he vetoed that. With food in her belly, she might not get as inebriated as he needed her to be. "When in Vegas, baby," he'd said as he'd steered her back to the hotel room and unpacked the bottle of tequila and wedges of lime from his overnight bag. Convinced her it had been a major fantasy of his for her to do body shots off him while he watched in the overhead mirror.

"Kevin," she'd protested. "I haven't eaten all day."

"Soon, baby, soon. Body shots first, then sex, then dinner." Made her do the shots over and over until "she got it right." Aka was drunker than a skunk and having difficulty managing basic motor skills. Perfect. Had a quickie, as promised, slam-bam-thank-you-ma'am. Watched the clock. Timed it. Got off in forty-eight seconds, a new record. Yanked up her panties, called a Lyft, still had her ID from his earlier outing. Half dragged, half carried her down the hall, into the elevator, through the lobby, and into the waiting car. They arrived at the twenty-four-hour wedding chapel fifteen minutes later and got married right and tight.

The whole time she was bawling like a baby that, no, no, no, she wanted a real wedding, with flowers and a beautiful gown. She wanted her mom and dad, poor little baby girl. Had to slip a couple of extra hundreds to the wedding officiant when it looked like he was going to balk. Suddenly, the man became very compliant, cracked jokes, slapped Kevin on the back, wasn't too picky about her portion of the vows. They all signed. Sarah's hand needed a little guidance, and then it was done. Married. Until "death do us part." No prenup.

Granted it wasn't the most romantic of nights. The Lyft driver had to pull the car over twice on the return trip to the hotel so she could barf her guts out by the side of the road.

She was still pretty green when they flew back to JFK International Airport the next morning as Mr. and Mrs. Hawkins, and there was not a damned thing her parents could do about it.

Beeeeeeeep! Someone in the car behind him was leaning on his horn, jolting him back to the present. Phillip's dry voice was droning on. "I'd be more inclined to believe Sarah was indeed alive if she had withdrawn funds from your joint account. Has she?"

Kevin fed his parking ticket into the machine, and the traffic arm lifted. "No," he said as he pulled into traffic.

"Any charges on the credit cards?"

"No."

"Any activity on her cell phone—"

"As I told you during our last meeting, she left her phone and credit cards behind." Kevin kept his voice level, the impatience out, but he could feel tension building. Needed to remove his hand from the steering wheel, crack his neck to disperse it. "However, a woman on the run—"

"And again, we circle back to my original question. Why would she be on the run?"

"I wish I knew," Kevin replied, keeping a tight leash on his fraying patience. "I've been so damned worried. I can't imagine how Sarah's coping. She's always been so fragile, prone to tears and bouts of depression."

"I never noticed any signs of depression."

"Of course you didn't. She's a very proud woman, didn't want family and friends to worry, but behind closed doors . . ." Kevin sighed heavily. "I should have known. She'd been acting strangely for several months before she disappeared. Must have had a psychotic break of some kind." Some jackass was traveling forty miles an hour in the fast lane. "Idiot," he muttered, swerving around the slowpoke and continuing on his way.

"I beg your pardon?" Clarke's voice grew even chillier.

"Not you." Kevin managed to squeak out a laugh. "A crappy driver on the road." It was an effort to eradicate any telltale trace of anger in his voice. "Look, Phillip. I don't know why Sarah took off, but I plan to find out. It breaks my heart to think of her out there, defenseless and vulnerable in this crazy-assed world. Look what happened with that madman on that yacht. I left a copy of the articles with your secretary. You read them, yes?" Phillip didn't respond. Didn't need to. They both knew he had pored over them just like Kevin had. "Sarah needs to come home, where she will be loved and protected. I won't rest until she is. The trip to Solace Island was fruitful. Apparently, she'd gotten herself a vehicle. The apartment manager had the license plate number in his files. I'll be back on the job Thursday, will put in a BOLO then."

"A BOLO?"

"Be on the lookout. More precisely, an ATL—an Attempts to Locate. With technology and the automated license plate readers installed on the roofs of most major city police cars, it's only a matter of time before a cop drives past her car. When that happens, an alert will show up on the system, along with the precise spot her vehicle was sighted. The instant that occurs, I'll"—Kevin cleared his throat—"I'll track her down."

13

USING EVERY OUNCE OF CONTROL AT HIS DIS-
posal, Phillip Clarke managed to place the receiver gently
into its cradle before slumping into his high-backed leather
office chair in an effort to absorb the psychological blow
without undue agitation to his heart. *Is it possible the girl
is alive? Lieutenant Kevin Hawkins could be bluffing, but
just in case . . .*

Phillip sighed. He was tired and old and had no stomach
for this type of foolishness. However, this was too important. He would need to follow up. The stakes were too high,
couldn't afford to make a mistake. He pressed the intercom
button on his phone.

"Yes?" Phillip closed his eyes and let the warmth of
Vicki's voice wash over him. "Mr. Clarke?" She always addressed him formally in the office. In the early days, sometimes a "Mr. Clarke" would accidentally slip out when they
were in the throes of passion. *Ah, those were the days when
he could wield his mighty sword at the blink of an eye.* He
sighed. *No more.* Type 2 diabetes had robbed him of that.
Now it was the sweet, calm tenderness she provided that

caused him to fabricate excuses to his wife before hopping into his cashmere-white Mercedes S-Class and making the furtive journey across the bridge to Brooklyn. He'd grab an hour or two at their little hideaway. The love nest he had purchased for her decades ago. Then, reluctantly, he'd head back to hearth and home. "Mr. Clarke . . . ?" Vicki's voice interrupted his reverie. "Are you all right?"

For a second he couldn't remember why he had called her. *Oh yes. The girl. Sarah Rainsford.* "I . . . I . . ." He was having difficulty catching his breath. He heard the scrape of her chair, the sound of her sensible shoes hurrying to his door. Vicki used to wear the most glorious spiky-heeled pumps in the old days. She had sashayed into his office, a fresh-faced nineteen-year-old looking for a job. For him it was love at first sight. He'd hired her within the hour. Took a little longer to cajole her into his bed. She'd made him wait, but it was well worth it.

The door to his office swung open, and there she was, standing in the doorway. His angel. She looked worried, hurried toward him. "You're pale," she said, almost an accusation, as if she'd caught him trying to sneak an extra serving of banana custard. She moved to the bar and poured him a tumbler of water. "Take a sip," she ordered, her two fingers now resting lightly against his carotid artery, her eyes on the lovely Cartier watch that he'd bought her to commemorate their tenth anniversary eighteen years ago. She had wept when she'd opened the box and had worn the watch every day since. He'd lost count of how many watchbands she had worn through.

Vicki frowned. "Your pulse is a little elevated." She pulled open his desk drawer on the side. He missed the feeling of her cool fingers against his skin. "Wouldn't hurt to take a baby aspirin." She popped open the bottle and fished one out. "Open up," she said, and then placed the aspirin under his tongue. He made a face. It was bitter but nothing he couldn't bear. Just made a face because it always caused her to make soothing noises and gently ruffle what was left of his hair.

"I need you to—"

"Uh-uh." She shook her head. "Wait till it's dissolved."

Suddenly impatient to get on with what needed to be done, he worked the bottom of his tongue against the pill and crunched the last vestiges of it.

"I need you to book—"

"Show me," she said, crossing her arms to let him know she was taking no guff.

He opened his mouth, lifted his tongue. She nodded. "Vicki, I need you to book me transportation to"—he glanced down at the pad of paper he had scribbled notes on—"Solace Island. I need to leave as soon as possible."

Vicki's mouth tightened. "Do you really think it's wise to travel? You clearly aren't feeling well."

"I don't have a choice. Kevin Hawkins claims Sarah Rainsford was there. He's put out a bulletin that will show up across all police jurisdictions with the license plate of the car she's supposedly driving. If she *is* still alive, we need to get to her before he does."

Vicki's hand rose to her throat as if the collar of the rose silk blouse she wore had suddenly gotten too tight. "Good Lord." Her eyes wide, mouth agape. She swallowed hard. Once. Twice. Then her lips firmed. Her spine straightened. "I'm coming with you," she said, just as he had hoped she would. She turned without waiting for his answer and hurried through the door to her computer to book their trip.

14

"ARRGH!" MICK KNEW THE LAYOUT OF HIS STUDY, hadn't bothered switching on the light. Had made the journey to his desk many times in the dark. But apparently that meddling woman had subtly rearranged the furniture in front of his desk, and he had rammed the little toe on his right foot into the wooden box with brass fittings that was supposed to be under the window. "Goddammit!" It would have been satisfying to hop around on one foot clutching the injured toe, but he couldn't even do that, because God knew what else had been shifted around. No. He had to shuffle his feet slowly, the script tucked under one arm, the other outstretched until his fingertips landed first on the back of one of the leather armchairs in front of his desk and then onto the desk itself. Once there, he was able to find the desk lamp and switch it on. He blinked, his eyes adjusting to the light. The room looked the same, but different. The two armchairs had been angled slightly, and the wooden box was now acting as a side table. There was a small crystal and silver bowl with almonds in it. She had dragged a rug from somewhere, woven with warm earth tones, a few small tweaks that made a room into something more. He dumped the screenplay on the desk, hobbled to the bowl and snagged a few almonds, rattled them around in the palm of his hand, trying to decide if he was pissed off or delighted. He popped the almonds into his mouth. They tasted good—smoky and salty. That's when he noticed a bottle of his favorite whiskey on the bookshelf, sitting on a silver tray with two crystal tumblers like a minor miracle. He smiled, rounded the armchair forgetting to limp, poured a finger of whiskey into a crystal tumbler, and then returned to his desk and settled in to work.

Mick had idly browsed through the Columbia screenplay while eating dinner. He had picked the script as company, a dinner companion so he didn't have to face another meal alone. He wasn't looking for a new project, but Ron Berg, the Columbia studio head, had bulldozed his secretary, Lois, into booking a conference call for ten a.m. Mick decided to skim a few pages so he could be semi-articulate when he turned Ron Berg down. There was no way Mick was going to dive into another project. He planned to take a couple of months off after the press for *Retribution* wrapped up. Go somewhere tropical. Laze in the sun. Swim. Fish. Down a couple of frozen cocktails with pointless paper umbrellas that he liked to grump about but privately adored.

The *Crushed Dandelions* screenplay started out better than he had expected given the synopsis that had come with it. Mick finished thumbing through the script while watching the Las Vegas Golden Knights skate their asses off. The Knights had lost in the shootout, which sucked. Just like the screenplay, which had quite a few good components but three-quarters of the way through took a hard right into ludicrous. He had deposited the script on the discard pile, relieved it was an easy no and his tropical holiday was still on deck. He tossed back the remains of his whiskey, switched off the TV, ambled down the hall to the bathroom, brushed his teeth, and went to bed.

But was he sleeping? No. The damned script had niggled at him like a splinter trapped under the skin. So he had dragged his sorry ass out of bed and was sitting in his damned study trying to fix the problems in a script he was pretty certain he didn't want to take on. He had decided to jot down the ideas that were swirling in fragment form so his brain would shut up and let him sleep. In the morning, when he got to the office, Lois could type them up.

After half an hour he had accumulated an ever-growing stack of marked-up Post-its, and that's when he realized there was a fundamental flaw in his plan. He should have numbered the damn things or stuck them on the corresponding pages of the script. *What you really need to do is learn how to type. Then you wouldn't be dependent on other people.* He reached for the phone to call his assistant and then remembered it was Rachel. *Crap. I can't call her.* Mick exhaled, plucked a couple of Post-its from his desk. He flipped through the screenplay to find the scenes he'd made the notes about. He would transcribe them in the margins. If he ran out of space, he could use the backs of the pages. He was able to figure out what scene the top Post-it was about and stick it on the appropriate page. The next two Post-its were a lost cause. His handwriting was messy on the best of days. In the dead of night it was damn near indecipherable. Didn't make fucking sense. "Dammit." He balled the offending Post-it notes in his fist and attempted to chuck them against the wall, but they had no weight, no heft, and the scraps of yellow paper floated ineffectually through the air for all of a foot and then descended as delicately as rose petals to rest on the top of his desk. "If the damn agency had sent me a male assistant as I requested, I would have already dictated the notes and gone back to bed," he muttered, glaring at the mess on his desk. The very fact he was sitting up in the middle of the night, attempting to work without success, avoiding calling Rachel because he didn't want to disturb her rest irritated him. Mick exhaled. He plucked another fistful of Post-its off his desk and attempted to read the scribbled notes. "A final—what the hell is this word? A final . . . blankity-blank . . . before the elevator. Make sure to . . . something . . . red haze through window." He slapped the Post-its down. "That's it. I'm calling her."

A SHRILL NOISE JERKED SARAH TO A SEATED POSItion, the taste of panic in her mouth. "What the—" *Ring . . . ring . . .* Wrestling her way out from under the covers, she freed an arm and grabbed for her burner phone from the bedside table. "Yes?" she croaked, swiping the screen, her brain groggy from being wrenched out of a deep sleep. "Hello?"

Ring . . . ring . . . "Damn!" She staggered out of bed and sprinted through the darkened apartment. Following the sound of the ringtone to the kitchen. *Ring . . . ring . . .* She could make out the shadowy shape of the old-fashioned landline phone attached to the wall by the fridge. She lunged for the receiver; her heart was pounding and highoctane adrenaline was coursing through her veins. "Hello?" She covered the mouthpiece and puffed out a breath, trying to dispel the frenetic panic in her voice. "Hello?" Her parents were already gone, four years now. But in the dark of the night, yanked from sleep, time had morphed, played a trick on her, and it felt like she was going to get the bad news all over again.

"Need you to get over here, pronto." The sound of her employer's voice acted as a foghorn and tugged Sarah back into the present.

"Yes. Of course," she said, modulating her tone. "Give me five to change out of my pajamas."

"Don't bother. You're coming over to type, not participate in a fashion show. And I don't want to hear any bellyaching. I warned you this would happen a lot."

So, the man is back in asshole mode. Fine. "Very well," she said, exhaling softly, trying to dispel the leftover effects of the fight-or-flight panic that had surged through her body. "I'll be right there."

"Thanks," he said curtly, and the phone went dead.

Sarah flipped on the light so she wouldn't break her neck on the journey back to her bedroom. She shoved her feet in a pair of sneakers, grabbed her robe, which used to belong to her mother, and tugged it on as she sprinted across the apartment and out the front door. On the landing, she remembered her eyeglasses on the bedside table. *Confound it*. She whirled around and ran back into her apartment.

15

SHE WAS WEARING A VINTAGE PALE-PINK ROBE. IT was a well-worn quilted satin with delicate clear pink flower petals with rhinestone pistils. When Rachel had rushed through the front door in her worn cotton pajamas and that robe, it momentarily knocked Mick on his ass. The robe was such a contradiction to the contained, constrained, almost inhuman efficient exterior that she had presented in all their prior encounters. It was as if he had stepped into the pages of an enchanted storybook, and on some cellular level, that pale-pink robe that she had wrapped around her slender body was the key.

"We're in here," he said, with a jerk of his head toward his study. Aware that his voice was gruffer than it should be. He followed the gentle sway of her body into the room, leaving a healthy distance between them, so she wouldn't be spooked. There was an innate grace to the way she moved. Perhaps she had studied ballet as a girl. Easy to imagine, long, lean legs encased in pastel-colored tights. Who was she before the world had left those ever-present shadows in her eyes? Once in his study, she turned and looked at him from where he was hovering in the doorway. The room that had seemed like a trap five minutes ago suddenly felt inviting. Intimate. He stayed where he was, propped against the doorframe. "I need you to take notes."

"Very well. I'll need a pad of paper and a pen." Her face looked different without the skillful application of subtle makeup. She looked younger, more vulnerable behind those dark-framed glasses. There was a slight imprint along the left side of her face. She must have been sleeping on her side when he woke her.

"Right." He pushed away from the safety of the doorway and ambled across the room as if her presence was having no effect on him whatsoever. He crossed to his desk, rummaged through a drawer, found a pad of paper and a pen and slid them across his mahogany desk. He was aware of a hint of the scent of lemon and wax rising from the desk's freshly polished surface. That was the bass note of comfort and home, but the melody was all her. The faintest scent of her warm skin clad in freshly washed light-blue cotton pajamas with a white piping trim. The worn pale-pink robe with buttons, which was both fanciful and yet elegant. There was something about her that dangled the impossible promise of hope and redemption. "Dammit," he muttered.

"Pardon?" She looked at him inquiringly.

"I apologize." His voice sounded stiff, slightly pissed off. *Better that than drooling on her.* "I hadn't thought it through. Should have given you time to get dressed. With my previous assistants, always men, it didn't . . ." He shrugged, feeling uncomfortable. "Anyway, next time, even if I sound grouchy, take the time you need to get dressed." He wasn't used to apologizing. Mick busied himself gathering the scattered Post-it notes. He was going to toss them across the desk, but Rachel extended her hand. She had elegant fingers. Perhaps she'd played piano or some other musical instrument. Maybe a cello cradled against her body, held in place with her thighs. A light grasp of her fingers holding the bow as she drew it across the strings, filling the listener with sweet melancholy music.

"Oh." She started to withdraw her hand. "I'm sorry. I thought those were for me."

"They are. I was . . ." He dropped the Post-its in her palm, careful not to make contact with her skin. Didn't matter. His fingertips had entered the space surrounding her, and electric tingles leaped from her hand to his fingertips. "Lost in thought." He put his hand behind his back. It didn't help. The sensation continued up his arm, to his torso, where the tingles expanded, radiated outward, filling his chest cavity with an unfamiliar, unsettled feeling. He didn't like it. Who was she to march into his home and turn it upside down, causing him to long for things he could never have? "Have a seat." He gestured to the chair in front of his desk.

She sat, uncapped the pen, her eyes on the yellow legal pad. Her unbound hair fell forward, partially obscuring her face. "Ready."

Mick wanted to lean across the desk and nudge the silky strands behind her dainty seashell ear so they wouldn't obscure his view of her face. He sat in his leather desk chair, picked up the script and flipped through it. "At the top of the page. Heading. *Crushed Dandelions Notes.* Page seventy-one, scene one forty-two, this is where the script starts jumping the shark. The screenwriter"—Mick flipped to the title page—"Ed Swartz, made certain promises to the moviegoers at the start of the script. The setup was great. Unique. The characters were for the most part engaging." He could hear the scratch of her pen on the pad. "I kept reading because I was intrigued by said promises and was curious about how the characters were going to solve them. Then something happened. From page seventy-one onward, it reads as if the screenwriter scored some potent BC bud and wrote the rest of the script stoned."

WHEN MICK FIRST STARTED DICTATING, HE HAD seemed uneasy, distracted, but within a minute, he had shifted into another gear. *Work mode*, Sarah thought, her pen flying across the page. He had become engaged, laser-focused. She could sense his talent roaring to the forefront, and there was something very addictive, almost seductive in seeing him like this. "The scene in the cave, on . . ." She could hear the sound of him flipping through the script. "Page seventy-three. What the hell is that about? Felt like filler. On page seventy-six there is the addition of a fucking mountain lion? *That's* what happened to Lance? Give me a break. The man is described as six foot six and built like a tank, and a mountain lion is going to take him down? First off, bees kill more people than mountain lions. Secondly, the man survived three tours of duty, is skilled in hand-to-hand combat, and he's done in by a mountain lion?" Mick sounded so outraged on Lance's behalf. "On page . . . sixty-nine, there is a long, drawn-out scene—Derek's messed-up relationship with his father. It felt like an afterthought. If you leave the scene in, it needs to be woven into the fabric of the script. It's a dramatic scene, but there is no mention of it afterward or any hint of foreshadowing. What do you get for it? Does it change Derek? Does it change the trajectory of the script and color his actions and motivations going forward? No. So why is it there? Page eighty-two— What are you smiling at? No. Don't write that down. I'm asking you a question."

Sarah's gaze jerked up from the page, and there he was, looking at her with those tawny, gold-flecked eyes. "I . . ." Suddenly she was aware of the late hour, the fact that she wasn't wearing a bra or underwear. Had grabbed the robe and dashed out of the door. She swallowed and forced her gaze back to the page, trying to ignore the liquid heat coursing through her. Sarah tipped her chin down so her hair shielded her from his scrutiny. "I was enjoying the work." A partial truth. "Hearing your insights on the script. It made me want to read it." She could see through her makeshift curtain that he was still watching her as if she were a puzzle he was trying to solve. *What would it be like to not have to hide, disassemble, to be able to stand tall in who I am, to hold a man's gaze and proudly invite him to do more than look?* The thought was as effective as pinching the lit wick of a candle, snuffing out the flame. A wave of weariness washed over her. *Will I ever be able to be more than a mirage?* Sarah felt her eyes heat but stuffed the emotion down. Clamped her teeth together, poised her pen over her paper and awaited his next note. She felt like a ghost, hovering on the fringes of life, constantly being forced to reinvent herself. Living an imaginary life where everything she did, every word she uttered was tinged with the acrid taste of falsehoods and lies in her mouth. And the odds of being able to return to who she was, to anything familiar, seemed highly unlikely.

16

IT HAD BEEN ONLY A WEEK SINCE SARAH HAD landed on Mick Talford's doorstep, and yet it felt as if she had been living there much longer. There was a familiar comfort to the place. It felt as if the home and the grounds, with their lush, fragrant gardens, had scooped her up into their embrace, making her feel safe and cared for.

Sarah was folding the top sheet over the comforter on Mick's bed when the dryer chimed down the hall in the laundry room. She hastily pulled the fresh pillowcases over the pillows, fluffed them. Then she propped them up against the headboard, gliding her hands over them to smooth the pillowcases. She tweaked the corners so they would stand correctly, then placed the small accent pillow just so. Stood back, looked it over. Good.

She scooped the pile of old linens off the floor and headed down the hall. The whole ritual, stripping his bed, remaking it, felt oddly intimate. That he had slept in that bed. She knew from his laundry hamper that he didn't wear pajamas. And no matter how hard she tried, her mind would go to the image of his long, lean, sun-kissed limbs lounging in the front doorway with an insolent smirk on his face. How she wished she didn't know what he looked like without his clothes. Once seen, it was impossible to forget. His body reminded her of Michelangelo's statue of David. She had seen it in Florence with her parents when she was twelve and curious. It was the first naked male body she had seen. It was magnificent. The marble seemed to breathe, to glow with an inner light as David paused for a second in that moment before a tremendous output of energy that would determine if he were to live or die.

Mick's naked body framed in the doorway had reminded her of that work of art, but Mick's sleek muscles were made of warm flesh and blood. At night, sometimes sleep would refuse to come and she'd find herself staring up into the darkness, her traitorous body heating with the knowledge that he was sprawled naked among his sheets. If she closed her eyes, she could almost taste the salt of his skin.

She hadn't seen Mick since the night he'd had her come to his study to work on the script, but she would hear him arrive home. Watch the lights in the house flick on. She'd imagine him going into the kitchen, opening the fridge and cupboard doors, finding all the tasty options she had placed in there. In the morning, she'd listen to him depart again, the purr of his high-octane sports car. The man might present himself like a lowlife, but he was no slacker, she'd give him that. He worked incredibly long hours. When Sarah had accepted the post, she had expected a steady stream of disreputable people marching in and out of the house. But as far as she could observe, once Mick came home, he kept to himself. *Although,* she thought with a huff of laughter, *it is Friday. Who knows what craziness the weekend will bring.* And on the heels of that thought came a tiny flare of jealousy, which didn't make any sense at all.

Sarah turned into the laundry room. She enjoyed how her days were falling into a peaceful pattern, which allowed her to daydream that she was someone else and had a regular life. After eating breakfast, she'd enter Mick's house and begin the day's work. She'd always start in the kitchen and add to the list she had created with notes on which foods had been eaten. She was getting a pretty good idea of what foods he preferred and how much to purchase. As she worked through the day, she could feel his presence. It was like having a conversation, a relationship with an imaginary friend. He didn't have any photos lying about, which was odd; but then, she didn't have any either. Hadn't had a chance to grab some before she ran. Every now and then she would duck into a public library and look her parents up online to see their beloved faces at a past gala or a fund-raiser. She would magnify the photos and trace her fingers over the familiar planes of their faces, longing to print them out so she would have something concrete, but it was too risky. Someone might discover them. All she had was her mother's robe, which Auntie Jane had brought to the hospital the night before she ran. Why didn't Mick have any family memorabilia lying about? Did he have brothers and sisters? Were his parents alive? Maybe he was an orphan. That would make sense, as there was a wounded wild wolf quality wrapped around him like a cloak, a loneliness beyond the brash mask he wore, which seemed to have burrowed bone deep. She did find a worn hard copy of the children's book *Amelia Bedelia* tucked in the bottom of his underwear drawer when she was putting away laundry. The library's borrowing card was still tucked in the pocket toward the front. Goldfield Elementary School. Did he go there? And why this book? But other than that the only personal objects were his clothes and a couple of books on his bedside table: Rilke's *Letters to a Young Poet*, Ingmar Bergman's *The Magic Lantern*, Andre Dubus's *The Times Are Never So Bad*, George Saunder's *Tenth of December*, and Charles Baxter's *Burning Down the House*. In his office was a Golden Globe and an Oscar for the movie *Run*, and another Oscar and Golden Globe, as well as a Prix de la mise en scène and a Palme d'Or, for *The Spider's Kiss*. But the rest of the objects in the house, the cut crystal, the choice of furniture, the artwork and decorative touches, seemed at odds with the man. It felt almost as if Mick had arrived with a suitcase and a couple of books and was squatting in someone else's home.

Sarah opened the door to the washing machine and stuffed the armload of linens inside, feeling oddly bereft as she closed the washing machine door on the subtle scent of him lingering on the linens. She added soap to the dispenser, turned the cycle to sheets, and started it up. Then she took the load of darks from the dryer and began to fold his things, her hands sliding along the fabric, folding jeans, T-shirts, socks, briefs.

Mick had reiterated the other night that she could hire a cleaning service, and she would. Eventually. But for now she was enjoying the solace of solitude, the puttering around, putting the place to rights. There was a pride to be had in a job well done. Plumping the pillows, polishing the furniture, cleaning the windows, making things shine. It felt almost as if the home and the contents were living, breathing entities. And in the doing and caring, she was receiving as well. Earning her way and showing her gratitude for the safe haven this place provided in her small day-to-day gestures of goodwill.

Once the laundry was folded, she began ironing his shirts and hanging the completed ones on the back of the laundry room door. Her mind wandered past her musing on Mick to alight on her parents, and the sudden stab of sorrow had her hand pressing hard against her chest, as if trying to cauterize a wound. Grief was like that sometimes. Four years since the accident. Four years since she lost everyone and everything that meant anything to her. For the most part, time had softened the ragged edges of her sorrow, but every once in a while, it would sneak up and grab her from behind, steal her breath, and force her to her knees.

17

"I'M SORRY I CAN'T BE MORE HELP," THE ART EXPRES-
sions Gallery owner said to Phillip, her hands neatly folded
on the desk before her. The artwork in Zelia Thompson-
Conaghan's gallery was quite impressive. Surprising, considering Solace Island was quite small. Who were her
clients? Driving through the small town of Comfort, Phillip
doubted any local resident would have the means to acquire
the art showcased in her gallery, let alone the taste. How
did the woman afford the overhead? The staff? "This Sarah
Rainsford looks nothing like my ex-employee Mary Browning. I can say with confidence I've never met this woman."

"I suppose it was too much to hope for." Phillip sighed.
He had squandered two days chasing a ghost. He shook his
head. "Lieutenant Hawkins was certain they were the same
person."

"No." The abrupt way the woman answered had him
studying her more closely. He could see tension around her
mouth, her eyes.

Vicki must have noticed too, because she spoke up,

which was unusual when they were in a professional capacity. "I can't stress enough"—Vicki leaned forward, her hand out, palm upward—"how vital it is that we reach Sarah before Lieutenant Hawkins does. He is a dangerous predator on the hunt. We believe she is in extreme danger. Indeed, her very life could be at stake."

The art gallery owner's sharp intake of breath was audible.

"So, if something springs to mind . . ." Vicki gentled her voice. "A coincidence or additional information, please don't hesitate to text, email, or call. Anything that you can think of that might be helpful in our search."

The gallery owner nodded. She seemed pale as she carefully placed the business card Phillip handed her into the top right-hand desk drawer.

VICKI HAD BEEN SILENT SINCE THEY'D LEFT THE ART Expressions Gallery. Come to think of it, she hadn't spoken much that morning either, and when she had, her responses had been rather sharp. Clipped. Perhaps she was on her monthly. In a day or two, the grumpiness would pass.

Phillip took a deep breath of the brisk ocean air. He had tucked her hand through the crook of his arm. What a pleasure it was to be out in public as if they were a couple, as if she were his wife. He enjoyed the warmth and vitality of her body nestled next to his. Phillip patted her hand with his free one. The texture of her skin had changed over the decades. The veins in her hand were more prominent now. A multitude of minuscule lines rippled outward as he caressed the back of her hand with his thumb. Vicki's hand twitched. Reminded him of a horse attempting to rid itself of a pesky black fly. He ceased the movement, suppressing a sigh as he turned his gaze to the ocean and the multitude of small islands beyond. Their relationship had changed in the last few years. She was more impatient. Found him clingy. Odd that. The more she pulled away, the more deeply and desperately he loved her.

"She was lying." Vicki sounded almost angry. She was such an emotional creature, so full of fire and passion, unlike his wife, who was placid as a cow in the field chewing her cud. "Sarah Rainsford *was* here. One hundred percent. You told me she was dead."

"No. I remember quite clearly. I said I *thought* she was dead. After all, no one had heard hide nor hair from her. She hadn't touched a cent of her money."

"Well, clearly she's alive."

Phillip nodded. Maybe Sarah was. Maybe she wasn't. It wasn't worth getting in an argument over.

"What next?"

Phillip tucked down a little deeper into the comfort of his cashmere coat. The March wind off the ocean had an insidious damp chill that crept into his bones. "I was thinking a nap might be nice."

"No, you old goat." Vicki took a jerky step backward, placing her fists on her hips. "I am *not* in the mood for a snuggle. I've worked too hard and too long and I'm tired, I tell you." Her voice had gone sharp and shrill. "Tired!" She turned abruptly and started walking away from him, but not before he caught sight of the angry tears filling her eyes.

"Vicki, what's going on?" He hobbled after her as best he could, the damp air aggravating his hip, causing it to flare up.

She turned on him, teeth bared. "Everything you've ever said to me has been lies. 'I love you.' 'I'm going to leave my wife. I promise.' But did you? No! Twenty-eight years. Twenty-eight years of my *life* I've wasted on you."

"I'm going to—"

"Shut up!" She jabbed her finger into his chest hard. Her face thrust up close into his. Scared him a little and turned him on as well, all that rage and passion. "There was always some damned excuse. 'The boys are going through a rough time.' Then they were at university, but your wife got cancer. Of course you couldn't leave then. What kind of monster would? But now I wonder, did she actually have ovarian cancer? Or was that just another thing you lied about?"

He felt rather like he was drowning. Tried to bluster his way through. "I don't lie to you. I never have."

She laughed, brittle as glass. "'You'd need to get licensed with FINRA,' you said, 'in order to pull a salary on the trust accounts.'" Her face was bitter and her voice high-pitched and mocking. "Well, I worked *hard*, all those nights and weekends that I sat waiting around for you to show up for an hour or two. I got licensed with the Financial Industry Regulatory Authority. Still you hesitated, so I took an online course and got my CFP. I'm a frigging certified financial planner. 'Ah,' you said. 'Wonderful! Congratulations, my beloved! Let's crack open a chilled bottle of Dom Perignon.' But did a damn thing change? No." Suddenly all the fight seemed to drain out of her. She seemed smaller. Older. Depressed and defeated. And he felt ashamed for having turned the bright, loving, trusting person she had been into this. She looked at him. No artifice. No smile. He could see the sorrow and disillusionment in her eyes. "You thought I'd never know, didn't you? You thought I'd take your word. That I'd trust you." She shook her head, her face wet with tears. "And I did. But all this time you've been running a con on me."

"What are you talking about, Vicki?" he asked, but he knew. The stew of guilt in his stomach was churning in overdrive. "Let's go back to Mansfield Manor, have a nice cup of tea." He reached out for her arm, but she shook him off. Turned away, both of her hands gripping the rough wooden railing as if she were contemplating hurling herself over it into the frigid ocean below. "Vicki, my lovey-dove-dove—"

"Don't." There was no bite in her words, no accusation, which was somehow scarier. "I never would have known if I hadn't pulled the Rainsford trust documents. I thought maybe you would need them to verify who you were to the authorities. I glanced through them this morning while you were in the shower, wanting to make sure everything was in order for you. Surprise. My name doesn't appear any-where on that trust document. There is no codicil or addendum. I've been doing all the work, and it's all in your name. Legally, only you are entitled to the bragging rights, the credit, and most importantly, the fees. Now, I'm curious, as you can imagine, so I pulled up other trust documents on my laptop. The Smith trust, the Davidson one, the Phil Stork trust. All these, mind you, are documents you'd told me I was now co-trustee on. Nothing." Her voice quiet, flat, emotionless.

"Vicki, I can't add your name as a trustee. You should know that. It's basic 101. Only the person who set up the trust or the courts can add or change a trustee. Barbara and Ryan are dead. The only way the terms of the Rainsford trust can be changed or a co-trustee added is if Sarah is found and she applies to the courts to make a change. Same goes for the other trusts I handle—"

She whirled to face him, anger flooding her face, which oddly was a relief from the flat detachment. "Then why did you send me on that goose chase? Why encourage me to get my FINRA and CFP designations?"

"I didn't think you would." She took a step toward him, her mouth tight, fists clenched. Phillip made the decision to take a couple of steps back. She looked magnificent in her fury, as if she might actually haul off and slug him. "And then," he added hastily, appealing to her reason, "when you actually started . . . I don't know." He turned his hands upward, aware of the pleading quality that had entered his voice. "I guess you were so excited and proud, and I was, too." He attempted to reach for her, but she jerked away, her arms crossed.

"So where did the extra salary come from? The bump in pay, since I wasn't actually entitled to collect a fee on those accounts."

"Out of my pocket."

"So I was an amusing little charity case? The safety net I thought I'd built for my future—the ongoing monthly fees from managing the trusts that were supposed to keep me fiscally safe when you passed away—was all an illusion. You die and the cash cow dies with you, the probate court steps in, assigns their person to the Rainsford trust, and I'm left out in the cold. How you must have laughed at me. 'Stupid little Vicki, how gullible she is—'"

"No. It wasn't like that."

"I'm done." Her words hit him like a sledgehammer to the gut. "I quit." Her face was pale and determined, her eyes red-rimmed, her nose, too, and he had never loved her more. "Get yourself some other sucker to gaslight. You and I are done. I will write myself a glowing reference letter using your letterhead and courier it to your office. You *will* sign and return it along with the contents of my desk, which you will box up and send to me."

"Vicki—"

She held up her hand, palm out. "Don't even, old man. Seriously, after everything you've put me through? It's the least you can do." Vicki didn't wait for a response. She turned on her heel and strode away.

PHILLIP LEFT THE DOOR OF THEIR HOTEL ROOM UN-locked, stayed up late pretending to read, but she didn't return to their room. He tossed and turned all night, and in the morning, when the limo arrived with her inside, quiet and unresponsive, her face turned to the window, he knew what he needed to do. No more words. It was time for him to step up, be a man, or he would lose the only person he'd ever loved.

18

SARAH'S HAND HOVERED OVER THE BOXED PIES. *Cherry or apple?* Since rereading *Amelia Bedelia*, she'd gotten it in her head that perhaps Mick, like Mr. Rogers, would appreciate some pie. She picked up an apple one. It looked kind of tired. How long had it been sitting on the shelf? Her mind flashed to the delectable home-baked pies that Maggie whipped up daily for the customers of the Intrepid Café on Solace Island. On the heels of that sudden mouthwatering craving came an image of her last boss, Zelia Thompson, bustling into the gallery carrying *Intrepid's* signature white pastry box wrapped in red string. "When I fall off the wagon, I do it with gusto!" Zelia had exclaimed. "I bought out the shop, so you better be hungry." Her head had tipped back, infectious laughter bubbling out.

Sarah slapped the boxed pie down, and the next thing she knew, she was in the produce section stuffing apples into a bag. *Why not?* she thought with a shrug. *How hard can pie be? And if I mess up, who cares? It's the weekend. My time is my own.*

Once the apples were in her cart, Sarah trundled to the

baking aisle, snagging some butter on the way. She threw a bag of flour, some sugar, and cinnamon into her cart. She'd never made pie on her own. The idea of attempting it was both scary and kind of thrilling, too. Sarah had helped her mom make it when she was young, standing on a chair so she could reach the countertop. Her mom didn't cook often. But every once in a while, she'd take Sarah's hand and they'd venture into the kitchen, where their elderly cook, Berta, reigned supreme.

"You got the cooking bug again, ma'am?" Berta would say, her face a wreath of smiles.

"I sure do," Sarah's mom would say, opening a drawer and tying an apron around her waist.

"Me too," Sarah would say, and her mom would smile as she tied another apron around Sarah's waist and dropped a kiss on the top of her head. Berta would "leave them to it." By the time they finished baking, the kitchen would be filled with the cozy smells of loving goodness. Sometimes it would be peanut butter cookies, sometimes a raspberry trifle, and every once in a while . . . pie! Didn't matter what kind. Dad loved them all. Granted, the desserts created during their kitchen forays never looked as nice as Berta's offerings. A little charring or a soggy crust was not unusual, but Sarah, her mom, and her dad would dig in with gusto, and her dad would always declare that he could taste the love embedded in the creation. Over the years, they had attempted chocolate cream pie, lemon meringue, peach, and apple. Sarah wasn't certain what all went into apple pie. Hopefully, she had gotten the majority of the ingredients. Would have to Google a recipe when she returned to the house and had access to a computer.

At the cashier, Sarah separated the pie ingredients from the rest of Mick's groceries. She paid for it with cash Mick had left on the kitchen counter Friday morning. An envelope stuffed with cash, her first week's pay. If the pie didn't turn out, Sarah would eat it anyway. But if she were able to pull the culinary feat off, the homemade apple pie would be her thank-you gift to Mick, and hopefully—even though the gesture was small—it would help her feel less beholden. She had to do something because that extravagant dinner at The Palm restaurant had been an act of charity on his part. It embarrassed her to think about that night, how hungry she'd been, how noisy her stomach, but remembering also filled her with a sense of gratitude. When they'd arrived home, Mick had insisted she take all the leftovers. There were a *ton* of leftovers. Sarah had demurred at first. But he'd marched to the side of the house where the garbage cans were, lifted the lid, and insisted that if she didn't want the food, he was going to throw it out. Said he'd "just asked the waiter to wrap the extra food up so the cooks in the kitchen wouldn't be offended." Sarah had snatched the food from him. Hadn't realized until the food was safely in her arms, clutched against her beating heart like a lost child, that the "throw the food away" had been an elaborate bluff. It wasn't anything he said that clued her in. It was the sudden happiness beaming out of his eyes. Pride was insisting she shove the bags of food back at him, but she didn't. She'd said, "Thank you." Granted her tone had been a little stiff and her cheeks flaming, but at least she had thanked him before she turned and fled up the stairs to the safety of her little apartment, the door locked securely behind her.

That food had saved her. No doubt about it. Sarah had carefully divided the food into seven portions. Kept the first three portions in the fridge, froze the other four so they would stay fresh and she'd have enough food to last her until payday.

Once Sarah had paid for both hers and Mick's portion of the groceries, she gathered up her grocery bags and headed for the exit. She stepped out into the bright Los Angeles sunshine so caught up in her baking plans that she was halfway across the parking lot before she noticed the black-and-white backing up. *Don't freak out,* she told herself. *This is probably nothing to do with you.* Even so, she veered to the right, heart pounding, yanking the rubber band from her ponytail, tipping her face downward so her hair fell forward and shielded her face. She forced her body to move slow and steady as she pushed through the panic. *Keep walking. That gray van there would be good cover. Two more cars. You can do it. Hopefully the cop is just stopping to pick up some lunch.* She tucked behind the van and watched the reflections in the grocery store window. The cop car glided to a halt directly behind her vehicle, blocking it in. *Oh shit.* Inside the cop car, the policeman tugged his computer screen toward him and started inputting information. Even from her limited vantage point, it was clear he was focused on her car. *Move. Move now!* By the time she reached the sidewalk, the cop was getting out of his vehicle. He circled her car, scanning the parking lot behind his mirrored sunglasses. A city bus pulled to the bus stop in front of the store. *Psshhhh* went the air brakes, and the door folded open. It felt like a sign. A promise of momentary safety.

Sarah melded into the line of people getting on the bus. *Four people to go . . . Three now . . .* She didn't look back. Didn't dare. Nausea, acidic and sour at the back of her throat. *Two people until safety . . . One.* Trying to keep her body language relaxed. *Nothing to see here. Just a woman with her shopping bags heading home.* She stepped onto the bus, half expecting a heavy hand to land on her shoulder, yank her back, and slam her to the ground.

Psshhhh. The bus door shut behind her, and the bus lurched away from the curb, causing Sarah to stumble. She grabbed the pole, and her grocery bags thumped hard against the metallic barrier. She felt a momentary flare of worry that the apples would be bruised. On the heels of that thought, embarrassment bloomed for worrying about something so inconsequential. "How much?" she asked the bus driver. Her voice sounded odd, as if she were listening to someone else speaking. It was raw and ragged, more like a croak.

"Dollar seventy-five. We don't make change."

"Okay." Sarah nodded, rummaging in her purse, watching out of the corners of her eyes as the grocery store parking lot, the cop, and her car glided past the smeared windows. The cop wasn't chasing the bus down, banging on the door. He had his hip resting against the side of her car, arms crossed, his face fixed on the grocery store doors. Sarah jerked her gaze away, dropped her coins into the fare box, then lurched to a seat. Her breath was unsteady as she placed her bags between her feet, tipped her head back, and shut her eyes. Her heart pounded like a brick in a dryer. *Kevin must have been to Solace Island. It's the only way he would have found out about my car, been able to trace my license plate. Stands to reason he knows what I look like now—*

"You okay, missy?" she heard a voice say. "You seem kind of pale. You need some water?"

Sarah opened her eyes. A middle-aged woman was looking at her. There was concern in the woman's faded brown eyes as she extended her water bottle. Sarah shook her head, managed a smile. "Thanks," Sarah said. "I'm fine, I just . . ." She trailed off, unsure what to say. She could feel a trickle of sweat making its way down the side of her face, beads of perspiration on her upper lip. Sarah swiped her forearm across her face. "Got a few more groceries than I had planned on carrying. Heavy."

Sarah could see the woman was still worried, but she nodded as if they both had agreed to pretend Sarah wasn't lying. "If you change your mind . . ." There was compassion in the woman's soft smile. She gave Sarah's hand a gentle pat, then faced forward again, her shoulders slightly rounded, as if the world and all its problems made her unbearably sad.

Sarah turned her face to the window, biting her lip hard so no noises could escape as she stared out with hot, unseeing eyes. *What now . . . ? What now . . . ?* A nonstop litany banged away in her head as the bus took her farther and farther away from where she wanted to be.

19

AFTER REREADING THE SAME PAGE FOR THE THIRD time that evening, Mick tossed the script from Paramount on the coffee table in disgust. Attempting to work was pointless. Night had fallen and still Rachel hadn't returned. He stood, scrubbed his face and scalp with his hands, hoping the massaging motion would dispel the unease that had been building in his gut since midday. The movement didn't disperse it. *Shit. This woman is too much of a distraction.* Normally he would have plowed his way through a couple of scripts in the amount of time he'd spent stuck on this one. He glanced at his watch. *Nine forty-five. Does she have a boyfriend? Is that where she is? A husband, perhaps? That's probably it. She's having a day with family or friends.* He sat back down, made his body relax. *It's crazy how little I actually know about her.* He leaned forward and picked up the script. *What a weird world I now inhabit,* Mick mused. *Open my door and let an absolute stranger live in my house.* Naturally, the employment agency would vet any applicant they sent over. But how thorough were their checks? *She could be a bloodthirsty psychopath, for all I know.* The thought made him smile. If there was one thing Rachel wasn't, it was a bloodthirsty psychopath. The woman was an intriguing mix, the bulletproof veneer with a bruised vulnerability and an almost innocence underneath. Mick's mind flipped to the memory of Wednesday night. He couldn't enter his study without seeing her there in that pale-pink robe, sneakers slipped off, feet tucked under her, cheeks flushed as she scribbled down notes. Rachel had typed the notes after he had returned to his bed, and they were in a neat pile, along with a USB flash drive, waiting in the entryway hall when he left for work the next morning. The notes were perfect. On the heels of that memory came the image of Rachel leaving that morning. He had cracked open his bathroom window to let the steam from the shower out and saw her exiting her apartment. There had been a bounce in her step. It was as if he could feel joy shimmering in the air around her. He had watched her, razor in his hand, suds on his face dripping down his neck. The towel wrapped around his waist was no match for his body's visceral reaction to her. There was something about this woman that captured his attention and made it difficult to look away. He'd watched her descend the stairs, looking lighter and more carefree than he'd previously seen her. For a split second he'd found himself holding his breath, hoping she would cross the driveway, knock on his door, and invite him to ride shotgun. She hadn't. Of course. She'd gotten into her car.

When she started the engine, soft music spilled forth, tumbling out of her windows. "Blue Moon," an old Cowboy Junkies recording that flung Mick back to being a nine-year-old kid. Chastity from Desert Rose used to play that song. She hadn't stayed at the ranch long. A couple of months and then hopped on a bus and never came back. She'd been young. Said she was nineteen, but he was pretty sure she was lying. Saw her coming out of the bathroom once without her makeup on, didn't look more than fourteen, fifteen tops. His grandma had put her in the bedroom next to his. The walls were thin. He could hear everything.

Wasn't spying. Couldn't help it. She didn't like being a prostitute; that was for sure. But the johns sure loved her with her pale-blond hair and gangly limbs. More often than not, she was the one they picked out of the lineup. Got so when she would bring a customer in, Mick would grab a book, go sit outside. He'd know when her trick was done. She'd put on that song, play it after the john had left, while she remade the bed, wiped out the sink, rehung the towels, singing along, crying by the end. Always. And Mick wondered now, as he had then, what was her connection to that old song? Had it been her mother's favorite? And if so, was her mother dead? Is that why Chastity was on her own so young?

"Blue Moon." The song haunted Mick. Except it sounded different when Rachel sang along as her car disappeared down the driveway. There was more a sense of celebration as she sang, a freedom to her voice and her movements that morning that was at odds with her conservative apparel and yanked-back, constricted hairdo. *Why did she yank it back like that? It had looked beautiful unbound.*

Mick hadn't heard her vehicle return, but it was possible he missed it. *Who was she? Obviously the woman was highly skilled, so how did she end up working for me? What circumstances propelled her to take this job?* And then, like a homing pigeon, his thoughts returned to *Where did she go?* Followed by the refrain *It's none of your business where she goes or what she gets up to on her days off.*

Nevertheless, after pacing the living room floor for a while, he found himself in the entryway. The cool night air poured through the open doorway as he stared into the darkness. He looked up first. He wasn't checking on Rachel. Was just getting a breath of fresh air. No stars were visible. Not tonight. Too much haze. However, there was a fuzzy silver sliver of the moon hovering in the branches of the large eucalyptus tree. He heard the far-off yips of a pack of coyotes closing in on their prey, and Mick's mind alighted on Rachel again. Hoping she wasn't lost or in trouble. Finally, he let his gaze wander to the spot where she usually parked. It was empty. The windows of her apartment were dark. *Odd the little things one gets used to.* Mick hadn't realized until that moment how much he liked seeing the apartment lit up. Sometimes her silhouette would pass by a window. It was comforting. Felt sort of like a hello-you-aren't-alone-in-this-big-wide-world. *Where the hell is she?* He glanced at his watch. *The Lakers game will have finished taping.* Mick closed the front door, went into the kitchen, snagged a beer and a bag of salt-and-pepper kettle-cut potato chips, then continued on to the home theater.

A little after midnight, passing by the window on the way back to the kitchen, he saw her apartment lights were on. Mick felt the knot in his stomach loosen. She was home. Finally. He could stop worrying, would go to bed now and get some blasted sleep.

20

PHILLIP STARED AT THE ELEGANT SPORTS CAR—LIT UP by his headlights—that had snagged his preferred parking spot directly in front of Vicki's town house. Generally, on Sunday evenings that space was free. During the day was iffy, because of the graveyard up the block, but Sunday evenings no one parked there. There had been a spot farther back, but he had been hoping. In the old days, he would have shrugged and backed up illegally. Never mind it was a narrow one-way street. He'd found cars would honk, but they'd get out of the way if he moved aggressively enough. Show no mercy. Show no fear. Hit the gas and go. However, the last time he tried that maneuver had been at least a decade ago. Torqueing his body to get a good view out the rear window had caused him to slip a disc, one of his lumbar vertebrae. It had been quite painful. He'd had to call Vicki from his car phone. She'd raced outside to help him out of his car. Somehow they managed to maneuver him up the stairs to her front door. It had been painted a robin's-egg blue back then. He'd had one of his arms around Vicki's shoulders, his other hand gripping the black wrought iron banister. Every movement caused debilitating, hot-dagger-like pain to shoot through him. By the time they got him inside to his armchair, he was sweating profusely. On the upside, Vicki had fussed around him like a mother hen. She had stuffed a bag of frozen peas down the back of his pants, then rustled up a martini for him, a dish of warmed mixed nuts, a muscle relaxant, and a glass of water to wash it down. Returning home that night had been impossible, the next night, too. He'd spent three full days and nights of painful bliss with Vicki in their love nest before he was capable of making the drive home. *Memories,* Phillip mused, making a right-hand turn onto McDonald Avenue. An SUV swerved, horn blasting. "Get off the fucking road, Grandpa!" By the time Phillip had his window open and his middle finger hoisted, the SUV was well down the road. With all the drama, Phillip had missed his turn, so he drove another block and then turned right, made another right and another. Luckily, no one had pulled into the parking spot he'd spied down the block from Vicki's house, and he claimed it for his own.

He glanced in the rearview mirror, attempted the thankless task of smoothing down his eyebrows, which over time had taken on a life of their own. Then he grabbed the bouquet of flowers lying across the passenger seat and exited his Mercedes. Even after all these years, Phillip still took great pleasure in the fact that he could walk onto any car lot in the world and purchase a top-of-the-line luxury car, no problem. He tucked the bouquet under his arm, freeing up his hands to give his slacks a hike and tighten his belt. Unlike his contemporaries, he hadn't let his body turn to fat. He still had his basketball player's build, long legs, and bony ass.

Once everything was in order, he stepped onto the sidewalk and headed toward her house, humming Paul Anka's "Puppy Love" under his breath. It seemed apropos. Physically, he was a seventy-two-year-old man, but Vicki made him feel like a teenager in love.

He was pleased to see that Vicki was home. Her porch

light was on, and light spilled through the cracks of the drawn curtains in her upstairs bedroom. She wasn't expecting him to arrive uninvited, but what other option did he have left? He had to see her. They needed to talk face-to-face. The anxiety was killing him. When they had landed at JFK, she had refused a ride home. Vicki had marched to the AirTrain, stepped inside, and as the doors were sliding shut behind her, she informed Phillip not to expect her in the office on Monday. She refused to answer his numerous texts and calls.

Phillip climbed the front steps and rapped on the door, which was, at present, a fire-engine red. How long this color would last was anyone's guess. It was one of the things he loved about Vicki—her passion and her joie de vivre. He listened for a moment but didn't hear the sound of her footsteps approaching. He could hear soft music drifting through her cracked-open window, the sound of voices. *She must have the TV on.* He rapped harder on the door, leaning on the doorbell for good measure. "Vicki," he bellowed, which was so unlike him it made him smile. *Who is this new man of action?* Phillip felt a sense of power surge through him as if he were channeling Marlon Brando and had become Stanley Kowalski, getting his Stella back. "Vickeeeeee!"

A dog barked down the block. A window flew open across the street. "Shut the fuck up! I got kids sleeping in here."

"Make me," Phillip called back, putting his dukes up, bouquet still under his elbow, doing a little one-two step. He might not have done it, because the guy was built like a gorilla, but he could hear Vicki sliding the safety chain off the door, unlatching the locks.

"Seriously, old man," the guy snarled. "Don't tempt me."

Phillip heard the door swing open. Vicki grabbed his elbow and yanked him inside. "What the hell are you doing?" she hissed as she slammed the door shut. "Trying to get yourself killed?" Her hair was tousled, and he could smell a hint of gin on her breath.

"I needed to see you. Life is meaningless without you. I think of you morning, noon, and night—"

She didn't look swept away by the romance of his gesture. She looked royally pissed. "I *live* here. These are my neighbors. Just last month Rocco chased away a crackhead who was attempting to break into my home." She jabbed a finger in his chest. "He looks out for me. Which is more than I can say for you."

Phillip blinked, thrown by the ferocity of her response. He needed to recalibrate. There was a thump overhead. Probably Angel, her overweight Persian cat, had knocked something over. Pain-in-the-ass cat that required Phillip to keep a sticky clothes roller in the trunk of his car to remove copious amounts of long white cat hair before he headed home. "I brought you carnations. Your favorite." He handed them to her, but instead of taking them and burying her face in their petals to inhale their scent, she crossed her arms and the bouquet tumbled to the floor. This was not how he had imagined things playing out. "Lovey-dove-dove," he said soothingly. "Don't be angry with your teddy bear. I can't take it. I brought you a reference letter. I wrote it myself this afternoon. Just needs to be signed." He reached into the interior breast pocket of his cashmere tweed sports jacket and pulled the letter out and opened it so she could see he wasn't lying. Phillip saw her glance at the letter in his hand, her expression softening slightly.

"You did?" There was a cautious hope in her voice, in her eyes.

"That's right," he said. "You get me a pen, I'll sign it right now, on the spot. However"—he held up a finger, then carefully replaced the letter in the envelope and slid it back into his breast pocket—"I am hoping that first you will grace me with five minutes of your time." He could see her mouth tightening. He had to speak fast, before she got it in her mind to throw him out. "I've left Jane."

She snorted in disbelief. "That old story? Seriously?"

"It's true. I told her you were the love of my life, always have been, always will be. I am going to file for divorce. At present I am staying at the Plaza Hotel." Something wasn't right. Vicki wasn't falling into his arms, laughing and crying, overcome with joy. She looked almost sad. Weary. "Did you hear what I said?" Phillip was starting to feel scared. "I've left Jane. I want to be with you. For us to start a new life together—" He heard the back door slam and froze. Vicki did too. The two of them a tableau suspended in glass, listening to the sound of leather-soled shoes descend the wooden porch steps that led to the back garden. The garden he paid his own gardener to maintain. "Who the hell is that?"

Vicki swallowed, then lifted her chin, brazening it out. "I don't know what you're talking about." Her eyes locked on his as they listened to the sound of the pea-gravel path crunching under swiftly moving feet along the side of the house. As Phillip headed toward the window, Vicki grabbed his arm. "I can explain," she pleaded, desperation in her eyes. "He said he knew of a job. A friend looking for someone with my skills—"

Phillip yanked free of her grasp, got to the window in time to see the figure of a man with close-cropped dark hair step off the path onto the sidewalk. Phillip couldn't see his face as the man's head was turned away, but there was something about him that was triggering memory bells. An itch he couldn't quite reach. The usurper was tall, well built, and moved like an athlete. *Could probably fuck for hours on end.* Phillip watched, jealousy consuming him, his gnarled hands gripping the windowsill. *Probably had.* The man crossed the sidewalk and got into the sleek midnight-black Maserati that had stolen his parking spot. That was *his* spot. His! It was the last straw. Phillip whirled to face her. "Who is he?" Phillip demanded, anger rising hot and fierce, snatching his breath from his chest.

"It doesn't matter. Phillip, you need to calm down. Your blood pressure is—"

He shoved her away. Not hard, but she must have been off-balance, because she gave a little cry as she fell to the floor. And the guilt of accidentally hurting her made him angrier still. "Who is he? You slut. You whore." As soon as those words were out of his mouth, the caring, pleading expression on her face slammed shut like a steel door. All that was left was a blank, numb sort of grief. A sorrow. As if he had once again disappointed her. But he didn't care. He was hurting too bad. Needed her to hurt, too. "And to think," he said bitterly, "that I left my wife for you. What a fool I am." She was sobbing now, and he was glad. "Tell me who he is!"

She didn't answer, so he grabbed a fistful of her hair and yanked her head up so he could see her lying, duplicitous face. "Who *is* he, goddammit?!" That was where he had made his mistake. Got too rough. Should have known better, because her leg shot out and swept his feet out from under him. He landed flat on his back with a thud, knocking the wind out of his lungs. Vicki stood towering over him now, filled with all the fury of Medusa herself, and he'd never loved her more.

"Don't you ever," she spit out, her eyes narrow slits, "*ever* lay a hand on me again, old man, or I will beat the crap outta you. Capisce?" She jabbed a deep-red manicured finger into his bony chest. "You. Don't. Own. Me. *No* man does."

Logically, he knew he should probably shut up, but he couldn't help himself. "Are you fucking him?" He knew he sounded pathetic, but he didn't care. He needed to know.

She bent even closer, her beloved face twisted in a sneer. "Look, you." She said it as if he were dog shit on her shoe. "I could welcome the entire male population of New York City between my thighs, and it would be *none* of your business. Now . . ." She yanked him to his feet, then stormed to her front door and opened it wide. She was magnificent in her rage. "Get out. Of my. House!"

21

MONDAY, MICK ARRIVED AT HIS OFFICE TO A SHIT-
storm. The phones were ringing. Lois wasn't at her desk.
Bob, Paul Peterson's new intern from USC, was running
around like a chicken with his head cut off. He was banging
cupboards open, rifling through them, letting out a groan
and then racing to the next one to repeat the process.

Ring . . . Ring . . .

"What the hell are you doing?"

Bob froze. Then slowly pivoted and swallowed hard. His
eyes wide, hands up in the universal gesture of don't-want-
no-trouble-here. *What does he think? I'm going to body-
slam him to the floor?* Mick sighed wearily. "Why are you
rummaging through my office?"

"I . . . uh . . . Well, you see, sir, it's like this. The writer
sent over new pages for Mr. Peterson's *Fatally Yours* project. He wants them printed on blue paper and incorporated
into the script pronto. However, Harmony says she forgot to
replenish the supplies and sent me over here to get some."
Figures. Paul's new secretary, Harmony, was another instance of Paul letting his libido do his hiring. It seemed,

where Peterson was concerned, bra size figured more prominently than brains.

Ring . . . Ring . . .

"Where's Lois?"

"Haven't seen her. Don't think she's in today," the harried intern replied. There was a slight sheen of sweat beading on his forehead and upper lip. "Look, I'm so sorry for the inconvenience, sir, but do you happen to know where she keeps the blue paper—"

"Wait a minute. Back up. Lois didn't . . . show up?" In the fourteen years Lois Caplan had worked for him, she had never missed a day. "Did she email or call?"

The intern blanched, started backing toward the door. "I . . . I wouldn't know." Mick heard a peal of feminine laughter drift in from the hall, a deep baritone rumble of a laugh that could only belong to one man. A second later Bradley Reed, in all his mega-movie-star glory, ambled in with his arm slung over his co-star Lauren Taylor's shoulders. Mick hoped for Lauren's sake that it was just Bradley being Bradley and didn't point to a more intimate relationship. Bradley was gold at the box office but a narcissistic dickhead off-screen: self-involved, temperamental, and very married.

"Hey, Mick." Bradley swaggered over and clapped him on the shoulder as if they were buddies. "Sorry we missed your party. Heard it was a wild one."

"We were planning on coming," Lauren said apologetically, sliding her long blond hair away from her face. Her English accent was more pronounced now that the cameras were no longer rolling.

"Oh, we were *coming*, babe." Bradley wiggled his eyebrows at Mick over the top of Lauren's head. "That's why we didn't show up, if you get my drift."

A blue-assed baboon could get his drift. Mick managed not to roll his eyes. Barely.

A flush of color rose in Lauren's face. She batted at Bradley. "That's private."

Ring . . . Ring . . .

Grateful for the distraction, Mick reached for the phone. "Gotta get this. Lois is out. Catch you guys later." Luckily, they took the hint and headed through the connecting door into Peterson's office. Mick exhaled, sank into Lois's chair, and brought the receiver to his ear. "Yes?"

"Hello, Mr. Talford, please."

"Speaking."

"This is Ruth Parker. I'm a nurse at St. Joseph's Hospital. Lois Caplan asked me to give you a call."

THE ELEVATOR DOORS WERE CLOSING, BUT MICK lengthened his stride and managed to slip inside. The accelerated movement caused some water to slosh out of the large vase of flowers he was carrying, soaking the lower portion of the sleeve of his jacket. Luckily, his stainless-steel Rolex was waterproof. The button for the fifth floor was already illuminated. *Excellent. Fewer germs to pick up.* Hopefully, this thing with Lois wasn't anything too serious. Perhaps she had caught that flu bug that had been making the rounds and had gotten dehydrated. He propped his hip against the wall, tipped his head back, taking advantage of a rare moment of stillness. He had not slept well. Hadn't had a good night's sleep ever since Rachel had moved in. He'd come home at night, dog-tired, have a bite to eat, a shower, then slip between the fresh sheets and sink into his comfortable bed. However, sleep refused to come. His mind wouldn't stop churning over the plethora of press and TV interviews he'd been slogging through for *Retribution.* Also, gnawing at his peace was the realization that he was rapidly becoming accustomed to the cozy creature comforts Rachel had imbued his house with. The troubling fact that he found he was looking forward to stepping through his front door. It bothered him that he would catch himself daydreaming about what treat she would have left out on the kitchen counter to greet him when he came home. After that first night, there had always been something: a plate of fresh cookies or brownies, a wedge of chocolate seven-layer cake, milk in the fridge to wash them down.

Then the weekend had come. And there were no new surprises left on his counter. He understood in his logical brain. She had weekends off, for Chrissake. She wasn't about to traipse over, barge into his house to drop some delicious delight off. He was the one who had told her he wanted privacy, solitude on the weekends. Not to mention, she was probably a little apprehensive about what—or whom—she'd find. But he found he was waiting, hoping anyway. Didn't like the feeling. Reminded him of Christmas, all the other kids talking excitedly about Santa this and Santa that and what Santa was going to bring to them. Mick knew Santa didn't exist. Hell, his grandma had disabused him of that notion when he came racing off the school bus, a glitter snowflake he had made in his kindergarten class trailing behind him on a string. He'd been bursting with the news of this magical being called Santa Claus and how he brought the most marvelous toys and candy to the good little boys and girls. He'd informed his grandma that the only reason Santa had never visited them was because they hadn't known to hang up their stockings on Christmas Eve. She had laughed that raspy laugh she had, full of venom, a trail of stale cigarette smoke escaping from between her lips. "Better hang up that pipe dream, kid," she said, wafting the smoke aside, thin bangles jangling on her bony wrist. "You ain't getting nothing from no Santy Claus. Bad kids don't, 'specially ones like you, who are rotten to the core."

But Mick had gone to bed that Christmas Eve with an empty sock in his hand, hoping, praying. The next year, too, but he'd stolen a thumbtack from the school bulletin board so he could attach the sock to the wall above his mattress on the floor, just in case Santa hadn't been able to remove it from Mick's hand without waking him.

But in the morning there was nothing. Not even a lump

of coal. That's how bad he was. After that, he'd stopped waiting. Stopped hoping. Stopped participating in that fool's game.

And these new expectations Rachel had conjured of a cozy, safe haven and a loving home's embrace? The way he was unable to sleep until he knew she was home safe and sound? They stunk. Were dangerous. He'd ridden that train a million times before. Every time his mom showed up at the ranch, sometimes on her own, sometimes with a new guy in tow. She'd coo over Mick, how big he had gotten, wrapping him in her perfumed arms, kissing and hugging him with tears in her eyes. She made all kinds of promises. Talking about how she was saving up, and one day she was going to take him home with her. A real home and he'd have his own bedroom, a bike, and maybe she'd even be able to get a place with a backyard and a swing tied to the branch of an old oak tree. Yeah. She spun pretty pictures, his mom. Carrying them out? Not so much. He fell for it, over and over, and then one day he just knew it was never going to happen. The next time she came to visit, he didn't bother coming out of his room to say hello. Mick heard her arrive, greeting all the girls. She had her party voice on because she had a new boyfriend in tow. Mick had seen them pull into the parking lot and get out of the car. "Where's Mick?" his mom had said. "Where's my darling boy?" He waited until they entered the front door, and then he climbed out his bedroom window and started running. Missed dinner. Didn't matter. Every once in a while, she'd stepped out into the parking lot, shielding her eyes from the sun, hollering his name, but he didn't come. No point. Couldn't stomach playing the game, hearing the lies, pretending he believed her. He stayed on his rock, hidden from the ranch by a creosote bush that smelled like rain. The moon came out, the stars, too. Finally she and her "friend" left. He had waited for another half hour in case it was a trick. But it wasn't. She was gone. And when he stopped crying, he wiped his face, returned to the ranch, climbed through his window, and crawled into bed.

No. Mick knew not to believe in fairy tales. Not anymore. They needed to be stamped out before they could take root and do permanent harm.

He needed to let Rachel go.

He would.

Just not yet.

The elevator *bing*ed for the fifth floor, and the stainless-steel elevator doors slid open. A woman with a cane slowly shuffled out. Mick stepped around her, glanced at the hospital map in his hand, then turned right.

When he inquired at the nurse's station at the end of the hall, a young nurse with a ponytail slipped out from behind the desk and led Mick to Lois's room.

There was something about hospitals that freaked Mick out, as if death, illness, and pain were lurking around the corner, waiting to pounce. And yet here he was. He stepped through the door of Lois's room, rounded the corner, and saw her lying there. He stared at his secretary, worry coursing through him. He didn't know what he was expecting, but it wasn't this. It was immediately clear that she would not have the mobility or desire to type, file, or answer phones. Casts encased both of her forearms and wrists; only her fingers were visible. Her leg was in a cast as well, strung up in the air. "How the hell did this happen?"

Lois mumbled something.

"Sorry, I didn't catch that." Mick's concentration was thrown off by the fact that an embarrassed rosy hue had bloomed across the face of his elderly, gray-haired secretary. "What did you say?"

Lois lifted her chin. "Hang gliding," she said, meeting his eyes. "Been feeling in a bit of a rut, so for my sixtieth birthday I decided to try something new."

"And you thought it would be a good idea to jump off a cliff clutching a glorified kite? Seriously?" It was hard to wrap his mind around the idea. Lois was always so pragmatic, so systematic and unemotional.

"It wasn't my fault. Everyone said so. The wind changed direction at the last minute. These things happen."

"You're an idiot."

"Thanks for the support. You have a lovely bedside manner. Why am I not surprised? Anyway. As you can see"—she held up her cast-clad arms—"I will be out of commission for a while. You'll need to find someone to take over. Stop glaring at me. I didn't do this just to inconvenience you."

"I'm not glaring at you." He was. He could feel scowl lines digging furrows in his face. Mick plopped the vase of flowers on the wide window ledge, a splash of color that brightened up the beige room. "I'm just trying to figure out what the hell we're supposed to do."

"I don't know what you're going to do, but as you can see, my options are limited. It's binge-watching *The Great British Bake Off* and bonbons for me. The doctor says it's going to be anywhere from eight weeks to six months off the job, depending on how fast I heal, rehab, et cetera."

"Eight weeks to six months?!"

"Stop bellowing—"

"I'm not bellowing." He was.

"And heads up, I'm not sure if at the end of rehab I'm going to want to come back."

"What?"

Her familiar face softened, as did her voice. "It's not you, Mick. For all your bluster and shenanigans, you've been a great boss. Best I ever had. Actually, it's because of your generosity that retiring a few years early is even an option. You see, in those split seconds between hopping off that cliff and realizing it was all going very wrong, I thought of all the things I've always wanted to do and have never done. It's true what they say, my life did flash before me, and it was short and uninspiring. I haven't lived, Mick. Not really. I've existed. Have meandered through life being dutiful and reliable and boring as hell. You see, none of us know how long we have, Mick, but by God, I want to make sure I begin to live fully."

He nodded, his throat a little tight. He felt lost. Cut adrift. "Where will you go?"

"Not sure." She smiled at him fondly. "I'm thinking maybe to get a little cabin by the sea. Watch the waves lap the shore, listen to the wind in the trees."

"Okay." His mind spun with images of Lois hang gliding intermingled with thoughts of the present and memories of the past, the workload waiting at the office. "Tell you what, let's not make any drastic decisions." He couldn't imagine his office without her. Lois had been by his side from day one. Helped him navigate the shark-laden waters. "You've had a bit of a shock. Focus on getting better. Get some rest. We'll deal with what comes next once you're back on your feet. No pressure. But you might feel differently after lying around for six months." Hopefully she would.

"Mick." Her voice was soft. "You're going to be fine."

"I just think it's best if we leave your options open. You want some time off. Fine. We'll check in with each other in September. If you still feel the same way, I'll accept your decision. Until then, I'll make do with temporary help."

22

SARAH WAS DOING A DEEP CLEAN ON THE OVEN when Mick blew into the kitchen like an electrical storm lighting up the place with his presence. "Why did you scream like that?" he demanded. "Made me feel like a fucking ogre."

"I didn't scream—"

"Damn right you did. Nearly gave me a heart attack."

"Well, you shouldn't sneak up on people."

"Whatever." The man was in a mood. Again. "Why didn't you pick up the phone? I was calling all morning."

"In my list of duties, you never mentioned answering your personal house phone—"

He impatiently waved her words aside. "If you had picked up the damn phone, I wouldn't have had to drive all the way back to get you. Grab your purse and whatever else is necessary," he barked. "I need your help at the office."

"What, right now?"

"Yeah, my secretary, Lois, is . . ." He huffed out a breath, ran his hands through his hair, not for the first time given that it was sticking up every which way. "She's out of commission for a while. Maybe longer than a while. I need you to step in while the agency finds an appropriate replacement."

"Okay." Sarah pushed to her feet and stretched out the ache in her lower back as she plopped the blackened sponge in the bowl of soapy water and pulled off her yellow rubber gloves. "I'll be ready in ten."

"Ten? Where's your purse, Timbuktu?"

Sarah could feel her eyes narrow. She was not in the mood for any of his bullshit. Had spent Sunday freaking out, cutting, dyeing and then redyeing her hair, trying to come up with a new look to keep her safe. Invisible. She hadn't gotten into bed until after three in the morning, and even then sleep hadn't come until the night sky started to lighten and the early birds had begun to sing. "Look . . ." It took everything she had to keep her tone civil. "I am willing to come to your office and bail you out in your time of need. But if you think I am going to show up in a professional capacity dressed like this . . . you are *sorely* mistaken."

"You look fine."

"Seriously?"

Mick stopped pacing, raked his gaze down the length of her. She forced herself not to squirm. Yes, she looked like something the cat dragged in. Big deal. His oven had needed cleaning. Besides, her brain worked better when her hands were busy, and she needed to figure out what to do next. A puzzled look crossed Mick's face, as if he was only now noticing how grimy she was. His gaze rose to her face, continued upward. His eyes widened. "What the hell did you do to your hair?" He said it accusingly, as if her hair were part of his domain.

Sarah crossed her arms so she wouldn't be tempted to strangle him and lifted her chin. So, perhaps the "midnight brown" hair color had turned hers black. Instead of the various subtle tones shown on the box, the dye had erased all nuance and left her hair looking like mud. Adding insult to injury, the bob cut she'd attempted looked nothing like supermodel Kaia Gerber's hair. No. Sarah had been unable to cut the hair in an even line. Kept tweaking—aka hacking away—but it just made things worse. Worse and waaay shorter than she had planned. Finally, when her arms were literally shaking with fatigue, she'd laid her scissors down in defeat, crawled into bed, wrapped her arms around Charlie's warm, furry body, and had a good cry.

So, yes, perhaps her hair looked like a hungry horde of rats had been gnawing on it while she'd slept. That was neither here nor there. A gentleman wouldn't gawk with the expression of someone who had just been smacked over the head with a baseball bat. "It's damned hard to cut your own hair."

"I gather," he said, the right corner of his mouth quirking upward. "Why'd you dye it?"

"I felt like a change. Stop smirking. I'd like to see you do any better."

"I wouldn't." Now the other side of his mouth was quirking upward as well, and she could see laughter dancing in his eyes. "That's why *I* employ a qualified hairdresser."

"Shut up," she growled.

Which just unleashed the laughter he'd managed so far to suppress. Watching Mick Talford laugh loosened something that had been locked deep inside. She could feel the low rumble of it rocketing through her. His face was so different in laughter. The unguarded expression made her think of wide-open wheat fields, fresh and full of hope and goodness. Laugh lines she hadn't noticed before fanned outward from the corners of his eyes. His head was thrown back, exposing the column of his neck. Tan and strong, begging for her to start at the hollow at the base of his neck and caress, lick, nibble her way up to his gorgeous mouth.

She stood there in his kitchen starving for human touch, human connection. Wanting so badly to step closer, press her hands against his warmth as if there were a blizzard outside and his unfettered enjoyment were a roaring fire. Sarah stood there feeling unbearably sad and yet joy filled, too. Spirals of heat and emotion flared upward, warming the tips of her ears, her cheeks, her neck. The heat then shimmied its way downward, dancing through her like droplets of light in a fireworks show to pool in her lower abdomen. Finally, his laughter subsided. He was leaning against the granite countertop for support and was wiping his eyes. "All done?" she inquired oh so politely, as if she were addressing the queen of England instead of this ill-mannered lout whom she so desperately wanted to knock to the floor and have her wicked way with. Apparently, she was losing her touch, because rather than being chastised by her tone, Mick laughed even harder.

"Here." Still chuckling, he grabbed a pad of paper and scribbled something down, ripped it off, and extended the paper to Sarah. "This is the address of the office. Input it in Google Maps. If you need to grab a quick shower, have at it. I'll meet you back there. If I'm at a meeting, Paul's secretary, Harmony, can show you around. And in the future, if the house phone rings and I'm not here, answer it; take a message."

Sarah stared at the piece of paper in his outstretched hand. "I can't." She took a step back. "Sorry."

"Can't what?"

"Meet you at your office."

The lightness the laughter had caused in his face had dissipated. "Okay . . ." he said slowly. "I'm a little confused here."

"I'm happy to help. Truly. I just . . ."

His eyes narrowed. "You are something else." His tone wasn't admiring. It was anything but. "Fine. I'll pay for your damn gas. Mileage. Figure it out and bill me."

"It's not that. My . . ." She inhaled. Huffed it out. "I don't have access to my car at present." She kept her gaze firmly fixed on the mirrored sunglasses he'd latched on the neckline of his gray T-shirt. She saw him still. Could feel the intensity of his gaze studying her. "Stop staring at me," she snapped. She could feel a flush of embarrassed heat suffuse her face as the vivid memory of Saturday roared to the forefront. The cop. The shakes. "It's not my fault." She should shut up. She didn't have to answer to him or to any-

one for that matter. She closed her eyes briefly in an attempt
to block out the memory of the hours she had spent on the
Los Angeles bus system, aimless at first, and then trying to
find her way back to Mick's house. The long arduous walk
home along winding canyon roads. Dusty. Uphill, lugging
heavy bags of food in the dark. The continuous stream of
cars roaring past, the feeling of helplessness and anger, too,
running from the law when she had done nothing wrong.

"What happened to it?" His voice cut into her thoughts,
yanked her back to his kitchen.

"To what?"

"Your car? Did you sell it? That's crazy. You can't get by
without a car in LA. Seriously. If you needed money, you
should have asked for an advance—"

"It's *in* the shop," she snapped, in an attempt to shut him
up. The moment the words were out of her mouth, she regretted them. The man was not without eyes. Sooner or
later he was bound to notice that her car was still AWOL.

Mick studied her face for a moment longer and then took
a step back. He leaned his hip against the kitchen counter,
all relaxed awareness now, thumbs slung through the front
belt loops of his faded jeans. "Okay," he said. His voice was
gentle. If it had been someone else, she might have even
described it as kind. "You can ride with me. How much
time do you need?"

She blinked at him, still flagellating herself for the stupidity of her gaffe. "Pardon?"

"I'll drive. How long will it take you to"—he tipped his
head toward her and raised an eyebrow inquiringly—"clean
up? You said ten minutes?"

"Ten. Fifteen tops." She took a step toward the hall
when his voice stopped her.

"Before it slips my mind again, how would you prefer to
be paid? I shouldn't have paid in cash this week. Laziness
on my part, and it's not fair to you. My mistake, but honestly, I didn't expect you to last. Anyway, my business manager can either set up automatic deposit into your bank
account, or she can cut you a check."

"I haven't gotten around to opening a bank account. I'd prefer to be paid in cash."

"You'll need to get on that. It's better if you're on the payroll, Rachel. Yes, you'd have to pay taxes, but it balances out. You'll get medical coverage. Also, our company has a very good employer-sponsored retirement plan. We match our employees' contributions up to three percent of their salary—"

"Thank you, but I want to be paid in cash. If that's not possible, I'll need to look for work elsewhere." His brow furrowed, his eyes narrowing slightly, as if he were activating his X-ray vision. She averted her face so she wouldn't have to see the suspicion—or worse, pity—in his eyes. It was hard to stomach. Mick probably thought she was so hard up she wanted to cheat the government out of their fair share. Why wouldn't he, given he also appeared to believe she'd sold her only means of transportation for cash? *Although, I wish to God I had. Such idiocy.* The cop would have made contact with Kevin by now. Undoubtedly, her ex would be on the next plane out.

"Okay," Mick was saying. "Cash it is. I'll leave it at the same place, kitchen counter every Friday."

God I'm so weary, Sarah thought as she placed a serene smile on her face. "Thank you," she said as she forced her body to saunter past him as if she didn't have a care in the world. Pretending the relief that the payroll wrangling hump had been resolved wasn't making her knees weak. *You are in control,* she told herself. *Cool, calm, and collected. Everything will be fine.* However, she must have let her guard down, because as she approached Mick, her senses were still in hyperaware mode. The intensity of his force field reverberated along her skin, caressed the tiny hairs on her arms, on the nape of her neck, as surely as if he had reached out and touched her. But she'd kept moving, brisk efficient steps, into the hall, the foyer, and out the front door.

Once she'd closed the door firmly behind her, she broke into a run. She needed every second in order to take a quick shower, drag a brush through what was left of her hair, and throw on some clean clothes.

TEN MINUTES LATER, ON THE NOSE, RACHEL SLID into the passenger seat of Mick's car. He quickly angled his phone away so she couldn't see the screen, hit the home button, and then slid the phone in his jacket pocket. Didn't know why he felt guilty. He'd been googling her. So what? Should have done so right off the bat. Hadn't yet found a match. It was going to be like searching for a needle in a haystack because there appeared to be a shitload of Rachel Joneses in the world. As Rachel's car door shut, a hint of her scent wafted over the center console to torment him. She smelled like spring, fresh scrubbed, cool water with a hint of honey-milk soap. Her hair was wet and slicked back. The darker color accentuated the milky creaminess of her skin, and the cut highlighted the swanlike length of her neck. Mick noticed a droplet of water quivering in the shallow hollow above her collarbone. She must have missed it in her dash to towel dry and get into clean clothes. And the impulse to reach out and capture that shimmering droplet of water on his fingertip, to taste it, was almost overwhelming. Mick forced his gaze forward, shifted into drive. It wasn't until they were halfway down Benedict Canyon that he was able to shake off the temporary lust-driven insanity. "Thank you," he said in the most reasonable of tones. "I appreciate you helping out on such short notice."

"A thank-you? Oh, my stars." She smirked. "There, now," she said, as if addressing a recalcitrant four-year-old. "That wasn't so hard, was it?"

Mick managed to choke back unexpected laughter. Barely. He glanced over, but Rachel had turned forward again. Her profile reminded him of a cameo brooch he had seen in a pawnshop window as a boy. She was dressed in the same nondescript outfit that she'd arrived on his doorstep wearing: conservative cream-colored blouse, black slacks, and sensible footwear. An outfit designed to keep a person at arm's length. Unfortunately, it seemed to have the reverse effect on him. *Why?*

No answers were forthcoming. Although, maybe it wasn't her wardrobe that was the issue, as her pink robe and pajamas had had a similar effect on him. He turned left onto Coldwater Canyon. When he did a shoulder check to switch into the right-hand lane, he noticed she wasn't wearing glasses. Must have left them behind in the rush. He cursed softly under his breath.

"What?"

My fault. Shouldn't have hurried her out the door. "Your glasses." He kept his voice flat so she wouldn't think there was any implied criticism.

She blinked, then lifted her chin in that way she had, her hands clasped neatly in her lap. "I'm wearing contacts."

His bullshit meter pinged again. For a split second, he was tempted to pull to the side of the road, take her face in his hands, look closely at her eyes to see if the telltale clear rims of contacts were visible. He didn't. Just as it was inappropriate to have lascivious thoughts toward his employee, it was equally against his moral code of ethics to manhandle one. He nodded his acknowledgment, as if he believed her, and kept driving. Turned right onto the 101 East ramp, merged onto the 101 South, stayed left to pick up the 135 East, and still neither of them uttered a word. Unspoken thoughts were thick in the air. *Who the hell is she and what is she hiding? Doesn't have a bank account. Needs to be paid in cash. Something's fishy about her car, and I'm pretty sure she's lying about the contacts. The question is why? Is she in trouble? Does she need help? Help.* He snorted. *Right. Like you're so good at that.* He had to make a conscious effort to loosen his grip on the steering wheel. *Her private life is none of your business. You're getting obsessed, man. You've got to let it go.* It wasn't until he had taken the Pass Avenue exit and pulled up next to a cop car that he glanced over and noticed she had unbuckled and slid her body down so it wasn't visible from the outside that the *ping* became loud alarm bells clanging in his head.

23

INSTEAD OF TURNING LEFT INTO THE WARNER'S LOT, Mick swung his vehicle onto a side street. Snagged a parking spot halfway up the block. Rachel had returned to her seat and was playing it cool, as if she hadn't just been plastered against the floor of his car. Didn't matter. Enough was enough. Mick parked, switched off his engine, then turned to face her.

Rachel avoided his eyes. She made a show of glancing out the window at the small dusty houses on the residential street, then twisted to peer at the shabby strip mall they had just passed. "Oh," she said brightly, reaching for the door handle. "We're here. Funny, it doesn't look at all like what I pictured . . ." He hit the lock button. Her voice petered out.

"I need answers."

She stilled. Her head tipped downward as if the weight of it had suddenly become too heavy for her neck to bear. Her eyes closed almost as if she were praying. He could hear her breathing go shallow and shaky.

"I'm not an idiot, Rach. You gonna tell me what's going on?"

No answer.

"All right. Let's start with something simple. What's your real name, and who are you running from?"

Still no answer. He shifted back in his seat, crossed his arms, and waited. He would wait all day if need be. The tension in the air vibrated on a knife's edge between them. "You might as well tell me, because we are not leaving this car until you do."

It was a matter of a split second. Caught him off guard. She moved like some kind of superhero, lunged forward, hit the unlock button, snagged her gray purse from between her feet.

"Rach . . . wait!" He reached for her, but he was too late. She'd already unstrapped, yanked the door open, and had tumbled out.

SHE RAN. KNOWING IT WAS POINTLESS. KNOWING she had nowhere to go. Knowing the walls were closing in fast. And yet she ran. Could hear the thump of his feet gaining on her. And then he was there. His body was like a brick wall, stopped her in her tracks. His arms, like steel, surrounded and encased her. Wouldn't let go, no matter how violently she fought. And she fought like a cornered animal with nothing left to lose. Striking, clawing any surface she could reach. He managed to capture her hands, but she still had her teeth, could kick. Too close, held too tight to manage a knee to the groin, but it didn't stop her from trying.

"Rachel . . . Rachel . . . Please." Through the thick fog of her fear, it dawned on her that there was no malice in his voice, no anger, even though he had to be hurting. He wasn't fighting back, either. The blows her body had instinctually braced for never landed. "Please, Rachel. I mean you no harm . . ." But it was the gentleness with which he contained her, the kindness in his voice, the concern and worry that caused the fight to drain from her body and left just the tears.

He cradled her into his chest, tucked her head in close. She could hear his breath, ragged, too, his heart thumping hard beneath his shirt. His head bowed over hers, his warm breath on her hair, and she could feel his hand making gentle circles on her back, as if she were a child that needed soothing. The comforting, safe scent of him made her weep all the harder. For all that she'd lost and all she'd never had.

MICK STOOD ON A SIDEWALK THAT HAD SEEN BET-ter days, the constant L.A. traffic streaming past, the noise a steady thrum in his ears. He could taste the slight tang of fear on his tongue, and smog and car exhaust. And an over-whelming sense of relief as well. He stood with his heart and his arms full of a woman he knew nothing about. And yet in a fundamental instinctual way, he felt that he did. Rachel was no longer sobbing. Thank God. The intensity of the storm seemed to have passed. Slight tremors shuddered through her slender frame, accompanied by little hiccuping gasps of breath. A skinny teenager on a skateboard with a mop of long hair whizzed toward them on the sidewalk. "Hey, guys," the kid called as he breezed past. "Get a room." The skateboarder crouched low, jumped the curb, leaned his body to the left, rounded the corner, and disap-peared from view.

Rachel straightened, wiped her eyes with her hands, and then took half a step back. His arms fell away from her body, missing her already as she dug into her purse and pulled out a tissue. "I'm so sorry. I was totally out of line, never should have struck you. I just . . ." She blew her nose. "I freaked out. Everything got jumbled, mixed up in my head, and you weren't Mick anymore. You became some-one else . . ." Rachel exhaled, her breath still shaky.

"Rachel, you know we can't go on like this?" He kept his voice gentle. Didn't want to spook her. "Who are you?" She froze for a heartbeat. "What are you running from?" Avoid-ing his gaze, she slowly, carefully placed the tissue in her purse. Took a long time closing it. He waited patiently, wasn't sure if she would answer. "I can't help if I don't know what the problem is. And, obviously, I need more information to make an informed decision whether it's safe to let you reside at my house." She stumbled another half step back, torso compressing inward, as if she had taken a body blow. Made him feel like a brute. "I will pay you for the time you've worked. I'm also prepared to put you and Charlie up in a short-term rental for two weeks to give you time to find a new job and accommodations."

Her eyes lifted from her purse to study his face. "Why would you offer to do that? I'm practically a stranger. You owe me nothing. Less than nothing." Rachel stilled, her breath seemed to catch, and then there was a flicker of something that looked like sorrow or self-loathing. "God." Her voice dropped to barely a whisper. "I'm . . . I'm sorry about your face, for"—she exhaled—"for flipping out like that."

"Forget about it. I have. You asked why am I offering to help?" He shrugged. "There's been times when I could have used a random act of kindness. I want you to have options, to not feel pressured to tell me more than you are comfortable with. However, you have to understand, if you can't trust me with the basic truths like your name, why seeing the cop freaked you out, I, in turn, will be unable to trust you."

She nodded slowly, still searching his face. He could see the fear and indecision in hers. A minute passed, then another. Finally, she seemed to come to some sort of decision because she squared her shoulders, her chin lifting slightly. Such bravery in spite of the fact that her body was trembling again. "My name"—her voice was clear, determined—"my real name is Sarah." She tore her gaze away from his, exhaled, pressing a fist to her chest. Then she lifted her gaze to look him straight on once more. "Sarah Rainsford."

Her name. She'd told him her name. He hadn't been aware that he'd been holding his breath. "Thank you." Her face was blotchy and her blue eyes swollen and bloodshot. Her nose was red, and yet he'd never seen anyone so beauti-

ful. There was truth shining out from her face like a beacon
of light. The walls were down. There was vulnerability, and
behind that he could see inklings of hope and the tender
shoots of a cautious burgeoning trust.

It started to sprinkle, a light misting rain. There was
something about the smell of rain on dry concrete that felt
to Mick as if God were washing away all the sins of the
world, making it fresh and clean again. New beginnings.
"Sarah Rainsford?" He tried her name on his tongue, and it
felt right.

She nodded, her eyes welling up. "Dammit." She swiped
her eyes dry. "I never cry. Seriously. It's just . . ." She exhaled, then smiled shakily. "It's been four years since anyone has called me by my real name. Didn't realize how
much I missed it."

"Suits you." The rain had transitioned from mist to large
splattering droplets.

Sarah nodded again, appeared to be bracing herself,
her breath coming out jagged and slightly shallow again.
"I'm . . . I'm on the run."

"I guessed as much." She was looking pale, as if she
might keel over. *Has she eaten lunch?* It hadn't crossed his
mind to check when he'd barged into the kitchen and demanded that she help out at his office. Mick tipped his head
toward the strip mall. "I could use a coffee and a bite to eat.
How about we get out of this rain? We can continue the
conversation inside."

She glanced around, eyes widening. The expression on
her face made Mick smile. Clearly she hadn't noticed the
rain until now. "Lunch is on me. We'll sit down, chat inside,
where it's nice and warm and most importantly . . . *dry*."
She smiled then, and he felt like a king because it was a real
smile that lit her up from the inside, and the beauty of it, of
her, hit Mick hard, like a blow to the solar plexus.

"Well, what are you waiting for?" she drawled, the shadows momentarily banished from her eyes. "In case you
hadn't noticed, it's *raining* out here." And the impish expression on her face caused laughter to come for the second

time that day. Unexpected, it rumbled upward from his belly, a stew of laughter and joy. The rain was now thundering down. Running was pointless because they were already soaked, but he snagged her hand in his and they ran anyway, hand in hand. And Mick felt young, like how he'd imagined love would be before he grew up and realized love was for fairy tales and fools. They ducked into the first restaurant they came to and dripped on the rubber mat by the front door.

"Hope Mexican's okay with you?" he said, wiping the rain from his face, taking in the decor and the smells of cooking that had permeated the premises.

"It's the perfect food for a rainy day," Sarah replied. The waitress bustled over, guided them to a booth, and placed worn menus on the Formica tabletop. The seats were red pleather. A strip of black gaffers tape covered a tear in the material, but the food coming out of the kitchen smelled good, as if it were made with care. They slid into the booth facing each other. Sarah shoved her hands in her rain-plastered hair and ruffled it in an attempt to corral her hideous haircut into some kind of shape. The movement of lifting her arms above her head stretched her shirt taut across her chest. The rain had rendered the cream-colored fabric see-through. *Holy crap.* He whipped off his WWII worn leather flight jacket, his arm getting tangled in his haste, and thrust it across the table. *She's your fucking employee.*

She jumped, startled.

"You were . . . uh . . ." He croaked, his mouth and throat suddenly parched. A few droplets of rain fell from his jacket and splattered on the tabletop. He was reluctant to tell her that her blouse was see-through. She would be embarrassed and was vulnerable enough as it was. "You were shivering," he growled. "Put it on."

"Are you sure? You aren't cold?"

"Hell no." *Put it on. I'm dying here.* "I'm running hot right now." *No lie there. And who the hell made her so skittish?* She'd flinched when he'd first extended his jacket, as if she were expecting a fist. "Go ahead. Put it on." He picked up the menu with his other hand, flipped it open, and studied it intently, trying his damnedest to be a gentleman, but it was too late. The image of her pert, uplifted breasts was permanently imprinted on his brain. The delicate lacy bra she was wearing beneath her blouse. He would have thought she'd go for more sensible undergarments, but no . . . He exhaled, trying to erase the knowledge that her areolas were a dusky rose, that if he glanced up he'd get another glimpse of her nipples straining against the fabric, hardened from the cold and the wet, seeming to be begging for the warmth of his touch, his mouth. He shut his eyes, stifling a groan, could hear her sliding his jacket on.

"Oh. Nice." She exhaled like a woman who had just been satisfied. "It's warm from your body. Feels so good." He could hear her snuggle into his jacket, and he wished it were him she was snuggling into. "Thanks." Her voice was breathy, slightly husky.

"Do it up."

"Pardon?"

"The zipper," he said, his voice gruff. "Will keep the heat in."

It was with regret and gratitude that he heard the zipper travel upward. He opened his eyes. Needed to blink to bring the menu in focus.

"You okay?"

It took him a second to order his thoughts before he was able to glance up and hold her gaze with a neutral expression on his face, as if he weren't sporting the monster boner of all boners under the table. She was looking at him quizzically. "Couldn't be better," he said, congratulating himself on managing a reasonably normal tone of voice. Thankfully, the waitress appeared at their table, tugging Sarah's attention to her.

"What can I get for you?" the waitress asked, her order pad at the ready.

"Oh." Sarah flipped open her menu and waved at Mick. "You order first."

"I'll have . . ." Mick glanced at his menu. "The number four combination plate. You want to share a tamale, some guacamole?"

"For sure." Sarah shut her menu and handed it to the waitress. "I'll have what he's having and some hot coffee."

Hmm . . . I don't think that's physically possible—the image of Sarah sporting a gigantic boner under the table made Mick grin—*but I'd be happy to share.*

"What are you laughing at?"

"I'm not laughing." Mick passed his menu to the waitress as well. "Ditto on the coffee. Please. Thanks!" The waitress nodded, tucked the menus under her arm, and completed writing down their order as she headed to the kitchen.

"You are internally," Sarah replied, looking at him inquisitively. "I can see it in your eyes."

"Ah." Apparently that answer didn't suffice because Sarah had raised her slender eyebrows. "Guess I'm just delighted to be out of the rain." Truth was Mick was feeling obscenely happy to be sitting there, soaking wet, across the table from her.

24

KEVIN FOLLOWED DETECTIVE LUNA AS HE STUMPED through the West Side LAPD car lot. The man was covering it well, but his gait was uneven. He favored the left leg. Kevin was sure the cold rain thundering down wasn't helping matters. The man's head was tucked into the collar of his jacket, as if that would help keep the wet at bay.

"You mind me asking why you towed it?" Kevin would have preferred if the LAPD had left the car where they had found it. He could have lain in wait at the grocery store parking lot, and if the car was Sarah's, eventually she would have shown up again. By towing the vehicle, they made it highly unlikely she'd use that store again. She had proven to be a worthy opponent in the game of chess they had embarked on.

"The vehicle was unregistered and had no insurance."

Kevin didn't want to put Luna's nose out of joint, but Jesus Christ, the incompetence needed to be addressed. "Out of curiosity," Kevin inquired politely. "A BOLO was placed on this individual for a reason. Rather than impounding the car, why didn't the officer use the car as bait to lure the individual into police custody for questioning?"

Kevin veered to the left to avoid a lake-sized puddle. Detective Luna plowed doggedly through it. "Officer Hatley stayed at the site for several hours. The grocery store has a two-hour parking limit. This car exceeded that. The parking lot attendee was preparing to call a tow company. Officer Hatley made the decision to bring the vehicle here."

"Has anyone contacted West Bureau to inquire about the vehicle?" Highly unlikely, but he had to ask.

"Not yet."

Figures. If it was Sarah, and she'd seen the officer sniffing around her car, odds were she would have slipped away. A more optimistic scenario was perhaps Sarah had used the grocery store parking lot while shopping at chichi boutique stores nearby and had lost track of time. Returned to discover her car was missing. But even in that innocuous scenario, Sarah wouldn't be stupid enough to sally into a police station to reclaim her vehicle. The lack of registration and car insurance meant the owner of the car was probably using fraudulent ID. Things would be much more difficult if the car was indeed Sarah's and she'd realized the cop's appearance meant Kevin had knowledge of her whereabouts, her vehicle, and plates. It wouldn't be a big leap for her to conclude that he also knew about the changes she'd made to her appearance. And she would be right. Kevin had commissioned a sketch artist to create a new composite drawing, which he had uploaded the day after the BOLO was put in. If this was her car, chances were she realized he was closing in. She would change her look and run again. Kevin needed to move fast before her trail got cold.

Detective Luna stopped and jerked his chin toward a gray Honda Accord. "That's it, there." The car was wedged between a lime-green Lamborghini and a rusted-out white 2005 Chevrolet Express.

"Thanks. Appreciate it," Kevin replied. He eyed the two-door, gray Honda. It was an older model, maybe 1995 or '96, a piece of junk. Had a hard time imagining Sarah behind the wheel.

"No prob." Detective Luna slapped a thin metal tool into Kevin's hand. "Lock it up when you're done and drop the slim jim at my desk." Detective Luna didn't wait for a response. Turned on his heel and headed back through the parking lot full of impounded cars toward the building. Kevin didn't blame him. It was pissing cats and dogs.

Kevin stared at the vehicle. He could feel his blood pressure rising. He'd taken a leave of absence from the job, been flying since the crack of dawn. Two flights for this? He'd been so goddamned certain he was closing in on his prey. What a laugh. Kevin felt like beating the crap out of someone. He walked to the back of the car and glanced at the plates. The numbers matched with the information he'd acquired on Solace Island. He shook his head. This was looking more and more like another wild-goose chase. Sarah had exquisite taste. She wouldn't be caught dead in this rust-ridden beater with its peeling paint and dent in the rear fender. He felt the acid rising in his gut, stuck his hand in his front pocket and flipped another Rolaid off the roll with his thumbnail, popped the disk in his mouth, and ground it into a chalky powder on his back molars.

He watched Detective Luna disappear into the building, then ambled to the driver's door. Dead end or not, he was there. Might as well check the damned car out. Unlocking the door took thirty seconds max. That was the beauty of those old cars' locks, so easy to unlatch. He opened the door and got in, more for protection from the rain than anything. It was pelting down at an angle, so he slammed the door shut behind him, leaned back in the worn seat, and exhaled long and loud. He swiped the rain from his face, refilled his lungs, and that's when his instincts started tingling. *At last!* Adrenaline rocketed through him. The last four years of searching were finally paying off, because he was pretty damn certain he was sitting in Sarah's car. He turned, slid down, his knees hitting the floor so he could press his face into the seat. He inhaled again, long and deep, his eyes narrowed, focusing hard. *Yes.* He could smell the scent of her embedded in the upholstery. *She must have been driving this old clunker awhile.* He settled back into the driver's seat, laughed out loud, feeling as though he'd just snorted a line of pure cocaine. His wife was in the Los Angeles area . . . and so was he. It was only a matter of time.

Kevin shook the rain off his briefcase. Then he snapped the locks open, pulled the fingerprint set out, and got to work. His gut told him it wasn't necessary, but additional confirmation never hurt.

25

SARAH TUCKED HERSELF DEEPER INTO THE WARMTH of Mick's jacket, which smelled of leather and rain. A delicious, beautiful, impossible pleasure, to have the fabric warmed from his skin, the spicy, clean male scent of him encasing her. It was as if, through his jacket, he was caressing her shoulders, her arms, her breasts, back, and chest, her belly and hips. She was tall for a woman, but being in his presence made her feel petite, delicate. The sleeves of his jacket covered all but the very tips of her fingers.

Sarah knew she was going to have to explain her situation. That was the deal, and even though she was dreading it, she knew it had to be done. Underneath the dread was a weary relief as well. She was tired of running. Tired of hiding. Tired of living a lie. Once the waitress had left, silence descended, and the laughing lightness had vanished from Mick's face. He seemed to be struggling with something. Was he angry with her? Sarah didn't blame him if he was. The man had wanted a simple life, an assistant to type up some notes, an organized house, a few homey comforts, and what did he get? Sarah shook her head. *A lunatic. A liar.* He had been nothing but kind, and how had she repaid him?

Sarah exhaled shakily, snuck a glance at him through her lowered lashes. His head was averted. Probably the sight of her lying face made him ill. His jaw was clenched. Holding back a slew of angry words, no doubt. She had gone crazy punching, kicking, and clawing at him, and for what? Why? He'd done nothing to harm her. Had only shown her a gruff sort of kindness. Sarah squeezed her eyes shut as embarrassment and regret roared through her. Something inside had snapped when he'd run her down. It was as if a fuse had blown in her brain and he wasn't Mick anymore. He had somehow morphed into a weird mutant combination of Kevin and that madman Guillory and she was hurled into the past, but this time she was fighting. Fighting for her life.

Poor guy. No good deed . . . Luckily, his leather jacket had deflected a lot of the damage, and hopefully her teeth hadn't broken skin. However, Sarah could see the angry tracks her nails had slashed across his throat and the red mark high on his cheekbone where her fist had made contact. She felt her face grow hotter at the visual evidence of her outburst. "I'm sorry." Her voice tugged his gaze from the swinging kitchen door to focus on her. The intensity in his gaze made the anxious butterflies in her stomach stage a full revolt. But instead of running or backtracking or averting her eyes, she stayed put, straightened her spine, and continued on the path she'd laid before her. "I freaked out. Some kind of PTSD, got stuck in a flashback, but that's no excuse for the way I behaved. I shouldn't have struck you."

"I meant what I said out there. No apology is necessary." A rueful smile flickered across his face, as if he were the one who had dealt the blows. "I figured it was something like that."

Sarah felt like he was constantly seeing beyond what she had told him. It was an odd feeling. "I imagine you have some questions."

He regarded her steadily. "A few."

She nodded. "As I mentioned on the street, my real name is Sarah. Sarah Audrey Rainsford. Ryan and Barbara Rainsford were my parents." Her throat felt tight, constricted. This was harder than she'd thought it would be. Putting words to her situation.

"Were?" Of course he would pick up on that. She had to look away. The compassion in his eyes was making it hard to continue, and she had only just started. "They've passed away?"

"Yeah. Four years ago." Lord, how she missed them.

"I'm sorry." He sounded as if he truly was, for people he hadn't even met. She shut her eyes, bit down hard on her back teeth. Determined not to start weeping again. "Do you have brothers or sisters?" she heard Mick say.

"No. It's just me now." She forced her hands to loosen their death grip in her lap. Blew out a breath long and slow, trying to get her breathing regulated. Then she inhaled, and on the next exhale, she looked up so that her gaze met his once more. "Actually, you're the first person I've told my real name to in almost four years, so if you would please not share it with—"

"Of course not." He cut in, his voice harsh, definitive, and she knew by the way he said it that she could trust him. The man wouldn't be telling a soul.

"It's weird how saying my name out loud makes me kind of emotional."

He was focused intently on her face. Didn't speak. His eyes seemed darker than usual. Maybe it was the lighting, but the amber color appeared almost black. "So," he said, breaking the silence. "You've been on the run for four years?"

She nodded.

"And your parents died four years ago?" His voice was measured, almost emotionless.

She nodded again.

"Is there a connection?" he asked.

The question was innocuous enough, but it felt as if

she'd just been bowled over by a wrecking ball. "No. God no. I had nothing to do with it. They were in a car crash, snuffed out by a goddamned cement truck. I *loved* my parents. Loved them deeply. They were the *most* important people in my life. We were looking forward to the future, to the baby, to the—"

SARAH FROZE, HER HAND FLYING UP, CLASPING hard over her mouth. A low keening noise forced its way past her hand, her head bowing to her chest, but not before he saw the tears fill and overflow from her blue, blue eyes. By the time he'd rounded the table, her body had started rocking back and forth as if the grief was too big to contain. He gathered her in his arms for the second time that day, holding her. No words were sufficient, so he just held her close.

The waitress quietly placed their food on the table with her eyes averted, then silently slipped away. "And then what?" Mick said, because it was clear, no matter how difficult it was, Sarah needed to talk things out. "What happened?"

"Nothing. There were no arrests. The driver had probably been drunk or high on amphetamines. Didn't even stop. Just mowed them down and kept going. They never found him. He went on living his merry life, but me . . ." Her voice broke. "One day"—her voice so soft now, weary—"my parents were there, and the next day they were gone. Didn't get to say goodbye. Tell them how important they were to me. How much I loved them . . ."

"They knew."

"You don't know that."

"They knew." Mick didn't know why he was so sure, but he was. It was a bone-deep certainty, and she must have felt it, too, because her body softened, as if the agitation was physically draining out of her. She turned her face into him. He could feel her hand clutching his T-shirt, her warm breath fanning across his chest.

"Thank you," she whispered. They were silent for a while. Just breathing in and out. When she spoke again, her voice was muted. "After we buried them, there was the reading of the will. Kevin was angry. They had tied everything in a trust and—"

"Kevin?" Mick managed to say, calm and steady, as if his heart hadn't started thundering like a stampede of wild horses, as if there weren't a sudden rushing in his ears. "Who's Kevin?"

"My husband," she replied.

26

SHE'S MARRIED. MICK HAD AN IRONCLAD RULE RE-
garding inappropriate behavior with employees and anyone
who fell below the legal drinking age. Recently he'd made
the executive decision to expand his hands-off policy to
include married women. No way he was *ever* going to invite that kind of mess into his life again. *Shit. Shit. Shittity
shit.* And to make matters worse, his body cared dick-all
for his rules, and even now, while comforting a distraught
woman, his nether regions were revving up like a frat house
on a Friday night.

"He had thought they were going to leave the money to
me outright," she was saying. "But they hadn't trusted
Kevin, you see." Now that her story was spilling out, that
iron core of strength she had was starting to reassert itself.
She straightened. Although a few rogue tears still clung to
her eyelashes, she wiped her face and no longer seemed to
need the comfort of his arms. He lowered his hands to rest
on his thighs, palms down. "So they put everything in a
trust that Kevin couldn't access. Which really pissed him
off." She reached for her coffee. Mick used the momentum

of her movement to stand and round the table. He slid back into the booth opposite her, even though every cell in his body was insisting he return and gather her into his arms once more.

The pleather felt cold under his butt, against his back. Mick reached for his mug of coffee. Instead of picking the mug up by its handle, he wrapped his hands around it, needing the warmth. Took a slug of the bitter brew, swallowed, scalding his throat. Took another gulp.

"Kevin thought I'd put them up to it. Accused me of colluding, but I didn't." Her face was pale. She was putting up a brave front, but he could see the slight tremors running through her body. *You aren't going to be her lover, but there is nothing stopping you from being this woman's friend.* The thought dropped into his consciousness, and he felt a loosening of the knot in his belly. *You will be a friend to her, because clearly she needs one.* "I knew Kevin was upset. I could feel his anger building while we were in my parents' lawyer's office reading the will. He would get that way sometimes." Another tremor coursed through her. "Like a bear with a sore head." She said it lightly, almost like it was a joke, with a faint smile lifting the corners of her mouth, but her eyes looked tormented and dead serious. "I was hoping once we left the office his foul mood would dissipate, but it didn't. If anything, the waves of anger swelled into a tsunami of animosity toward Phillip, my parents . . . and me, too."

"And Phillip is?" *A friend? A lover?*

"My parents' lawyer." She shut her eyes briefly, then opened them again. "Phillip Clarke handled their legal affairs and mine. Actually, he met his wife at my parents' wedding. She was my mom's maid of honor. He was a bit older than her, but it didn't matter because it was love at first sight. I've known the two of them my whole life. They were always coming over for dinner with their two boys. They were present for any big celebration, or party. A constant. But—" She broke off. Glanced down at her hands. "Guess you never really know someone, do you?" Then

Sarah shrugged, as if throwing off whatever thought was weighing her down, picked up a tortilla chip and poked it in the salsa. "But I should talk, right?" Sarah looked at him and smiled wryly. "Pretty much everything I told you up until now was a lie."

"What?" Mick said, raising his eyebrows and clutching a hand to his heart. "You mean you can't type a hundred words a minute? You bitch!"

She laughed, which was what he'd been hoping for. "No, that, actually, I can do, but everything else? Total bullshit." He laughed along with her even though his mouth had a slightly metallic taste that made him reach for his mug of coffee and take another slug. This was what he wanted. To keep her loose and talking so he could unravel the mystery, discover what was hiding in the very deep waters of her psyche. Once he knew the whole story, perhaps it would help dissipate this infatuation he had with her. "And my car's not in the shop. I had to ditch it at the supermarket." The words were tumbling out of her now. "A cop had spotted my car and staked it out. That's when I realized a BOLO must have been issued." She gestured toward her face. "That's why I changed my hair again, took off my glasses—which are fake, by the way—there's nothing wrong with my eyes." The fingers of her right hand drummed lightly on the table. Mick was reeling from this newest nugget of information. *So what does she really look like? And cops? What the fuck?* And on top of those thoughts, he also found himself wondering once again if she'd taken piano lessons as a girl, which was really messed up because that thought had absolutely no bearing on the seriousness of the situation. "I figure," she continued, blithely unaware of the chaos her revelations were wreaking. "If the police have my car license plates, they've got to have my physical description as well. That's why I hit the floor of your car earlier."

"And a BOLO is?" Mick kept his face expressionless, not letting on that his stomach was in knots. He carefully dunked a chip in the salsa.

Sarah made a face. "A police term. Be on the Lookout."

Mick's stomach clenched even tighter. Being infatuated with someone inappropriate was one thing. Being obsessed with someone who the police were hunting down took fool-hardy recklessness to a whole new level. "So . . ." He re-moved another corn chip from the red plastic basket on the table before him. He was acting casual, but his mind was leaping from one hair-raising explanation to another. *It's not something innocuous like a missing person, because she's in hiding. What other reasons could there be? Bank robbery? Extortion? Murder? The very idea seemed ludi-crous. However . . .* Mick exhaled. Looked at the chip he was holding and realized there was no way he could man-age to chew his way through another. "Why"—he gently laid the chip on his plate, wishing it were as easy to place his worries down—"are the police on the lookout for you?"

"It's complicated."

"Try me." Mick could feel tension in his jaw.

Sarah heaved a sigh. "I didn't do anything wrong, if that's what you're thinking."

"Fine." Mick crossed his arms and leaned back. "Then it should be easy to explain why you're on the run. Why you changed your appearance. Why you left your only means of transportation in a grocery store parking lot." Sarah dumped a dollop of sour cream on her cheese enchilada, stalling for time. He waited.

She poked her food with her fork, then placed the utensil down and met his gaze dead-on. "Kevin works in law en-forcement."

"Your husband is a police officer?"

She screwed up her face as if tasting something bitter and nodded. "A lieutenant. Look, I know I said 'my hus-band,' but he's not. Not really."

"You're divorced?" He leaned down hard on the hope that had flared up. He needed to deal with the facts. Spe-cifics.

"No."

Damn. "Separated, then?" After all, divorces could take a while if things were acrimonious.

"Not legally, no. I tried to, but as I said before, things are complicated . . ." She trailed off.

Mick shook his head, trying to clear it. "I'm a little confused here. You say you *were* married, but you're neither divorced *nor* separated. I don't understand what that means. You told me your husband is a lieutenant, but that doesn't explain why the police are looking for you. I can't . . ." He felt like he was being asked to run full tilt through a maze blindfolded. "This isn't . . ." Mick forced himself to pause. The woman was obviously traumatized and feeling vulnerable. He knew from a decade of dealing with emotional actors that getting frustrated with her would only exacerbate the situation. He took another sip of coffee to buy the necessary time needed to tamp down the disappointment. She was attempting to gaslight him once again. "Sarah. It's best if we deal in facts, not shadowy half-truths."

By the way Sarah's eyes flashed fire, Mick realized he hadn't been as successful in tamping down his frustration as he'd thought. "You want facts?" she growled, practically baring her teeth at him. "Okay. Here's a *fact* for you. I don't give a *damn* what a piece of paper says. What matters is how I feel in here." She slammed her clenched fist against her heart. "And in *here*, I am divorced." She thumped her fist against her heart again, fierce and strong. "In here, he has *no* right to me, *no* right to my body or my life. And for the record, I'm not some frikkin' criminal. I didn't do a damned thing wrong other than have the misfortune to marry an abusive dickhead who is using every resource he has to stalk me. That is the *only* reason I'm on the run."

"Are you telling me there is nobody who would help you? Give you a place to stay while you sorted things out?"

"Ha! You are so naive. You have no idea the kind of power and sway my ex has within the NYPD, do you? It's terrifying. I couldn't risk endangering anyone I cared about. I had to disappear completely. Because, believe me, my ex would ferret me out and *destroy* their lives. And here's another fact to chew on. I happen to be worth a hell of a lot of money. Kevin will stop at *nothing* until he has me back under his foot. Literally." Mick could hear truth in her voice, could see it shining out of her eyes, a cleansing, powerful truth. And it had helped to loosen the knot in his gut.

Mick nodded. "Okay."

Sarah jabbed a forkful of food off her plate and stuck it in her mouth, chewing harder than the soft food required. Mick picked up his fork even though his appetite had flown. As a director, it was clear to him that the food had become a prop, a way to give her a little emotional distance from what she had shared with him. "Kevin is a duplicitous, pathological liar." Sarah speared another forkful of food. "He can put on a *real* good show. So convincing. The loving husband whose unhinged wife needs to be located for 'her own safety.' *That's* why the cops are looking for me." She lifted another forkful of food, and then, instead of completing its journey to her mouth, she angrily slammed the fork down. "I feel so ashamed I was ever involved with him. What the hell was I thinking?" Mick knew there was no right way to answer that question. "When I look back over the things I went through. The way he treated me. How rude he was to my parents. How he mocked and alienated all my friends. How he—" Sarah broke off. Her mouth compressed into a flat line, as if forcing herself to hold back additional words. She snatched a chip and bit into it, as if she wished the chip were Kevin's head. "And you want to hear something real pathetic? We got married, all right, but I don't remember a damn thing about it. Nothing. Not the preparation or making the decision to elope rather than follow through with the big wedding that was in the works— which, by the way, I was having serious reservations about. Literally. I was this close"—Sarah held her index finger and thumb a millimeter apart—"to canceling the whole damn thing. I was working up my courage to break the news to him. You see, since the engagement, I had witnessed a different side to the charming, charismatic man who had proposed to me, and it scared the hell out of me." She shivered, looked lost for a moment, then picked up her mug of coffee, her hands wrapped around it tight. Took a sip. Kept the cup in her hands. "Yeah. Don't remember getting married. Don't remember going to the church, saying my vows, my wedding night. Nothing." Sarah looked up from her mug. Her gaze met his, her eyes bleak. "That's why I don't drink alcohol anymore. I never want to be in a position where I'm that vulnerable, where I make such a life-changing colossal mistake like that again."

"Were you a heavy drinker before?"

"No. Would have helped if I had been. Would have built up a tolerance. Nope. He flew us to Vegas for a surprise getaway, and the next day we're flying back to New York, I'm sicker than a dog, and married."

"If you were drunk enough to black out your memory, I'm surprised city hall issued you a license."

"I didn't go to city hall."

"You must have. Can't get married in Vegas without a license."

"We must have gotten one at the chapel."

Mick shook his head. Hadn't lived in Nevada all those years and learned nothing. "Nope. The wedding venues aren't certified for that. For a marriage to be legal, you'd have had to obtain a marriage license from city hall."

Sarah slowly placed her mug down on the table. She did it cautiously, almost as if the mug were in danger of detonating.

"You okay?"

She looked up at him, eyes wide and slightly wild. "I'm pretty sure . . . I didn't go to city hall. I mean . . . unless in Vegas the city hall stays open late?" She reached across the table and clutched his arm. "Can we check on your phone?" Her face was intent. He could see hope and caution duking it out.

He tipped his chin toward her. "It's in my jacket." Her hands scrambled over his jacket. "Lower pocket. On the right." She tugged his phone out, and Mick belatedly remembered that he had been googling her before she got into his car. Had he cleared the screen? *Shit.* He extended his hand, palm up, with a calm he didn't feel. *Who is the asshole now?* "Here. I'll do it." As she dropped the cell phone in his hand, her cool fingers made momentary contact with his and sent electrical currents zinging through him. Keeping his phone screen angled away from her view, Mick swiped up, removing the Google search of Rachel Jones, then tapped Safari and typed "Las Vegas, city hall, hours."

"What does it say?"

He felt like a prick, the way she was looking at him so trustingly. "Seven a.m. to five thirty p.m."

She paled even more. Looked as if she were about to faint, her hands rising to her mouth. "Holy Mary mother of God," she whispered. And then joy, pure unadulterated joy seemed to fill her entire being. "I . . . I don't think I'm married, Mick." Her voice started gaining in strength. "I *can't* be. I never went to city hall."

"Hold on a minute." He wanted nothing more than to jump on board, but one of them needed to be practical. "You might have gone. You told me you were drunk, didn't remember the ceremony. Maybe you went, but don't remember—"

"No." She shook her head vehemently. Both her hands landed on the Formica tabletop, adding emphasis to her words. "It's *impossible*. We were on a morning flight, arrived in Vegas around midday, took a Lyft to the hotel and checked in. We dropped our suitcases in the room, and then Kevin hustled me out the door. He'd booked a special spa day for me. Herbal wrap, massage"—she counted off on her fingers—"facial, and mani-pedi. I didn't get dressed and back to our room until six fifteen, six twenty p.m. at the earliest." She leaned back, dazed. "I'm not married," she repeated. "I didn't apply for a license at city hall, so there's *no* way. Wait. Unless"—she stilled, looking at him, the worry back in her eyes—"only one of us had to go to city hall? Because Kevin would have had time to."

"I don't think so." Mick's mind flipped through what he thought was true. However, he didn't want to give her false hope. "Let me check." He plucked his phone off the table and tapped it on. He opened the Las Vegas City Hall website, tapped on Permits & Licenses, selected Marriage Licenses, and read. He could feel Sarah's eyes boring into him as if all of her focused energy would bring forth the answer she wanted. He skimmed through the information again to make sure he'd gotten it right. Then looked at her straight on. "Nope. Both parties must appear in person with proof of identity. Government-issued photo ID."

"Oh my Lord," she whispered. "I'm free." She looked almost like she would weep, so deep was her joy, her relief. *Her husband must have been a piece of work to get this kind of response,* Mick thought as he watched emotions dancing across her face like fast-moving clouds. "It's hard to take in. My mind is spinning. He has no rights to me, then? I'm free? Like, I'm truly free?" The expression on her face was almost that of a child discovering that no monster actually lived under their bed. In that split second she looked so vulnerable and heartbreakingly innocent that it caused something inside him to *ping.* Something sort of like love, if he'd believed in that kind of thing. Which he didn't, of course. Growing up in a brothel would do that to a man.

"Before you get too excited." He hated how brutally brusque his voice came out. "We'll need to go to Vegas to confirm. Go to city hall. They must have records of all the marriage licenses issued that day. We'll go to the chapel the ceremony was held at, check their records—"

"We'll . . . ?"

"Stop looking at me like that," he growled.

"Like what?" she said softly.

"All hopeful, like I'm some kind of goddamned hero. I'm not. I'm an asshole through and through, and you'd be wise to remember that."

But instead of scaring her off and creating some distance, her expression just softened even more. "Sure," she said. "You're a big, tough guy. I know." And then she smiled the sweetest smile he'd ever seen. Made his knees feel weak, made him grateful to be seated.

Then, as if by mutual agreement, they both tucked in to their food, surrounded by the comforting noises of the restaurant and the rain pounding down outside.

27

KEVIN ENTERED THE GROCERY STORE AND GLANCED around. There was a skinny, dark-eyed kid wearing a green apron restocking the lettuce section in produce. Couldn't be more than nineteen or twenty years old. His attempt to grow a mustache was not meeting with much success. He was working conscientiously, was a pleaser, easy to intimidate. Kevin strode over, flipped open his badge wallet, and flashed his shield at the kid. Did it quick, with his thumb across the city designation and department. "Lieutenant Hawkins, LAPD." Mentioning he was actually NYPD would open a can of worms.

The kid's eyes widened and then darted to the side, as if he was considering making a break for it. "I . . ." The kid's voice came out high and reedy, and then he flushed to the roots of his hairline and swallowed hard.

A coworker, female, midforties appeared next to the kid. "Carlos," she said, her eyes half-shuttered, mouth a straight line. "Miguel needs you up front."

The kid turned toward her, his hand rising like a limp fish in Kevin's direction. "But he—" The flush that had suffused his face was rapidly fading, leaving his skin with a chalky look to it. Pretty clear he was an illegal immigrant, working without documentation.

"I'll take care of it. Go on." The woman clapped her hands. "Quick, quick. He's in a bad mood. You know how he gets." The kid scurried away, shooting a grateful glance over his shoulder at his savior, who now stood, feet apart, arms crossed.

"How can I help you, sir?"

"I'm Lieutenant Hawkins from the Los Angeles Police Department."

She nodded. "Figured as much."

"We have reason to believe a person of interest was in your store yesterday." Her face was a mask, but he could see her shoulders relax slightly. Chances were she was undocumented, too. He was mildly tempted to toy with her. What kind of compensation would she be willing to forfeit to convince him to look the other way with regards to her and/or the kid working in produce?

However, as enjoyable as that would be, the clock was ticking, and Kevin had a bigger fish to fry. He flashed the search warrant he had printed. "I'll need to take a look at your surveillance video. Both in the store and the parking lot." He didn't let the warrant leave his hand, as it was bogus and wouldn't withstand close scrutiny.

Her eyes flickered over the document too fast to actually be registering any of the content. Her pupils were slightly dilated, and he could smell her fear. She hid it well, but nevertheless it was there. He could see her accelerated pulse beating in her neck. *Too bad . . . So tempting. Would love to take her out back and fuck her in the alley by the dumpsters.* The woman gave a short nod, her face shut, mouth tight as if she'd read his mind. "Best I take you to our manager, Joseph. If you would follow me, sir."

KEVIN HAD BEEN FAST-FORWARDING THROUGH THE security video feed from Saturday, March 20, two days ago, when Sarah's vehicle had been spotted and towed. There were multiple cameras throughout the store, which meant a lot of footage to sort through. He'd been sitting at the store manager's crowded desk in the back for a couple of hours, now. His shoulders were tense, his ass tired from the flight, the drive, and now this. He heard the scrape of a foot in his peripheral vision. He could see the store manager, Joseph, with his greasy strands of hair ineffectually combed over his bald, shiny pate hovering in the doorway. "How much longer do you think you'll be?" It was a polite enough question, but Kevin could feel the man's rising concern, his desire to have the use of his workspace back.

Kevin didn't bother turning around, hoping the man would take the hint and leave. "As long as it takes. I apologize for the inconvenience." Like he really gave a crap, but no point in pissing off Joseph. He might demand to take a closer look at the badge, the search warrant, or call down to the LAPD for confirmation.

"It's just, I don't want to rush you, but I have orders to place, inventory tallies to do, and I am going to need access to my computer soon."

"I underst—" Kevin was just about to drag his gaze from the computer when something on the screen captured his attention, a woman toward the far end of aisle eight. Her head was tucked down, but there was something familiar about her. It was more of an instinct that had him staring at her, as it was hard to make out details. The images were a little pixilated and a blurry black and white.

"You what? Sorry I didn't catch—"

Kevin cut the manager's question off with an abrupt wave of his hand. He leaned his face closer to the screen, backtracked, zoomed in, and hit play. And there she was walking down the aisle as if she didn't have a care in the world. He watched her bend over and pick up a bag of something off the lower shelf.

"Flour," Joseph said. He had edged closer to see what had caught Kevin's eye. "Ten pound . . . white flour. Not whole wheat—that's farther down."

Kevin paused the tape, impatient irritation flaring as he

swiveled in the cheap office chair and stared at him. "What in the world are you babbling about?"

"I . . . I . . ." The store manager blanched and took a quick step backward. "I like . . . uh . . . reading mysteries, suspense, crime fiction, and . . ." He shrugged, embarrassed. "Sometimes in the books, the most inconsequential details are the most important." Once Joseph's mouth started flapping, he seemed unable to stop it. "I don't know if that's the case here, but it looks like she picked up a ten-pound bag of flour. From where she's standing, I'd say it's a toss-up between Gold Medal or King Arthur." Joseph tipped his chin toward the screen. "Is she the one you're looking for? What'd she do? Murder? Robbery? Is she a con artist? A drug dealer on the run?"

No. She's my lying, cheating, two-faced wife, Kevin wanted to bellow, but he didn't, just bit out between clenched teeth, "Sorry. It's classified." He turned back to the computer and clicked play.

"I get it." Joseph took a step back, jiggling the spare change in his khaki slacks. They watched in silence as Sarah continued down the aisle. She stopped again and put a smaller object into the cart. "Sugar," Joseph murmured. "Five-pound bag."

Kevin ignored him, kept his gaze trained on Sarah as she approached the overhead security camera. It was her. No question about it. The glasses obscured her eyes, the hair color was different, but that was the way she moved. *That's how she tilts her head . . . That's her smile . . .* On the heels of that thought, anger crashed white hot, like a bolt of lightning incinerating everything in its path, because as her image became clearer and clearer, one thing was inescapably obvious: she seemed happier, lighter than he'd ever seen her, and how fucking dare she.

"This is so fascinating," Joseph chirruped. "You'd never guess that chick's got the law on her tail. Looks like a frikkin' Sunday school teacher. I'd tap that for sure. Bet she's wild as all getup between the sheets." It took everything Kevin had not to plow his fist into the dipshit's face and rearrange his features.

28

"HEY, MICK." THE GUARD AT THE STUDIO GATE beamed at Mick. "Me and the wife already got the babysitter booked for the Thursday after next! Every morning while I'm eating my breakfast, I make another check mark on the calendar. Counting down until the big day!"

"Going to paint the town, huh? What's the occasion, big birthday coming up? Anniversary?" Mick's head was turned away from her, but Sarah knew he was smiling. She could see the creases fanning outward from his eye, the portion of his cheek that was visible lifted upward. Yes, the man swaggered around with a tough-guy veneer, but underneath his gruff growl, she could now discern the warmth and genuine goodness in his voice.

"Seeing *Retribution*, that's what we're gonna do! Opening weekend. The buzz on the street is it is *amazing*! The lines at the box office are going to be massive. I'm gonna bring folding chairs. The wife, she wanted to see some chick flick, but we know who's the boss." The guard laughed heartily, and then he tipped his hat back and peered into Mick's car at Sarah. "Who you got with you?"

Mick glanced at Sarah. She could see his whole face now, and it was as if the cloud had moved on, revealing the full glory of the sun. "A friend," Mick said, his gaze still locked on her.

Over Mick's shoulder, Sarah could see the guard wiggle his eyebrows. "Nice to meet you, friend," the guard said. "I'll need some ID."

She saw Mick's eyes widen slightly before he turned his focus back on the guard. "Is that necessary? We're going to be five minutes tops. Just picking up some work and heading back out."

"Sorry, Mick." The guard straightened and pushed his hat back in place. "Would love to accommodate you, but it's not worth my job. The little lady needs a pass."

"No worries." Sarah dug in her purse and pulled her counterfeit ID out of her wallet, acting casual, feeling clammy under her blouse. She placed a polite smile on her face as she leaned across the center console and handed her fake driver's license through the window.

The guard glanced at it. "Rachel Jones?" She nodded. "Just a minute please." He took her ID into his booth. Sarah could feel tension radiating off Mick. Could see the guard typing stuff into his computer. *He's just a guard at the studio. Not a cop. It is highly doubtful his system is tied to the police.* Logically, she knew this. Internally, she was freaking out.

"Sorry. I forgot about this," Mick murmured. "Do you need us to leave?"

She gave her head a slight shake. "Should hold up," she replied quietly, her lips barely moving. She kept her gaze nonchalant as she looked unseeingly through the windshield. "I paid enough for it. Besides, cars are behind us now. No way to go but forward."

The guard printed something out, then returned to the window. "Here you are." He handed her ID and visitor pass to Mick. "She should peel that off and stick it on her jacket. Have a good day, you two." He gestured to the next car as the boom barrier lifted and Mick drove through. Sarah peeled the visitor pass with Rachel Jones scribbled on it in blue ink. She noticed her hands were trembling slightly as she stuck the pass on Mick's jacket, which she was wearing. She shoved them deep into its pockets, hoping Mick hadn't noticed as well.

He pulled into a parking spot, where his name was printed in large dark lettering on a white sign. Sarah unstrapped and was reaching for the door handle when she felt Mick's hand alight on her arm. It was unsettling how the mere touch of his hand would cause such heat to course through her. "Yes?" She turned to face him. "Oh. That's right, I'm wearing your jacket. Yeah." She laughed. "That might make things a little awkward at the office. Sorry." She peeled her visitor's pass off his jacket, then reached for the zipper.

"No. Keep the jacket. You're shivering."

"People will assume—"

Mick cut her off with an abrupt wave of his hand. "I was thinking you might want to wait in the car."

The guy was nuts. "I can't really handle your office work in the car." She unzipped, shrugged out of his jacket, and handed it to him. He seemed angry. Had jerked his head away, his jaw clenched, crossed his arms, refusing to take his jacket. Which was crazy, because seriously, she was not going to waltz into his office wearing the boss's clothes. That would look bad, and she'd lose all credibility with anyone who worked there. "Take the damned thing." She dropped it in his lap.

MICK BRACED HIMSELF AND TURNED TOWARD HER. "Sarah. First. Put my jacket on. The rain made your blouse . . ." He waved his hand in the vicinity of her chest while keeping his gaze firmly fixed on her face. "I mean, it's way better than it was, but you can still . . ."

Sarah glanced down and then her eyebrows shot upward. "Oh God." She snatched his jacket and had it back on and zipped in record time. "Right." Her face had gotten quite rosy. "You could have told me."

"I just did."

"What am I going to do? I can't saunter in there wearing this."

"Not only that." He grinned. "Your nose is red—eyes, too. People will think I'm the heartless brute who made you cry."

"That's ridiculous." He could see the beginning quirks of a smile teasing the corners of her lips. Lips he wanted to taste, to explore.

"Second. I'm not sure what PR and Peterson have booked for today. We've been doing a lot of press for *Retribution*. A couple of the actors were there when I left, so it's possible media is in there."

Her eyes widened. "Seriously?"

"Yeah." He nodded. "Given what you've told me, it might be an issue. No need to tempt fate. I'll go up, grab some work, cancel a few appointments. Be back in fifteen minutes tops."

"Sounds like a plan." She settled into her seat. The color of her eyes reminded him of lying flat on his back, staring up at the deep blue of a cloudless Nevada summer sky. Could almost taste the grit of dust in his mouth and hear the chirping of the grasshoppers. "You okay?"

"Sure." He tugged his mind back to the present. "We'll swing by the house, pack overnight bags, take a quick flight to Vegas, and do some sleuthing."

"If possible, I'd rather not fly. Haven't put my fake ID to the test yet. It might withstand the scrutiny, but then again, it might not."

"Right. Fancy a road trip?"

She grinned back at him. "I'd love one."

29

THE FARTHER THE I-15 NORTH TOOK THEM FROM LOS Angeles, the lighter Sarah felt, as if there was no way her worries could run fast enough to keep up with Mick's Porsche. The mood as they sped down the highway had almost a holiday feel. She nestled deeper into the low-slung, natural leather espresso seats that hugged her body. She enjoyed the deft way Mick drove, how he handled the car, took the curves, changed lanes. He seemed effortlessly aware of the vehicles around them, as if he knew what they were going to do before they made their move and he responded accordingly. They had fallen into a comfortable silence, watching scenery pass and the sun slowly sink in the sky. The whir of the tires on asphalt added a peaceful continuity that reminded her of Charlie's purr. Sarah had contemplated bringing him, but Charlie hated riding in cars. A road trip with Charlie meant cleaning up cat vomit and listening to him yowl 24/7. That was asking a lot from a cat person, which Mick was not. So she had filled a casserole dish with cat food and another one with water. It was overkill, probably would take Charlie two weeks to munch his way through all that food, but just in case there was a delay, Charlie would be okay.

As she'd left the apartment, Sarah had given Charlie a snuggle and a scratch behind his ears. Then, with Charlie draped over her shoulder impersonating a fox stole and purring like a tractor, Sarah had switched on the TV to the cats channel and set the volume on low. "There you go. Your favorite show, Charlie, and I'll be back before you know it."

Sarah gazed at the flat landscape whizzing past. Part of her was already in Vegas sorting out her marital status. The other half of her was missing her makeshift apartment and her temperamental cat already. Hopefully they would return tomorrow, but even if they got delayed, they would certainly be back in LA by Thursday night, or Friday morning at the latest. And then Mick would be flying to New York for a press junket and the premiere, as his new movie was opening that following Thursday.

Sarah liked watching Mick's hands on the wheel, tanned, sure, and strong. His fingers were blunt-tipped with fingernails cropped short and clean. A beam of sunshine forced its way through the tinted glass and caused the sprinkling of hair on his forearms to turn golden, like Rumpelstiltskin turning mundane everyday straw into pure spun gold.

Mick glanced over, as if he had felt her eyes on him. "What were you thinking just then?"

"Why do you want to know?"

Mick shrugged, a rueful smile on his face. "Curious, I guess. The director in me." He shrugged again, the tips of his ears flushing as if he regretted the question the moment it escaped his mouth. And there was something about his sudden vulnerability that had her answering honestly, even though she had honed her skill at keeping people at bay.

"The sunshine on"—she smoothed her fingertips along her own forearm so she wouldn't be tempted to reach out and skim them lightly along his—"on your forearms makes the hair look almost golden." She smiled. "Reminded me of an old fairy tale my mother used to read to me when I was a little girl. *Rumpelstiltskin*."

When Mick laughed, the low sound rumbled through her like a fast-passing train, filling her belly with warmth. "Rumpelstiltskin, am I?" He shook his head, still laughing. "Slick move, Rainsforth. Way to polish my ego. Isn't he a malevolent, tiny, hunched-over creature with a big belly and large bugging-out eyes who spun straw into gold?"

"Yes, but that's not"—it was hard to get her explanation out because her own laughter was bubbling forth—"what I meant."

"Woooooweee. I'm coming up in the world!" Mick grinned happily as he shook his hand in the universal sign for hot. "Keep with the flattery and my swelled head will suck up the remaining oxygen in this car."

Still giggling, she waved her hands toward his arm. "I was talking about the hair on your arms—"

"My hairy arms now?" he said with mock indignation. "So I'm a Rumpelstiltskin *and* a great hairy beast. Wonderful. That's just swell."

"Never mind," Sarah said, wiping moisture from her eyes. "Just forget I said anything."

"I think," he said, in a wounded tone of crushed dignity, "that would be"—he paused and tipped his face heroically heavenward with the slightest quiver of his lower lip—"for the best." Which started her laughter all over again.

"IT'S RAINSFORD, BY THE WAY," SARAH SAID, BITING into a double burger with all the fixings. Night had fallen, glossy black beyond the window, creating a cocoon-like atmosphere. As if the world beyond Daisy's Diner had ceased to exist. Mick watched Sarah take another bite. He didn't know why it made him so damned happy to feed her, but it did. He liked watching her eyes go hazy as she savored her food. Her eyelids fluttered shut, and he noticed that her eyelashes didn't match her newly dyed hair. Her lashes were pale, almost invisible toward the tips, and there was something so beautiful, so vulnerable about seeing them like that. Made him want to reach across the table and run the tip of his finger in a barely there touch along the delicate hairs, as if gently caressing the wings of a butterfly. A soft moan escaped from between her lips, as if she wanted him to touch her, too. His logical mind knew her moan was one of enjoyment for the meal she was eating. Nevertheless, the breathy sound of it had his cock swelling.

"What is?" His voice had caused her eyelids to open. He tugged his gaze away from the spell of her gorgeous violet-blue eyes, picked up his burger, and took a bite. It was as good as he remembered. Big, flavorful, and sloppy, everything you could want in a burger.

"My last name. Earlier, you called me 'Rainsforth.' It's Rainsford."

"Ah." He nodded. "Rainsford. Got it." He watched her take another bite. A trickle of juices escaped and moved down her wrist. The tip of Sarah's pink tongue darted out and lapped it up, and he needed to lay his burger on his plate so he could discreetly readjust himself.

"Sooo good," she moaned, taking another bite. He felt sometimes almost as if she were a starving, stray kitten he had coaxed out of a dumpster with a saucer of cream. Terrified and pretending to be fierce, back arched, tail bushed out and sticking straight in the air, claws extended, lips drawn back, hissing ferociously, as if attempting to pass for a tough Halloween tomcat. Sarah smiled at him as if slightly drunk from the combination of delicious flavors.

"Try the chocolate shake." He nudged it toward her. Yes, he wanted her to taste it because the milkshakes at Daisy's were a revelation, but he'd be lying if he didn't admit that a part of him wanted to watch her suck the thick shake through that red-and-white-striped paper straw.

She obliged, and it was everything he imagined and more.

"Rainsford," he repeated thoughtfully, as if the blood hadn't rushed to his nether regions.

Sarah looked at him, her elegant eyebrow arching. "Yes?" So perhaps he wasn't pulling the wool over her eyes.

"I'm just repeating the correct pronunciation of your name so it will be stuck in my—" He broke off because the repetition of her surname had tugged forth a faint memory from his brain. "Wait a minute." He felt his eyes narrow as he tugged a little harder. "Four years back . . . It was all over the news." His mind was dropping Tetris pieces into place. "There was a missing heiress . . ."

"Everyone presumed was dead? No body found." Sarah shrugged and took another slurp of the milkshake. "Yeah. That's me." She said it as if she were talking about the color of her socks.

Mick shot to his feet, needing to move, jammed his hands in his pockets. "You're *that* Rainsford? The missing Rainsford *heiress*?!"

"The one and only," she replied, calmly dunking a French fry in the ketchup and stirring it so two-thirds of the fry was coated in the sauce before eating it.

"Holy crap." He shook his head, trying to clear it. "I was obsessed with that case. Kept hoping she would be found, safe and sound."

"And here I am."

Mick was finding it difficult to wrap his mind around this latest revelation. Hell, the entire day had been pretty bizarre. He cast his mind back, flipping through magazine and news images. He could see similarities in her profile. Sarah had the same color eyes, and her hair was obviously dyed. However, the woman could be running an extremely sophisticated con on him, or perhaps she was mentally unstable and suffered from delusions. "So you're actually blond?"

She smiled ruefully and tugged at her dark hacked-up hair. "Yeah." She studied him across the table. "You don't believe me, do you?"

"I'm not sure." Mick knew he was being surly, because her being *the* Sarah Rainsford actually made a weird sort

of sense. From the second he'd laid his eyes on her, he'd had
the feeling that he knew her from somewhere. Had initially
attributed the odd sense of deja vu to the erroneous sup-
position that she was a scheming actress or an undercover
reporter.

"Why would I lie?"

There were a million words hovering on the tip of his
tongue, but what came out was "Why in the hell are you
scrubbing my toilets if you're so filthy rich?" His words
sounded harsh, angry to his ears, which didn't make sense.
What did he care? "You can buy and sell me a million times
over."

"You say that like you're accusing me of a crime."

"You should have told me."

"I just did." She dunked another French fry. "Sit down
and eat your food. It's going to get cold."

Mick sat down. Not because she was the boss of him. He
sat because he was drawing attention by looming over their
table, and the last thing Sarah needed was more eyes turned
her way.

"Look," she said. "If it's bothering you how I've
nickeled-and-dimed you, I had to. I don't have access to my
funds at present. But if it will make you feel better, I'll pay
you back plus five percent interest once I get everything
sorted out."

"It's not that," he growled. "I don't want the damned
money back." He could feel his ears and the back of his
neck heat up. He'd known she was a class act, but it had
never crossed his mind that she had grown up in a super-
wealthy rarefied household. There wasn't the slightest stench
of a spoiled, pampered rich kid about her. "You worked hard.
Earned every cent."

She looked at him, the intelligence shining out of her
deep blue eyes. "Then why are you angry?"

"I'm not ang—" He snapped his mouth shut. Sarah tilted
her head, a small, barely discernable movement that suddenly made him ashamed of the lie that hovered along the
inside wall of his lips. "I guess," he said slowly, feeling his

way to the truth, "I feel as if I've been sucked up in a tornado and have been set down in an entirely different locale, different customs, language. I don't know how to navigate it. The status quo is all screwed up."

"How do you mean?"

"I'm not . . ." He shrugged as if it were no big deal. "I'm not . . ."

"In charge?" Her voice was gentle, her face, too. "I'm still your employee . . ."

"Yeah, about that—"

She cut him off as if she knew what he was about to say. "And you're still the big man, bossing me around. I'm strapped for cash. No joke." He could see compassion in her eyes, and humor was there as well, in her gaze and at the slightly tilted-up corners of her lips. "And I want you to know how very grateful I am. You gave me a job. Took time out of your busy schedule to travel with me to Vegas. All these things you did—for no ulterior motive—but because that's who you are. I don't know how you got the reputation of a degenerate, dissipated playboy. You are such an honorable, decent, kind human being."

"I'm not," he growled. He felt naked.

"You can say what you like." She wagged a finger at him. "But your actions prove otherwise. Want an example? That abundance of food you bought me at The Palm. It was the first good meal I'd had in a very long time. I was literally dizzy with hunger when you insisted on taking me out. The leftovers sustained me until Friday when I got paid. Your random act of kindness meant a lot to me."

"Woman, you better take off those rose-tinted glasses. I was being the big man, Mr. Moneybags, patting myself on the back for helping out the poor unfortunate peasant. Hell, I bet you ate food like that all the time. There I was sitting in that booth opposite you secretly congratulating myself on my largesse. I was so pleased, so full of my own consequence, proud that I wasn't a starving kid anymore and had the means to help out. And if I'm being totally truthful, I wanted to impress you."

Her hand covered his. He could feel the scrape of calluses. Had scrubbing his house put them there? Did her strong, slender hands used to be unmarred, manicured, and soft as silk? Perversely, he found a beauty in the slightly rough texture. It was a tribute to her strength of character—her willingness to buckle down, work hard, and do whatever it took to ensure her safety and independence. "You did impress me," she said softly.

She was gazing at him like he was some kind of saint, when the truth was, he would have gladly given up his worldly goods to bend her over the diner table and take her eight ways to Sunday. "Don't look at me like that." His voice sounded like it was being filtered through gravel. He shook her hand off and picked up his burger to keep himself from reaching for her. "I'm not to be trusted. Fair warning, I'm an unprincipled bastard, through and through."

"Good to know." Sarah moved to the chair next to him, her thick, lush lashes obscuring his view of her summer-sky eyes.

He could smell the fresh scent of her and longed to lean into it, into her. "Seriously. These noble motivations you are affixing to my persona are incorrect. What you see as acts of kindness were nothing more than me being self-serving and driven by lust."

"Lust? Oh my." Her hands rose to his shoulders, a slight smile teasing the corners of her lips.

He edged back. "What are you doing?"

"I've been curious about the taste of your lips." Her lashes lifted, revealing the scalding-hot heat in her eyes. "Any objections?" The tip of her tongue moistened her upper lip, causing what blood was left in his brain to rush downward like a flash flood. She laughed low in her throat, as if something she was seeing on his face delighted her. "You seem nervous. Come on. Let me have a little amuse-bouche of that terrible lust. Just one taste. That's all. I promise."

Nervous? She had him breaking out in a hormone-crazed sweat. She leaned closer. "No objections, then?" Her voice was a husky purr that promised untold delights.

"Wait," he croaked, his cock so hard it was causing him pain.

Her gaze flickered down to his crotch, and she smiled, sultry, like Aphrodite incarnate. "Yes?"

"We can't . . ." His lungs felt like they were going to burst. "You're married."

There was a flicker of uncertainty in her gaze, and then it was gone. Her chin rose a millimeter. "I'm not. You'll see. But let's say the information we turn up on this trip doesn't go my way. The fact of the matter is Kevin and I have been living separately for four years. The actual filing of the paperwork is a mere formality. I am *never* going back."

"Okay, makes sense, but there's an additional"—he sucked in another gulp of air—"line I don't cross. You're my employee." This was dead serious, but he had the sense she was laughing at him. "I have a rule," he insisted as much for his benefit as for hers.

"And if I weren't your employee?" Her forefinger rose and gently caressed the swell of his lower lip. "Would you let me kiss you then?"

"No question. One hundred percent."

"Wonderful." She slid closer. "I quit," he heard her murmur, and then her mouth was on his with a moan. The world fell away as liquid heat and the taste of her roared through him. Her fingers gripped in his hair, as she demanded, insisted on more, and he gave, and he took, his heart thundering in his chest. So effortlessly he tumbled off the cliff of his ironclad rules. And it was worth every second he would spend in hell to be caressed by the scent of her, to luxuriate in the plump softness of her lips. Drowning in sensation as the erotic slick of her tongue danced with his. Another soft moan, he wasn't sure if it was his or hers, so drunk on the taste of her. Then her fists released their grip on his hair. Her palms gently traversed his face, her fingers trailing in their wake until they came between his

mouth and hers. "One. I said one. Oh God, I want more."
She leaned her forehead against his, their breath intermingling, harsh and ragged as if having completed a fifty-meter
dash. "I never should have promised just one," she moaned
as her hands traveled down his neck to rest over his beating
heart. Then she raised her head, and he saw such longing in
her eyes before her eyelids fluttered to half-mast, shielding
the naked beauty of her thoughts from him.

"Sarah . . ." He reached for her, but she was already
gone. Had rounded the table and was back in her original
seat, her face flushed, her lips rosy and swollen. He shut his
eyes momentarily, every cell in his body throbbing. Trying
to permanently imprint that mind-blowing kiss into his
memory bank so he would have it for this lifetime and into
the next.

30

"YOU'RE CERTAIN THE RESERVATION WAS FOR TWO separate rooms, Mr. Talford?" The stout desk clerk stroked his Vandyke beard worriedly. He tapped something else on his keyboard, his head jutted forward as he studied the screen with a pale unblinking gaze.

"Absolutely." There wasn't an ounce of give in Mick's voice. Sarah saw a muscle jump in his jaw.

The desk clerk dragged his glance away from the computer. A slight sheen of sweat had appeared on the man's forehead and around his nose. "I'm so very sorry, but there appears to have been a miscommunication. Perhaps your secretary made a mis—" The steely, uncompromising look in Mick's eyes had the desk clerk's voice petering out. The man flinched, blinked, and then swallowed hard, as if he'd realized he had mistakenly tugged the tail of a tiger.

"I. Made. The reservation."

"Oh dear."

"Two rooms."

"Okay. Got it." The desk clerk's fingers tapped nervously on the padded desktop, and his gaze darted back to his computer screen. "By the way," he said almost apologetically. "I'm a huge fan of your work. I studied filmmaking." He laughed nervously. "And look how that turned out. Anyway, I'm happy for you, dude." He punched something else into the keyboard, looking anything but happy. He shook his head, eyes squinting as he scanned the screen and scrolled down. Sarah was pretty sure whatever the desk clerk was looking at wasn't promising, as his lower lip was caught between his teeth and the sheen of sweat on his forehead was now beading. "Okay . . . All our single rooms are booked for the night. Let me just . . ." He pushed back from his desk. "I need to have a word with our manager. One second, please." The desk clerk held up a finger, eyebrows launched upward as he disappeared through an almost invisible door at a trot. He returned a few moments later beaming from ear to ear. "Have I got a treat for you!" he declared, rubbing his hands together. "Our manager is going to upgrade you to one of our exclusive two-bedroom villas. He was holding it open for a high-roller, but I explained how huge you were, told him what happened. You are going to freak out when you see this place. Three thousand, two hundred square feet of unadulterated luxury, two bedrooms, a living room, three bathrooms, a massage room, your own private pool—"

"No thanks." Mick plucked his credit card off the desk and snagged the crook of Sarah's arm. "Let's go."

"Mick." He gave her arm a little tug, but Sarah set in her heels, refusing to budge. "Why in the world—"

"We need separate rooms," he growled.

"We would have them. Two bedrooms, not to mention all the other stuff." She turned to the desk clerk. "Thank you so much. That would be absolutely wonderful. So kind of you to arrange that."

"And doors that lock," he gritted out.

"Don't worry," she said with an airy wave of her hand. "I'm not going to jump you. I'm pooped. Am planning on taking a steaming-hot shower and then crawling into bed."

"It's not *your* self-control I'm concerned about."

"It's remarkable how you can squeeze words through those clenched teeth," she said cheerfully, as if what he'd said hadn't sent a bolt of lust coursing through her. She plucked the credit card from Mick's fingers and handed it to the desk clerk with a smile. "Here you go. Write that puppy up." She turned and leaned in toward Mick, not so their bodies were touching. Just close enough so the heat of his force field would shimmer along her skin. "However," she murmured, "tomorrow, when we obtain proof that I am not a married woman"—she leaned in even closer, rising on her toes—"all bets are off," she whispered, her mouth barely skimming his ear. She heard his breath hitch, which filled her with delight and a wonder, too. The words had slipped from her lips with an ease that astounded her. And where had that husky rasp come from? Never had she felt this kind of freedom before, this feeling of safety, of stepping into her power and sexuality without fearing reprisals or a fist. She lowered her heels, placed her hand on his chest, and tipped her head toward him in a confidential manner. "Because four years is a hell of a long time to go without." Watching as heat flared in his eyes, reveling in the fact that an answering response was pooling low in her body where her legs met her torso, a pulsing, swelling, hungry wanting. "That is"—she could feel the accelerated thud of his heart against her palm—"if you're up for it?" she said, a sultry smile dancing on her lips. Then Sarah stepped away, letting her hand fall gently from his torso. She tugged her gaze back to the desk clerk, who was sliding paperwork across the desk, but not before Sarah had the pleasure of seeing Mick swallow hard and his irises darken even further.

31

SARAH CLOSED HER EYES, LETTING THE HOT WATER from the rain shower pummel her back, her buttocks, and cascade over her sensitized skin. It had felt so good to wash the day from her body. Visualizing all of her troubles flowing off her to join the water spiraling into a whirlpool and disappearing down the drain. The gorgeous shower was a thing of beauty, all white marble, glass, and chrome. It even had a steam component, which she had switched on so it could heat up while she'd shed her clothes. When she'd stepped inside, the warm steam particles surrounded and embraced her.

Sarah turned languorously and let the water beat against her upturned face, her breasts, her abdomen. *Luxury.* She sighed contentedly, savoring every molecule of comfort. *When I am finally able to extricate myself from this mess, I will never, ever take for granted the multitude of blessings my parents gifted to me by the sheer luck of my birth. I will give back and share my blessings with those less fortunate. I promise.*

And as the water soothed and caressed her, Sarah

thought of other blessings that had come her way. Surviving the deranged madman on Solace Island who had thought she was his sister. Meeting Mick, who, for all his gruffness, had an inner core of such generosity and kindness that it humbled her. *Prior to Kevin, would I have gone out of my way to help a stranger in need? Would I have even noticed? Been aware?* She didn't bother digging through her memory bank. She knew the answer. And Zelia was another blessing the universe had gifted her. Zelia had known Sarah was lying when she'd applied for work and yet had given Sarah the job at the gallery anyway. Befriended her. Helped Sarah when she had needed to run again, gave her money, no questions asked. "I miss her," Sarah whispered in the empty bathroom. She missed Zelia's laugh, her joie de vivre, the sound of her voice. And on the heels of all that, a wonderful idea began to form. *It's nighttime. Zelia won't be at the gallery. She'll be home. Tucked in bed, cozy and warm in Gabe's arms. You could call the office and listen to her voice on the message machine. It wouldn't endanger either of us because even if Kevin has managed to bug Zelia's phone, I won't leave a message, so he won't know it's me. And if he's tracing calls, who cares. We're checking out tomorrow morning.*

MICK WAS NURSING HIS SECOND WHISKEY ON THE rocks when Sarah blew into the common living room like a summer storm, wrapped in one of the hotel's thick white terry-cloth robes, barefoot. He had been mulling over their conversation from the Mexican restaurant. She had mentioned a baby right before she fell apart. Where was her child now? Had she run and left the baby with her violent ex? *Who would do that?* And on the heels of that thought, *My mother would.* He felt bile rise up in his throat. He couldn't imagine Sarah doing something like that; but then, what did he truly know about her? She had said everything she'd told him was a lie. *Ask her. If she did, it's yet another reason to keep your distance.* Mick opened his mouth. "I thought you were going to stay in your room," he said. *Good going. Way to tackle the subject head-on.*

"Don't worry." She smiled like a siren luring him to the rocks. "Your precious virtue is safe with me." She was rubbing her wet hair with a towel.

His body, taut with need, was urging him to cross the room and take possession of her mouth. He took another slug of whiskey and felt it burn all the way down. *But what if she didn't abandon her baby? What if something terrible happened? Maybe she miscarried, or the baby died.* Sarah had looked so heartbroken, so devastated, when the subject had come up. *Are you going to be the asshole who rubs salt in the wound?*

"I'd like to make a long-distance call," Sarah said. He nodded to acknowledge he was listening. Didn't look over. Didn't want her to read his thoughts. "Will be only a minute or two. Would you mind if I used the phone?"

"Sure." Mick set his drink down on the mahogany-and-granite wet bar. The ice cubes clinked against the crystal tumbler. *Besides, it's none of my goddamned business. I'm helping her sort out a problem. That's it.* "Be my guest." He nudged his cell phone along the bar top, keeping his eyes on his forefinger pushing his phone. It was self-preservation. Couldn't look at her straight on, knowing she was likely naked under that robe. It would be akin to staring directly at the sun—tempting, but one runs the risk of permanent damage to the corneas.

She shook her head. "I know hotels charge an arm and a leg, but it would be better if I used their phone. Just in case, so the call can't be traced to your cell phone."

He tipped his head at the phone sitting on the desk in the living room. "Have at it."

Sarah crossed the room. He tried not to notice the gentle hypnotic roll of her hips and failed miserably. "I'll pay you back someday," she said, tossing the damp towel over her shoulder. "I swear."

He waved her off. Forced his body to swivel around on the barstool so he was facing forward. Could still see her reflection haunting him in the damned mirror. He wrapped his hand around his ice-cold drink and took a healthy swallow, relishing the burn as he watched her sit at the desk. She crossed her legs, leaned forward to pick up the phone, and began to dial. Her robe, tightly cinched at the waist, gapped open slightly, revealing long, slender limbs, her knees, and a portion of her thighs. Mick tore his gaze from the mirror and stared at his drink, watched condensation trickle down the side.

Sarah was listening intently now, eyes wide—her hand rose to her mouth as if holding words back. Then abruptly, she hung up the phone, her body motionless. Her hand was still on the receiver, as if she was reluctant to break the connection.

"Are you okay?"

Her hand left the phone as she turned to face him. There was a sadness and a longing in her eyes. *Who had she needed to call? What did that person mean to her?* "I'm fine."

"No one was home?"

"Something like that." She rose to her feet. "Thanks for letting me use the phone."

He tipped his drink to her. *"Mi casa es tu casa."*

She smiled wanly at him. "You're very sweet." As she passed him on her way back to her room, she gently brushed the knuckles of her left hand along his cheek, leaving a tingling of heat in their wake. "Again, I'm so sorry about the scratch marks, about hitting you this morning."

"Don't worry about it."

"It was wrong." Her eyes were dark with regret.

Mick shrugged. "Believe me, I've had worse."

"I hate that. You're starting to bruise, right here." She placed a gentle kiss high on his cheekbone, bringing the faint scent of lemons and springtime to tantalize his nostrils. "So sorry." She straightened, sorrow in her eyes as she scanned the rest of his face. "And here . . ." Her cool, slender fingers were now on his neck near his carotid artery. "I must have scratched you. Again. I'm so sorry. There is no excuse." Her fingers started to traverse ever so lightly along the angry red mark. Pure torture.

"Forget about it. I have." Mick shifted slightly so her fingers fell away.

"All right." She stood there for a second. He could feel her eyes heating his skin. "Good night," she finally said. Mick could feel the air shift as she stepped away. The sense of loss was almost crippling as she headed down the hall, but he forced his body to stay glued to the barstool, his hand clenched around his drink. She was vulnerable and in a precarious position. He threw back his drink, could feel the liquid fire's journey all the way down as he poured himself another. It was going to be a long night.

32

PHILLIP CLARKE HADN'T PLANNED ON SPENDING his evening sitting in his darkened car, staring at Vicki's town house. He was supposed to be across town having dinner with clients. But when Phillip left the office, instead of heading to Daniel Boulud's restaurant on the Upper East Side to sup on exquisite French cuisine, he found himself in Brooklyn again. He pulled out his cell phone, dialed, and made his apologies. "I'm terribly sorry. Was heading out the office door when I was laid low with a vicious bout of dysentery. Racked with stomach pains, squirting like a goose. Am trapped on the potskie. Yes. It's very inconvenient. You go ahead. Give my regrets. It's all taken care of. Vicki already gave them my card—" And saying her name caused the lie to become the truth, because unbelievable pain doubled him over with its intensity. "Sorry," he croaked. "Have to go." He switched his phone off and dropped it on the seat beside him. Had to wrap his arms tightly around himself and rock back and forth as he waited for the grief to subside. He'd always known he'd loved her. Just hadn't realized how much until it was too late.

A woman with a large black standard poodle passed the car, paused, and then backtracked. She rapped on the window of the passenger side of Phillip's car. "Are you all right, sir? Do you need me to call 911?"

He managed to unwrap one arm from his abdomen to shoo her away. "I'm fine. I'm fine."

"You don't look fine, sir. Is there someone I can call for you? A family member, perhaps?"

"Go away! I'm fine. Just need a little space. A little peace and quiet!"

"All right." The woman straightened and backed away.

He watched her scurry off. *Nosy bat*, he thought as he pulled a handkerchief from the inside breast pocket of his jacket. He mopped his eyes and then blew his nose long and hard as he tried to figure out what his next move should be.

33

"WOW. I'M AMAZED." SARAH GLANCED AROUND THE relatively empty Marriage License Bureau. "I'd figured that, Vegas and all, this place would be swamped." She seemed better this morning. The shadows in her eyes had retreated.

The lack of people had surprised Mick as well. Weddings in Vegas had always been big business. The metal barriers were set up for people to queue, but there was no line. A few couples were at various kiosks, a family was near the wall watching a younger man who was typing something into a computer. Mick studied Sarah's face. "This place triggering any memories?"

"Nope," Sarah replied with absolute certainty. "Never been here in my life."

He felt some of the tension easing out of his belly. "You ready?"

"Wait." He could see a flicker of sudden panic in her eyes. Her hand shot out and wrapped around his wrist as she turned to block the view of their faces from the clerks sitting in their kiosks. Then Sarah noticed the cameras over the main door and in the corner, so she moved even closer, almost as if stepping into an embrace. The delicate floral hint of her shampoo and the uniquely feminine scent of her surrounded him, snatching his breath. "What if they need to see my real ID?" He had to study her lips to make out what she was saying, her voice barely a whisper.

"Do you have it?" he murmured softly.

She shook her head. "Just the fake Rachel Jones one." He could see a slight tremor run through her, could feel it in her hand that had gripped his wrist. "I . . . I left everything behind when I ran." From the expressions chasing across her face, Mick would put money on Sarah's thoughts being momentarily trapped in memories of the past, none of them good. He had the urge to punch something. Preferably Kevin's face, but he would be content with doing damage to any part of the scumbag's anatomy.

"Then we'll brazen our way through." His instinct was to lead the way, fight her battles, to throw his body between her and any dragons that might arise. However, he could tell by the tension around her eyes, the slight tautness around her mouth, that she was scared. The only cure for that was for her to take control. Step into the fear so she could move past it. "And if it doesn't work." He shrugged with a nonchalance he didn't feel.

"Right." Sarah nodded, raising her chin. "I've got nothing to lose by trying and everything to gain." She was slightly pale as she threw back her shoulders. "Let's do this." Sarah sucked in a breath, turned, and headed along the winding path formed by metal barriers. Mick followed in her wake, so proud of her courage, her strength in facing the multitude of challenges life had thrown her way. Sarah stepped up to kiosk four. Mick flanked her.

"What can I do for you today?" The clerk was behind a bullet-resistant glass window with a metal speak hole. She looked to be in her late thirties, early forties. She was a large, comfortable-looking woman with dangling earrings and light-brown hair piled on her head with a sparkly clasp.

"Hello." Sarah's voice cracked slightly. She cleared her throat and started again, a pleasant, calm smile on her face. "Hello. I'm hoping you can help me. I was—"

"Oh. My. Holy kamoley!" The clerk rose to her feet, cutting Sarah off, and was staring at Mick with a dawning smile on her face. *Must be a fan,* Mick thought. Sometimes being a famous director could be a pain in the ass, but in a circumstance like this it could be quite helpful. "Mick Talford . . . is that you?" She said it with a familiarity to her tone. As if she knew him.

Mick didn't want to contemplate the possibility of his ugly past rubbing up against Sarah's predicament, even peripherally. He was tempted to grab Sarah's arm and haul her out of there, marriage license be damned, but he didn't. He stayed put. "Sure is," he said. "How are you doing?" *A generic enough response. Covered all bases.* He hoped he'd read the situation wrong and the clerk was indeed a movie buff.

"Look at you. All grown up, and my goodness you look fine." *Shit.* "I haven't seen you in a coon's age. But I've been following you in the papers." *Maybe we went to school together?* He stared at her hard, racking his memory bank but coming up blank. The woman was dressed in a paisley cotton dress, a white cotton sweater with the sleeves pushed up. Her face was pleasant enough. Forgettable. He'd almost swear he didn't know her, but something about her voice niggled at him.

Sarah faced Mick. The hope and relief in her smile almost blinded him. "You guys know each other?"

The woman laughed, good humor dancing in her eyes. "He has no idea who I am. Do you, Mick?"

"Well, I . . ." There was no good way to answer that.

"That's okay. You were young, and I . . ." Another hearty belly laugh tumbled out. "It would be an understatement to say I look a little different. Popping five kids out will do that to a woman."

"Five kids?" Mick was stalling for time. "Incredible."

"Yep." She extended her left hand toward the bullet-resistant window and wiggled her fingers, the simple gold wedding band catching the light. "Got married to a real nice man. Has a steady job with NV, our electric utility company. You still don't recognize me, do you? Want me to give you a hint." She smiled big, and that's when he noticed the missing molar and a memory flashed to him. In the party room at Desert Rose, a john had been throwing back drinks when Chastity approached. The guy flipped, hauled off, and decked her. Knocked out her tooth.

"Don't need one," Mick replied. "Good to see you, Chastity."

Chastity's grin grew even wider. "You do remember." Her face lit up as if he had just given her a diamond necklace.

"Of course I do. Just took a minute to place you."

"Well, bless your soul." Chastity turned to include Sarah in the warmth of her smile. "You got yourself a good man here." She returned her attention to Mick. "Mr. Hollywood, working with movie stars and shit. Who would've guessed?" Chastity tipped her head toward Sarah. "Did you take her by your old stomping grounds?"

"Hell no."

Chastity let out a hoot of laughter. "Don't blame you. Flo's ghost might be lurking around those charred old ruins. Don't mean to speak ill of the dead, but that decrepit scary bitch was harsh."

Sarah looked at him. He could see curiosity in her eyes. "Who's Flo?"

"His grandma." Chastity leaned toward the speak hole in a confidential manner. "And believe me, darling. You can thank your lucky stars she's dead—"

"Okay, enough with the reminiscing," Mick cut in.

Chastity looked at him, her head cocked. "You haven't told her, have you?"

Mick's stomach clenched. His face felt like a mask. "It's not relevant."

"Told me what?" Sarah asked.

Chastity kept looking steady at Mick. "For what it's

worth," she said, "it's better to tell the truth. Otherwise you're going to be starting off the most important relationship of your life with a lie. That's a foundation built on quicksand."

"Thanks, Oprah," Mick said dryly. "Hate to burst your bubble, but we aren't here to get married."

"You aren't?" Chastity seemed slightly crestfallen.

"No."

"I got married here in Vegas," Sarah said. "We came to get a copy of my marriage license."

"Oh." Chastity glanced at Mick with an apologetic shrug. "Sorry about jumping to erroneous conclusions, but in my defense . . ." She extended her hands outward, laughter in her eyes again as she lifted her overplucked eyebrows. "One needs to take into consideration the venue."

"An easy mistake to make," Mick replied. "Can you help her out?"

"You can get a copy of your marriage license," Chastity told Sarah, "but you came to the wrong place." She scribbled an address on a notepad. "You need to go to the Clark County Clerk's Office. It's right around the corner—Two Hundred Lewis Avenue. Three-minute walk, max." Chastity ripped the note off and handed it through the slot to Sarah. "There you go, love. Out the door, make a left, another left on Third, and left on Lewis, and again, sorry about the mix-up. It was great to see you, Mick. You're looking good."

"You, too," Mick said. He stepped away from the kiosk.

"Wait." Sarah touched Mick's arm, stopping him in his tracks. Even in a sterile institutional setting, her touch set his body humming. He scanned her face. Thought he saw an answering flare of heat in her eyes in that split second before she turned back to Chastity, but it could have been a trick of the light. "Is it difficult to get a copy?" he heard Sarah ask, the sound of her voice washing over him like a whiskey bath. "Do I need documentation?"

"Her husband was unable to make the trip with us." Mick added.

Chastity smirked. "I get it. What happens in Vegas stays in Vegas."

"Get your mind out of the gutter. We're friends."

"Mm." Chastity's smirk broadened into a smile as she circled her hands in the air. "From the sparks I see zinging around, you two will be doing the horizontal hula any day now."

"Will Sarah need to show ID or anything like that?" Mick asked, his voice curter than it needed to be, which apparently Chastity found hilarious.

"You're something else, Mick. Still such a prude." She shook her head in mock sorrow. "And after all these years, still charging windmills, saving kittens from drowning—"

A man in an inexpensive suit crossed behind Chastity. "Chas, when you finish up here, Nora could use your help?"

Chastity straightened. "Sure," she replied over her shoulder. The man continued his journey to the copy machine. Chastity turned her attention to Sarah, all business now. "No need for IDs, documentation, nothing like that. It's public record. You just request it. Easy-peasy. There's no forms to fill out. Fifty cents for a plain copy, six dollars and fifty cents for a certified one."

"What's the difference between the two?" Sarah asked.

"Both of them are printed off the original license. The certified one is printed on special paper stock that incorporates security features and will have a raised seal on the front."

"Thank you so much." Sarah beamed at Chastity. "You've been such a big help."

It wasn't until they were walking along Third Street that Sarah turned to him, her hand shading her eyes against the harsh sunlight. "You used to live here?"

"Drop it," he growled. Normally when he used that tone of voice, people shut up and backed away fast. Not Sarah. The corners of her generous mouth twitched upward, as if she were suppressing a grin. Her short, spiky hair and laugh-filled eyes made her look like a mischievous elf. All she needed was a green and red tunic and a hat with a pom-pom.

"Sure, Boss." She paused on the sidewalk, then mock frowned and wagged a finger at him. "Wait a minute," she said accusingly, as if he'd been trying to slip a fast one past her. "You're *not* my boss. I fired you. You are, however, if Chastity's to be believed, a prudish, windmill-chasing, champion of kittens earmarked for a watery grave. Weird, huh? Considering you're supposed to be the wild bad boy of Hollywood." She grinned at him like a sunny day as she tucked her arm through his. "Let's move along, my country vicar," she said, giving him a little tug. "We have places to go, documents to obtain."

"WOULD YOU LIKE A RECEIPT?" THE CLARK COUNTY clerk asked.

Sarah stared at the copy of her marriage license in dismay. "Excuse me. This is the wrong one. It's the marriage license that was signed at the chapel. What I need is a copy of the license that was issued at city hall."

The balding clerk's mouth tightened. "This is a copy of the marriage license issued by city hall."

"But my *signature* is on it."

"Yes." The clerk was looking at her as if he suspected Sarah was missing a marble or two.

The man's listening skills could use a little polishing. "This isn't"—Sarah spoke slowly and clearly so there could be no mistaking her request—"what I needed. You gave me the one from the chapel. I need a copy of the license that was issued *at* city hall."

"Again, ma'am. This is the license from city hall. You then took said license to the chapel, got married, and signed the license. This *is* your marriage license."

"My understanding is in order to get legally married, we both had to be present at city hall to get the license. Had to fill out a form. Show ID. Yes?"

The clerk crossed his arms and huffed out a breath, glancing at the ceiling as if his fraying fragments of patience could be found up there. He must have found the reset button, because when he looked at her again, his face was placid once more. "That is correct. And your point is?"

Sarah exhaled slowly, forced herself to walk the intensity back a few notches, to think clearly. "My point is I didn't apply for a wedding license. Somebody else must have been acting in my stead. Which I believe would render my marriage invalid." Her mind was flipping through information. She was grateful for Mick's steady presence behind her. "However, in order to pursue this avenue further, I came here to get documentation, to get proof. The man who is/or is not my husband is a violent, abusive man. I live every day"—she had to swallow hard, then exhale slowly—"scared for my safety. I intend to sort this mess out." It was difficult to keep the shakes from taking over. "I *know* for *certain* I didn't go to city hall. We were in Vegas for one night. I was at the spa until *after* city hall had closed. Yes. My signature *is* on the marriage license, but I have no idea how it got here. No memory of agreeing to get married, or the ceremony." Sarah's heart was pounding. She could feel the blood rushing in her ears, but she spoke calmly, was determined not to plead to this officious bureaucrat. *You have every right to be here. To ask for what you need.* "I need your help. I want to find proof of whether I am actually married or not. I need a copy of the *original* application."

To Sarah's surprise, the clerk's face had softened, his brow furrowed in consternation. "Oh dear." He wrung his hands. "I'm so sorry." The man was looking at her with such worry and sorrow in his eyes that she wondered what his backstory was. Did he have a daughter or a sister trapped in an abusive situation? Or maybe he grew up under the specter of abuse and witnessed brutality firsthand. "Unfortunately," he continued. "Once the copy of the signed marriage license is received by us from the wedding venue, we scan the updated license into our system and then shred the corresponding paperwork."

* * *

SARAH SLUMPED INTO HER SEAT, THE SOLID DOOR of Mick's Porsche shutting behind her.

Mick rounded the car and got in the driver's seat. "What now?" He turned to face her. His relaxed wrist was slung over the top of the leather steering wheel, the sunlight catching the soft hairs on his forearms, turning them the color of cognac. For a split second she longed to lean over and run her cheek over his arm, to feel the heat, to see if those sun-kissed hairs were as downy soft as they looked.

"I don't know." She jerked her gaze away, wishing for a moment that things were different between them, that the warmth of his body could offer a welcome distraction from the crushing disappointment. *I shouldn't have let my hopes soar so high.* She stared blindly forward, determined to find an alternate solution. *The registration forms for the marriage license have been shredded. Yes. There is no way to prove your marriage was fraudulent. That sucks. What's your next step?* Her mind flashed to the hotel spa. Maybe the spa's computer would have a record of her spa day. *A long shot but worth a try.* Sarah straightened. "Would you mind swinging by the Hard Rock Hotel & Casino? I'd like to visit the spa and see if they have a record of my spa day."

Mick shook his head. "Sorry. Can't do that."

"Okay. Fine. I get it." She kept her voice light. "It's a long shot and you have people to see, things to do." She opened the car door. "I'll grab a taxi and meet you back at—"

"Sarah, put the porcupine quills down. You should know by now that I'm happy to drive you wherever you want to go." Mick reached across her and pulled her door shut again. "The Hard Rock shut down."

"Oh." She slumped back into her seat. *What is the matter with you? Always expecting the worst of people. Is this who you are now?* A wave of weariness rolled over her. She wanted to go back to the hotel, crawl into bed, and pull the covers over her head. Unfortunately, they'd already checked out, so that wasn't an option. Sarah shut her eyes, trying to find her balance. *So proving the marriage was fraudulent didn't pan out. You aren't any worse off than you were yesterday.* The internal pep talk wasn't working. Usually she was like her childhood Bozo Bop punching bag. No matter how many blows that clown received, it would always bounce back up. But then, one day, the toy got a leak, could no longer bounce up, and was taken out with the trash. The one-two punch of the morning had drained all the air out of her. Odd how such a small setback—after all she had been through—had laid her so low.

"The Hard Rock closed its doors in 2019," Mick continued. "Richard Branson bought the resort and did a big renovation. It's the Virgin Hotel now."

"I see."

"It was a good idea though."

Sarah scrubbed her hands through her shorn hair, attempting to activate her brain. *What now?* She was tired. Tired of running. Tired of the uncertainty. Tired of doors shutting her out.

"Where to?" Mick's voice nudged through her downward spiraling thoughts.

"I don't know." She felt as if she too were ready to be taken out with the trash.

MICK STUDIED SARAH'S FACE. SHE LOOKED SO LOST and small. Unsure. She had been ready to think the worst of him, hop out of his car at a moment's notice. Clearly trust was still an issue. *And why wouldn't it be? She's shared so much with you. What have you shared with her? Nothing of any importance. Why? Because you're scared shitless that if you let her see past the veneer, she'll no longer look at you with that glow in her eyes.* "Bullshit."

"Sorry. I wasn't . . . What did you say?" She looked so weary.

"Nothing. Didn't realize I'd spoken aloud." *You had the*

perfect opportunity when Chastity brought up Flo, and what did you do? Shut her down, and Sarah, too.

Dammit.

Mick could feel bile rising in his throat, fear, too, but he knew what he had to do. "Right." He pulled his car into the traffic. "There's something I want to show you before we head back to LA." She gave a slight nod, her eyes still closed. Mick got into the left lane. At the traffic light, he made a U-turn and headed out of town.

34

MICK PULLED OFF ROUTE 266 ONTO THE POUNDED dirt and gravel parking lot, the tires of his Porsche spitting up clouds of dust. He jerked his chin toward the view of the burned ruins of the collection of double-wides through the windshield. His heart was thundering in his chest. "You asked about where I grew up." He felt slightly disoriented, almost nauseous. A car like his would have caused quite a stir back in the day. Big money. "There she blows. Home sweet home."

Sarah looked at him, her eyes wide with surprise. "Oh, Mick," she said, a soft smile dawning on her face as if he'd just gifted her with something very precious. "You want to get out?"

"Not really," Mick replied as he yanked open his door and exited the vehicle. He forced himself to do it fast, his breath held as if he were jumping off a pier into a glacier-fed lake. He could hear Sarah get out as well. Mick didn't look at her. Kept his eyes firmly on the building. Acting relaxed, but he could feel the tension gripping his jaw.

"It's beautiful land in a stark sort of way."

He shrugged. Could feel heat rising on his neck. *Whatever.* The smell was so familiar. The air, crisper than in Vegas, comingled with the scent of dust, disappointment, and the spicy, bitter tang of the big sagebrush that speckled the desert landscape. He was experiencing a feeling of vertigo. Never had taken anyone here, but Sarah had looked so desolate. So he had come up with the poorly conceived idea that by showing her this place, as repulsive as it was, he might somehow gain a little of her trust. *Either that or she'll run screaming for the hills.* Mick sucked in a breath of air, seemed to be having difficulty getting oxygen into his damned lungs.

Sarah tipped her chin toward the weather-beaten sign out front, peeling white backdrop with red lettering. THE DESERT ROSE RANCH. "This is where you lived?"

He nodded.

"Looks like those photos of . . ." She paused, then said in a matter-of-fact tone, "A house of ill repute."

He shoved his hands deep into the front pockets of his faded jeans. "It was." His voice came out flat. He ambled across the drive. Tufts of cheatgrass and red brome had pushed their way through the hardened earth, looked as if they were determined to take over and thrive. As he approached the front door, he was aware that the building was smaller than he remembered. However, the feeling oozing out of the ruins was just as bleak.

"What happened to it?" he heard Sarah ask from over his shoulder.

"Fire." He nudged the charred steps to the front door with his foot. There were four steps, which he used to hop up and down when he was a boy. Feet together, knees bent, then launch into the air and land with a thump. When he was really bored, he'd wrap his legs and arms around the rough wooden banister, mindful of splinters, and hang upside down like a monkey, all the blood rushing to his head. Those steps had been good for sitting on, too. Hot summer days, an ice cube melting slowly in his mouth as he watched the occasional car whiz by. Sometimes the cars would slow

down on the approach and Mick would disappear around to
the back like a ghost before they had pulled into the lot.
Grandma Flo had strict rules about that kind of thing.
Would whup the hell outta him if any of the johns caught
him out front. Didn't want them to be scared off by the
sight of a dirty-assed, snot-nosed kid.

"Wildfire?" Her voice was like a clean light surrounding
him, somehow keeping the worst of the memories at bay.
He shook his head. Another shrug, nonchalant, as if all the
moisture hadn't evaporated from his mouth. Sarah stepped
next to him, the scent of honey and milk radiating from her
sun-warmed skin. She slipped her hand into his, intertwin-
ing her slim, elegant fingers with his brutish ones. If he had
any shred of decency, he would have moved away, not tar-
nished her further with his presence. But the terrifying pull
of his childhood, the bombardment of memories, had him
tightening his grip on her hand. "Tell me," she said. And so
he did. His throat constricted, his voice sounding odd to his
ears. Ragged, hoarse, as if he'd been gargling battery acid.
He told her about that night when he was ten and had woken to the sound of a crash. Didn't know what it was. Sat up
in bed. There was a whooshing, roaring sound. Crackling.
Could smell gasoline and smoke. "I could see a glowing
orange imprint outlining the door and the inset of the panels. I guess because the wood was thinner there. Thick
black smoke was streaming in through all the seams and
crevices like a bad horror movie. The windows in the trailers had been jerry-rigged. They could only be opened two
inches max, enough to let in air, but nothing more. 'A safety
measure,' Grandma Flo had said. She didn't want johns or
boyfriends creeping in on the sly, fucking for free. It was
those windows that had turned the Desert Rose Ranch into
a firetrap. The gauzy hot-pink drapery ignited like dry
summer grass. Turned the Ranch into a hellish inferno."

"But you got out," Mick heard Sarah say, her voice
bringing him back to the present, to the feel of the desert
air moving across his face.

"Yeah. I got out."

"How?"

"When I turned nine, Jewel, one of the girls, had given me a Swiss Army knife. I loved that thing. Was always looking for ways to use it. I figured out how to remove the screw Flo had driven horizontally through the track that stopped the window from sliding open. Even with the safety screw removed, an adult would have had a hard time getting in or out. But I was a kid, so it was different. I had practice. At night, sometimes, I'd sneak out the window. It was a tight squeeze. Had to turn my head and body sideways. The first night I'd tried sneaking out, I landed on my face, got a bloody nose. But after a while I got it down pat. Over the next year, the ridges wore down. I didn't have to use my screwdriver anymore. Could lift the screw right out with my fingers. Tucked it in my pocket, replaced it in the window frame when I got back inside. So that's how I got out. Wasn't thinking. Just ripped out that screw, yanked open the window, tumbled out, choking, eyes burning from the thick smoke."

"And then what?"

"I ran." Acid guilt ate the lining of his stomach as he spoke. "I should have stayed. Got people out, but I didn't think of it at the time. Was so scared. I tumbled out that window, hit the ground, screaming 'Fire! Fire!' at the top of my lungs while my legs were running faster and faster. I ran and I ran, yelling 'Fire! Fire!' Didn't stop until I reached my rock. Looked back and the whole ranch was in flames. Didn't hear any screaming anymore. Just the roar of the flames shooting higher and higher into the night sky."

Sarah had her arms wrapped around his waist. Holding him tight, as if he were still that little boy and she was keeping him safe.

"Your rock?" she said. Her voice was slightly muffled, her face burrowed against his chest.

Mick exhaled shakily. Dragged the back of his wrist across his damp eyes. "I had a rock." He inhaled deeply and then exhaled again. "It was my safe place. My secret."

"Tell me more."

He knew what she was doing. Made the knot in his gut soften slightly. He swiped his eyes again, then wrapped his arms around her as well, holding her gentle as a springtime prayer of thanksgiving. "It was large and relatively flat." He laid his cheek against the top of her head, her hair soft. He breathed in the beguiling scent of her, fragrant, womanly, and totally unique. As she filled his lungs, the thundering of his heart slowed to a gentle trot. "The rock was far enough away from the ranch that my thoughts were my own. The trailer and all its troubles receded and became a batch of fairy lights twinkling in the distance. I'd lie on it, cool and smooth, solid under my back. I'd look at the night sky and the millions and millions of stars and feel, for a moment, clean again. Sometimes I'd go there in the day, too. When school was out and my chores were done. It was a good place to read uninterrupted. Or to watch ants crawl across to obtain a few cracker crumbs. A good place to dream grandly as the clouds and the sun traveled across the wide-open sky."

They stayed there like that, arms around each other, listening to the sounds of the desert, the whip of the wind, the beating of each other's hearts.

"And then what happened?" she asked. "With the fire. Was everyone okay?"

He'd known it was coming. Had dreaded it. And yet now that it was on him, it was just one more segment of the story. "I was the only one who made it out." He heard her sharp intake of breath, felt her arms tighten slightly around him.

"The only one?"

"Mm-hm."

"God. That must have been tough."

It had been. "They tracked my mom down, but she didn't want me, so I was put in foster care."

"Oh, Mick." There was sorrow in her voice. He absorbed it by osmosis through all points of contact. Chest. Torso. Arms. Cheek.

"Wasn't so bad." It was. "Gave me drive and a determination to carve out a better life."

"And you have."

Mick laughed, the sound dry, almost bitter. "In some ways yes, in some ways no. In many ways I'm still trapped in the skin of that ragamuffin kid that ran away. I should have stayed. Should have shaken everyone awake. Should have dragged people out."

Sarah pulled back. She looked him dead-on. There was a ferocity to her expression that he'd never seen before. "And you were *how* old? *Ten*, I believe you said. How were you going to manage that? Hm?" She didn't wait for him to answer. "It was a raging fire."

"You don't know that."

She snorted dismissively. "You said you could *see* orange glowing through the panels of your door, and there was smoke *seeping* around the creases, so the hall. Was. Full. Of. Fire," she said briskly. "Keeping that in mind, how were you going to save them all? Was there access to the rooms other than through the hall?"

"No."

"You yelled, 'Fire, fire,' correct?"

"Yes."

"What more could you do? You were ten. Years. Old." She crossed her arms and looked at him sternly. "You wouldn't have had the body strength to physically haul anyone out of that house. You were too small. If you had tried, you would have died, too. Do you understand? Are you hearing me?"

"They could hear you down in Vegas, woman."

"Good. And I for one am glad that you found a way to save yourself." Then she nestled into his chest again. "So very, very grateful." She hugged him for a moment longer and then stepped back. "Now, you know I'm not going to be able to leave this godforsaken place without a visit to your rock."

WHEN THEY GOT TO HIS ROCK, SARAH INSISTED THEY needed to clamber up onto it.

So he did.

They lay down with the hard, smooth stone under their backs, their arms outstretched, hands clasped. They stayed that way, words having fallen by the wayside as they let the sounds and healing scent of the dry desert air wash over them, gently caressing their bodies. He shut his eyes but could still see the glowing outline of the afternoon sun shining so bright and fierce overhead, could still see it through his closed eyelids. He heard Sarah shift before he felt her, rolling onto her side to nestle into his body. He wrapped his arm around her shoulders, tucked her in close. The beat of her heart, the warmth of her breath fanned against his chest, filling him with contentment and a bone-deep gratitude.

35

KEVIN WATCHED A MIDDLE-AGED WOMAN ENTER the room. Her hand rested on the doorknob as she glanced up from the clipboard in her hand. "Lieutenant Hawkins?"

He stood. "That's correct." This was the fifth employment agency he had visited thus far.

She waved a hand toward his chair. "Please have a seat." She left the door ajar and strode to the chair behind the desk, sat, and folded her hands. "What can I do for you?"

"I am working on a missing person's case. The woman is extremely unstable and is a clear and present danger to herself and others. We have reason to believe that this fugitive is living and working in the Los Angeles area." Kevin snapped his briefcase open and slid several photos of Sarah across the woman's desk, along with the news clipping photo from Solace Island. "You'll need to look closer than surface details as she has changed her hair color, cut, et cetera. She has been using an assortment of aliases. Her most recent identity is Mary Browning—"

He had been watching the woman's hand pick up the

photos. Her gasp drew his focus to her face as it drained of color. "Rachel Jones," she croaked. The woman's gaze flew from the photos to meet his, her expression slightly wild. "Rachel Jones," she repeated, her voice louder, almost strident in the bare-bones office. "Oh, shit. What have I done?"

36

MICK WAS BEHIND THE WHEEL. HE AND SARAH WERE tearing down Highway 95. The windows of his car were open wide, desert air rushing past. He felt lighter, cleaner somehow. He glanced at Sarah, who had been pretty quiet since they'd left Desert Rose. "Yesterday you mentioned you'd tried to get a divorce. What happened with that?"

"Once I was safely away, I contacted the family lawyer who was handling my parents' estate."

"Phillip Clarke?"

"Yes. I asked him to prepare the paperwork for a legal separation. I rented a post office box so I could receive the paperwork. Phillip told me he'd sent the documents by express post. However, when I arrived at the post office to pick up the package, my ex was waiting for me." She shrugged, feeling the betrayal fresh in her belly. "The only person who could have given him that information was my lawyer."

Mick nodded, deep in thought. "So that's why you never filed."

"Yeah."

"You believe your lawyer sold you out. That he's in cahoots with Kevin."

"I don't know. I don't want to believe he would do something like that. He was an old, deeply trusted family friend,
but how did Kevin get that information?"

"This Phillip Clarke, he's not the only lawyer in the
world. Why didn't you ask another lawyer to file for you?"

"You think that didn't cross my mind? I would have
loved to get this whole mess over and done with. Unfortunately, in order to file divorce papers, one needs ID. Phillip
has copies of everything: my birth certificate, social security number, copies of every single passport I've had since
I was a baby. Someone new?" She shrugged, feeling weary.
"Why would they believe me when I have no ID proving
I'm who I say I am?"

Sarah saw something flicker across Mick's face. "Why
don't you have ID?"

She felt heat rising up her neck, flooding her face. "After
we married, Kevin purchased a safe. He said it was to keep
our important documents secure in case of a fire or a robbery." Her stomach hurt just thinking about it. How gullible
she had been. "He had me gather my jewelry, passport,
driver's license, credit cards, birth certificate. We put everything inside. He shut the safe door, latched it, and spun the
lock. I asked for the combination. He told me I didn't have
to worry, that he had the number sequence stored in his
head. I could feel the panic rising as he exited the closet,
me standing there with all my valuables locked up tight. I
heard the TV in the living room switch on to the football
game. I had hoped that he'd left the safe combination in the
top drawer of his bedside table along with his gun, ammo,
and stuff, but it wasn't there. I followed him into the living
room and asked again. He accused me of not trusting him
and he kinda"—she swallowed hard—"flipped out . . ." She
smoothed her suddenly damp palms along her thighs.
Shrugged. "I learned to stop asking."

"Why didn't you tell your parents? Ask them for help?"

It was a good question. One she had repeatedly turned over in her mind. Sarah looked Mick straight on. She was done cowering from the truth. "I was ashamed," she said. One of Mick's hands left the steering wheel and covered hers, warm and solid, giving her courage to keep talking. "My parents took an instant disliking to him. Said they didn't trust him. They felt he was a player, a manipulator. At the time, I thought they were being unfair. I was young, foolish, and headstrong. We got into a terrible argument. I accused my parents of being elitist snobs." She shook her head. "But my greatest stupidity was, once I learned how very right they were, I didn't back down, ask for their help. The arrogance of youth and pointless pride made it impossible to admit I had made a mistake, to ask for help. Instead I made a multitude of excuses for Kevin, to myself and to them."

"For what it's worth—keeping in mind I don't know the various parties involved—it is possible that you are correct and your lawyer and ex are in cahoots." Mick's cell phone buzzed, but he didn't answer it. Kept talking. "However, there might be a couple of other possible explanations."

Sarah tried to clamp down on the tiny seedling of hope-fulness. "Really? Like what?"

"You mentioned Kevin was abusive. Has your lawyer ever done anything that made you feel unsafe or made you question his loyalty?"

"Other than giving Kevin the information about where I was hiding?" Her tone came out a little sarcastic, but he didn't seem to take it personally.

"Yes. Other than that."

Her mind flipped through memories. "No," she finally said.

"Off the top of my head"—his phone buzzed again—"you told me Kevin was in law enforcement." *Buzz . . . Buzz . . .* How could the man let his cell phone ring and not pick it up? *Buzz . . . Buzz . . .* Sarah was tempted to reach over and an-swer it herself. "Wouldn't that give your ex the skills and

know-how to do surveillance?" Sarah's attention snapped
from the sound of the phone to what Mick was saying. "It
would be child's play for him to bug your lawyer's phone,
to trace his incoming calls, emails, et cetera. So that would
be one possibility." He glanced to the right. A small cluster
of gas stations and a coffee shop were fast approaching.
"I'm going to grab a coffee. You want one?"

"Sure."

Mick steered onto the off-ramp. Thankfully, his phone
had gone silent. "Also, since your lawyer handles major
estates like your parents', he would have staff." He pulled
into a parking spot. "What'll you have?"

Sarah opened her door. "I'll come with you. Will be nice
to stretch my legs."

They headed toward Starbucks. "All Kevin would have
needed to do," Mick continued, "was convince one person
in that office to assist him in obtaining information."

SARAH GRABBED MICK'S ARM, TUGGING HIM TO A
stop. She was staring at him as if he'd announced that ele-
phants could fly. "Do you think?" she whispered. There
was a spark of vulnerability in her eyes, and hope, too. "Oh
my, Mick. Kevin *could* have bugged the phones. He *could*
have paid someone off in Phillip's office." Her clasped
hands rose to her mouth, almost as if she were praying.

His phone started vibrating again. The only person
Mick knew who was that persistent was Peterson, and he
could wait. Mick watched as Sarah's fingers extended to a
form a peak, which she tapped against her lips. Her eyes
flickered shut for a moment, as if she were absorbing these
new ideas through the molecules of her skin, a plant con-
verting carbon dioxide into oxygen. When she reopened her
eyes, the internal metamorphosis was astounding. She extended her hands to cup his face. "Thank you," she said.
"Of course." Her eyes were glowing, happiness and relief
shining out. "I can't even begin to tell you what this means
to me. Thank you so much." She leaned forward and placed

her lips on his, soft, gentle, and warm. A kiss of gratitude, and the tenderness of it had Mick reeling. Never had he experienced the pure sweetness of a kiss like that. And then her mouth lifted from his, and her hands followed suit and returned to her sides. But her eyes, the glorious gaze of her beautiful glowing sapphire eyes remained fixed on his.

"Can you answer that now?" she asked.

"What?" His mouth was still tingling, and his brain was mush.

"Your phone," she said with a laugh. "It's been driving me nuts."

"Oh. Right." He tugged his phone out of his pocket and swiped his finger across the screen. "Yes?"

"Mr. Talford?" A woman's voice, vaguely familiar, but he couldn't place it.

"Speaking." He kept his face and voice neutral.

"Thank goodness I got ahold of you. This is a very difficult phone call to make. I hope you won't be too angry with me, but I've made a terrible mistake." The woman sounded agitated. Mick wasn't sure why, but internal alarm bells were ringing. He could feel Sarah's gaze on him.

"Who is this?"

"Sorry. I should have—I'm a little unnerved, you see." He heard her exhale heavily. "It's Ellen Davis from the Windham Employment Agency, and I've done you a terrible, terrible disservice. I didn't check thoroughly enough the credentials of the assistant I sent to your house."

Crap. This did not bode well. "I beg your pardon?"

"A Lieutenant Hawkins is in my office."

Fuck.

Sarah raised her eyebrows. *What?* she mouthed.

Mick shook his head, tapped a finger against his lips. Sarah nodded, her eyes intent on his. Mick put his phone on speaker. "A who?" he replied, keeping his voice disinterested.

"Lieutenant Hawkins." Sarah froze. Every cell in her body appeared to have revved to high alert. Mick captured her hand with his free one. Her fingers were cold. "Appar-

ently, the employee I sent to you is—" Mick heard the
woman on the other end of the line swallow hard. "She's a
fugitive. The police are looking for her. There is no excuse
for not having vetted her more carefully. I am so sorry . . .
Hold on a second." He heard the woman from Windham
Employment cover the mouthpiece of the receiver. Could
hear the muffled murmur of voices. Could see a tremor
course through Sarah, so he wrapped his arm around her
and tugged her to his chest. The woman came back on the
line. "I'm going to put Lieutenant Hawkins on the phone.
He'll be able to explain the situation more concisely." A
barely audible moan emerged from between Sarah's lips.
She slapped her hand over her mouth. Her eyes, which had
locked on his, were dark and drowning in panic.

"Mick Talford. Lieutenant Kevin Hawkins here." The
man's voice had an amiable, authoritative quality to it. "I'm
a fan of your movies. Hey, look, we've got a situation here.
I'm hoping you can help me out."

Mick could feel tremors running through Sarah's body.
He ran his hand in slow circles on her back, letting her
know she was not alone. "What's going on?"

"I'm sorry to inform you that the woman you hired under the name Rachel Jones is mentally unstable. She is a
risk to herself and possibly to others. Not to worry. Now
that we've located her, it will be a simple matter of removing the fugitive from your property. It would be best for
everyone's safety if you vacated the premises."

"I'm not at the house now."

"Wonderful. Perfect." Mick could hear the satisfaction in
the man's voice. "Hold on a second." There was the sound
of Ellen murmuring something. Kevin answered. Mick
couldn't quite make out the words. He heard a "Great . . .
Helpful . . . My thanks." Then Mick and Sarah could hear
Kevin's voice again, strong and clear. "Ms. Davis has
kindly given me your address. I'll be able to remove the
fugitive within the hour. Again, sorry for the inconvenience, and thank you for your cooperation. Please, for

your safety, don't mention anything to your employee, as she might get violent." Mick glanced at Sarah's face. Yes, it was drained of color, but she looked furious, too. Like she would kick serious butt if required.

"Lieutenant Hawkins." Mick kept his voice bored, dry.

"Is there an alarm system I need to know about?"

"There is a state-of-the-art alarm system."

"Can you disable it remotely?"

"No." He could.

"Not an issue." Hawkins rolled right over him. "You can give me the code and password. Do you have an emergency key stashed somewhere? It would be preferable not to have to break open the door—"

"Lieutenant Hawkins," Mick cut in. "I hate to be the bearer of bad news. This all sounds quite fascinating, almost like the plot of a Hollywood movie. However. First. Rachel Jones no longer works for me. I specifically told the Windham Employment Agency I wanted a man. A *man*. What did they do? They sent me an incompetent female with a bad attitude and a fucking mouth on her to boot. She didn't last out the day. I fired her sorry ass and switched to a different employment agency, one that actually *listens* to a client's requests. Secondly. With all due respect, unless I am shown a search warrant, I will not be handing the key to my house or my password and code to anybody. If that is all, I'm quite busy right now. Sorry I couldn't be of more service." Mick disconnected the call, switched the phone off, then wrapped his other arm around Sarah's trembling body and held her tight. "I think it's time to go to New York and meet with your lawyer."

She nodded. "You're right. I need to sort this mess out, or I'll never be free." Sarah's voice was subdued, her breath slightly shaky.

"You okay?"

"I'm scared." She exhaled. "Scared, but I'm going to do it."

"And that is the mark of true bravery." He wrapped his

arms even tighter around her, his head bowed over hers. "You humble me." She felt his lips brush her forehead, and then he placed a finger under her chin and nudged it upward, his face visible now. His eyes were determined. "I'm coming with you, Sarah." His voice was gentle but firm. "No way I'm letting you face this alone."

37

SARAH HANDED HER BOARDING PASS AND ID TO the flight attendant at the gate. The attendant scanned her boarding pass, his eyes flicking to her ID and back to her face, and gave her a cursory smile. "Thank you, Ms. Jones," he said as he handed her ID and boarding pass back. "Have a good flight."

Sarah walked past slow and steady, busying herself with tucking her fake ID back into the zipper compartment of her purse. "Thank you, Mr. Talford," she heard the attendant say to Mick. "Have a good flight." A moment later she felt Mick's solid, strong presence beside her, safe and comforting. *This is how a relationship should be,* she thought, and she flashed to her parents again. They were always there for each other, too, a united front. And for a moment the longing, the pain of their absence, rose to the forefront.

"What are you thinking about?" Mick's voice murmured. "You look sad."

Sarah turned and looked up at his face, a face that had somehow in the last two weeks become so familiar and dear to her. "I was thinking of my parents," she said. "And how much they would have loved you."

A puff of air escaped Mick's lips as a shadow crossed his face. "I can say with certainty your parents wouldn't have 'loved' me. If anything, they would have run screaming in justified terror and locked you in a gilded tower for a good forty-five years."

"You're wrong," she said, taking his hand in hers. "My dad was an excellent judge of character. He. Would. Have. Loved. You." Mick probably would have argued some more, but they had arrived at the door of the plane.

The stewardess glanced at their boarding passes. "2A and 2C. Welcome aboard." She gestured with her hand. "Straight ahead and to the left."

They settled into their seats. The steward double-checked their names, handed out menus, and offered a choice of champagne, orange juice and/or mineral water before takeoff.

"Orange juice for me, please," Sarah said.

"Same. And would it be possible to get some of those warmed nuts?"

"We generally distribute those after takeoff. However, I'll check and see if we can make an exception, Mr. Talford."

"It would be greatly appreciated. We're ravenous."

The steward nodded regally. "Consider it done." He placed two glasses of cold orange juice between them and disappeared into the galley with his silver tray. He was back a moment later with two generous servings of warmed mixed nuts and a saucer with two warmed chocolate chip cookies on it. "Enjoy," he said before straightening and moving on to greet the other passengers in first class.

"Well played, Mr. Talford," Sarah said as she dug hungrily into the salty warm nuts. She was happy to see that there were no peanuts, just plump cashews, perfectly roasted almonds, pecans, and only one oily Brazil nut, which she ate around.

Mick tried unsuccessfully to suppress a smile. "I aim to please, Ms. Rainsford," he drawled. His gruff baritone caused a warmth to surge low in her abdomen and a plump wanting feeling in her breasts.

"Thanks for arranging a cat sitter for Charlie as well."

He patted her hand. "Don't worry." The man had an uncanny ability to read her mind. "Harmony is always rescuing some stray or another. She'll get the key to my place from Pete and will swing by after work to pick up your furry monster."

HARMONY WAS WENDING HER ANCIENT TOYOTA Corolla up Mulholland Drive. She squinted through her windshield, trying to read house numbers. The approaching headlights were making it difficult to see past the streaks on the glass. She had planned on purchasing some window-washing fluid that morning when she'd gassed up, but by the time she remembered, she'd already cashed out and was running late. "Eleven forty-eight . . . Eleven fifty . . ." Harmony's cell phone service was spotty in the canyon, so she wasn't able to rely on Google Maps for navigation. This was not how she'd planned to spend her evening. To say she was not pleased was an understatement. She'd had to cancel a Tinder date with a guy named Scott. Had seemed promising. Super cute. Nice body, good haircut. At least that's how he looked in his photos. His Facebook page was full of photos of colleagues from the investment firm he worked at, and family and friends. But now that possibility was blown to hell. When she'd called to see if he would mind rescheduling for another night, he'd gotten pissed, accused her of blowing him off. Started to lecture her on "manners" and "etiquette." She'd hung up. The guy was a pompous dickhead, but still.

Harmony's hands felt slick on the steering wheel. "Why does Mick have to live up this stupid canyon?" she muttered. There was the dark body of a car looming ahead. She tapped her brakes so the asshole tailgating her wouldn't slam into her trunk as she slowed down and squeezed past the abandoned vehicle on the shoulder of the road. *What kind of jerk leaves their vehicle with the body encroaching on the lane?* And on the heels of that thought came another. *Must have run out of gas. Didn't have a choice.* She suppressed a shiver and glanced down at her fuel gauge. She still had a third of a tank. *Thank goodness.* Harmony lived in horror of running out of gas. Had happened to her once driving home from a set in East LA. Scared the shit out of her. And ever since then she was diligent about not letting her tank get low.

She rounded the bend, and there were the granite pillars and wrought iron gates with the curlicue design Paul had described to her. Discreetly embedded in one of the pillars and lit with a lantern was the house number she'd been looking for. With a sigh of relief, she swung her car into Mick Talford's driveway, the tailgating car roaring past, blasting its horn, as Harmony stopped before the elegant gates. Even with night having fallen, she could see that it was a beautiful property, tucked away and securely positioned behind a wall of hedges. She unrolled her window, punched the code into the keypad, then hit #, and the gates slowly swung open.

She drove past the gates and down the lushly landscaped driveway toward the sumptuous Spanish villa, which looked to have been built in the 1930s. She snorted. *God forbid Mick settles for anything but the best.* But as quickly as the thought arose, slightly acrid and bitter, she stuffed it down. "The man works like a dog," she murmured. "Deserves a beautiful place." *And what about you? You work hard.* She did. Damned hard. And what did she have to show for it? A furnished studio apartment with a Murphy bed and a kitchen the size of a small closet. *Where's* your *mansion?*

She pulled up in front of Mick's house and looked at her notes. The cat, Charlie, was in the apartment over the garage. Harmony exited her car and stretched the kinks out of her limbs. She hated driving in LA, dealing with the congestion, the crowded freeways, the smog. But driving the winding canyon roads was the *worst*, especially at night.

The streets were badly lit, with hairpin turns that if you missed would send you over a ravine, plunging to your death. People drove way faster than was safe, arrogant assholes in their fancy cars, tailgating too close, revving their motors.

As Harmony crossed the circular drive, she noticed through the darkened living room window of Mick's house, the lit pool, a shimmering blue that beckoned her like a monsoon rain after a drought. *And why not?* she thought, veering to the left, taking the flagstone path past the honeysuckle shrub whose delicate sweet fragrance had her plucking a tiny flower and tasting the droplet of nectar at the base. She rounded the side of the house, trailing her fingers along the glorious magenta bougainvillea that climbed the interior garden wall, feeling pleased with her decision but a little guilty, too. *No one is here, so if I take a quick dip, who does it hurt?* She stepped past the dark bark of a jacaranda tree, its branches bedecked with pale-purple blossoms, and out into the back garden. Fairy lights hung from the branches. There were garden lights discreetly placed among the flora and fauna, and beyond that was the pool, glimmering under the stars, steam rising in the cool night air. She twirled, arms outstretched, taking in the beauty and serenity of the garden. This was what she'd imagined when she'd packed up her car in Wisconsin and headed to LA to make her fortune, become rich and famous. *Ha.* And just like that the jubilation, the magical sheen of the adventure vanished. The sudden weight of reality had her arms dropping to her sides, and her eyes felt hot. *Fuck it,* she thought thrusting her chin out. *I drove all the way up here, canceled my date. At the very least, I'm gonna swim in that goddamned pool.*

KEVIN WATCHED, HIDDEN DEEP IN THE SHADOWS OF Mick Talford's living room, as the voluptuous strawberry blonde with the tight skirt and full lips stepped into the light, twirled once, twice, paused, seeming lost for a second, and then her shoulders squared and she marched across the back garden. An almost angry determination was present in every footstep. She shed her clothes piece by piece until finally, at the pool's edge, she discarded her bra, her thong, and dove into the water.

When the headlights of her car had flashed across the window, briefly lighting the interior of the darkened living room, Kevin's adrenaline had spiked into high alert. The "state-of-the-art" alarm system had been ridiculously simple to disarm, but perhaps he'd underestimated and there was a secondary silent one with a different panel. He'd flattened himself against the wall and watched through the glass as the flare of headlights swiveled, switched off, and the body of the vehicle was suddenly visible. Luckily, the car had been a civilian clunker, which had ruled out police, armed security guards, and the director. Kevin had surmised it was staff. He hadn't split on the off chance it was Sarah, because when Talford said he'd fired her, something in his voice didn't ring true. Niggled at him. So much so that Kevin had followed his hunch and had swung by Talford's residence to take a look around.

Once the woman had exited the car, it was immediately clear she wasn't Sarah. Hairstyle, clothes, those things could be changed, but the body type was wrong. Kevin had experienced a moment of doubt. Had his hunch been wrong? Was she the new assistant? The cook? A girlfriend? Kevin waited to see which door she would head toward so he could slip out the other, but she hadn't approached either. She'd disappeared around the side of the house. A moment later she'd reappeared in the garden. And once again the chess pieces had shifted in his favor. Instead of exiting the house and furtively making his way back to the vehicle he'd left on the side of the road. Kevin had waited. He'd watched. He'd made plans.

Flashlight in hand, with the power switched off, Kevin slipped out the kitchen door and silently made his way to the pool, keeping his eyes fixed on the prize. And a tasty prize she was, too. As the woman swam, the defiant anger she had entered the water with seemed to dissipate, and a languorous enjoyment of the water and the luxurious surroundings appeared to take over. Perfect. That she was naked and would rocket from a totally relaxed state to one of high anxiety would make his entrance and his interrogation all the more pleasurable.

It was time to make his move and find out who she was, and more importantly, what could she tell him about Sarah? He stepped out from the shadows, flicked his flashlight on, the beam trained on the back of her head. "Security," he yelled. "Get out of the pool." She spun around, eyes wide, pupils dilating in fear, which gave him an instant boner. Her hands rose in an ineffectual attempt to cover her muff and her porn-star-sized jugs. Had to bite down hard on his back teeth to keep from laughing. Dumb bitch. He'd already looked at the goods and planned on having an even closer inspection before the night was done. "Move!" he bellowed, drawing his gun, making sure the light spilling from the lanterns glinted along the barrel. Visuals were always helpful in establishing control over a victim. "Hands in the air. Get out of the pool. *Now.*"

Her eyes got even wider. Her hands shot in the air so fast, it was almost comical. She scrambled out of the pool, small whimpering sounds escaping from her lips, which made him harder than hell. "State your name and your business," he barked.

"My name's . . . Harmony. Harmony Albright." The words half-spoken, half-sobbed. "I work . . . for Paul Peterson." Like that meant dickshit to him. "He's Mick's partner. Mick Talford. He asked me to pick up a cat."

"His cat?"

"No. It belongs to his new assistant, but they needed to fly to New York."

"New York?" His senses sharpened.

"Yes. An unexpected trip. Paul's pissed off because there's a lot to do. They've got a new movie coming out and I'm . . . I said I'd take care of the cat."

"By swimming?" He leisurely let the beam of his flashlight travel the length of her body. "Nude? You have an odd idea of cat-sitting."

"I know. I'm sorry. Please don't tell him. I can't afford to get fired—"

He snapped the flashlight up. The bright beam was trained on her face, which was drained of color underneath her California tan. "And his assistant's name? The one he's flying to New York with?"

Tears streamed down her face as words stumbled past quivering lips. "I . . . I don't remember . . ."

"That's too bad." He cocked the gun.

"Wait a minute . . . Wait a minute . . . It's, uh . . . It's right on the edge of my—*Rachel*! Her name is Rachel. They needed to talk to some lawyer out there. I don't remember her last name."

"Rachel." *Eureka.* He smiled. Glanced down at his watch. *So the two-faced bitch was going to see Clarke to try to cut me free.* Kevin shook his head. *Over my dead body.* He made a few quick calculations. If he moved fast enough, he could catch a red-eye to JFK. "Thank you, Harmony. You've been most helpful."

She attempted to return his smile, still crying though. Tears, water from the pool streaming down her trembling body. He would have loved to dally, sample all that was on offer, but he was operating on a time crunch now. "Please don't tell. Please . . ."

"Life is full of difficult choices," he murmured.

"If there is anything I can do"—her tongue darted out in an attempt to moisten lips that had gone dry as dust—"to help make the decision easier, just say the word." Her hands were still in the air. She was trying so hard not to freak out, it was really quite luscious.

Too bad she had to die.

38

"YOU AREN'T HUNGRY?" MICK'S VOICE CUT THROUGH Sarah's tangled thoughts. She glanced at the slice of avocado toast in her hand. It was perfectly fine. The avocado was soft and silky. The crushed heirloom tomato confit added a nice touch of acid and color, so why was she having such a difficult time getting it down?

"It's delicious," she replied, taking another bite even though her stomach was in knots.

They were eating breakfast in the Garden at the Four Seasons on East Fifty-Seventh Street. When they were finished, they would head over to 450 Lexington. Sarah forced herself to chew and swallow. She needed to eat, to fortify herself, to ensure that she fed her body and mind so she was battle ready and sharp. She took another bite, chewed. Reached for her glass of fresh-pressed orange juice to help wash it down. "Although, when one considers that they are charging thirty-two dollars, and that doesn't include tax and tip." She looked at the piece of avocado-smeared toast on her plate. "If you cost out the ingredients . . ."

"I can afford it."

"Still. Doesn't make it right." Sarah was aware of her mouth opening and shutting, of inconsequential words coming out. Words that had nothing to do with the anxiety she was experiencing internally. After four years, she was going to be seeing one of her father's oldest friends, a man whom she had considered an uncle. She was going to look Phillip Clarke in the face, confront him with the facts, and find out whether or not he had betrayed her and, by proxy, her father. "I never noticed the price of things before going on the run. Wouldn't have thought twice about ordering something like this and then leaving the majority of the food on my plate." She made herself take another bite.

"You're trying to muscle that down, aren't you?"

"So?"

"And you don't want to leave it because of the cost."

"Can't take it to go. The avocado would go brown."

"I see," Mick said gravely. He tipped his head toward the other slice still on her plate. "You want me to eat that."

"Would you?"

Mick laughed. "Happy to oblige." He reached over and snagged the remaining piece of toast and took a bite, still chuckling. "You're such a weirdo. You look so relieved."

"I owe you."

"I'll add it to your tally." A minute later the avocado toast had disappeared down his gullet. He glanced at his watch, took another slug of coffee, glanced at the check, and peeled a few bills from his wallet. "You ready?"

Sarah's stomach lurched, but she rose to her feet, keeping her face serene. "As ready as I'll ever be."

THEY STEPPED OUT OF THE REVOLVING DOOR, PAST the doorman, and onto the bustling sidewalks of New York City, a mass of humanity streaming past in both directions, everyone seeming to have somewhere to go. Mick paused, taking it in. "Blindfolded, I'd still know I was in New York."

"The noise?"

Mick shook his head. "The smell." His cell phone buzzed. He pulled it out and glanced at the screen.

"Anything important?"

"Another message from Paul." He turned the phone toward her so she could see the screen. IMPORTANT, YOU SON OF A BITCH. ANSWER THE GODDAMNED PHONE! "Such drama." Mick slid the phone back in his pocket.

"You aren't going to call?"

He shrugged. "Later. Everything's always 'important' with Peterson. He gets especially wound up when we've got a new movie coming out. Loses sleep combing through the preview feedback forms, frets over the various projected box office estimates. Shits a brick at the slightest provocation. I'll give him a couple of hours to sort it out, calm down, and then I'll check in."

"Okay. And for the record, New York doesn't stink."

"That's not what I meant. There's something about the quality, the texture, and taste of the air here that is unlike anywhere else in the world. Breathe deep. Smell that? It's the scent of cultures colliding, the crush of humanity, humidity, pavement, automobiles, salted pretzels, warm toffee nuts, big dreams and broken ones. The city has got this unmistakable unique pulse that's constantly thrumming." He glanced up the road at the oncoming traffic. "Fewer taxis though. Used to be way more of them when I first visited. A sea of yellow cabs as far as the eye could see." He moved toward the curb. Sarah snagged the crook of his arm.

"Would you mind if we walk? It's not too far, and I think moving would help dissipate my nerves." She wasn't looking at him. However, she could feel his gaze scanning her face.

"Sure. Lead the way."

Sarah kept her hand tucked in the crook of his arm. *The better to steer him with,* she told herself, knowing it was a lie. The human contact, the strength she could feel under the fabric of his clothes, comforted and settled her. Made her feel safe. She wanted to bury her face in his chest and breathe in the spicy, clean male scent of him. She wanted to slide her hands under that fitted charcoal-gray T-shirt and imprint the texture and warmth, the contours onto her fingertips, her palms. "We'll take Lexington," she said, proud of how even-keeled her voice sounded. She gave his arm a little "we're just pals; nothing to see here" pat for good measure as they headed up the road.

"Hey," he complained, a grumpy bemusement in his eyes. "I'm not a dog."

No kidding, she thought, stifling a snort. *You are a hot-blooded, sexy man who is driving me wild with lust.* "Note to self," she said as they strode along the pavement at a good clip. "Mick Talford is *not* a dog." She smiled cheerily up at him. "Thanks for the clarification. Kind of hard to tell." She waved her hand in his direction. "What with your shaggy hair and the lolling tongue."

"Shut up and walk," he growled.

"Ooh. Tough guy."

He didn't respond. Didn't have to. The man had distracted her from the jangly nerves that had been plaguing her all morning, bless his heart. Sarah felt she could face anything striding alongside this man, enjoying the sunshine on her face.

39

MICK HAD KEPT THE CONVERSATION TROTTING along as they wended their way through the packed crowds, but once they stepped into the elevator, Sarah had fallen silent. By the time the button for the twenty-eighth floor lit, her chin was up, her shoulders were back, and her face was as serene as still water. However, her grip had tightened fractionally on his forearm. He didn't turn, could see her blurry reflection in the polished metal elevator door. Mick placed his hand over hers, just for a second, a fleeting contact to say, "I'm here. You aren't alone," before the elevator doors opened.

"Thanks," she whispered, facing forward as well.

The elevator pinged, the doors glided apart, and Sarah released her grip on his arm and sailed forth, spine erect, class, breeding, and grit emanating from every fiber of her being. There wasn't even a second of hesitation. Sarah knew exactly where she was going, and Mick followed, close enough to be backup, not so close as to draw attention or cramp her style. She strode past a corridor of occupied cubicles and desks. Mick was aware of heads turning, a building buzz of whispers, but Sarah didn't look right or left. It was almost as if she were unaware of the furor she was creating. However, Mick could see the slight tension in her jaw, the faint flush of color staining the tips of her delicate ears. As Sarah approached a set of large steel-gray doors at the end of the corridor, she glanced to the side at the fresh-faced young woman who sat at a desk to the left of the doors.

The woman looked up from her keyboard and smiled politely. "Hello. May I help you?"

"Yes. I'm a client of Mr. Clarke. Sarah Rainsford. I've lost my ID. Mr. Clarke has copies of all my pertinent papers: driver's license, passport, birth certificate, et cetera. If you could please gather them for me while I'm meeting with Mr. Clarke, it would be greatly appreciated."

"Certainly." The young woman was skimming through the day calendar on her desk. "Sarah Rainsford, you said? I'm new here." She clicked open a corresponding calendar on her computer and scanned it. "Don't have all the client names down yet." She lifted her gaze from the screen and shook her head, a helpful smile on her face. "I'm sorry. I can't seem to find you on his schedule. Perhaps you got the day wrong?"

Sarah hesitated for a split second. If Mick had blinked, he would have missed it. "Nope," Sarah said decisively. "Our meeting was scheduled for now. Not to worry." She briskly stepped past the young woman, grasped the door handle, and swung the door open. "I'll announce myself."

"Please hold Mr. Clarke's calls," Mick instructed to the startled secretary. He felt his cell phone buzzing in his pocket again as he followed Sarah into the large corner office. Mick shut the door behind him with a *thunk* and locked it for good measure. He could hear the scramble of the secretary's heels as she rounded her desk. Could feel the rattle of the metal door handle as she frantically tried to get it to open.

"Mr. Clarke," she called. "I'm sorry. I tried to stop them. Do you need me to call security?"

There was a shriveled old man with sparse strands of hair carefully arranged over his balding pate. He appeared to be in his early seventies and was seated behind the massive polished mahogany desk. His head had snapped up from the paperwork at the commotion. Irritation vibrated through his frail frame. "For God's sake," he barked at his secretary, who could be seen gesticulating frenetically through one of the glass panels flanking the door. "All I asked is that you man the goddamned desk." His annoyed gaze traveled from the glass panel to his unwanted visitors. His jaw dropped, and his rheumy eyes widened. "Sarah . . . ?" The old man rose shakily to his feet, and he clutched the desk for support. Dazed. "Is that you?"

SARAH DREW TO A HALT IN FRONT OF HER LAWYER'S desk. Her heart felt like a trapped bird in her chest. "Mr. Clarke." She gave a curt nod. Sarah could hear the new assistant secretary's shrill voice on the other side of the door. Was grateful for Mick's strong, solid presence standing sentry beside it, making certain she was not disturbed. She watched her old lawyer jab the intercom button. "I'm fine, Hannah," he said into the speaker. "Please carry on with your work." His eyes didn't stray from Sarah's face. "And hold all calls."

Sarah kept her face calm and expressionless. "Please sit. We have some things we need to discuss."

"Sarah . . . my dear . . ." His gnarled, birdlike hand extended toward her, palm upward like a beggar crying for alms. He had aged so much since she had seen him last, shrunken several inches, and lost that brisk vitality that had always seemed to crackle around him. Seemed skinnier, too, like a shell of his former self. Was he sick? *No,* she told herself firmly. *You can't allow nostalgia and emotion to cloud your judgment. You must approach this situation with a clear-eyed, logical pragmatism. That is the only way you will get to the truth.* "Thank God you are alive and well." There was a quaver in his voice. "I've been so very worried." Sarah's eyes felt hot. He started to round the desk.

"No." Sarah held up her hand to stop his approach. This was no happy homecoming, and she'd be damned if she'd pretend it was. The room was silent. She could hear the ticking of the antique clock her father had given Phillip. It was nestled on his bookcase among leather-bound books. Phillip was watching her cautiously. "Please. Sit."

Her father's lawyer sank to his seat. "Are you all right, my dear?" he ventured. There seemed to be genuine concern in his voice. "I didn't know what to think when you disappeared like that. I tried to track you down, but you'd vanished into thin air."

Anger flared in Sarah's chest at the duplicitousness of that statement. There was a time when she wouldn't have said anything. Not wanting confrontation. Scared to face uncomfortable truths. Not anymore. "Why did you tell Kevin where I was?"

An expression of confusion flittered across his face. He leaned forward with his brow furrowed, head tilted as if his hearing were fading.

"Kevin," she repeated louder, enunciating clearly, so there could be no mistake. She could hear the coldness in her voice and feel the stiff remove in her face, a mask to keep the hurt at bay, because he wasn't worth it. This old man whose hand she'd clasped so trustingly as a child. She had a memory of walking down the street, her father on one side, "Uncle Phillip" on the other, both of them big and strong. Her father would call out, "One . . . two . . . three . . ." and then the two of them would swing her up in the air, soaring, sailing, and then gently alighting on the pavement once more. "You told him where I was."

Phillip stared at her in consternation, blinking his pale, watery eyes. "I'm sorry, my dear, but I don't know what you are talking about."

Sarah kept her expression calm, her hands folded neatly in her hands. "I am not a fool, Mr. Clarke." He looked wounded. Good. She'd be damned if she'd address him informally. This was business, plain and simple. She'd made that mistake once. Trusted. Never again. "When I was on the run, I contacted you, asked you to send legal separation documents so I could begin the process of dissolving my marriage. I gave you the address of a post office box."

"Yes. I remember that. I filled out the forms as per your request and had them sent out that afternoon. Express post."

"And what else did you do, that same afternoon?" The acid bite in her voice had him stiffening slightly.

"It's hard to remember. Was a long time ago—"

"Shouldn't be hard to remember. Unless you make it a daily practice of backstabbing clients, breaking your vow of confidentiality, and putting their lives in danger?" The man was a good actor. He really gave the appearance of having no idea what she was talking about. "However, in the name of expediency, let me refresh your memory. You contacted Kevin—you remember him—the husband I was trying to discard? Told him my whereabouts. I hope he paid you well because you—"

"I did *no* such thing." Phillip Clarke rose from his chair. His face had turned an unbecoming shade of puce as he slapped his hand on his desk. He was doing a pretty credible imitation of a man who had been falsely accused—she'd give him that. However, there was no way she was going to remain sitting as if she were a misbehaving child in the principal's office. She was a woman grown, powerful in her own right. Sarah shot out of her seat, stepped forward, slammed her hands on the opposing side of his desk, and leaned toward him, teeth bared. Part of her hoping, praying that he would prove her wrong.

"Then kindly explain to me how Kevin magically managed to appear in the tiny town of Brimfield, Illinois, population eight hundred and thirty-four? Not exactly a thriving metropolis. Not exactly a place that Kevin would visit." Her words were spoken clearly and succinctly, smashing into him like a volley of well-placed blows. "And yet there he was, staked out in front of the damned post office where I was expecting to receive a package from *you*."

Phillip Clarke stared at her as if she'd produced a ghost.
"He was . . . waiting for you?" Sarah nodded, a bitter taste
in her mouth. "But how? He tracked you to Brimfield, Illinois?" And then a pained expression crossed his face.
"Sweet Mary, mother of God," he murmured as he sank
back into his chair. His breathing had become irregular
pants, as if he were suddenly having difficulty catching his
breath. His fist rose and pressed against his chest. He didn't
look good.

"Mr. Clarke . . . ?" His head wobbled back and forth on
his skinny stalk of a neck. The movement didn't succeed in
shaking any more words out. There was a slight sheen of
sweat glistening on the top of his head, his forehead, and
dotting his upper lip. *Shit. Is he having a heart attack?* She
rounded the desk. "Uncle Phillip, are you all right?" She
could see Mick in her periphery crossing to the water
cooler as she placed her fingers against the old man's carotid artery. His pulse was erratic. His skin felt clammy and
smelled of old age, sweat, and cologne.

"Vicki . . ." Phillip Clarke rasped as if all the moisture
had vanished from his mouth and throat. "Had to be her."
His eyes were like a drowning man's, tormented, as if he
had received a fatal blow. "She must have . . . told him.
She's the only other person who had knowledge . . . of your
whereabouts . . ." His eyes fluttered shut. "I'm sorry. So
very . . . sorry."

Sarah's mind was spinning as she wrapped her hand
around Phillip's shoulder to steady him. *Vicki? Did his secretary give the information to Kevin, and if so, why? It
didn't make sense.* The lawyer slumped forward slightly.
Damn. Sarah tightened her grip and tapped her fingers on
his shoulder to keep his attention in the room. "Uncle Phillip." Her voice seemed loud and slow to reach her ears.
"Nod if you can hear me. Can you hear me?" He nodded.
Thank God.

Mick appeared beside them, nudged a glass of water into
the old man's hand and curled his gnarled fingers around it.
"Take a sip," Mick said as he helped bring the glass to the

old man's trembling mouth. "Nice and easy." Phillip took a sip. A trickle of the water escaped his lips, dribbled down his chin, and dropped onto his cream-colored shirt like an oversized tear making a grayish spot.

"I'm going to loosen your tie." She was still talking overly loud, couldn't help herself. Was overenunciating, too. "Okay?" Sarah didn't wait for a response; she tugged at his navy silk tie, which was dotted with gold bumble-bees. She loosened the knot, then unbuttoned the top two buttons of his shirt. "There you go. Better?"

He nodded and smiled wanly, blinking his watery eyes. "Much better. Thank you." The color was starting to return to his face. He was able to hold the water glass on his own now.

"Take another sip," Sarah urged. Her voice was more normal now, but her heart was still racing. He raised the water glass and took another sip. There was something so vulnerable and almost childlike about his acquiescence. Then he placed the water glass carefully on the desk in front of him. Both hands wrapped around it, his eyelids half-shut, as if he were too weary to raise them.

"I'm a foolish old man." His voice was barely audible, his shoulders were rounded, and the expression on his face made him look as if he were a million years old.

"Uncle Phillip, I don't understand why you think Vicki would—"

"Sit." He waved his hand toward the chairs in front of his desk. "You, too," he said to Mick. "This might take a while. I have a lot to apologize for. You see . . ." He stared at his desktop, gathering his thoughts. "I was passionately, deeply, and totally in love with Vicki. Have been for the last twenty-eight years." His voice was low and filled with sorrow. "I will go to my grave loving her. She is my beloved. But." He lifted his head, and Sarah could now see silent tears were sliding down his face. "That doesn't mean that I am blind to the uncomfortable truths that now face us. Vicki has left me. And, Sarah, it breaks my heart"—he squeezed his eyes shut, paused as if bracing for a physical blow, reopened his eyes, his expression resolute—"to be the bearer of bad news," he continued. "But I've recently learned why. My precious Vicki has been carrying on a covert affair with your husband."

"With Kevin?" Shock caused her voice to leap a half octave.

"Yes." He swiped the back of his shaky hand across his damp eyes. "I don't know how long this has been going on. However"—he jabbed his forefinger onto the top of his desk with a good deal of force—"I recently discovered him sneaking out her back door. Now. It is very possible she was the one who gave him your information. Not out of malice, mind you. My Vicki doesn't have the capacity for that kind of betrayal. Kevin must have woven some kind of spell on her, as he did on you. I remember clearly how concerned your parents were." He shook his head, briefly lost in memories. "All of us were. I hadn't mentioned your parents' concerns about Kevin, or my own deep misgivings, to Vicki. You had already gotten married. The deed was done. Client confidentiality and all that." He sank back in his seat, a broken man. "I wish to God I had. It might have saved her from becoming entrapped in the center of this mess. I am worried, Sarah. I am worried for her safety."

"As well you should," Sarah murmured as a shiver of fear slithered down her spine. "He's a monster."

"I'm begging you. Please. Speak with Vicki. Warn her of his true nature. She won't listen to me. Vicki believes I am delusional, am speaking from a place of jealousy. And yes, the loss of her love breaks my heart, but even more important than that, I *want* her *safety*."

Sarah's tendency was to leap into the gap and rush in and help. *No. You're too soft,* she told herself sternly, clamping her mouth shut. *That's how you ended up married to Kevin. Take a moment to sort this through before you speak.*

"I can't sleep," he continued. "Can't eat." He tugged the waistband of his slacks from his body. "See here. I've lost seven pounds in the last five days. Seven pounds and I'm skinny to start with. I'm sick with worry."

Sarah held up her hand to interrupt the deluge of words. Phillip stopped talking. His eyes fixated on her like a starving mongrel. "I'll think about it." Phillip opened his mouth. "I'm not done." His lips snapped shut so fast, it was almost humorous. His expression reminded her of a toad who had just captured a fly. "I'm not making any promises. First there are some things I need sorted out. As I mentioned to your secretary when I came in, I want the notarized copies of all my identification documents you have in your files: passport, social security card, birth certificate, driver's license. Secondly, your secretary needs to draw up the petition for my divorce. Once we have signed, notarized, and mailed it, I will be able to contemplate whether or not I'll feel comfortable having a conversation with Vicki—"

"But drawing up the documents will take a while, my dear. Vicki could be in extreme danger."

Sarah felt her mouth tighten. Uncle Phillip might be an old family friend, but he was selfish asking her to visit Vicki, especially if her ex was lurking around. "Believe me, Uncle Phillip. I understand the gravity of the risk Vicki is putting herself in, being involved with Kevin. One could say I have firsthand knowledge of said danger, considering the abuse I and my baby incurred at his hands. Not to mention, I've been on the fucking run for the last *four* years." She heard Mick's phone buzz again, but she kept her eyes locked on Phillip's. Could see in her peripheral vision Mick glance at the screen and then flick it off. "So, you see, Uncle Phillip, my priorities are a little different from yours. Until my petition for divorce is filed, until I have proof of my identity in my hands, I am not going to do a damned thing."

"Maybe you could see her while we work on the documents?"

"No. I'm sorry, but this is nonnegotiable."

"But Vicki . . . ?" There was a tremor to his voice, and urgency. His eyes filled up again. "Time is of the essence."

"I agree," she replied, hardening her heart. "Time *is* of the essence, so you and your new secretary had better get working."

Phillip's mouth tightened fractionally. He was not accustomed to taking orders. Nevertheless, he jabbed the intercom button. "Hannah," he barked. "I need you in my office, pronto."

Sarah could hear the sound of scurrying feet. Mick unlocked and opened the door. The new secretary, Hannah, rushed in. She looked a little disheveled. "Mr. Clarke, I was looking—"

"Hannah. I need you to clear our schedule for the next few hours. We need to write up and file a petition for divorce for my client Sarah Rainsford Hawkins from her husband Lieutenant Kevin Hawkins. Also, I want you to go into the files and get the copies of Ms. Rainsford's ID."

"That's just it, Mr. Clarke. I've been searching all over for them, but they aren't there. Not only are the copies of her ID missing, but there are no legal or financial papers either. It's the darnedest thing."

Sarah met Mick's eyes over Hannah's head. He looked grim.

40

"I STILL CAN'T BELIEVE IT," SARAH SAID. MICK GLANCED at her. She had been dead silent since they'd gotten in the taxi at Lexington and East Forty-Fourth, deep in thought. "It will take a while for the divorce to come through. I'm sure Kevin will fight it, and there will be financial stuff for the lawyers to quibble about, but at least it's finally in the works."

"I didn't think it was possible for that old man to move so fast," Mick said. "Those papers were flying across that desk at record speed."

"I feel lighter now that the process has started. Feel so much better in here." She placed a fist over her heart.

Lighter was good. If Mick was being honest, he'd nudge his feelings past "lighter" to bordering on celebratory. As if delicate champagne bubbles were coursing through his bloodstream. With Sarah's divorce petition signed, sealed, and sent off, she was a free woman. *What was that she'd called him? A prudish country vicar . . .* Mick grinned. *Not for much longer.* "You deserve to feel good. You were amazing. Kicked some *serious* butt."

"I did, didn't I?" She grinned back at him, a spark of joy in the dim light, and then she fell into a brooding silence again. The darkness of the Queens Midtown Tunnel combined with the overhead lights had lit the interior of the cab a greenish-yellow tint. "Now all I have to do is get my damned ID. Uncle Phillip sure freaked out when he realized Vicki had cleared the office of all my files. I have so many questions zipping through my brain. Did she bring them home with her? Is she planning on using them to blackmail Uncle Phillip? Or maybe she's planning on selling them to Kevin? And the strangest thing is, it's hard to imagine her doing these things. You'll see when you meet her." Sarah shook her head. "What if she won't hand them over? That is what's worrying me the most. I can't get ID without having ID to prove I'm who I say I am. It's a catch twenty-two. If I don't get this mess sorted out, Sarah Rainsford could literally cease to exist. But then I circle back to why would Vicki do that? What's in it for her?"

Mick could conjure a million reasons why someone would want to make an incredibly wealthy heiress disappear. Maybe that person was Vicki. Maybe it was someone else. More information was necessary in order to have clarity. Hopefully, Vicki would have a reasonable explanation for why Sarah's documents were at her home and would be happy to hand them over.

"I've got to confess, I'm still reeling from the unwanted image of the two of them getting it on." Mick wasn't sure which possible affair Sarah was referring to. "I'd seen them at the office and at social functions as well." *Ah. Clarke and Vicki.* "I had *no* idea they were having an affair, and for *all* those years. I wonder if his wife knew, if my parents did." She shook her head in disbelief. "It's true Vicki was always there in the background, like a comfortable bookcase or old slippers, but Uncle Phillip seemed so solidly married."

"You called him that in the office as well. I wasn't aware he was your uncle."

"He's not. It was an honorary title, I guess, from way

back as long as I can remember. No blood relation. They were just Uncle Phillip and Auntie Jane. His wife is lovely. They've been married forever—thirty-five, forty years. Have two grown sons. There were photos of his family on his desk. Did you see them? Looks like there is a granddaughter now, too. He always carried photos of them in his wallet. How can he betray Auntie Jane like that? And how can she? Vicki deals with his wife all the time, making travel plans, dinner reservations . . . How can she look Auntie Jane in the face, knowing . . . ?"

Mick snagged her hand in his. "For what it's worth, I wouldn't."

Sarah exhaled. Curled her fingers around his. "Me either." They sat for a moment, hand in hand in quiet comfort. "Do you think he was telling the truth? He is getting old. Maybe he's confused—"

"If I were a betting man, I'd say the odds are they were involved. There were too many concrete details, no hesitation. Although, he could be an incredibly skillful con man."

"Yeah. I'm clutching at straws. Looking back, it seems so clear. Of course they were having an affair. You want to know what's grossing me out. He's old enough to be Vicki's father. And . . ." She attempted to suppress a shudder. "Now I've got this image of them"—she wafted her free hand in the air with a grimace—"getting it on. The more I try not to think about it, the deeper it gets embedded in my brain. And then there's . . ." Her voice trailed off.

"What Clarke inferred about your ex and Vicki?"

She nodded, subdued.

"Do you think it's a possibility?"

"I don't know. If you'd asked me yesterday, I would have said the idea of Vicki and Uncle Phillip was far-fetched." She worried her lower lip between her teeth. "Vicki's *really* not Kevin's type . . ."

"But if he wanted something from her?"

"If he wanted something from her, then all bets are off."

"From what you've told me, it sounded like Kevin was obsessed with having the ability to dominate and control you. What if this is a trap? What if Clarke and Kevin are working together, and this whole 'talk to Vicki' thing is a setup?"

"You spoke to Kevin yesterday." Sarah was gazing out the side window in a seemingly nonchalant manner, but her eyes narrowed slightly and her lips had compressed together. "He's in LA."

"As were we. And now we are in a cab on our way to Brooklyn." He lifted their entwined hands and turned hers over, his thumb gently grazing the delicate skin of her inner wrist. Then he replaced his thumb with his lips, imprinting the sweetness, the taste of her soft skin in his memory bank. He had her attention now. "Let me drop you off at a coffee shop." His voice was husky with longing and need. Her close proximity overwhelmed his senses, and the merest of tastes made him ravenous for more. He turned his head, laying his cheek against her soft skin, then exhaled slowly and lowered her hand. "Seriously, Sarah. I think it would be safer that way. You can write down what you want me to say to Vicki, the questions you have. I will get the information for you and return, pronto."

A tender smile gently curved her lips, her eyes soft. "I can't do that," she said. "Thank you for the offer though."

"Why?"

"Because if you—a total stranger—show up on her doorstep demanding she turn over my documents, she'll kick you to the curb. More to the point, she would be correct to do so. She'd have no way of knowing you were connected to me. Not only that, as far as she is concerned, I am missing, and possibly dead. No, the only way we have a shot at retrieving them is if I go. More telling than the words that will come out of her mouth is the smaller details, the emotional and physical clues. That is where the truth resides. I need to be in the room."

Sarah was right, of course, but it didn't make it any easier to swallow. She faced forward again. There was something about the sight of her profile against the glistening white, blue, and gold tiles whizzing past, so determined and strong in the face of such adversity, that moved him on a profound, fundamental level. *But is that who she really is?* the cynic in him whispered. *Or are you falling into that old childhood trap of idealizing and whitewashing because you'd rather live in a fantasy world than face the hard truths?* He released her hand, rubbed his face, trying to exorcise the unwanted thoughts. It didn't work. "Sarah?"

"Mm . . . ?"

"Can I ask you a question?"

"Sure." She turned to face him. "What's on your mind?"

"You've mentioned your baby a couple of times." He hated himself for the flash of sorrow he saw in her eyes, but he needed to know to put the demons to rest.

"Ah . . ." Her voice came out as softly as a leaf falling to the ground. She nodded. "Sorry. I kind of left you hanging, didn't I?" Her gaze dropped to her hands lying empty in her lap. Sarah exhaled as if steadying herself. "She didn't make it. Was stillborn. I was out cold when she was born. I didn't get a chance to hold her little lifeless body, to tell her I loved her. I would have liked to have been able to do that, but when I finally gained consciousness, she was already gone."

He felt like such a dickhead for bringing it up. "I'm sorry."

She reached over and patted his hand. "It's okay. The passing of time helps soften the jagged edges."

"Still." Mick turned his hand over so they were hand-clasped again.

Sarah managed a smile, a slight shadow of sorrow lingering in her eyes. She exhaled again and then turned to look out of her window, so he turned to look out of his window as well, both of them lost in their thoughts as the tunnel walls whizzed past. There was a hint of sadness, but mostly it was a sense of tranquility, a feeling of trust, friendship, and something more, that filled the silence that surrounded them.

In the distance, a small circle of daylight was approaching faster and faster, growing in size until finally their taxi shot out of the tunnel, leaving them squinting in the bright sunlight.

Mick's cell phone started buzzing. He glanced at the screen. "Peterson. Again. The man is like a dog with a bone."

"You better answer it. Otherwise he'll just keep on calling," Sarah said, still gazing out the window.

Mick sighed, swiped to answer. "What's going on?"

"What's going on?" Peterson was definitely freaking out. His voice was an octave higher than normal. "I'll tell you what the fuck is going on. Harmony's dead."

"Wait." Mick's lungs suddenly felt like they were embedded in ice, and his brain seemed to be having difficulty processing. "Back up. It sounded like you said Harmony's—"

"*Dead.* That's right, *d-e-a-d.* What are you, fucking deaf? Why didn't you pick up your goddamned phone? We've got a movie opening in eight days, and nobody's in the office! Lois is in the hospital, Harmony's dead, you're out of town, and I'm having to spend my fucking morning at your house dealing with the cops."

"My house?"

"Yeah, they are swarming all over the place. Harmony drowned in your pool. This is not going to look good in the press, dude. Naked secretary found facedown in your pool. You better really be in New York and have a fucking good alibi . . . Oh shit! I don't have a fucking alibi! I spent the night alone, with my dick in hand, watching reruns of *Be-fucking-witched.* Oh Jesus. I'm screwed." Peterson let out a low moan.

"Paul, I don't understand. What the hell were you doing at my house in the first place?"

"Harmony didn't show up at work this morning. Thought nothing of it. Figured she'd been waylaid, had the flu, some such shit. Called her phone. Got diverted to voicemail. I'm in my office, trying to work, but your damned phone kept ringing. Somebody's calling. Hanging up. Calling. Hanging up. Can't take it. Answered the damn thing. It's your gardener babbling at me. Can't understand half of what he's saying. Called Bob the intern in to translate. The gardener and his crew arrived to discover a dead woman floating facedown in the pool. I told him not to touch anything, called the cops, and met them at the property. I'm being a good guy, you see? I'm helping my friend who is out of town. You can imagine my shock when the cops flipped her over and I saw Harmony's face. Shit." Peterson's voice broke. "And you know the worst part of this whole clusterfuck? When I hired her . . . I'd had hopes of someday seeing her naked . . ." He was sobbing now. "But not like this. Didn't want to see her naked like this . . . Can't dislodge the image from my brain . . ."

"Too bad she's dead, denying you a chance to berate her for destroying your deviant fantasy life. Seriously, dude?"

"It's easy for you to take the moral high ground." Peterson swung from sorrow to rage, for which Mick was grateful. Anger was easier to deal with. "Women are always throwing themselves at you like handfuls of confetti. Me? I gotta work for every lay I get. And now you win again. Some chick dies in your pool, and who is here, cleaning up the mess? Me, that's who! You're off in New York, free and clear, bonking out the brains of your new assistant."

"I'm not bonking her—"

"And what do I get?" Peterson's voice was getting shrill. "My sexy assistant is dead. And they'll probably try to pin the damned thing on me!"

"You need to calm down, Paul. Seriously. There is no reason they would make such an erroneous leap."

"No, you dipshit! You don't understand. What they are *going* to do is *comb* through her damned phone and make a big deal out of a few drunken emails or texts I might have sent her in the wee hours of the morn."

"Hold on. You did what?"

"I get lonely, for Chrissake! What do you want from me? Can't blame a guy for trying." Then Mick heard the sound of someone speaking in the background. "Uh-huh." Peterson's voice was muffled, as if he'd lowered the phone.

"Okay. All right." Then Peterson's voice returned to full volume. "Look, Mick, I gotta go. They have a few more 'questions' they wanna run by me. I'm well and truly screwed. Why'd you have to ask Harmony to take care of that damned cat?" And then the phone went dead.

MICK'S FINGERS WERE STILL GRIPPING THE CELL PHONE that had fallen away from his ear as if it were suddenly filled with wet sand. It lay facedown on his thigh. His face was void of expression. His body was still, too still. Something wasn't right. "What did he want?" Sarah asked. He turned his head in her direction, an inch or two, max. His gaze was unfocused.

"Harmony's dead." His voice was flat, almost monotone.

"The Harmony who is taking care of Charlie?"

"Crap," he cursed softly. Jabbed at his phone screen, then held it to his ear and listened. "Damn. Not picking up. I'll text Peterson, tell him to grab the cat before he leaves."

"Don't worry about it. I'm sure he has a lot on his plate right now. Charlie will be fine." From what little she knew, Paul Peterson was one of the last people she'd trust with her cat. "I'm flying back tomorrow, and the food and water I left would last him a couple of weeks."

Mick nodded curtly. "Fine." He shoved his phone in his pocket. Exhaled.

"Was she sick?"

"No."

"What happened?"

"Drowned."

The taxi was silent. Just the tinny sound of the radio, music being sung in an unfamiliar language, the plucking of stringed instruments in high-pitched tones, accompanied by lots of complicated percussion. The hum and bustle of the city streets beyond the confines of their taxi created a constant background pulse.

"I'm sorry," Sarah said.

"We weren't close. It's a shock is all. She was a couple

of years younger than me, with her whole life before her." He turned toward her, his face bleak. "I know it's not my fault, but the fact that she died in my pool. She must have decided to take a dip, slipped, and banged her head. If I hadn't asked her to go there—"

"No. I'm not letting you put the burden of that woman's death on your conscience. She chose to swim in your pool. If you want to blame somebody, blame me. I'm the one whose cat needed looking after."

"Don't be ridiculous."

"I rest my case." She slipped her hand into his. Sarah could see the cabbie's curious gaze watching them in the rearview mirror. "I'm sorry though. That her life was cut short—" Sarah broke off, sudden nausea rising in her throat. There was something about the removed observational quality of the cabby's gaze that triggered a cellular memory. "Kevin," she whispered, staring at Mick with dawning horror. "It might have been him."

"You've lost me. What does Kevin have to do with—"

"He had a thing about water. Would hold me under. Remember, the woman from the Windham Employment Agency? Ellen Davis. She said she'd given him your address. He must have gone to your house. Been waiting for me, and Harmony accidentally stumbled into his web." Images, memories flashing before her, sunlight sparkles on the water, Kevin's face blurry through the ripples, enjoying her fear as she struggled against his grip for life, for breath. She'd come to, face-up on the lawn. Kevin was straddling her hips and doing chest compressions. Coughing, choking as water spewed out of her mouth and nose. The nausea worsened when she became aware of his erection. "I should have known he would go there." Suddenly, Mick's arms were around her, tugging her close. Holding her tight, a ballast in the storm.

"Not your fault," Mick said over and over. "This is not your fault."

41

"SARAH AND MICK EXITED THE TAXI. "IT'S NOT TOO late to switch plans," she heard Mick say. "Grab a coffee and a slice of pie."

She looked over at his wolfish face with his lean, carved cheekbones, the dark stubble that she longed to run her fingertips over. His expression was so serious, Sarah had to suppress the impulse to ruffle his hair. "I'm okay," she replied. "I'm ready to do this." She felt revved up, a boxer preparing to step into the ring.

It was a lovely residential block with lots of trees. In a few more weeks, the tight buds on the barren branches would unfurl new greenery to herald the arrival of spring. Charming historic houses lined the street in one of the more expensive parts of Brooklyn. Sarah could see a sprawling old graveyard down the road. She glanced at her phone, double-checked the address. "It's this one." She gestured to the gracious town house that was painted a pale gray with white trim except for the front door, which was a bold, fire-engine red.

"It would be difficult to afford this neighborhood on a secretary's salary," Mick murmured. They climbed the porch stairs, past a trio of flowerpots, where a cluster of tall daffodil stalks and what looked like crocuses were threatening to bloom.

"Maybe she rents, or has roommates." *Or maybe Uncle Phillip was telling the truth when he'd said he'd set her up in a little love nest.* Sarah pushed the thought aside. It was vital she keep an open mind, not jump to conclusions. Perhaps Vicki had been involved with Phillip, but age might have muddled his mind. It was possible the "affair" with Vicki was fantasy rather than fact, especially given the rather far-fetched Kevin twist.

There wasn't a doorbell, so she rapped on the wooden portion of the red door. Sunshine spilled through the rectangular glass pane on the top half of the door onto the old oak floors. Sarah couldn't see anyone, but she could hear the sound of someone clanking pots or pans around in the kitchen. She knocked a little louder.

"Hold on," a woman's voice called. A few seconds later Vicki appeared through the arched doorway of the kitchen, a cigarette perched between her lips as she squinted out of the doorway through a cloud of smoke. Vicki took a couple of unsteady steps in the direction of the front door, then peered at them again, one hand rising to rest against the wall for balance. She was wearing a worn flannel nightgown and a coral fleece robe. She didn't look like a woman bent on seduction, juggling two lovers. "Go away." She took the cigarette out of her mouth and waved it at them wearily. "I'm not interested."

"If we could just have one second of your time?"

"Look, lady, no disrespect, but I don't open the door to anyone I don't know." Vicki turned away.

"Wait. Vicki, it's me, Sarah Rainsford."

Vicki paused, her back still to them, then slowly pivoted and approached the door. "You look different," she said, eyeing Sarah through the glass.

Sarah's hand rose self-consciously to her head. "I cut my hair. Dyed it."

"You made a hash of it."

"I know," Sarah replied, running her fingers through it. "It's a hot mess."

The corner of Vicki's mouth quirked up. She took another drag of her cigarette, watching Sarah through half-closed eyes. "I'm glad to see you are alive and well. By the way, I don't work for Mr. Clarke anymore."

Sarah nodded. "He told me. We came from his office. Can we come in for a minute?"

"Nope."

"Mick can stay outside."

"Like hell I will," Mick murmured. Sarah gave him a discreet kick in the shins.

"It's imperative I speak with you."

"Not interested." Vicki crossed her arms. "Whatever you have to say can be said on the other side of that door."

"It's personal."

"Well, la-di-da. Spit it out, girl. I'm losing patience."

Sarah shrugged. "Okay. If that's the way you want to do it. Phillip asked me to tell you that he misses you. That he made a mistake. That whatever you want, he will do. He said he'd made promises. He didn't tell me what they were, but he wanted me to tell you that he will keep them." Vicki's face was like an impenetrable fortress, but the sadness in her eyes gave her away.

"But that's not all, is it?"

"No. I had gone to his office to collect the copies of my identification papers, passport, et cetera. His new secretary was unable to find my ID or any of my financial papers—"

Vicki held up a hand, a slight sneer on her face. "Oh, wait. Let me guess. He told you I stole them?"

"He mentioned it was a possibility. That you had been upset when he fired you."

"Oh. So now he fired me?"

"Look. I don't want to get in the middle of whatever is going on between the two of you—"

"And yet here you are." A mottled flush of emotion was rising in Vicki's cheeks. "I *worked* my *ass* off for that man, looking out for *your* family interests. Twenty-eight years, and this is my thanks? You come down here, accuse me of stealing your precious papers, act as a go-between for a two-faced lying bastard who you shouldn't trust any farther than you can throw. And you expect me to open my home to you? What else did he say?"

"He said . . ." Sarah's mouth tasted as if she'd downed a lukewarm glass of rancid milk. "That you are having an affair with Kevin, my ex."

And just like that, the last traces of lingering sadness in Vicki's eyes were replaced with white-hot anger. "*Really!* How fascinating. And you believed him?"

"I don't know. For your sake, I hope not. Kevin is a psychopath. He can charm the birds out of the trees, but once he has them in his hand, he will snap their necks and laugh about it. Please do not trust him. Your life and safety depend upon it."

Vicki shook her head, bitterness drawing deep grooves on her face. "You are something else. How dare you come to my home to spew the poison that son of a bitch whispered in your ear," she spit out. "We are done here." She turned angrily, took a few steps down the hall, then returned to the door. "You would think, after all I'd been through with that man, he would know me better than that. You tell that putz he doesn't know dick about love." She was furious, but Sarah could see tears lurking behind the rage. "Wait. Better yet, tell him you found me bent over the kitchen table and getting fucked from behind. Yeah. Tell him *that*." Vicki pivoted and stormed away from the entryway door.

A breeze kicked up and caused a shiver of goose bumps to ripple down Sarah's neck and spine. "Vicki," Sarah called. "I'm sorry I upset you. That wasn't my intent. However, I really, *really* need access to my files! I am willing to pay, and pay well, for my ID papers back. No questions asked. I'll leave my contact information in your mailbox. *Please.* Call me tonight. I fly out tomorrow morning—"

Vicki hoisted her middle finger high in the air over her shoulder. "Go to hell," she yelled, then disappeared around the corner into the kitchen. A second later loud music was switched on. They could hear Vicki singing along to Toni Braxton's "Un-break My Heart," accompanied by the energetic banging of pots and pans.

"Damn." Sarah shoved her hand into her gray purse and rummaged around for something to write on. Her fingers closed around the pen and a small pad of notepaper from the hotel's bedside table. She circled the hotel's address and phone number at the bottom and scribbled down her name, Mick's name, and their room numbers.

"Do you think that's wise? What if she's working with your ex?"

"Kevin's in LA. If she calls him now, he'll still have to book a flight, drive to the airport, add an additional two hours for security, and a five-and-a-half-hour flight. It will take him at least another hour to get into Manhattan. If she doesn't call me tonight, we can change hotels tomorrow morning. Make a deal with the front desk to forward messages to us."

"Sarah—"

She placed her hand on his arm. "Mick," she said softly. "I'm tired of running. I need my ID. If she has my documents and records, I need to give her every possibility to do the right thing." Sarah turned and quickly slipped the note through the metal mail slot in the door.

Damn. Mick stared at the slot through which the note had disappeared. His gaze dropped to the base of the door. There was a rubber weather guard at the bottom. No possibility of slipping something under the door to retrieve it. "How about we give talking to her another go? We could walk around the side of the building to the back. Bet there's a kitchen door."

"No. She needs space." Sarah turned and headed down the porch stairs. "Hopefully, tonight, once she calms down and thinks it over, we'll get a call from her."

"And if her sense of morality doesn't kick in," Mick said dryly, "maybe practicality will. She's unemployed, so your promise of financial compensation might soften her stance."

Sarah smiled at him. "Of course. That's why I offered. I'm a firm believer in covering all bases."

42

"THE FOUR SEASONS ON FIFTY-SEVENTH BETWEEN Madison and Park," Sarah told the cabbie through the scratched-up plastic partition. Mick slid in beside her, shut the door of the rattletrap vehicle, and had a momentary longing for the comforts of his Porsche.

"You got it," the cabbie said, slamming on the gas as if he were auditioning for the Indy 500. *Great.* Mick reached for the safety belt. It was sticky with God knows what. He made an executive decision to make use of the handlebar above the door.

Sarah strapped in, then turned and fixed those brilliant blue eyes on his. "So, what are your thoughts?"

"It was a fascinating peek into someone's life, an interesting character study, lots of complexities. Wish I had it on tape. Could use it to inspire my actors to dig a little deeper, not go for the obvious."

"You think she was acting?"

"If she was, she's damned good."

"In here"—she placed her hand over her gut—"I am certain Vicki was involved with Uncle—" Sarah broke off, exasperated. "I don't know what to call him anymore. For the last four years, I've forced myself to think of him as 'Mr. Clarke' or 'Phillip,' but now . . ." She scrubbed her hands over her face as if it would help clear her thinking. She looked troubled. "He was truly shocked when I accused him of selling me out to Kevin."

"When you think of him, what name pops to the forefront?"

"I don't know. When he collapsed, 'Uncle Phillip' came out, but that feels weird. Our relationship is in this limbo. I feel so uncomfortable about the whole cheating on Auntie Jane." She shook her head. "Whatever," she said. "It's not important."

"I do agree with you. Vicki was involved with your old lawyer. No question. There was too much anger and passion there."

"And hurt," Sarah said. "Like a deep sort of wounding had shaken her to the core. I've never seen her so undone. She's always been super pulled together."

"She seemed a little slurry, like she might have been drinking."

"I think she's self-medicating to tamp down the pain. What about when I mentioned Kevin?"

"What did you think?" Mick asked, watching her closely.

Sarah nodded. "She knows him." There was no hesitation in her response. "I could feel it. Could see it in her eyes. She knows Kevin, but I'm not sure if she knows him in a biblical sense." She caught her lip between her teeth, her head tipped to the side, a slight frown furrowing her brow.

The sight of her lush lower lip caught between her teeth. The primness of her saying "biblical sense" instead of "fucking" or "screwing" or a million other coarse words had his cock rock hard. Making it a struggle to focus on other matters. "Do you think she's the one who gave your information to Kevin?" He managed to keep his voice and expression neutral.

"Maybe. But then why did she say she was glad to see me alive and well?"

"That response could have been triggered by guilt."

"I suppose." Sarah glanced out the side window, exhaled. "Do you think she has my files?"

"I don't know."

"I just . . . I *want* my damned ID." Sarah's frustration was evident in her voice. "Once I have it, I'll have access to my funds and won't be beholden to anyone ever again." Mick hadn't thought past keeping her safe and helping sort things out. Hadn't thought much about the fact that she had a life she was going to return to that didn't include him. "I should have asked Phillip what happened to my parents' homes. I hope he didn't sell them." Her hand alighted on his knee. "They have a wonderful apartment in the Hampshire House on Fifty-Seventh with an expansive view overlooking Central Park. And the house in the Hamptons—I have so many memories tied up in those places."

"I'm sure they are very beautiful." His voice sounded stiff.

She tipped her head at him like a curious chickadee, her sky-blue eyes shining bright. "You okay?"

"Of course."

She studied his face, the joy in her eyes dimming. "I'm being insensitive. A member of your team passed away unexpectedly. I imagine it's a shock."

"Any life lost is one too many. However, I'd be remiss if I led you to believe I'm reeling in grief. I should feel something, but I don't. Numb really. Maybe it hasn't set in? Or maybe I'm just an insensitive brute, incapable of the higher feelings that other people have?"

"Bullshit."

"I beg to differ. Yes, Harmony was a relatively new addition. I didn't know her well, but shouldn't the news of her death have me reeling?" He shook his head. "Nope. There was a jolt of shock when Peterson told me, a dropping in my stomach, a sense of disbelief. But grief? You want to know the truth? I wasn't thinking about her just now. I had *forgotten* that she was dead." He saw Sarah blink. "Yep. That's the man you are sitting next to, painting him with noble colors that he doesn't deserve." She opened her mouth to say something, but he beat her to it. "You want to know what I was thinking? I was thinking about you. About how stupid I was not to have leaped into your bed when I had the chance. How's that for an enlightened male? Harmony's dead, and I'm obsessing about what an ass I was holding off making a move on you."

"You know, I've been curious about that. Why didn't you?"

"You'd been through a tough time, and I knew you were vulnerable. You'd mentioned your ex was abusive. You needed help. I could do that, for which you were grateful. I didn't want to take advantage."

"Take advantage?" She arched an eyebrow. "I offered."

"I know," he growled. "That's where the 'ass' part comes in. I was operating under some antiquated cockamamie belief that it would have been wrong, unfair to lure you into my bed when I held all the power."

"Aw . . ." The noise she made sounded sympathetic, but he could see amusement dancing in her eyes. "Hate to break it to you, Mick," she practically purred. "But you never held all the power."

"Whatever. We're arguing about semantics. What matters is that you are free now. Soon you'll have access to your funds and properties. Your petition for divorce has been filed. You hold the world in your hands." *And I have nothing left in my arsenal to tempt you with.* He managed a smile. "And for the record, I *am* happy for you. Truly, I am."

43

MICK SWIPED AT THE FOGGED-UP BATHROOM MIR-
ror with a thick hand towel. It didn't do much good, but at
least he could see a blurry version of himself and should be
able to manage a shave without slitting his throat. His mind
was still mulling over the long conversation he'd had with
Peterson. The man was shaken, balling his eyes out. Mick
had never heard him so undone. After he'd hung up, there
was the call to the police department. A promise had been
extracted. Mick would drop by the station when he returned
to Los Angeles. A hot shower was no longer a luxury but a
necessity. He needed the ritual of washing off the weight of
the day. The thought of Harmony with all her hopes and
dreams extinguished. Why had death chosen her? Didn't
seem fair.

Generally, Mick kept his showers short, doing his bit for
the environment, but this night a long shower was needed.
Steaming hot, with lots of soap. And in the shower, perhaps
there was a component of salt intermingled with the water
beating down, but if there was, it was nobody's business.

Mick had removed his travel-sized shaving cream from his toiletry bag and began lathering his face when he heard a knock on his room door. "No thanks," he called, figuring it was hotel housekeeping or minibar service.

"Hey, now," he heard Sarah retort from out in the hallway. There was a trace of laughter in her voice. "You haven't heard yet, sir, what's on offer." Her husky, honey-drenched tone wreaked havoc on his body. Mick adjusted himself so he wasn't tenting the towel slung around his hips and walked to the door, blood pulsing through his veins like a drumbeat.

He braced himself, then opened the door. "Yeah," he said with a nonchalance he didn't feel, because being in her presence snatched the breath from his lungs

She looked at him, her eyes narrowing. "Have you been crying?"

"Hell no. Got soap in my eyes. What's it to you?"

"Ah," she said softly. She glanced over his shoulder to the living room beyond. "I called the switchboard and had them forward any phone calls to your room. Thought we'd have dinner together. You good with that?"

The tightness eased in his chest. Grateful he wasn't going to face the evening alone. He leaned against the doorframe and drank in the sight of her, barefoot, scrubbed face, wet hair, wrapped in one of the hotel's thick white robes. Clean. Fresh. Like a new beginning. *Jesus, you're a goner, Talford.* He was glad he had something sturdy to prop him up until his knees lost their sudden gelatinous quality. "So, this offer you mentioned," he drawled. "Were you talking about dinner? Or . . . something else?"

She took a long, lazy perusal past his partially lathered face, to his throat, down his body, her gaze lingering as she took in the broad expanse of his bare chest, still damp from the shower. "Mm . . ." The pink tip of her tongue peeked out briefly, moistening her lips as if the sight of his partially naked body had made her mouth dry. A rosy flush stained high on her cheeks, but she didn't stop her downward trajectory. Her gaze paused at the front of his towel, and her eyes widened. "I remembered thinking you were big that first time I met you, but you're larger now."

"WOMAN." MICK'S EYES HAD DARKENED EVEN FURther, his voice a low growl. "You are playing with fire."

"Good." Sarah arched her back slightly, enjoying the knowledge that she was naked beneath her robe. She could see the exact moment he broke. Was unable to contain her satisfied smirk when he grabbed her hand, yanked her into his room. Gone was the restraint and cautious fragile care with which he had treated her, as if she were made from spun glass. He kicked the door shut and in two seconds flat had her against the wall, her face cradled in his hands as he lowered his head and took possession of her mouth. There was something so heady, so thrilling—as if she were dancing barefoot on the edge of a cliff in a rainstorm—about the way she had snapped his self-control, because she knew on the deepest, most fundamental level that in this man's hands she was absolutely safe. What a sense of freedom that knowledge created, after years of tiptoeing cautiously through life, to run full tilt into the waves, arms outstretched. She reveled in the animalistic hunger and urgency she had incited in him, her body writhing against his, needing to get closer. She fisted her hands in his hair, which was wet from his shower, pressing him closer still. Wanting everything he had to give and more. A groan erupted from deep in his chest as he captured her lower lip, dragged his teeth over her bruised flesh, then soothed the throbbing ache with his tongue. The slick slide and taste of him against her lips, dancing with her tongue was intoxicating. A revelation. When he pulled back, his breath was ragged and the wanting in his eyes caused her body to heat even more. His pupils dilated with passion, leaving only a narrow circlet of his amber irises visible. She reached up and, using the blade of her hand, tenderly removed the lather from his jawline. The contrast of textures, the thick silky lather against the rough scrape of whiskers was such a turn-on, she had to press her thighs together tight to try to ease the throbbing.

"I forgot that was on my face." A slight laugh in his husky voice, his eyes sleepy with lust. "You can wipe it on my towel." His hand guided hers down, down to the towel wrapped around his waist, to press against the straining hard length of him. She curled her hand around him, could feel the pulsing heat through the thick fabric.

Need, longing, and unspoken words built a logjam in her throat. "You're so damned beautiful," she murmured, when what she really wanted to say was *I think I love you* . . . And that realization caused her eyes to flutter shut and her head to fall backward to rest against the cool wall. *I love him. Oh God. I am in love for the first time in my life.* And the enormity of the revelation caused her eyes to fill with the beauty of it. Fear was there, as well, of the vulnerability and the possibility of being broken in two.

He left her hand wrapped around his cock and returned to his exploration of her face. "You slay me." His voice was a soft rumble as he brushed a gentle kiss on her closed eyelids, which made her knees weaken. She could feel him trace her eyebrows with his thumbs. His warm, sweet breath caressed her face, a hint of mint. He must have brushed his teeth. She still couldn't open her eyes. It would be too much, too overwhelming. He would see the truth in her eyes. The shaving cream was gone from his jawline, but she could still smell the scent of it on his face, could feel the creamy thickness of it on her hand, between her fingers. Bergamot and something else, apple, perhaps, mingled with his freshly showered skin. His callused fingertips continued their exploration of her face, down her cheeks and throat, causing tingling trails in their wake, as she memorized the shape and feel and heft of him through the towel. He returned to her mouth so his lips could caress hers, back and forth, as if by the lightest of touches he was better able to imprint the taste and texture of her on his lips. Back and forth, softly, sweetly, like a whispered prayer.

Her other hand released its grip on his hair and traveled the breadth of his shoulder, gathering intimate knowledge of his hard muscles and hot skin through the pads of her fingertips. Greedy for more as restless heat rampaged through her body and pooled low in her abdomen and lower still, thrumming with need and want. A soft moan escaped her lips. She slipped her hand beneath the flap of the towel and wrapped her fingers around his hot cock, so hard and yet the skin so very soft, silky-smooth. She slid her hand up the thick length of it. Her thumb explored the swollen head, the ridge, glided through the droplet of moisture at the tip, ripping a husky groan from his throat. Sarah felt a tremor run through him, which caused an answering ripple of need in her own body. His hands traveled downward and nudged the robe from her shoulders, his mouth tasting the sweetness of her skin, the shape of her collarbone, a lick and then a kiss in the hollow at the base of her throat. His mouth traversed outward, upward to the muscle leading from Sarah's neck to her shoulder, lightly, ever so lightly. A slight growl as his teeth bit softly down.

A cry flew from her lips as heat surged through her. Her hand tightened around his hot cock, which was getting slick from his juices.

"Too rough?" he murmured.

"No," she gasped. "No. I liked it."

"Good." Mick soothed the bite with a lick, a kiss. His hand slid underneath her robe to palm her aching breast, fondle her nipple. She felt his teeth biting down again, toying with her, his teeth scraping, then releasing. Another soothing lap of his tongue, and then his mouth latched on, sucking hard on her tender skin, marking her, branding her his, causing shivers to ripple through her. All the while his nimble fingers wreaked havoc on her, such knowledge in the way he caressed her body, taking her higher and higher. He pulled back and looked at where he'd been sucking. "Mine," he said, tracing the mark lightly with his fingertip. The primitive male satisfaction in his voice pumped through her like a shot of hot whiskey. "When you leave this room, everyone will know what we've been doing." With his other hand, he gently rolled her taut nipple between his forefinger and his thumb. "They are going to see that mark, look into those innocent baby-blue eyes of yours, and know that I have carnal knowledge of you. They will know that you had my thick, hard cock buried deep inside you." His dark gaze fixed on hers as the pressure on her nipple tightened and tightened, pleasure and pain intermingled. "And that you liked it." He released her nipple, and she found herself arching toward him as his thumb made a slow, soothing circle.

His other hand on the move now, traveling down, down, to caress the slick, wet folds between her legs. *Oh God . . . Oh God . . .* He dipped a finger inside her. More. She wanted more. Everything tightened around her. A moan escaped from between her lips. His face was taut with need, with longing. Sarah was unable to look away, drowning in his eyes, panting slightly, but it was impossible to contain the unfamiliar sensations that were roaring through her. Trembling, she was trembling as he caressed her most intimate parts with his knowledgeable fingers, which seemed to know just exactly where to touch.

"Mick," she moaned. "Please . . ." He caught her other nipple between his finger and thumb, giving it a soft caress. He slid another long finger inside, stretching her further, to join the steady pulsing in and out, slick with her juices. His thumb gently circling over the swollen quivering nub, pressing down occasionally, then circling again, as his fingers inside her mirrored what his cock would soon do. Higher and higher she traversed, past the moon and the stars. "Mick . . . I'm . . . I'm . . . going to . . ." Mick curved his fingers inside her and began stroking some kind of magical spot she didn't know was there, his other hand at her breast, ruthless now, his finger and thumb clamping down hard on her nipple. The sudden sharp sensation sent Sarah flying over the edge. Wave upon wave of pleasure crashed over her, and a startled cry ripped from her throat as her convulsing body shattered into a million pieces. A million pieces flying outward all in the safety of his arms. "Sarah. Oh, baby," Mick murmured. "You humble me." He swept her still-shivering body into his arms and strode through the living room to the bedroom beyond.

44

SOMEWHERE ALONG THE JOURNEY FROM THE LIVing room to the bedroom, Sarah had managed to loosen his towel. It dropped to the floor. Mick shoved it out of the way with his foot as she nuzzled her face into his neck. "Before we go any further, we need to have the talk." Her voice was low and throaty, the sound of pure sin, making coherent thoughts difficult.

"The talk . . . ?" *What was that? Some kind of womanspeak clearly, but for what?* And then an image dropped into his sex-muddled brain. Sarah in a wedding dress smiling at him as she walked down the aisle. *Oh . . . The Talk.* Once he had the thought, it made perfect sense. Mick had known from the moment he met her that she was not a oneand-done kind of woman. She was permanence and forever and a warm, welcoming home. Mick was used to making snap decisions based on his gut. His work required it. "Right. The talk. Consider yourself engaged. We'll go out tomorrow morning and shop for a ring."

She's laughing. Why is she laughing? Her arms wrapped around his neck, and she was dropping little kisses amid her laughter, on his shoulders, his neck, his cheeks, his forehead, his ears.

"You are"—*kiss*—"so damned adorable . . ." *Kiss.* "It kills me." *Kiss.* She was still laughing. "Oh God . . ." *Kiss.* "I love you so much . . ." *Kiss . . . kiss . . . kiss.*

Mick froze midstep. *She just said she loves me. But wait. She said, "Oh God, I love you so much." Was she talking about God? To God? Must be.* Love and Mick Talford was a contradiction in terms. There was the Hollywood "love you, baby," which meant jack dick, but *love*-love. Nah. Mick was an unlovable bastard, and he knew it. Never had it in his life and probably never would. *Whatever. Doesn't matter. What matters is now, and I am going to make love to this woman if it's the last thing I do. She didn't say no. And she's kissing me, so I'm going to take that as a hard yes on the engagement thing.* "So, we're all squared up? Good to go." She was still laughing, wiping moisture from the corner of her eyes, which had gone all soft and doe-like.

"Oh, Mick . . ." She took his face in her hands and kissed him long and deep. Pulled back and looked at him with this indescribable expression on her face that made him feel comfy and warm inside. "You." He waited for more words, but they didn't come. She just traced his lower lip with her thumb. He started moving again, toward the bedroom. "What I meant was," she said, still dropping tender little kisses on him, "the I-have-a-clean-bill-of-health-and-no-sexually-transmitted-diseases talk."

"Oh." *Of course. That talk. What a ding-a-ling.* Mick felt his face flush, as well as the tips of his ears and the back of his neck. But along with the embarrassment was another emotion he didn't want to look at too closely. A feeling akin to waking up and discovering his Christmas stocking was just the way he'd left it the night before, hanging loose and empty on its thumbtack. *Expectations. Frikkin' fairy tales bite you in the butt every time.* "Ah," he said. "Right." Mick shoved aside the childhood memory. *That has no bearing on this. You have a wonderful, warm, sexy woman in your arms. Stop looking up the ass of things. Speaking of asses* . . . Sarah's terry-cloth-clad bottom was brushing against the bobbing tip of his rock-hard erection with every step, a glorious torture. He cleared his throat, trying to sound like a normal person instead of a man crazed with lust. "I had a full physical at the beginning of September. Had a clean bill of health. I've never injected. Haven't had a sexual encounter for"—he paused; even counting backward was an effort, given all the blood from his brain had taken up residence in his nether regions—"in a little over a year." *A little over? Ha. Eighteen months to be exact. It was mind-boggling really.* He hadn't made a conscious decision to abstain. It had just happened. "So, health-wise, all clear on this front." All this "health" talk had done nothing to tamp down his erection. The memory of Sarah's sweet cries, how she'd shattered in his arms, had left him teetering on the razor's edge of sanity. Every molecule in his body, every nerve ending was demanding succor.

"I'm not a drug user either, and in the abstinence department?" Sarah's expression was wry as he set her down on his bed. "I've got you beat." A shadow flickered across her face, so quick he almost missed it, and then it was gone. "While I was in the hospital, I had the doctor run the works on me. Got the results in the evening, and the next morning I hit the road. Kevin and I hadn't been intimate in the seven months prior. Once we discovered I was pregnant, he'd lost all interest, and since he's the only man I've ever slept with . . ."

The need to possess, to be buried deep inside her was more than a hunger now. It was rapidly becoming more vital than the inhalation of his next breath. "You'll be sleeping with me."

"Haven't slept yet." A teasing smile played on her lips.

"Oh, we will." His voice summoned up from the very core of him and carried the weight of a vow. Her eyes darkened, her lips parted, as if an inhalation was caught between them, like a wish, while she waited for what came next.

He untied the sash of her thick terry-cloth robe and re-

moved it from her glorious body. He felt thick-fingered at
the sight of the creamy perfection of her skin. He couldn't
stop his hands from shaking. "You're so beautiful," he murmured. No lie. The unobstructed vision of her breasts had
caused his breath to catch in his throat. Her nipples were
ruched into little tight buds of pale peach. The color similar
to the delicate flush of a Bonica rose. The innocent, almost
virginal color created an erotic contrast to the sensual, satiated knowledge in her eyes and the slightly swollen pout of
her lower lip.

Sarah wrapped her hands around his engorged cock,
stroked up, one hand doing a swiveling rotation over the top
of the head, and eradicated any possibility for conscious
thought. Down her hands swooped, the finger and thumb of
one hand circling the base. "A cock ring," she murmured,
tightening around him, her thick lashes fanning against her
cheek. "To keep you from coming too fast." Her other hand
reached farther and cupped his contracted scrotum and
tugged gently.

"Oh God . . . Oh God . . . Oh God . . ." he moaned.

Her lashes lifted lazily, a sultry smile curving her lips.
"And with regards to a condom . . ." She leaned forward,
the tip of her tongue playing over the spot where her thumb
and finger met.

"A condom. Right. I picked some up," he croaked. "In
the bedside table." She had loosened her grip slightly to
slide her tongue through the gap. Flames of pleasure rushing upward, ready to blow, but at the last second her grip
tightened and pressed down slightly.

"What I wanted to say, before I was so rudely interrupted . . ." The sultry sound of her voice was intoxicating
enough, but the sight of her elegant fingers wrapped inti-
mately around his engorged prick, her pink tongue framed
by her swollen lips as she lapped his shaft was beyond
pleasure. It was like a religious experience. "Is that
pregnancy"—her tongue began traversing up the length of
him—"is not an issue." She reached the swollen head of his
cock. "I've got that covered." And then she took his cock in

her mouth and started humming. *Humming.* Causing vibrations to reverberate through him. *Unbelievable.* His breath was ripping in and out of his lungs like a freight train as her tongue, her mouth, and fingers made him weak-kneed and dizzy. "No more," he rasped, his voice hoarse. "Can't . . . hold out."

She looked up at him, her lips swollen and slick. "Sure you can." Her hand rose, to take the place of her mouth, a hint of pleased laughter in her voice as she did that diabolical twisting motion over the head of his cock, ripping another moan from his chest. He was shaking. Literally shaking.

"I need you, Sarah. Now."

"All right, then." She released her grip on him, scooted back on the bed, spread her arms wide, and fell backward as if preparing to make a snow angel. "I'm all yours. Take me."

NO SOONER HAD THE WORDS LEFT SARAH'S MOUTH than she felt the welcome weight of Mick's magnificent body on hers. All six feet four inches of hot horny male, lean, hard muscles, gentleness, and strength. The fire in his eyes, his ragged breathing, the light sheen of sweat across his shoulders and face made her feel like the sexiest woman alive. She dragged her nails down his back, over the taut mounds of his buttocks, then slipped her hand between their bodies to position his hard cock at the entrance of her core. She drew small circles with the ruddy, swollen head, making it even slicker with her juices. Then, with a slight upward thrust of her hips, she had taken the engorged tip inside her. "More. I want more." Need rising like a winter river after a hard rain. "I want you planted to the hilt, deep, *deep* inside me."

Mick thrusted his hips forward. His beautiful eyes locked on hers as he drove his cock into her warm, welcoming sex. "Like that?" he murmured.

"Yeah, just like that," she replied like a woman starving.

Slowly, he withdrew, even as everything inside her tightened, wanting, needing the feel of him filling her. Slowly, he withdrew until just the tip was still lodged in her. "Please," she moaned, and he plunged into her again and again, stretching, claiming every millimeter of her, and it felt so incredible, so very right, how she had imagined lovemaking would be before she'd hooked up with Kevin and discovered the truth. *But now* . . . A sudden groundswell of gratitude and emotion swept all thoughts aside, and there was nothing left for her to do but to wrap her legs around him tight, hold on, and ride the love, ride the cresting waves higher and higher until they obtained completion.

45

"YOU KNOW WHAT WE FORGOT TO DO?" SARAH said, trailing her fingers lazily through the scattering of hair on his chest, her palm settling over his heart. She could hear the comforting thump of it through the ear nestled against his skin. She was tucked around him, his arm holding her close. She loved the warmth of his hard body, the contained strength he possessed, and was reluctant to move. Mick had carried her into the bedroom as if she were a dainty five foot four, making her feel like a heroine in a movie. Heck, even the memory of it was causing a languid heat to course through her. However, she hadn't eaten since breakfast, and hunger was making itself known. She removed her leg, which had been resting across his thighs, enjoying the sensation of the slight rough texture of the hair on his legs, so different from hers, bringing a jolt of heat to her sex. She sat up and swung her legs over the side of the bed.

"What did we forget?" His voice was like warm toffee. His gaze was as wide open as the desert sky. "I aim to please, ma'am," he said with a cheeky grin. "Your satisfaction is paramount to me. Although . . ." He paused, looking like a mischievous fallen angel. "You did scream pretty loudly, more than once, if I recall, but hey, let's give it another go. Practice makes perfect." He reached a hand and tugged her back into his arms, rolling over so she was underneath him.

"You gotta be kidding," Sarah said, unable to help the smile that was spreading across her face as Mick positioned himself at her opening, which was still slick from their last encounter, and in one smooth thrust he was where he belonged.

Forty-five minutes later she lay boneless, breathless, and more satiated than one woman deserved to be. "Wow . . . if I'd known this was what I was missing, I wouldn't have waited so long." She heard Mick growl possessively, which made her chuckle. He spread his hand over her abdomen. She liked the way it looked, his long, tan fingers against her pale skin.

"Good thing you're on the pill. Made me come so hard, woman. No way that load wouldn't have impregnated you." And just like that, the sorrow came, for what would never be. "What?" He rolled to his side, pushed up on his elbow, concern in his voice.

"I'm not on the pill." Her voice was barely a whisper.

"IUD? Diaphragm?"

She shook her head. Squeezed her eyes shut to block out the worry on his face. It was easier this way, to say what needed to be said. "I don't need birth control. I'm unable to get pregnant."

He gathered her in his arms, holding her close. "Were children something you wanted?" She could feel his voice rumbling through his chest.

"Yes, of course. I always believed that one day I would be a mom." It was comforting being held by him. Made her feel safe, less alone. "And when I found out I was pregnant." She paused, words stuck in her throat.

"Go on." His hand made soothing circles in the space between her shoulder blades.

Sarah pulled back a little so she could see his face. "Even though I was in a terrible relationship, I wanted that baby. Wanted her so much. My mother was thrilled that she was going to be a grandmother. My dad . . . He was a little less ecstatic. I think he was enjoying having my mom's undivided attention, and that took a back seat once the baby was coming. My mother became a whirling dervish of activity. There was a nursery to set up, a layette, and maternity clothes to purchase. She was so happy. Came with me to every doctor's visit. Held my hand when we both saw the baby's heartbeat for the first time. It was the most amazing thing, this miracle of life growing inside me. My mother attended Lamaze classes with me so she could be in the hospital to help me through the birth . . ." Sarah stopped, unable to speak, the weight of all she had lost crashing over her.

Mick held her close to his chest, solid as a mountain. His head bowed over hers, and his heartbeat was a steady, comforting thrum. Great breaths of oxygen entering his lungs and exiting again, slow and measured, as if he were breathing for both of them. Time passed and still he held her, keeping her safe in the storm. And when it passed, he snagged some tissues, wiped her tears, and then stuck a couple in her hand. Didn't so much as blink when she blew her nose more than once. There was no way to do it delicately, not after crying that hard. And once she'd mopped up, he held out his hand and made her drop the soggy tissues in it. He got off the bed, and she watched his long, rangy body stride naked into the bathroom to toss the tissues away and was filled with gratitude that this man had entered her life.

When he returned, he sat cross-legged on the bed and took her hands in his. "So, then what happened?" He was right, of course. She couldn't stop there, no matter how much she wanted to pull the covers over her head.

"A cement truck plowed into my parents' vehicle. My dad died on impact. My mom passed away in the ambulance on route to the hospital. The driver of the cement truck must have been high or drunk, because the footage shows him backing up and taking off. The license plate was covered in mud and was unreadable. Every time I see a gray cement truck, this irrational rage wells up inside. I fantasize about dragging the driver out and punching him on the nose. It doesn't matter if the person was actually the one who killed them and then drove away, leaving my parents' car and their broken bodies discarded like litter on the road. I literally hate all drivers of gray cement trucks." Mick didn't look shocked or repelled by her revelation, but inside he probably wanted to run screaming from the room. Sarah exhaled slowly, suddenly weary. "The next few days passed in a blur. So much to set up, graves to purchase, coffins, headstones to order, a funeral to arrange, a memorial, food, flowers, what the readings should be, and on and on and on. Jane and Phillip helped. Vicki, too. But still there were so many details that only I could attend to." She paused, looked down at her hands encased by his. "After it was all over and everyone had gone home, there was the legal stuff that needed to be dealt with. Wills to be read. Papers to sign. Kevin took the day off work to come with me to Phillip's office."

"And . . . ?"

"And I'm not sure if I mentioned this before, but when the will was read Kevin . . . wasn't pleased."

"Because your parents tied their estate up in a trust? It shouldn't have been a surprise. Many people do."

"Yes, but this one had a caveat. It was to be kept in trust for as long as I was married to Kevin. If we ever got divorced or he died, the trust would be dissolved and I would own everything outright."

"Pissed him off."

"You could say that. He took it pretty personally. When we got home, he took it out on me. Me and the baby." She could hear her voice. It sounded flat, emotionless, just stating facts now, one after another, too tired and heartsick for any more tears.

"That son of a bitch." Mick's curse was a low growl that

had her gaze flicking upward to his face. Anger and a vow to avenge her and her unborn child were blazing from his eyes. *Good,* she thought. *Let Kevin know what it feels like to be hunted and scared.*

"I tried to shield the baby when he knocked me down"—her face felt slightly numb and masklike—"and was kicking the shit out of me curled up on the kitchen floor. Did the best I could, but it wasn't enough. After his fit, he slammed out of the house. I crawled to the phone, called 911, so worried for the baby. There was so much blood, and contractions were ripping me asunder. The last thing I remember is the ambulance crew strapping me onto a stretcher and starting an IV. When I regained consciousness, I was in a private hospital room. There were bouquets of expensive flowers, get-well cards, a box of chocolates from La Maison, but no baby. Phillip had brought Auntie Jane by, hoping her presence would help soften the blow." She turned her palms upward, stared at them. Felt almost as if they belonged to someone else. But she knew they were her hands because they were empty. Would always be empty. "I knew they meant well, but it was exhausting, meaningless chatter about the weather and such. Finally, I pretended to fall asleep so they would go. After they departed, the doctor informed me that the violence of the miscarriage had caused a lot of internal damage, which resulted in uterine adhesions, synechiae. Basically, fancy words for scarring. Scarring that would prevent any new embryos from implanting." She shrugged, attempted a light laugh, but it came out sounding more like a dry heave after one had vomited out one's guts. "So, you're safe. A baby won't take root." Her voice cracked slightly, but otherwise she'd managed to hold it together pretty well.

"I'm so sorry," he said, and she could tell he was, could hear it in his voice, see it in his eyes.

"Me too," she whispered. They didn't talk anymore. There wasn't a need to. Mick gently settled her back on the bed, retrieved the covers from the floor and pulled them over her. Then he climbed into the bed, opened his arms, and she snuggled in, her legs and arms wrapped around him tight. And they stayed like that. The past was behind them. There was only the present. Only the now. The two of them holding each other tender and sweet, their breath, their heartbeats intermingled as one.

LUCKILY, MICK AND SARAH HAD GOTTEN THEIR ORder in the nick of time. Ten minutes later and room service would have switched from the expansive all-day dining to the truncated overnight menu.

When they had awoken from their impromptu nap, Mick remembered a great mom-and-pop Italian bistro that was only a couple of blocks away, but Sarah had been reluctant to leave the room. She was still hopeful Vicki might call. Mick could have told her waiting for the phone to ring was a waste of time. A decade of directing had made him something of an expert at reading faces, and Vicki's was stone-cold shut. No call would be forthcoming.

The room service arrived twenty minutes later and was surprisingly good. They ate the perfectly grilled halibut with buttery mashed potatoes, "local" asparagus—which Mick had argued against because where in the hell were they growing asparagus in New York City—but Sarah won. He was grateful to see her appetite was better than it had been that morning. However, she still looked a little pale and had developed violet shadows under her eyes. It was as if they had made an unspoken pact and talked only about inconsequential things, like the premiere of his new movie, which would be a week from Thursday in New York. He floated the idea of the two of them staying the extra week. "We could make a vacation out of it, amble through the museums, take in some Broadway shows, shop for a fancy outfit, and you can attend the premiere with me."

She demurred. Her cat, Charlie, would be missing her. And even though he was disappointed, he enjoyed watching Sarah's face lighten as she described how her motley cat would insist on sleeping with his nose tucked into the nape of her neck, his paw draped across her shoulder. "Claws ready to extend," she said, raising her hand, arching her fingers into pretend kitty claws, her eyes sparkling with amusement. "To hold me in place, even in his sleep, to make sure I'm not preparing to vacate the bed."

"Sounds like a tyrant," Mick said, not in a complimentary fashion, but Sarah took it as one and smiled.

"He is," she replied, and scooped up another forkful of mashed potatoes.

Once they had noshed on the "healthy portion" of the meal, they tucked the dirty dishes and leftovers in the belly of the white-linen-covered trolley. Then, with fanfare, Mick had removed the organic carrot cake with crushed pineapple, the homemade chocolate peanut bar, and a pot of steaming-hot coffee.

"Oh my," Sarah half moaned, half sighed as she sank her fork into the cake. "You are a terrible, terrible man."

"Thank you," he replied with a gracious nod of his head. He watched her kiss-swollen lips close around her forkful of cake, and his prick sprang to attention remembering those warm, luscious lips wrapping around his engorged member. *Down, boy,* he told himself sternly. Every muscle in his body was insisting he bend her over the room service trolley and take her from behind. *You are not a wild beast. You are a civilized man*—Mick tugged his gaze away from her mouth—*who will let the woman eat her dessert in peace.* He speared a forkful of the chocolate peanut bar for himself with one hand and poured coffee into their mugs with the other.

"I like a man who can multitask." He wasn't sure if the husky undertones in her voice had been caused by the delectable taste of the dessert, or if she was suggesting another bout of mind-blowing sex as a possible aperitif? Didn't matter. There was only so much temptation a man could take. "How would you feel"—he set his forkful of chocolate peanut goodness down on his plate and rose from his chair—"about a change of venues?" He rounded the trolley. She used the side of her fork to slowly cut another mouthful, laughter and a make-me dare dancing in her eyes. His hand closed over hers, stilling her action.

"Mm . . ." she said, releasing her fork, which clattered on the china. "I take it you have a more satisfying dessert in mind?" She lifted her mouth to meet his, her arms twining around his neck.

The shrill sound of the phones ringing in both bathrooms, the phone in the bedroom, and the one on the desk jolted Sarah upright. Mick stifled an oath. *So much for dessert,* he thought, *although perhaps it's room service wanting to remove the dishes.* Whatever it was, the mood was broken. Sarah was no longer curled up in the armchair, a sultry Aphrodite incarnate, her elegant pink-tipped toes peeking out from under her robe begging to be kissed. The damn phone rang, and the day's tension came crashing back. All the languor and teasing laughter had vanished from her face. She looked at him, her eyes large. "Do you think?" she whispered.

Ring . . . ring . . .

"It's Vicki. It's got to be. Who else would be calling so late at night?"

Ring . . . ring . . .

Sarah shot to her feet, scrambled around the desk, and grabbed the phone. "Hello? Hello? Yes, this is Sarah." She was hunched over the phone. Both her hands were wrapped around the receiver, gripping it tight. One didn't have to be a hotshot director to read that body language. "Don't worry about the hour. Seriously. I'm glad you called."

Mick sighed. "Not room service, then?" he murmured. Luckily, he wasn't expecting an answer.

One hundred percent of Sarah's focus was on the person, presumably Vicki, on the other end of the phone. "Wow. Absolutely," Sarah said. "No. It's no trouble at all. I'm really grateful. I can be in a cab in five minutes. No traffic at this time of night, so it shouldn't take long. See you soon." Sarah hung up the phone and turned to him. "That was Vicki." He could hear the excitement in her voice, could see it emanating from her face. "She's just come back from Phillip's office. Located my files and identification papers in their storage room in the basement of the building and brought them to her town house. I have to get dressed."

He snagged her arm as she dashed past him. "Hold on."

"What?" She fisted her hands on her hips and tapped her toes impatiently.

"You're planning on visiting her now? It's after midnight."

"It's not important *when* she wants to hand my documents over. What matters is that she is *willing* to."

"Alarm bells are ringing, Sarah. This feels off to me. Feels like a trap."

The defiant expression on her face softened. "Mick," she said, her slender hand alighting on his arm. "I have to go. I've spent the last four years running from shadows, afraid and fearful. I refuse to be that woman anymore. If I have to visit Vicki in the dead of the night to regain my identity, so be it."

He studied her face. He could see the fierce intelligence shining from her eyes, along with determination and pure grit. Shimmering beneath the surface he also sensed a healthy dose of fear and apprehension. "All right. We'd better get dressed."

She placed her hands on either side of his face, rose onto her toes, and brushed a gentle kiss on his forehead. "Thank you," she said, smoothing an errant lock of hair from his eyes. "That means a lot to me. I'll bang on your door when I'm ready to go." She gave him a soft smile, as if he were the sun and the moon, then turned and darted out of his room.

46

AS THE CAB PULLED UP IN FRONT OF VICKI'S TOWN house, the unease Sarah had been feeling on the drive over seemed to heighten. "There is nothing that says we have to follow through tonight," Mick said. "We can arrange to come back in the morning."

"No. Vicki sounded like she had continued the drinking fest after we left. Tomorrow, when she's hungover and sober, she might rethink her generosity. She could change her mind, or demand an enormous sum of money for what she's offered to give me for free."

"For what it's worth, I agree with your lady friend," the burly cabdriver said, twisting in his seat. "My brother . . . Let's just say he's in the business of extracting information." The cabby cracked his neck. He seemed lonely. Certainly didn't appear to be in any hurry to have them exit his cab, although that might be in part because he hadn't turned the meter off yet.

"Let's settle up." Mick pulled out his wallet.

The cabbie jabbed a button on his meter. "Strike while you can." He was dispensing advice with a cocky grin, like he was a featured guest on *The Oprah Winfrey Show*. "Don't give her a chance to wise up, fly the coop, or receive a bigger bribe from another party. That'll be eighty-seven fifty, sir." He had been pretty chatty the whole ride.

"We aren't bribing anyone, sir," Sarah said stiffly.

"Although." The cabbie continued unperturbed. He tipped his chin toward the town house. "You sure you got the right address? Place seems pretty locked up for someone expecting visitors." Sarah glanced at the town house. The windows were dark. Even the porch light had been extinguished, leaving the building in murky shadows.

"Sarah—" She knew what Mick was going to say. She was thinking it herself, but she hadn't traveled across the country to turn back now.

"This is the right place. Thanks for the ride." Sarah exited the cab before Mick could use his damnable logic on her. Vicki had called her. Asked her to come. Sarah wasn't going to return to Manhattan without getting what she came for. She stepped onto the sidewalk and stared at the darkened building. An icy chill slithered down the back of her neck.

"Of course"—the cabbie continued as if he were discussing whether or not it might rain—"there's always the possibility that someone's already shut her mouth for her."

Another shiver rippled through Sarah. She glanced around. The street was deserted. The bare, witchy branches of the black trees silhouetted against the night sky. The harsh glare of LED streetlights illuminated patches of concrete. There was something about the quality of light, along with the drop in temperature, that made the area seem even more daunting than before.

She felt Mick step beside her. "Ready?" he asked. Sarah nodded. She could feel tension in her jaw, in her shoulders. They crossed the sidewalk. Mick flicked on his cell phone flashlight to chase the darkness from the steps leading to the landing and Vicki's front door.

It seemed unnaturally quiet. There was the whir of late-night traffic up the road at the intersection, but other than that the neighborhood seemed locked up tight. She was glad Mick had insisted on accompanying her.

Sarah rapped on the red door, which had seemed so cheery in the daylight but now, in the shadows, took on the hue of blood.

They waited.

No sound of feet approaching. No interior lights flicked on. "Give it another go," Mick said. Sarah knocked again, louder this time.

Still nothing. She cupped her hands around her eyes and peered in the window. The glass was cool against the sides of her palms, beginning to fog from the warmth of her breath. The sense of unease was building. "See anything?" Mick asked.

"Can't make out much, a few dark shadows." She squinted, trying to force her eyes to see more.

"Told ya," a male voice called. Sarah spun around, glared first at the cabbie and then at Mick.

"Did you pay him to wait?" she demanded, grouchy that she had allowed herself to get spooked.

Mick didn't take umbrage. Just shrugged. "For a couple of minutes in case nobody came to the door."

Sarah turned back to the window. "Let me have your phone for a sec?" Mick handed her his cell phone. "Thanks." She held the phone's flashlight up to the pane of glass, hoping to be able to see more clearly, but all she could see was the reflection of the bright light on the glass pane shining back at her. Mick wasn't saying anything. Didn't have to. She knew what he was thinking. Sarah knocked again, putting more force into it. "Vicki," she called, trying not to be too loud so she wouldn't wake the neighborhood. "It's me, Sarah." Her palms felt sweaty.

Nothing.

Reluctantly, she turned away from the front door. "She's not going to answer."

"Looks that way." There was regret in his voice, but relief as well, because now they could leave. The way he was scanning the area, his battle-ready alertness spoke volumes. As they descended the front porch steps, the light from Mick's phone fell on a wrought iron gate at the side of the town house. It was ajar. Seemed like a sign. So instead of making a right and returning to the waiting cab, she turned left through the open gate.

"Sarah," Mick growled warningly.

Sarah glanced over her shoulder without breaking her stride, placed a finger to her lips. "Shhh . . ." She was walking as softly as humanly possible. However, the crunch of the gravel underfoot sounded deafening to her ears.

"No kidding," he muttered, but he followed her, thank God. "What are you hoping to accomplish with this? Are you planning on adding breaking and entering to this night's agenda?"

"Maybe," she whispered. "I don't know. I just . . ." What *was* she doing creeping along the side of Vicki's house? "I'm not leaving without my documents." But even as the words fell from her lips, she knew it was a lie. She was operating on sheer intuition because the sense of urgency had built to a roar. Sarah broke into a jog. A litany pulsed in her brain. *Hurry . . . hurry . . . hurry . . .* Her heart had started pounding crazy loud in her chest. When she rounded the corner of the town house, she suddenly knew why. Everything screeched to a halt. Didn't even need the flashlight. Could see Vicki's body sprawled on the flagstone pavers beside the round bistro patio table for two.

"Is she dead . . . ?" Her words dropped almost soundlessly on the night air. Vicki's nightgown was hiked up. Her neck and back were arched. Only a sliver of her face was visible, but that, along with her exposed abdomen, bare hips and legs, looked an almost unnatural white in the moonlight. One of the delicately wrought chairs was overturned beside her. *Was she sitting on it? Did she have a stroke or a heart attack?*

Sarah felt Mick disengage his phone from her frozen hand. The movement broke Sarah's momentary paralysis.

By the time she'd reached Vicki's side, she could hear Mick talking to the 911 operators. "I'd like to report an emergency—"

Sarah shoved the upturned chair out of the way and dropped to her knees. "Vicki, can you hear me?" She shook the woman's shoulder. There was no response. Vicki's head was already arched back. Sarah checked that her airway was clear.

"Is she breathing?" Mick asked. Sarah stared at Vicki's chest.

"I don't know. It's hard to tell in this light." She tugged the hem of Vicki's nightgown down enough to cover her privates. "I'll see if I can find a pulse." She placed her fingers against the side of Vicki's neck. Her skin was cool and clammy to the touch.

"Hello? Yes. We're at Five Fifty Twentieth Street, in the backyard. There's a female down. We don't know the cause. Just arrived on the scene. She's unresponsive."

Under Sarah's fingers, she thought she felt a faint flutter. Suddenly, Vicki spasmed violently, her arms and legs rigid. A harsh, ragged gasp for air ripped out of her gaping mouth. The sudden movement, the inhuman noise, triggered Sarah's highly honed fight-or-flight instincts, but she forced herself back down to her knees. "She's alive," Sarah heard Mick bark into the phone. "But something is very wrong."

Another seizure ripped through Vicki. Her eyelids jerked open, her pupils were dilated, her mouth attempting to expel words through the harsh, rasping struggle for air. It sounded almost like "Why? I . . . loved . . . him," but Sarah couldn't be sure. "Sorry. I couldn't make that out. What did you say?" There was an anguished sorrow in Vicki's eyes so much deeper and more potent than the fear. The woman opened her mouth, her lips moving, but another painful spasm arched her body. Vicki's eyeballs rolled back in her head, and horrible choking noises were clawing their way out of her throat. It sounded like she was suffocating. Wasn't getting enough air. Sarah's mouth was chalk dry, and her heart was pounding a million miles an hour as she placed her hands at the center of the woman's chest and began doing compressions.

"Hang in there, Vicki." Sarah hoped on some level Vicki could hear her voice and that knowing she wasn't alone would offer comfort. "Help is coming." She was so grateful for the CPR course she had taken with her mother in the first months of her pregnancy. Vicki sucked in another rasping breath. "You're doing great. Good job, Vicki. Take another breath. Wonderful. And another." She could hear the faint sound of sirens wailing in the distance and prayed that they were heading their way.

"Yo!" A man's voice jerked Sarah's focus away from Vicki's face. The cabbie was standing at the entrance of the walkway framed by the gate, a beer-bellied silhouette back-lit by the streetlight. "Time's up."

"Hold on a second," Mick called. "We're dealing with an emergency situation here."

"And I'm tryin' to make a livin'. It's simple. Pay me to wait, or I'm leavin' to find another fare."

"Jesus H. Christ," Mick muttered under his breath.

"Go on. Pay him," Sarah said. "We aren't going to want the hassle of trying to find a cab once we're done here. Also, if this isn't a heart attack or a stroke, then we're going to need the cabdriver as an alibi/witness when the police and paramedics arrive."

"All right, time's up. I'm leaving," the cabbie called.

"Fuck me." She felt Mick's hand alight on her shoulder. "You okay here? It'll just take a second."

"Absolutely. Do it. Quick before we lose him."

Mick turned on his heel and jogged down the walkway. The cabdriver had already stepped back onto the well-lit city sidewalk and was moving toward his taxi.

"Wait up!" Sarah heard Mick call, and then he was swallowed into the shadows along the side of the house. She needed to pause her compressions for a minute to wipe the sweat from her forehead and then began again. The sirens were getting louder.

"Help is coming." Sarah said it as much for herself as to

comfort Vicki, because the moment Mick vanished, the sense of dread had increased exponentially. *There is a logical explanation for your fear. You are alone in the dark, doing compressions on a woman who is making horror film noises, her body is in spasms, and she's fighting to breathe. Or course you're a little freaked out.* "Help is on—" *No! It's more than that. Pay attention.* Sarah's head jerked up, full-fledged panic surging through her. But it was too late. The dark figure of a man launched through the back door. A hunter, moving low and fast. She had opened her mouth to scream, when his body slammed into hers like a thunderbolt, his arm wrapped tight around her neck, yanking her to her feet. She could feel the cold muzzle of his beloved Glock 17 nestled against her temple.

"Just like old times, huh?" His voice was a harsh whisper next to her ear. "I'm not one to look a gift horse in the mouth. You're coming with me, baby. One sound and you're dead." The familiar stink of his aftershave mingled with the smell of his skin made the taste of vomit rise in her throat. Sarah forced it down, along with the bone-numbing fear. *No!* a voice bellowed inside. *Enough!* She was not a scared, whimpering woman anymore. She refused to be.

"You won't kill me, Kevin," she said, keeping her voice calm and clear even though tremors were running through her body. Hoping her voice would carry through the night air to Mick and warn him of the danger. "If I die, you get nothing, and you love having all that money to roll in." The grip around her throat tightened. She tucked her chin to her chest, protecting her airway and making it much more difficult for him to crush her windpipe. Adrenaline coursed through her at these small acts of defiance. "Yeah, that's right, asshole," she rasped out through clenched teeth. "I've learned a few tricks since you last saw me. Not so easy to make me black out." She braced herself for a blow—insolence would never go unpunished—but it didn't arrive. His hands were full, and Sarah couldn't help the triumphant smile that curved her lips, even though she knew she would pay for it later.

"Shut the fuck up, bitch." He was dragging her toward

the alley at the rear of the garden. The sirens were quite loud now. And then, as if Mick had tapped her on the shoulder, Sarah knew he had returned. She could sense him silently, stealthily moving in the shadows, making his way along the perimeter of the garden to block Kevin's exit. The only problem was Kevin had a gun. He would shoot her as a last resort, but he would not hesitate to murder Mick in cold blood. "And I'm warning you now," her ex-husband continued. "You better have kept your legs clamped shut. Otherwise, no amount of money could wash off the stench, and the consequences would be dire." He was trying to intimidate her, but it created the opposite effect. She was *not* going to let Kevin permeate another second of her life with his abuse and fear. There was *no* way in *hell* she was going to let him endanger the man she loved. She would fight to the death before she allowed that to happen. She was strong. She was powerful, and enough was enough. Sarah, keeping her chin tucked to her chest, raised her hands to his forearm clamped around her neck, as if trying to loosen his grip. Once her hands were in place, she slumped toward the ground. The sudden deadweight caused Kevin to stumble, giving her the opening she needed. Quick as lightning, she grabbed the barrel of his pistol with both hands and yanked it away from her face.

"What the f—" She could feel his rage crashing over her, but instead of crushing her with fear, it was fuel. A shot roared out, ringing in her ears, a numb burning sensation in her left hand, both of them suddenly slippery on the gun. Through the ringing, she could hear Mick's battle cry. Felt the thump as Mick's body launched into Kevin, but still she didn't release her grip on the handgun, and the three of them went down in a pile. She wrapped her body tightly around Kevin's forearm, pinning it and the Glock to the ground, keeping Mick out of harm's way.

Another shot rang out. Heat skimmed along her rib cage. Her vision was blurring, but she didn't let go. She could hear sirens, dogs barking, vehicle doors slamming, people shouting.

There was a third blast, but still she didn't let go. She could hear footsteps pounding. Only a tiny circle of vision remained in the very center of her eyes, the rest was darkness. But it was all she needed to see the blessed first responders, the police, the paramedics and firemen flooding into the courtyard. "Thank God," she murmured. "Thank God," and then that fragment of vision slipped away as well.

47

SARAH REGAINED CONSCIOUSNESS AS THE PARA-
medics lifted her onto the gurney, just in time to see Kevin
being led away in handcuffs. "You are making the biggest
mistake of your career, Officer," Kevin shouted. "Fucking
heads are going to roll." His eyes were blazing.

Sarah turned her face away, but she could still hear him
cussing. "What happened?" she asked the female para-
medic who was threading a strap through a buckle to secure Sarah's lower legs to the board.

"You blacked out," the woman replied. "Shock, most
likely."

"I'm okay. I can walk." Sarah attempted to push herself
to a seated position, having forgotten about her injured
hand, and fell back with a cry.

Suddenly Mick was beside her, his hand on her shoulder,
his worried face filling her vision. "We're going to the hospital to get you patched up."

Mick rode with her in the ambulance. She was grateful
for his company, to not be going through this alone after so
many years of fending for herself. He brought her up to
speed on the trip to the hospital. The cops hadn't known

whom to believe, especially when Kevin pulled the NYPD lieutenant card. "It was touch and go for a moment. Fortunately, the cabdriver's version of the events corroborated my own. They agreed to let me accompany you to the hospital, but we both will need to drop by the police station tomorrow morning. I'll finish the rest of my statement, and they will need one from you as well."

Sarah nodded. Suddenly tired. So tired. She could see the residual flash of emergency lights through the window at the back. "They didn't put the sirens on."

"You want me to ask them to?"

Sarah shuddered. "No thanks."

Mick smiled at her, but she could see the worry in his eyes. "Might be exciting?"

"Ha." Her hand hurt like the devil, and her abdomen felt like a strip of skin had been carved away.

When they'd arrived at the hospital, the ER doctor deemed her wounds not life-threatening. Instead of treating her injuries immediately, the doctor called in a forensic nurse. Sarah stood on a piece of paper in a freezing-cold room and dropped her clothes, one by one, which were then labeled and stored. Photos were taken of the bruising around her neck, her damaged hand, the abrasions and powder burns on her abdomen. Her fingernails were scraped. Adhesive stubs collected gunpowder residue from her hands and her abdomen. Finally, Sarah had been given a thin hospital gown, a robe, and slippers and was led to a bed in the emergency room with a pale-green curtain for privacy. The nurse returned with a couple of warm blankets. "To keep away the cold," the nurse had said as she wrapped them around Sarah's shoulders. "You're shaking like a leaf." And then she was gone. But the kindness of that small gesture remained, warming more than her shoulders, and Sarah needed to momentarily close her eyes.

"YOU WERE LUCKY," THE ER DOCTOR SAID AS SHE sewed the torn flesh between Sarah's thumb and index finger with neat black stitches as if she were sewing on a missing button. Sarah's hand had been numbed, but she could still feel the tug. "Merely a surface wound across your abdomen where the bullet skimmed you, and the damage to your purlicue is not extensive." The doctor's hair was pulled back in a haphazard ponytail, and she looked tired, as if sleep was a commodity she couldn't afford. "Which is fortunate. If the bullet passed through a centimeter inward, there would have been significant nerve and vascular damage, as well as tendon disruption and multiple fractures."

Sarah nodded. "That's good," she replied. She was dog-tired. "I'm glad." *Lucky, the doctor said. Yes. I am.* And Sarah had had a hand in creating that luck. By grabbing the barrel of the firearm and controlling its trajectory, she had been able to mitigate the damage her ex had been able to do. *And Kevin is in police custody. Thank God.* Hopefully all the evidence they had collected would ensure that he was incarcerated for a very long time. Adding to her blessings, Mick was in the waiting room, and Sarah held on to that thought as she fought back waves of weariness and pain. Used the image of him to keep her grounded in the present, instead of sliding back into unconsciousness. Watched the delicate hand of the doctor, the needle puncturing her flesh and the thick black thread pulling tight. *Mick is in the waiting room safe and sound.* And the joy of that knowledge made her weak-kneed with gratitude and relief.

48

"IF YOU WOULD READ THROUGH YOUR WRITTEN statement one more time to make sure it's an accurate portrayal of the incident as you remember it," Detective Docherty said. The detective had taken Sarah to a specially equipped video suite. "We wanted to make sure to cover all bases." Detective Docherty was all business. Her ginger hair had been corralled back into a severe knot at the base of her head. However, Sarah could see rebellious wisps that had escaped their strict confines and created a soft halo around the woman's stern face that reminded Sarah of images of the pioneers as they crossed the Great Plains in their covered wagons. And for some odd reason, the added humanizing addition of the sprinkling of freckles across Detective Docherty's nose and dotting the crests of her cheek helped further to put Sarah at ease. There was something very fierce and trustworthy about this woman. There was a gentleness underneath the gruff exterior, a soft underbelly of kindness. Sarah could feel it in her gut, and it was such a blessing, because she hadn't been able to eat breakfast. The dread of visiting a police station had her stomach in knots. She had felt extremely vulnerable walking up the stairs and through the front doors, as if Kevin would come striding around the corner in full regalia and take her back into custody. "Feel free to make changes if there is anything that needs clarifying"—Detective Docherty, still sitting, rotated her shoulders as if she had worked out too hard and was feeling the effects—"to include any additional details or redact anything that is incorrect."

Sarah read over her statement. "It's fine," she said.

"Good. Now, if you would sign and date it?" Sarah signed. "Wonderful." Detective Docherty stood, then switched off the video recorder. "Well, that should wrap it up for now."

Sarah got to her feet, suddenly tired. Her painkillers must have worn off, because her hand and abdomen were throbbing. "Do you know how Vicki Orsini is doing?"

A flicker of regret flashed across Detective Docherty's face. "I regret to inform you, she passed away this morning at approximately three thirty a.m."

Sarah's stomach dropped. "Oh." A sense of numbness set in, as if she were watching from above. "I'm sorry to hear that."

"Appeared to have been poisoned. The symptoms point to strychnine. We're waiting on the autopsy and the lab results on her drink."

"I see." *Poisoned.*

The detective watched her for a moment, then fished out a business card and handed it to Sarah. It was embossed with all the detective's details on it. "If you think of anything else—maybe an important detail, a conversation, or something of significance that might have slipped your mind—please don't hesitate to get in contact with me. Sometimes it's the little things that will connect the dots for the judge and jury and lead to a conviction."

"Okay." Sarah nodded. "I will." She tucked the detective's card into the back pocket of her jeans. When she returned to the hotel, she would transfer it into her wallet in the zipper compartment of her purse. She didn't want to fumble one-handed with the task in front of an onlooker. "And if one of you comes across my ID and files while you are processing the crime scene?"

"Whatever is needed for evidence, we will keep until the court has ruled on the case. However, copies can be made and notarized so you'll be able to obtain new documentation."

"Thank you."

"Appreciate you coming in." Detective Docherty headed for the door. "If you would follow me, I'll show you the way out."

Sarah followed Detective Docherty through the open door and into the noise and commotion of the corridor. Police officers were escorting handcuffed detainees, officers were talking, entering, and exiting the rooms, thundering down staircases. There were the sounds of boots, utility belts, curses, and laughter. It was overwhelming, and Sarah found she was tucking into herself, attempting to make herself small, invisible. *Kevin is probably here. Is he locked up? Or did he convince them to let him go, as a favor from one jurisdiction to another?* "Excuse me?" Sarah sped up her steps to catch up with Detective Docherty's brisk clip. "I was wondering . . ." Her voice sounded higher pitched and a little too breathless for her liking. "If Lieutenant Hawkins is still in custody? Or if"—she swallowed hard, her heart pounding—"he was released on bail?"

Detective Docherty stopped walking so abruptly that Sarah almost crashed into her. She turned and looked at Sarah with eyes that had seen too much and were way older than the late twenties that she appeared to be. "Don't worry," she said. "Lieutenant Hawkins is in custody. I expect he will remain there. However, if for some unknown reason, a decision is made to release him on bail, I have your contact information and I will let you know."

"Okay." Sarah nodded, trying to get her breathing more ordered. "Thank you."

"Anything else?"

Sarah shook her head, straightened her shoulders. She

exhaled, long and slow, forcing her fists to unclench. "No. That's everything. Thank you."

"Right." Detective Docherty turned briskly and continued down the corridor with Sarah—still coursing with the aftereffects of panic adrenaline—following in the detective's wake.

49

MICK WAS SITTING IN THE LOBBY OF THE POLICE STA-
tion in one of the green plastic bucket chairs that were
bolted to the floor. The detective that was supposed to interview him had gotten called away. Mick had his phone
out and was responding to emails when something had his
gaze lifting from the screen. It was Sarah, walking into the
lobby, her face pale and shoulders back as if she'd just
bravely run the gauntlet through enemy territory. He rose
to his feet. Every protective instinct he possessed urged
him to sprint to her side, scoop her up, and remove her from
the premises, but he forced himself to stay put. He watched
her shake hands with the female detective, saw the second
her gaze found him, rejoiced in the way the rigidity of her
body and the suppressed panic in her eyes seemed to soften
slightly. *I love her,* he thought as he watched her make her
way to him. *I love her so damned much.*

"What are you smiling at?" She looked weary.

"You," he replied, wrapping an arm around her shoulders, dropping a soft kiss on her head.

"You finished giving your statement?"

Mick shook his head. "Haven't gone in yet."

"Oh dear." He felt her shoulders slump slightly. Could see faint lines of strain around her eyes and mouth.

"Painkillers worn off?"

She nodded.

"I don't know how long this is going to be," Mick said. "You should go back to our room and get some rest."

"I can wait with you," Sarah said. And Mick knew she would, but it wasn't necessary. "Vicki died. They think she was poisoned." A faint tremor ran through her. "Kevin's such a monster. He was probably with her when she phoned, forced her to call."

"Maybe. Look, Sarah, I don't want you hanging around here by yourself while they're taking my statement." What Mick didn't mention was his worry that Kevin was in the building. She didn't need the extra stress of crossing paths with her psychopathic ex.

"Hang on," Mick said, holding up a finger. "I'll be right back." He jogged over to the receptionist. "Mick Talford. I'm waiting to speak with Detective Kostas. I have to go out front for a second but will be right back."

"Fine." The receptionist barely looked up, fingers flying over his keyboard. Mick returned to Sarah, wrapped his arm around her shoulders, and steered her toward the metal-framed, thick glass doors.

"I'm going to pop you in a taxi. I want you to return to the hotel and wreak havoc: raid the minibar, order room service, flip channels, read a book, whatever. Enjoy some downtime. Let your body heal. Get some rest. I'll join you just as soon as I'm done."

"Okay," she said softly, lifting her mouth for a kiss. "I'm going to do that. And when you come back, I'll be all rested, and then I'm going to wreak havoc on you."

"Promises . . . promises . . ." Mick pushed open the door, and as they stepped out of the building, it seemed to him that Sarah's shoulders relaxed even further. He flagged a yellow cab, tucked her inside, shoved a wad of cash in her hand as he brushed a light kiss across her lips. "Love you," he said, then stepped back onto the curb and swung the door shut.

"What?" Her mouth had fallen open as she stared at him through the window with a look of wonder on her face.

"You heard me." He grinned as the taxi pulled away from the curb. "Strap in!" He stood and watched as she and the cab became smaller and smaller. Finally, the cab made a right-hand turn and disappeared from view. Mick returned to the police station with a buoyancy in his step and a smile in his heart, thinking about Sarah. He let the receptionist know that he had returned and then reseated himself in the green plastic chair to await his interview with Detective Kostas.

50

SARAH STEPPED INTO THEIR HOTEL ROOM, WEARY TO the bone. The numbing effect of the meds had definitely worn off. Her hand and abdomen were throbbing with pain. She dropped her purse on an armchair and entered the bathroom. Her hand hovered over the Tylenol, but she felt like crap, so she tipped a pain pill out of the prescription medication container, saying a silent blessing to Mick. He'd had the foresight to remove the childproof lid when he'd brought the pills back from the twenty-four-hour pharmacy last night. She swallowed it dry. Then she returned to the living room, hoping the numbing effect would set in shortly. On the taxi ride to the hotel, Sarah had decided she was going to tuck into the new Nora Roberts novel she'd purchased at the airport, raid the minibar, and possibly take a nap. She perused the selection of goodies in the minibar, finally settling on peanut M&M's. It was awkward ripping it open, had to use her good hand and her teeth. A blue one and a yellow one escaped. They rolled across the carpet and under the coffee table. Normally, she would have plucked them up, citing the five-second rule, but it was too much

hassle to risk aggravating her stomach and hand to try to
fish them out of their hiding place. She placed the opened
packet of candy on the end table beside the sofa within easy
reach, returned to the minibar, removed a can of Coke and
placed it by the M&M's. She padded into the bedroom.
Sarah was glad they had consolidated rooms and Mick had
moved her stuff into his when he'd woken up. She was
plucking Nora's book off her bedside table when the phone
rang. The unexpected noise caused her to levitate. *One day,*
she promised herself as she reached for the receiver. *One
day, all that's gone on will be a distant memory and you
will no longer jump at shadows.*

She brought the receiver to her ear. "Hello?" Her voice
was a little breathless. Her heartbeat was still recovering
from panic mode.

"Sarah? Is that you?" It was Phillip Clarke, his voice
sounded ragged, as if he hadn't slept all night.

Oh shit. He doesn't know about Vicki. "Hi there. Yes,
it's me."

"Did you talk with Vicki?" *Damn.*

Sarah knew the peace and quiet she was longing for was
rapidly fleeing in the rearview mirror. *This is important,*
she told herself sternly, but her inner child was flat on her
back, pounding her heels into the floor and wailing, *Not
fair!* "Yes, I saw her."

"What did she say? Does she miss me? Did she say she
would consider coming back?"

It would be heartless to tell him about Vicki over the
phone. *Tempting but unkind.* Sarah could feel the meds
kicking in. She forced her brain to focus. She could do this.
Granted she might be a little slurry, but hopefully he
wouldn't notice. Sarah reluctantly tugged her gaze from
Nora's book, exhaled. "Phillip," she said. "We need to talk."

"I would love that. I've just broken for lunch. You want
to grab a bite? I'll get us a table at Eleven Madison Park.
Your mother adored that place."

Sarah had been hoping a quick coffee would do it, but

he sounded so hopeful, and he was going to be heartbroken when he heard about Vicki. "Sure," she said gently. "That would be lovely."

"Wonderful!" He sounded chipper now. Sarah could just see him rubbing his hands together as he did when he was excited. She was not looking forward to breaking the bad news. "I'll pick you up at the Fifty-Seventh Street entrance of your hotel. I'll be driving a Mercedes-Benz S-Class, cashmere white. If I'm not out front, that means the door-men shooed me away and I'm circling the block. Wait by the curb and I'll be there shortly."

"Sounds good—"

"Better yet, if I'm not there, walk up half a block to Park Ave. I'll pull to the side and put my blinkers on. That way I won't have to battle the traffic endlessly circling the block."

"Okay. I'll head down."

"Don't forget, a Mercedes-Benz S-Class, cashmere white. See you soon!" The line went dead. Sarah stood there for a moment with her eyes squeezed shut, the phone still gripped to her ear. *This is going to be a hellish conversation*—she exhaled heavily, opened her eyes, and replaced the receiver—*but you will get through it. And so will he. Life goes on.* A resigned Sarah returned to the living room, scribbled a note for Mick, and placed it in the center of the coffee table. "Dammit," she said, but there was no heat in her words, as she grabbed her purse, a room key, and the bag of M&M's. It wasn't poor Phillip's fault that she was injured. Wasn't his fault that she was now faced with the unpleasant task of in-forming him that the love of his life was dead. As Sarah passed by the minibar, she thought, *What the hell,* and snagged the overpriced mason jar of gummy bears and stuffed them into her purse. Took a couple of steps, then returned to the minibar for the jar of roasted cashews in case she needed something salty to wash down all the sweet. *Wash down. Hmm . . .* It was overkill, but she re-turned to the side table and plopped the can of Coke in her purse as well. However, even the extra treats in her purse didn't tamp down her reluctance for the unpleasant task that awaited her. She sighed again, then straightened her shoulders and exited the room, her overstuffed purse clanking heavily against her thigh.

51

WHEN SARAH HAD RETURNED TO THE HOTEL, IT WAS in the bright sunshine, but by the time she stepped through the lobby doors, it was clear that the wind had picked up, bringing with it a drop in the temperature. Sarah hesitated for a second, wondering if she should return to the room for a coat. The wind had whipped a white plastic bag into the air. When gravity brought it to the earth, the bag began rolling, helter-skelter, an urban tumbleweed. The doorman returning from depositing a couple into a Lincoln Town Car had his head tucked down and was at a slight tilt from leaning into the wind.

"Can I get you a cab, miss?" the doorman asked, his head tipped inquiringly.

"No, thanks." Sarah attempted a smile, but it probably came off as rather lame. The meds had kicked in pretty good. The pain was now a distant thrum. Goose bumps had risen all over her body, but the idea of slogging all the way back through the lobby, up in the elevator to the forty-second floor to wrestle her way one-handed into her coat did not fill her with enthusiasm. No. She could manage the

cold for half a block, where Phillip would be waiting in his
toasty car for her. Pleased with her decision, Sarah stuck
her hand into her purse. She had the strap slung across
her body with the purse in front of her torso to deter
pickpockets . . . also to give her easier access to the treats
inside. She managed to wiggle several M&M's from their
pouch, everything a little more complicated with only one
hand. *Dang, it's cold!* She popped the candies into her
mouth and crunched through the sugar-candy coating into
the chocolaty peanut goodness. *Amazing how the mere act
of tossing a couple of morsels of candy into your mouth
can make the world a little brighter,* she mused. *Ah!* There
was Phillip's car, tucked around the corner, emergency
lights flashing. *I wonder why it's called "cashmere white."
Cashmere can be any color.* The tinted passenger window
in his vehicle glided down. "Get in. Get in," Phillip said,
one hand on the steering wheel, the other gesticulating vig-
orously. *I used to have the use of two hands. It was lovely.*
Sarah thought she heard someone chuckle. Sounded like it
came from her mouth. She opened the passenger door and
got in, closed the door behind her. Was a good thing she
had done it quickly, because Phillip had pulled into traffic
with a sudden lurch, causing several vehicles to honk
irately. Sarah strapped in. She might be drugged out on
pain meds, but she wasn't senseless. She had never ridden
in a car with him before. *Hopefully, I'll survive it. Wouldn't
that be hilarious? I sail through all these challenges and
am done in by a little old man behind the wheel of a luxury
sports car.* He was a very bad driver; he oversteered and
was incredibly jerky. The erratic movements were making
Sarah feel a little nauseous.

"Hello," she murmured, shutting her eyes and leaning
her head against the headrest. Maybe if she took a little
snooze on their way to the restaurant, she'd wake refreshed,
rested, and ready for conversation.

52

MICK GLANCED AT THE LARGE CLOCK BY THE PO-
lice receptionist's desk. Another twenty minutes had passed
since he'd stuck Sarah in a taxi. How long was he expected
to wait for Detective Kostas? He'd been feeling perfectly
fine sitting there, but now agitation had started stewing in
his stomach, an unexplainable sensation of foreboding. As
if an unseen danger was lurking just beyond his view. He
stood and walked over to the receptionist. "Do you have
any idea how much longer Detective Kostas will be?"

"No idea." The receptionist didn't even bother looking
up this time. His face was like a brick wall.

"Oh, okay." Mick returned to where he had been sitting,
but his seat had been usurped by a man in a hoody, who
grinned at him cockily.

"You snooze you lose," the guy said, flashing a gold
front tooth. The guy's oversized crony sitting next to him
cackled. The Mick fresh from the scrabble-hard deserts of
Nevada would have enjoyed cracking their heads together,
bloodying their noses, and then tossing them out of the
front door on their insolent asses. However, experience had

taught him that acting on those impulses was one thing when one was young and broke but quite another when one had a high net worth and was in the public eye. Mick had no intention of having his photo splashed over the tabloids and putting up with the inconvenience of another drawn-out lawsuit so some greedy bastard could claim a hefty cash restitution. There was an empty seat across the room. Mick took it and ignored the high five the two bozos gave each other. When Mick made his first million, the world had changed around him. Even people who he had considered friends ceased to see him as human. Looked at him more as an ATM, resented him when he loaned or gave them money. Got angry when he refused. *Cash. Screws things up. Look at Sarah and what she's gone through. Caused Kevin to force her into marriage, to stalk her when she ran. Did he love her? Or was it all about money?*

The woman in the seat next to him looked as if she were homeless. She smelled of urine and had very bad BO. Mick stayed put. Didn't want to hurt her feelings by leaping out of his seat and racing to the far end of the room. He clicked on his cell phone, opened an email from his production manager, Andre Burns, and skimmed through it.

So, I've been putting the budget together for FREEDOM. It's coming in around 5.6 million high. Either you return to the backers and get them to ante up some more cash, or you'll have to cut the stadium and chase sequence. All those stunts and damned extras are as expensive as hell.

Andre

Mick reread the email. Why was the word "cash" coming up in his brain over and over that morning, niggling at him? And there it was again. The word "cash" in the email had jumped out and attached itself to his psyche like a coastal sandbur embedded in his sock, refusing to be ignored. Mick put his phone away, tipped his head back against the white tile wall, shut his eyes, in the hope that his subconscious mind would take over. And then he saw it, a forgotten image from the night before. He was following the paramedics carrying Sarah on the gurney around the side of Vicki's town house. They had already raced Vicki into the night. It was like someone had tapped him on the shoulder. Mick turned back. Nothing so unusual. He could see the patio, the overturned chair. The police were bagging and labeling the empty glass tumbler that had been lying on the bistro table. Vicki must have been drinking out of it when she'd had her collapse. "Got this off Lieutenant Hawkins," Mick had heard a cop say. The cop crossed into Mick's view, and he had two bundles of something in each of his latex-clad hands. He dropped them into a paper bag that the other cop held out and labeled the bag. *Cash dropping from his hands like a ripe plum. Great whopping stacks of cash. For what? Why did Kevin bring that kind of money to Vicki's house? Drugs? Payoff for information? And if Vicki was expecting a huge cash infusion from Kevin, why did she botch it up by inviting Sarah to drop by? And if Kevin arrived fully prepared to pay for information, why did he bother killing Vicki?* Mick's mind was whirling. *Unless Kevin agreed to pay Vicki to get Sarah there?* Mick shook his head. Didn't add up. Last night, just before drifting to sleep, Sarah had mentioned Kevin had said he "wasn't one to look a gift horse in the mouth." *What did that mean? What gift horse?* Mick shot to his feet. *Sarah! Sarah's the gift horse.* Last night Mick had overheard Kevin insisting he had been set up. Had nothing to do with Vicki's collapse and now subsequent death. Mick had figured the dickhead was lying, but what if he wasn't? *If so, that third party is still at large, and Sarah is alone.* The dread that had been pulsating in his gut turned into a loud drumbeat now.

"Mick Talford." The receptionist's voice came over the PA. "Report to the reception desk."

Damnation. Mick strode across the lobby to reception. "Mick Talford here. Look, I gotta—"

A large man with a weather-beaten face stepped forward. "Mr. Talford? I'm Detective Kostas." He extended his business card. "I apologize for the delay—"

"Sorry," Mick cut in. "A family situation has arisen." Mick plucked the business card from Detective Kostas's fingers. "I have to run." He was already jogging backward. The sense of urgency was building. He waved the card over his head. "Will call and reschedule as soon as I sort it out." Mick pivoted, sprinted through the lobby, out the doors, and spilled onto the street, flagging down a taxi while he punched the hotel number into his phone. "Hello, yes. Room 4207 please."

"I'll connect you," a woman's voice said. "One moment, please." A taxi pulled to a stop. Mick climbed in as he listened to the phone *ring* and *ring*. No answer. *Shit.* Hopefully, she was in the shower. "Four Seasons Hotel, Fifty-Seventh Street," he said, his mouth dry as dust. Her name was pounding like a pulse. *Sarah . . . Sarah . . . Sarah . . .* All the while praying this feeling was a case of frayed nerves. Praying she was safe.

53

SARAH DRIFTED IN AND OUT OF SLEEP. IT WAS VERY restful. She had reclined her comfortable seat. Music was playing softly. Tommy Dorsey and his Orchestra, "Cocktails for Two." Very civilized. She pried her heavy eyelids open. Her vision was a little blurry but not so much that it was worrisome. The pain was gone, and she felt such a sense of pleasure and well-being. She could see greenery zipping past the window. Made her laugh softly to herself. No wonder she couldn't hear the sounds of the city anymore. "Where are we?" she asked, turning her head, stifling her yawn.

Phillip glanced over. "Oh, you're awake," he said cheerily. There was an excited, happy twinkle in his eyes. "You were sleeping so soundly, and then I thought, to heck with dining at some stuffy restaurant. A picnic would be much more fun. I called your auntie Jane on the car phone—had to turn the volume way down so I wouldn't wake you. She was over the moon yesterday to hear that you were alive, safe and sound, and wouldn't you know it, she insisted on seeing your dear face with her own two eyes. So! I decided to zip you out to our country home in Westchester."

"That will be nice," Sarah said, feeling a little dreamy. It had been so long since she'd last seen Auntie Jane. *When was it? Oh, at Mother and Father's funeral.* The buoyant feeling abated slightly, but the grief wasn't as intense, was just a wistful sort of numbness. *Funeral. No, that's wrong. I saw her at the hospital after the miscarriage. But there's something else I'm supposed to remember . . .* And then the image of Vicki's contorted body with her gaping mouth slammed into Sarah's consciousness. *Oh shit.*

"Uncle Phillip," she said. "Before we get to Auntie Jane's house, there is something I need to tell you."

"Yes, dear?"

Sarah pressed the electronic seat adjuster and returned her seat to an upright position. The lovely drifty feeling was not quite so lovely anymore. Not only was she going to have to sit across from Auntie Jane knowing her husband had been carrying on an affair for years, but she had to tell Phillip about last night. "It's about Vicki."

"Did she say she misses me, that she's coming back?"

"Uncle Phillip, I am so sorry to inform you that there has been a terrible accident, and Vicki . . ."

"Yes? Yes, what about her? Is she okay?"

"She passed away, Uncle Phillip. There is reason to believe that there was foul play."

"Foul play?" He looked so lost.

"Yes. The police are looking into—"

A harsh cry rang from Phillip's throat, and then another, and another. He started punching the steering wheel over and over. "My darling . . ." He sobbed. "My precious . . ." It was fortunate that there wasn't a lot of traffic on the Bronx River Parkway because his Mercedes was swerving erratically.

Sarah reached out to steady the steering wheel. "Uh . . . maybe we should pull over? Uncle Phillip?"

"No. No," he panted, dragging the sleeve of his tweed sports jacket across his eyes. "Jane is waiting for us. She has a meal prepared. We can't be late. She would worry. Oh my God. This is terrible news. My poor lovey-dove-dove." He fished his handkerchief out of his pocket with two fingers and then blew his nose violently. "Don't mention this to your auntie Jane. It would upset her greatly. She hasn't gotten over your parents' death, and this would undo her completely."

"Yes. Of course." *The affair or that Vicki's been poisoned?* Either way, neither was a topic she was going to spring on Auntie Jane over lunch. "But, about that picnic you mentioned, I was thinking it's rather cold and I left without a jacket."

"You can borrow one from Jane. Lord knows she has enough of them. Besides, I think the fresh air would do us all some good." Phillip stuffed his snotty handkerchief into his breast pocket. Sarah was grateful she wasn't responsible for doing his laundry. Suddenly his head jutted forward as he squinted through the windshield, his chest almost lying on the steering wheel. "Dagnammit!" he hollered, jerking the wheel hard and swerving across two lanes of traffic, barely making it onto exit 15. Even with the softening effect of the drugs, Sarah found it a little hair-raising. Phillip turned left at the stop sign. Swung wide onto Fenimore Road but managed not to clip any of the other cars. "Do they know who did this terrible thing to my precious Vicki?" he asked, oblivious to the chaos his driving created around him.

Sarah swallowed hard and with a concentrated effort was gradually able to corral her eyebrows from her hairline back to their normal position on her forehead. "Well," she managed to say conversationally. She didn't want to hurt his feelings. He couldn't help that he'd gotten old, lost his reflexes and spatial relations. "Kevin, my ex, was at Vicki's town house. The police took him into custody."

"So, he *was* having an affair with her. That bastard! I hope they beat the crap outta him before they threw him in the slammer."

"Well," Sarah said wryly, holding up her bandaged hand. "Someone got the crap beaten out of them."

Phillip glanced over, his wrinkled face furrowed in concern. "Oh dear. I'm so sorry. I noticed that when you were sleeping, and the bruises as well. What happened?"

"We struggled; his gun went off."

"Ouch. Painful."

Sarah shrugged. "I'm not hurting too badly right now. Meds have kicked in, so I'm feeling pretty good. Except, of course . . . the upsetting news about Vicki."

"Yes." Other than the emotional outburst upon receiving the news, Phillip seemed remarkably cheerful. "Heartbreaking. I shall miss her. Although, I must say I'm very glad they caught your psychopathic husband. He's been making my life a misery for years. Snooping around, asking questions, poking his nose where it wasn't wanted." He pulled onto a long, paved drive flanked with imposing brick gateposts and lined with trees. The interior of the property was hidden behind tall American holly shrubs. "It is a relief to know he is safely behind bars where he belongs. We shall all sleep a little easier tonight." He pulled up to a stately Georgian brick Colonial with white trim, dark shutters, and a lovely slate roof. The first garage door in the three-car garage glided open. "Home sweet home," he chortled, pulling to a stop. He switched off the ignition and turned to face her. He seemed a little flushed, and there was a rather unwholesome twinkle in his eyes that made Sarah feel a little nauseous. There was something that felt wrong, almost unhinged, reverberating around him. *Is he getting off on the fact that I'm going to have to visit with Auntie Jane knowing the truth about him and Vicki?* And not for the first time that afternoon, she wished she had been selfish and just blurted the news about Vicki over the phone. Refused lunch. Rested. Tucked in with her stash of candy and Nora Roberts's book. "Come on. Out we get," he said, clapping his hands together. "Don't want to keep Auntie Jane waiting." He hopped out of the car, was quite agile for an old guy, and did a modified cha-cha shuffle to the garage door. Sarah reluctantly unstrapped, got out of the car, and followed him into the house.

54

MICK'S HAND WAS SHAKING SLIGHTLY AS HE TAPPED his room key on the pad. *Red light*. "Damn." He tapped it again, slower this time. *Green light*. He turned the handle and opened the door. "Sarah?" he called, even though he could feel the vacant emptiness of the room. "Sarah!" He jogged through the living room to the bedroom.

She wasn't there.

"Sarah!" He burst into the bathroom even though it was pointless. He knew before the door bashed into the door-stop that the bathroom was empty. "Dammit." He ran his hands agitatedly through his hair, rubbing his scalp in an attempt to force his brain cells to think . . . *Think!*

Nothing.

He reentered the bedroom, his eyes scanning for clues. *Her purse is gone. Her shoes are, too. Not her coat, though. Why didn't she bring her coat? Must have stayed in the hotel. Downstairs maybe, in the restaurant getting a bite to eat!* He was on the move, back out of the bedroom into the living room, heading for the door, when he saw out of the corner of his eye a piece of paper placed on the coffee table. He snatched it up.

Mick,

Phillip called. I'm meeting up with him. Have to break the news about Vicki. It's not going to be fun. Love you. Hope you weren't stuck too long at the station.

—Sarah xo

Was the messy printing of her handwriting because of her injury, or was it a result of the drugs? *Probably it's a combination of the two,* he thought as he sprinted down the hall. He jabbed the elevator call button. *She's with Phillip. Phillip Clarke. Should be safe. A longtime family friend. So why was the notion of that filling him with dread?* The elevator doors glided open, he stepped in, and pressed the button for the lobby. The couple already in the elevator took one look at him and drew closer together. Mick turned his back to them and focused on the illuminating floor numbers above the door, as if that would make the elevator move faster. *Where is this feeling of panic coming from? Am I freaking out? Is this some sort of anxiety attack? Sarah's ex is in jail. She should be safe. Or maybe this unease is tied up with the Vicki mess?* Mick had read enough newspaper articles, seen enough true crime shows to know that it's usually someone close to the person. A family member, a friend, or a lover . . . Mick's stomach clenched further. *Was it a crime of passion, for monetary gain, or to silence someone, or all of the above? Phillip Clarke ticks at least one of those boxes, maybe more. That Sarah knew about Phillip's relationship with Vicki might put her at risk as well.* The elevator doors opened. Mick tore out into the lobby, through the front doors, out onto the street, and ran full tilt up the block, turned right on Lexington. He didn't have the address, but he knew the distinctive building that somehow managed to blend the grandeur of a historic old post office with a sophisticated modern flair.

Mick had clocked it because he'd thought it would make a good visual backdrop when shooting in New York. He would figure out the floor when he was in the lobby. Then the memory of standing in the elevator with Sarah yesterday flashed before him. When the floor number twenty-eight lit, her back had stiffened and her chin had lifted. Phillip Clarke's office was on the twenty-eighth floor.

55

"JANE," PHILLIP CALLED IN A SINGSONG VOICE. "I brought you a little surprise!" He was acting odd, but grief presented itself in strange ways. *Perhaps this frenzied excitement is a coping mechanism*, Sarah thought as she followed his slight, bird-legged frame through the mudroom, which had a door leading to the back garden. Two pairs of muddy Wellingtons sat neatly on a rubber mat by the door. One adult-sized, and a miniature pair, that were pale pink with a sparkly bow at the back. There were also two pairs of gardening gloves. Both items looked damp, as if Auntie Jane and her mini-me had recently been mucking around in the dirt. *One of her boys must have had a little girl. How nice for Auntie Jane. She'd always bemoaned the fact that she'd only had boys*. A wide-brimmed straw gardening hat hung on a hook. Oversized dark movie-star sunglasses that were quite fashionable a decade ago dangled from the hat's adjustable chinstrap. A smaller straw hat hung on a lower hook and had purple plastic sunglasses with specks of glitter embedded in the frames. Sarah paused, taking in the cozy tableau. Kevin was incarcerated now. She didn't have to run anymore. The future was wide open. Someday, perhaps she would open her parents' house in the Hamptons and re-create the memories of her past with her future children. She could always adopt. There were plenty of kids who needed homes. And she and the children would dance on the beach at dusk with the fireflies, have hot dog roasts, and go to The Palm as she did with her parents, sun-kissed, sticky with sweat and particles of sand. She bent over and gave the little pink boots a gentle pat. *When I have children, I will tell them stories of their grandparents and cook and garden with them, too.*

"What is wrong with you, woman?" Phillip's angry voice cut into Sarah's daydream. "Can't you follow the simplest instructions?" Sarah's head jerked up, guilty, as if she'd been caught stealing candy, but Phillip hadn't been talking to her. He was glaring into the kitchen. *Awkward.* Sarah heard Auntie Jane murmur something but couldn't make out what she was saying. Nevertheless, it wasn't appropriate for him to be taking out his frustrations on Auntie Jane, who was a dear little soul. Sarah straightened and hurried forward. "I specifically requested that you lock the kid in her room."

"Be reasonable, Phillip. You called Mrs. Bailey an hour ago. Hadn't checked with me before instructing our housekeeper to give our entire staff the rest of the day off, even the gardeners. You *knew* I was planting. And the nanny? Seriously? You can't expect the child to spend the entire day locked in her room by herself. It's inhuman."

Sarah rounded the corner and looked into the kitchen over Phillip's shoulder. "Hi, Auntie Jane," she said with a jaunty wave, as if she weren't plopping herself in the middle of a marital minefield. "And who is this little cutie?" Sarah asked, because there was a small child with pale-blond pigtails and large blue, blue eyes peeking out from behind Auntie Jane's legs.

"Goddammit." Uncle Phillip smacked the back of his hand against his palm. "Get her *out* of here."

"Sarah . . . ?" Auntie Jane had turned pale, as if she were seeing a ghost. "Is that you?"

"*Now*," Uncle Phillip hissed out through clenched teeth. Auntie Jane hoisted the little girl onto her hip and ran from the kitchen. *Okay. That was just weird.* Sarah could hear the little girl crying and Auntie Jane attempting to soothe her as her footsteps fled down the hall, up the circular staircase. "I'm surrounded by incompetence," he muttered. Sarah turned to look at him. His face was mottled with suppressed rage. People dealt with the death of a loved one in different ways, but this was unacceptable. Sarah could hear the tread of footsteps overhead, fainter and fainter, and then the far-off thud of a door closing. Suddenly, Phillip hitched up the waistline of his slacks and then stormed through the kitchen to the arched doorway Auntie Jane had just exited through. *I really wish I'd stayed at the hotel and enjoyed my book.* Sarah stepped into the kitchen. There were crayons and a partially finished drawing on the breakfast table in the nook.

"Jane," Phillip bellowed. Sarah glanced over. He was standing at the foot of the stairs. "Dump the damned kid and get your ass back down here. I need your help." He strode back into the kitchen, smoothing the strands of his gray hair back into place.

"Sorry about that," he said, attempting to smile congenially, as if he hadn't just had a meltdown. "Can I get you a drink?" He smoothed his shirt into his pants as he strolled to the refrigerator. He swung the fridge door open and peered inside. "Cider, white wine, juice boxes, mineral water . . ."

"I'm okay for now. Look, Uncle Phillip, I don't mind the little girl. Seriously. She's welcome to stay down here with us. If you want to know the truth, I really adore children. Had always planned to have a ton of my own someday. So, you'd be doing me a kindness. Truly."

Sarah heard a gasp and turned to see Auntie Jane standing in the doorway staring at her, her hand rising to her throat. "He . . ." Her gaze darted to her husband and then back to Sarah again, her eyes wide. "He said you didn't—"

"Jane." His voice cracked like a whip. "A *picnic*. We *need* a picnic."

"Yes . . . Yes, of course." She crossed the kitchen to the pantry as if in a daze. *Okay,* Sarah thought. *These painkillers are messing with my mind. I feel like I'm missing half the content of these conversations.* Auntie Jane reappeared from the pantry a moment later with a wicker picnic basket. She placed it carefully on the white marble kitchen counter as if it were made of glass. Her gaze flickered up from the basket to lock with Sarah's, only for a moment, but the impact was like a fist to Sarah's gut. The expression in Auntie Jane's eyes was almost luminous with sorrow. Then her head tipped downward like the broken stem of a flower. She moved to the fridge and opened it like a sleepwalker. "We have some nice cold fried chicken," Auntie Jane said to Uncle Phillip in a tentative voice. "Would that do?"

"Fine." He seemed agitated. He was standing in the breakfast nook staring out the window at the rear garden beyond.

Auntie Jane took a Tupperware container of chicken out of the fridge and placed it in the basket. "There's also some leftover chocolate layer cake. Would you like some of that?"

"Woman, I don't care what you put in the basket. Just pack the damn lunch and let's get on with it. I've got to return to the city later today." He turned from the window. "Excuse me." He crossed the kitchen. "I need to grab something from my study. I'll be right back." He disappeared into a room down the hall. Sarah caught a quick flash of lovely mahogany paneling and bookcases before the heavy wooden door swung shut behind him.

"Can I give you a hand, Auntie Jane?"

"No . . . no . . ." the elderly woman murmured. The color still hadn't returned to Auntie Jane's cheeks. She seemed suddenly old, shaken. The kitchen was quiet, just the sound of Auntie Jane packing a few more items into the basket, Uncle Phillip thumping around in his study, and the faintest sound of the soaring score of a children's movie playing upstairs.

A wave of melancholy swept over Sarah. She had always thought of Auntie Jane as relatively content, with a good marriage. Apparently, nothing was as it seemed. *One thing is for certain. I'm going to start shopping for a new lawyer. I refuse to have abusive people in my life. Perhaps the man is polite to me, but how he treats his wife speaks volumes.* Once her divorce was finalized, the trust her parents had set up would be dissolved. *For the time being . . .* Sarah slipped her hand into her purse and pulled out the package of M&M's. "I know we are eating soon, but . . ." Sarah shrugged and managed a grin, trying to lighten the mood. "Would you like a couple? You know, an amuse-bouche?"

"No, thank you, dear."

"Is there anything I can do to help?"

"No. Don't worry, dear. He gets like this sometimes. I'm so glad you dropped by. Seeing your face reminds me of happier times. When you smile, you look so much like your mother."

"I miss her," Sarah said softly.

"Me too." Silence fell over them. Just the distant sound of Uncle Phillip banging around in his study. Then Auntie Jane straightened her shoulders. She seemed to come to some sort of decision. "Sarah." There was an urgency in her voice. "There is something you need to know—" A door slammed, jerking both of their heads in the direction of the hallway where Phillip was fast approaching. "Later," she whispered, then busied herself with the latching of the picnic basket. She looked demure as always, the dutiful wife incarnate, but Sarah could see a stubborn set to Auntie Jane's jaw that spoke of rebellion. Sarah hoped so, not only for Auntie Jane's sake, but for the small granddaughter who was living with them as well.

56

"I'M SORRY, SIR, BUT MR. CLARKE IS NOT IN THE OF-fice at present." Mr. Clarke's secretary smiled at him perkily.

"Yes. I am aware of that," Mick replied. "Mr. Clarke is with Sarah Rainsford. I was supposed to go with her, but I got held up at a meeting."

"You must be mistaken," Hannah said helpfully. "He's not with your friend. He had to go to his home in Westchester. His wife needed his assistance with something. A plumber or gardener, I can't remember."

Mick had wiped his face in the elevator, but he couldn't do anything about the cold sweat congealing under his jacket. He kept a pleasant smile on his face even though his insides were vibrating with tension. "Ah, yes." He snapped his fingers. "That's right. I was supposed to meet them there. Mr. Clarke and his wife are contemplating selling the family home and making the apartment in New York their residence since the"—his brain scrambled through conversations with Sarah, then flashed to the photos on Phillip Clarke's desk, tossed up a Hail Mary, and went with it—"boys are grown. Sarah remembered the lovely old home from visiting as a child and wanted us to take a look at it since we are relocating here."

"Oh!" Hannah brightened, her mouth shaped into a little circle. "How wonderful. I've never seen it, but I heard it's simply beautiful."

"However, I've misplaced the address." He smiled at her with all the boyish charm he could muster. "You wouldn't happen to have it, would you?"

"I do! Here, let me write it down for you." She called up Phillip Clarke's address on her computer, scribbled it down on a piece of notepaper, then handed it to him. "There you are. Enjoy!"

"Thank you," Mick replied. "You've been so helpful." He spun on his heel and headed for the elevator.

"If you get a chance, would you let Mr. Clarke know?" he heard the secretary call after him. "I'm a new hire, and I need all the brownie points I can get."

"Absolutely," Mick called over his shoulder as he broke into a jog. He yanked out his cell phone and got to work. By the time he'd exited the building, he had a helicopter waiting to fly him to Westchester. He stepped off the curb, hailed a cab, and hopped inside. "How long will it take to get me to Pier Six? Located at South Street and Broad?" Mick asked the cabdriver.

"Twelve minutes."

"I'll give you a hundred extra if you can make it in six."

"You got it, Mister," the cabbie said with a wild look in his eyes. "Better hang on tight." As the taxi peeled out into the traffic, Mick inputted Detective Kostas's number on his phone keypad and listened to it ring. It went to voicemail. Mick called his precinct and had him paged.

57

PHILLIP SEEMED TO HAVE A CERTAIN SPOT IN MIND
because he'd had them cross the backyard at a quick clip.
They had passed the lap pool, went through a gate, and
were now tromping across an elaborate garden with an
abundance of flower beds, mature shrubs, and trees. Auntie
Jane was lugging the picnic basket. Sarah offered to help
carry it because it was clear Phillip wasn't going to assist,
but Auntie Jane waved her off. "I'm stronger than I look,"
she said. Sarah was grateful for the navy waxed rain jacket
with a quilted tartan lining Auntie Jane had draped over
Sarah's shoulders as they had followed Phillip out the back
door. The jacket was quite effective at cutting the wind.
Sarah tipped her head and rubbed her cheek against the
corduroy collar. It reminded Sarah of her mother, who had
worn the exact same raincoat but in sage green. Had she
and Auntie Jane purchased the raincoats together on one of
their famous shopping sprees? Sarah's purse was banging
against her thigh, and the weight of all the extra junk inside
was starting to make her shoulder ache.

Phillip was striding ahead of them in a businesslike

manner, as if he were Hitler inspecting the troops. His fisted hands were shoved into his sports jacket pockets, causing his elbows to poke out in an odd fashion. *Must be hard for him to march around with that stick up his ass all the time.* Sarah pulled her attention back to Auntie Jane, who had the picnic basket hugged to her chest and was huffing a little. Her cheeks were flushed. "My right hand is strong and able if you'd like to take a little break?"

"I'm fine. Truly."

"Okay. Let me know if you change your mind." They walked a little farther in silence. "Is your granddaughter going to be okay, left alone in the house?" Sarah asked.

Auntie Jane's gaze darted over to Sarah like a startled sparrow. "I . . ." Her lips parted as if the inhalation she'd just taken was trapped halfway down her throat. She blinked, then fixed her eyes on her husband's back. "I turned on *Frozen*." Auntie Jane glanced over again. "It's her favorite movie. She would watch it over and over if I let her." A sad smile graced her lips. "Listen," she whispered softly. "There is something you need to know."

Phillip turned abruptly. His eyes were cold, hawklike. "What are you two talking about?"

Sarah saw a slight tremor ripple through Auntie Jane, but she met her husband's gaze straight on. "Lilly," she said in a clear, calm voice. "A terrible misunderstanding has happened. I'm not sure how it came to pass, but it needs to be rectified."

"Bullshit." Phillip stormed over, grabbed Auntie Jane's arm. "You will tell her *nothing*," he hissed as he dragged her away from Sarah. The picnic basket tumbled from Jane's arms, the contents scattering on the ground. He stopped near a large deep hole hidden by a copse of trees. There was a good-sized northern red oak tree lying on its side. The root ball was wrapped in burlap and wire mesh. There was also a large bag of fertilizer, a spade, and a backhoe. Auntie Jane started crying, obviously upset about the fallen basket.

"Hey, dude, seriously?" Sarah dropped to her knees,

causing her injured abdomen to complain. She didn't care about the damned picnic, but clearly her aunt did. Sarah turned the basket right-side up. "Just because you're feeling crappy," Sarah said, anger flaring as she returned the fallen food to the basket, "doesn't give you the right to manhandle Auntie Jane."

"Shut up, you spoiled brat!" The viciousness in Phillip's voice jerked Sarah's attention from the fallen food to him.

"Wow," she said, getting to her feet. "Nice to know how you really feel."

"Phillip, no!" Auntie Jane cried. "Put that away. What are you doing?" And that's when Sarah noticed the snub-nosed pistol in her uncle Phillip's hand.

"Cleaning up loose ends," he replied, his pistol trained on Sarah. "I had imagined that when Kevin saw this little slut show up last night with a man she was obviously shtupping, he would have taken care of my little problem for me. No such luck. Oh well. Needs must."

It took a moment for his words to penetrate Sarah's brain. She was still trying to wrap her mind around the fact that her parents' trusted lawyer and friend appeared to be holding a gun on her. "You . . . you were the one who forced Vicki to call?" Sarah was hoping she had heard him wrong, that there was no gun and the painkillers were making her delusional.

"That's right." He rocked back on his heels with a smirk on his face, so pleased with himself.

"And it wasn't Vicki. You're the one who sicced Kevin on me."

"Ding . . . ding . . . ding . . ." He crowed like he was running a bingo hall. "We've got a winner!"

"You sonofabitch," Sarah ground out, but Phillip just grinned and did a half bow as if she had paid him a compliment. The odd thing was, Sarah discovered she wasn't scared at all. *Must be the meds.* No, she wasn't scared. She was seriously *pissed* off. "And now, oh my. Look at you. Eeek." She raised her hands in the air as she took a casual step backward, sarcasm dripping from her voice. "Bet you feel like a real big man standing behind that gun. One problem, asshole, you shoot me, how are you going to drag my body over to that hole to bury it? Notice the slight incline." She dropped her hands, using the movement to take another step back. She was still too close. Odds of survival wouldn't be good if she ran. *Five or six rounds in the pistol's chamber. At such close range, even a crappy shooter would probably make contact. Stall. Increase the distance. Then run. Serpentine.* "That's going to make your job even more difficult. Don't think your puny little arms are up to the task." He blinked. "Yeah. Good planning, big shot," she drawled. "With those inferior strategy skills, it's hard to believe my parents trusted you with their fortune. But that's the way they were, trusting and loyal to the core, and look how you repay them."

Phillip's face turned puce. "Is that right?" he sneered. "Well, I hate to burst your little rose-colored bubble, but your father was *interviewing* people to replace me. He said 'it was time for me to retire.'" He raised his hands and made quote marks with the fingers of his left hand and over the barrel of the gun with his right. "He said I was 'slipping up' 'making mistakes,' that he had noticed 'discrepancies in the accounts,'" his voice shrill and mocking. "That is who your *precious* father was. Someone who would *fire* a loyal retainer who had worked tirelessly to increase *his* net worth, who was at his beck and call, who looked after his interests *day* and *night.* And how did he plan to repay me? With *enforced* retirement! By *elbowing* me out of the way. Ageism plain and simple."

"He . . . he offered you a very generous pension, Phillip," Auntie Jane said, her voice reedy, wavering slightly.

He turned on her. "Shut up! What do you know? Nothing!" While he was distracted, Sarah took two more large steps and casually eased the strap of her purse over her head, careful not to make any sudden movement to draw his attention. She would be able to run faster if she wasn't weighed down. "My *job* was my *life.* And *he* wanted to steal it from me!" The old man was sobbing now. Sarah took another step back, her body braced, ready to run. "Your father left me *no* choice," he wailed. "He had to be dealt with."

Everything in Sarah froze. "What?" fell from her numb lips. Her chest felt like an iron fist was wrapped around her heart. "Dealt with? How?"

"Your mother wasn't supposed to be in the car." He shook his head, dragging his arm across his wet face. "She was supposed to meet Jane for an early dinner and an evening at the ballet. But *you*"—he turned on Jane with a look of disgust—"*canceled*. Had 'a headache.' You fucked up, like you always do, and thus signed the death warrant for your best friend."

And suddenly running was no longer an option. This fucker had killed her parents, and she would make him pay or die trying. She wrapped the strap of her purse around the fist of her good hand. "So, you killed my parents," she said conversationally. "I never suspected foul play." Sarah could see Auntie Jane was staring at her husband in abject horror. Jane staggered back a couple of steps, as if recoiling from the toxicity emanating from him.

"Nobody did." Phillip's face was still wet, but his chest swelled with pride. "I was tricky. Made it look like an accident."

"So, you hired the cement truck driver to make the hit?"

"Yes, siree," he said smugly. "I was surprised at how easy it was to arrange. Cheap, too." And that's when Sarah charged, the raincoat falling from her shoulders to the damp ground. She heard a shot ring out, but she'd gone low, swinging her weighted purse like a mace, making contact with his crotch. A stream of soda pop fizzed out of her purse as her belly hit the ground. Phillip screamed in pain and fury, the blow doubling him over. Sarah rolled quickly to the side as another shot rang out, sending a hunk of sod flying a few inches from her face. She'd scrambled to her feet to launch her body at him again when she was halted by the sound of a loud *thunk*. Phillip staggered, the pistol falling from his hand. Another *thunk*. Phillip's eyes rolled back in their sockets as he pitched forward, landed in the pit, and lay motionless, his neck bent at an unnatural angle.

Sarah stared down at him. "What the hell just happened?"

"I did." Sarah turned. Her auntie Jane had moved to stand beside her, the wooden handle of the shovel resting against her shoulder, a smear of blood on the spade. "I don't care if I go to jail," she said shakily, her eyes welling up. "I had to stop him." She stared into the pit at his broken body. "I . . ." She swallowed hard, as if battling back nausea, her chest rising and falling like a trapped bird. She wrenched her gaze away from her husband, but it settled on the blood-stained shovel in her hands. "Oh my Lord." She dropped the shovel in horror and backed away, wiping her hands frantically on her dungarees. "What have I done?"

Sarah took the trembling woman in her arms. "What you did, Auntie Jane"—Sarah kept her voice gentle, as if soothing an injured fawn—"took tremendous bravery. I am forever in your debt. You saved my life."

"I couldn't let him kill you. I couldn't." She clung to Sarah like a woman drowning in grief. "You are the daughter of my dearest friend and . . ." Her gut-wrenching sobs were ripping Sarah's heart asunder. "And . . ." Auntie Jane pulled back slightly and met Sarah's eyes dead-on. Breath-catching shudders had possession of her body. Tears continued to flow down her face, but there was a fierce determination as well. Auntie Jane's trembling hand rose to gently cup Sarah's face. "The mother of . . ." Auntie Jane said softly. "My precious little Lilly-girl, who has been such a ray of sunshine in this dark, bleak world."

58

SARAH STARED AT HER AUNTIE JANE, STUNNED. HER heart was thundering like a runaway horse, and she could hear the seashore in her ears. "You need to sit down, dear." Auntie Jane's voice seemed to be coming from far away. "You look pale. The shock. I understand." Typical. Auntie Jane was still crying, but Sarah could feel her gentle hands guiding Sarah to a sitting position. "Put your head down between your knees . . . There you go . . . Take deep breaths, nice and slow." Sarah could see both of their feet dangling in the pit above her uncle Phillip's body, could feel Auntie Jane's hand making shaky circles on her back as Sarah gulped in air. She noticed a small clod of dirt falling from her shoe onto Phillip's cheek and then rolling off to join its brethren dirt clods, leaving a streak behind. The skies opened up, and it started to rain, and still they stayed, feet dangling, breathing in the smell of wet earth, and being alive, and freedom.

Once Sarah had managed to catch her breath and the dizziness had subsided, she lay back and stared at the gray skies overhead. "My daughter, you say?" Sarah said, breaking the silence now that her heart was beating properly again. "That beautiful little girl who is in your house right now watching *Frozen* . . . she's my daughter?"

Auntie Jane leaned back on her elbows and looked sky-ward as well. "Yes. And she is a wonderful child, loving and kind. Smart as a whip. Generous. Everything a mother could desire."

Sarah rolled on her side to face her. "I thought she hadn't made it. I was told she died."

"I realized that today, coming back from taking Lilly upstairs. I overheard you talking with my husband about your desire for children, and the world as I knew it came crashing down around my shoulders. You see, my dear." Sarah felt Auntie Jane's weathered hand cover hers. "Phillip had told me you didn't want to be a mother, refused to see your own baby or hold her. He told me that Kevin was abusive and that you hated everything to do with him, including your baby. You needed us to bring money, were running away. Refused to take refuge with us, because we were the first place that Kevin would look. That you were terrified at what he would do to us. And Phillip told me you'd instructed him to put Lilly up for adoption."

"I never would have left her behind. I wanted her *so* very much."

"I know that now. When we arrived at the hospital, Phillip insisted that I not mention the baby to you. He said you'd been through a terrible ordeal, and talking about it would only distress you further. When I entered your hospital room, I fully intended to disregard his orders, but when I saw your face." She shook her head, lost in the past. "Sarah, my heart broke to see you that way. There were so many bruises and such a weary bleakness in your eyes. I figured the beating, the premature birth of your baby on the heels of the strain of your parents' untimely deaths had been too much for you. When we left the hospital, we took the baby with us. In hindsight, I'm not sure how he managed that."

"He had legal and medical power of attorney," Sarah said. She could feel the raindrops cleansing the past. "Must have paid someone off, or convinced them I was mentally unsound."

"But why? Why would Phillip do such a thing?"

Sarah laughed, the sound bright as a bird in flight, feeling oddly happier and lighter than she had in years. "Money. Pure and simple. My parents left a huge estate behind. When I disappeared, that was a huge boon for Phillip because Kevin had no access or control over the estate. He just received a monthly stipend. If I was dead and had no heirs—that's where getting rid of Lilly came in—for Phillip it would be even better. That would give your husband unfettered access to do what he liked with the funds from the estate for the rest of his life, with very few checks and balances."

Auntie Jane nodded. "That's it. He was always jealous of your father. Why did I believe him?"

"He was your husband. Of course you believed him. But why didn't the doctor at the hospital tell me Lilly had survived?"

"Phillip must have given him the same spiel he told me. He *was* your legal and medical representative. Or it's possible the doctor was corrupt and Phillip bribed him. Who knows? But I should have known better. Rather than handing over the envelope of money he told me you'd asked for so you could run, I should have found a way to discuss the baby with you. Should have made sure." Auntie Jane exhaled deeply. "Anyway, I refused to let him take Lilly to a safe haven drop-off location to put her up for adoption. I insisted we take her home and raise her as our own. She was Barbara's granddaughter. Barbara had been so delighted that she was going to have a granddaughter to dote on. I just couldn't let Lilly be raised by strangers. In the back of my mind, there was the belief that perhaps you were suffering with postpartum depression and that in a week or two you would find a way to come and see me. I'd ply you with tea, you'd tell me you regretted your decision, I'd produce Lilly, and all would be well. But you never came."

"I'm here now," Sarah said softly.

"Yes, you are." Auntie Jane's face was filled with a quiet joy, and wistful, too. "Do you want to go meet your daughter?"

"Oh yes." Sarah's words came out almost as a prayer. "So very much." They got to their feet, helping each other so they didn't slip in the wet mud. They gathered the borrowed raincoat, the scattered picnic items, and the two of them headed back to the house.

59

AUNTIE JANE HAD TUCKED A SOFT THROW BLANKET around Sarah's shoulders. She had spread a dish towel over her lap and handed her another one, which Sarah tucked into the top of her blouse before Lilly climbed onto her lap. Sarah would take a shower later, but her daughter's little body was nestled into her. Sarah's arms were holding her child for the very first time, and she was wrestling back tears of joy. Lilly gently glided her finger over Sarah's bandaged left hand.

"You have a bad boo-boo?"

"Not too bad," Sarah replied. "Just have to be careful not to bump it is all."

"You guys are muddy." Lilly grinned mischievously, as if she'd caught them being naughty.

"We're super muddy," Sarah replied.

"Were you making mud pies?" Lilly asked.

"No. I make really good ones though. We'll have to do that someday."

"I like making mud pies." Lilly reached up and patted Sarah's cheek. "And I like *you*."

"I like you, too, honey." Sarah's voice was thick with emotion. Auntie Jane was bustling around the kitchen, keeping her hands busy while they waited for the police, brewing a pot of tea, and placing butter cookies with rainbow-colored sprinkles onto a plate. Lilly snuggled in. Sarah bit her lip from the pain of the warm little body pressing on her injured abdomen, but she wouldn't have shifted her precious daughter for the world. Lilly plopped her thumb into her mouth and sucked contentedly as she smoothed a corner of the dish towel between her tiny fingers. Sarah bent her head and inhaled, filling her lungs and her being with the fresh scent of Lilly's downy soft hair and the warm wiggling sweetness of her child's little body. "My child," Sarah murmured, and suddenly she was filled with awe and wonder and the glory of God. She raised her eyes and met Auntie Jane's gentle gaze over Lilly's head, sharing with her the preciousness of the moment, the sheer simplicity and the beauty of the pleasure. *Thank you*, she mouthed. Auntie Jane inclined her head and placed her hand over her heart.

Lilly's thumb popped out of her mouth. "What's that noise?" she asked, her head tipping like an inquisitive baby chick.

"What noise?" Sarah asked.

"That noise," Lilly said, gesturing toward the ceiling with her wet thumb. And then Sarah heard it, the sound of helicopter blades overhead, getting louder and louder.

Auntie Jane froze, teapot in her hand. "The police," she whispered, all the color draining from her face. "They've come for me."

"The what?" Lilly asked, looking from back and forth between the two of them.

"Maybe not," Sarah said, but she knew she was probably whistling in the wind, because the sound of the helicopter was now a deafening roar. "Does one of your neighbors own a helicopter and commute from the city?"

Auntie Jane shook her head. There was the sound of running feet, pounding at the door. Auntie Jane gently placed the teapot down. Straightened her spine and sailed into the main hall as if she were in a comportment class and had a stack of books on her head. *Never mind that she's muddy as hell,* Sarah thought, unable to hold back the smile even though the consequences were dire. *Mother was right when she said Auntie Jane had class bred into the very marrow of her bones. Well* . . . Sarah stood and plopped Lilly on the chair. There was no way she was going to let Auntie Jane deal with the police on her own. "You stay here, okay? I've got to go talk to the people at the door for a second." She dug into her sticky soda-soaked purse. Her fingers closed around the little mason jar of gummy bears. She pulled it out, tore off the plastic seal, opened it, and placed it on the table in front of her daughter. "You see that clock on the wall?"

"Yes."

"You see the big hand?"

"I can tell time," Lilly said proudly.

"Wonderful. This is what I need you to do." Sarah reached across the table and slid the scattered crayons and paper over to Lilly. "While you are drawing, out of the corner of your eye, I'd like you to keep an eye on the clock for me. When the big hand moves to the next number, then you get to gobble up a gummy bear."

Lilly's little face lit up. "Okay," she said with a happy wiggle. "You can count on me."

"Wonderful!" Sarah dropped a kiss on the top of Lilly's head. The little girl already had a purple crayon clenched in her fist. "Stay put. I'll be back in a jiffy," Sarah said, and then swiftly left the room. She could see the slender figure of her aunt at the end of the hall, her hand on the door. "Wait for me," Sarah called, but her voice was drowned out by another thundering volley of knocks.

60

THE DOOR FELL AWAY FROM MICK'S FIST. STANDING in the opening was a fragile-looking elderly woman. Her gaze skittered past him, taking in the helicopter on the front lawn. It seemed as if she had expected to see something else. Something unwanted. Her shoulders relaxed slightly. "Yes?" she said in a cultured mid-Atlantic accent. "May I help you?" The woman reminded him of Sarah, how she carried herself like royalty despite the fact that there were streaks of mud across her face, on her knees and thighs.

"I was told Sarah Rainsford is here." Mick had to work to keep his voice steady, when all he wanted to do was charge inside and rip the place apart until he found her. "I've come to fetch her."

"And you are?" the woman asked as protective as a mother bear, but who was she protecting? Phillip Clarke? Was Sarah okay? Was she safe? Suddenly Sarah appeared behind the woman, her hand settling on the woman's shoulder, and relief tore through Mick like a flash flood.

"Mick." Sarah smiled. Her warm gaze alighting on him made him feel like he was standing in the midst of a brilliant rainbow bathing him in love. He swore he could hear birds start chirping in the trees like some cheesy soundtrack. "What are you doing here?"

Mick suddenly felt a little foolish. *What am I doing here? Sarah is obviously fine.* "I . . . uh . . ." he said. "I had a feeling, was scared you were in danger, so I tore out of the police station like a madman, went to the hotel, Phillip's office, and ended up here." But instead of laughing at his imaginings, Sarah got misty-eyed.

"Mick," she said. She stepped forward, and he wrapped her in his arms, no matter that her clothes were soaking wet, covered in mud, and she had a tea towel tucked in the neck of her blouse like a bib. She nuzzled her muddy face into his neck and inhaled deeply. "Thank you. You are such a sweetheart, racing here to try to save me. Did you hire that helicopter?"

"Yeah."

She beamed at him. "You're the best. I'm so glad you're here. There is so much to tell you! So much has happened, but first"—Sarah gestured to the elderly woman behind her—"there are a couple of people I want you to meet. Mick, this is my auntie Jane. Jane, this is Mick."

"Lovely to meet you," her aunt said. Sarah's aunt seemed to be a real sweetheart.

Sarah tugged his hand. "There's someone else I need to introduce you to. Come inside." Her eyes were sparkling like the brightest of sapphires, full of joy and love. And he didn't want to tamp it down, but there were things she needed to know.

"Wait. Sarah." Mick glanced over her shoulder down the hall. No telling where in the house Phillip was, but if his suspicions were founded, Sarah might be in danger. "We need to talk first."

She looked bemused. "Out here in the rain? Wouldn't it be nicer inside with a warm cup of tea?"

"It's about Phillip," Mick said. "I was at the police station and—"

A low moan escaped the older woman's lips. "Oh no.

What else has he done . . . ?" Her elegant posture had evaporated. Her chest was caved inward slightly, as if the weight of the world had descended upon her shoulders.

"I'm not sure, ma'am, but I . . ." Mick turned to Sarah. "I'm concerned," he said, not wanting to worry the older woman unnecessarily. "I was thinking about last night. When the police first arrived at Vicki's house, they took Kevin and me to different areas to question us. But I overheard a little. The man can yell pretty loud."

"Tell me about it." Sarah rolled her eyes.

"Anyway, sitting there in the police station after you left, a few questions started niggling at me with regard to Vicki."

"I didn't get a chance to tell you before you popped me in that taxi, but Detective Docherty told me she died at the hospital. They believe she was poisoned. They're waiting to get confirmation from the lab."

Mick nodded. "That ties into what I was thinking as well."

Sarah's aunt took a half step back, clearly stunned. "Vicki's . . . dead? Oh, dear Lord . . ."

"I'm sorry, Auntie Jane," Sarah said. "Everything happened so fast, I didn't get a chance to tell you."

"Oh no . . . Poor Vicki." The elderly woman started to weep. "Phillip killed her, didn't he? My husband was a monster. How could I have lived with him for all these years and not known the depths of his depravity?"

The woman was obviously very distraught. "I'm sorry, ma'am. Didn't mean to cast aspersions. Nothing's for certain. However, I did contact one of the detectives who are looking into the matter. They should be here shortly to speak with your husband. A few questions have popped up is all—"

"No." Sarah's aunt's voice was bitter, but it carried the ring of conviction. "He killed Vicki, all right. Just like he murdered Ryan and Barbara in cold blood, and he would have killed Sarah if we hadn't stopped him."

Mick felt as if someone had poured a keg of liquid nitrogen over his head. Took a moment to unfreeze his brain, his ears, and his lips. "I'm sorry, *what*?" he said slowly. "Come again?"

"That's what I wanted to talk with you about," Sarah said. "Come inside where it's warm. We're having a cup of tea while we wait for the police to arrive."

61

THE MYTHICAL CUP OF HOT TEA NEVER MATERIAL-
ized. No sooner had they shut the front door than a plethora
of cop cars squealed into the circular drive with their lights
flashing and sirens wailing. When Sarah peered out the
window, an officer's voice came blaring over the PA system, ordering her to "step outside with her hands up." She
complied. However, Mick and Auntie Jane exited with her,
complicating the matter. She didn't know where to look.
There were so many police officers. They were spread
out, their guns yanked from their holsters and trained on
the three of them. Another cop was in ready stance, super-
vising Mick's helicopter pilot's descent from the aircraft.
The pilot nonchalantly swung out of the helicopter cabin as
if gun-wielding police were a daily occurrence. "Are any of
you armed?" The policeman's voice boomed over the PA
system, startling Auntie Jane, who emitted a little shriek,
her hands fluttering like autumn leaves into the air.

"No," Sarah said, her voice clear and strong. Determined not to be scared, to never cower before a member of
the police force again. "None of us are."

"What about you, sir?" came over the PA, as if Sarah's answer was suspect.

"I'm unarmed," Mick replied, all three of them keeping their hands in the air. "What is this about?"

"And you, ma'am?" the police on the PA asked, as if Mick hadn't asked a question.

"No. I'm not packing a gun," Auntie Jane quavered. Under normal circumstances, Sarah would have found that statement from her sweet little aunt hilarious. "Or anything else that could do bodily damage." And suddenly Sarah's mind flashed to Phillip's body with its bashed-in head, and the humor of the situation vanished. She and Auntie Jane were in deep shit.

"We received a report that shots were fired at this location. Which of you fired the shots?"

"None of us fired any weapons," Sarah replied. "Officer, we called 911. Maybe someone else called in as well—"

"Is the shooter inside?"

"No," Sarah said. She refused to be scared even with all the saliva in her mouth having beaten a hasty retreat. "He's in the back garden—"

"Secure the area," the head cop yelled with a jerk of his head. Some of the cops started moving; others stayed where they were, guns still trained on the three of them.

"The shooter is—" Sarah started to explain, but the front doorknob rattled. "There's a child inside. Please, put away your weapons. You're going to scare her!"

"Get down on the ground," the cop on the PA boomed. "Hands behind your head." It was a little more difficult than it sounded, getting facedown on the ground with one's hands in the air. Sarah managed, but she was pretty sure there were going to be colorful bruises on her elbows, and it was extremely uncomfortable given the recent burn marks on her stomach. Several cops had swiveled. Their weapons were now trained on the opening door.

"Please, I beg you, put your weapons away." The police didn't move from their ready stance. "Lilly!" Sarah called.

"Shut the door. Stay inside!" She didn't hear the door shut, but she was praying that Lilly hadn't come outside.

"Mommy?" Lilly's voice piped up. Sarah's heart stopped. *Oh God. Lilly is on the front stoop.* And on the heels of that horror came an odd sort of joy. *She called me Mommy. We didn't have a chance to tell her. How does she know?* But then Lilly padded over to Auntie Jane. "Mommy, why are you lying on the ground? Is this a game?" And then Lilly carefully lay down on the circular driveway between Auntie Jane—whose face was looking a little gray—and Sarah, and with an angelic smile, Lilly put her chubby little child arms behind her head, too.

62

"I STILL CAN'T BELIEVE THEY DIDN'T ARREST ME,"
Sarah's aunt Jane said for the millionth time that week.

"If they had, Auntie Jane"—Lilly had picked up on the
change of names and status with remarkable ease—"we
would have come to visit you, and I'd have let you have my
favorite blanket to comfort you so you wouldn't be scared."

Jane chuckled and covered Lilly's little hand with hers.
"You're such a little character. Thank you, Lilly. Luckily,
there was no need for such heroics."

Mick looked at the faces of the people seated around the
dining room table in the Four Seasons Gotham suite. *Family,* he thought. *This is what it's like to have a family.* They
were having a quick bite of pizza before heading out to the
New York premiere of *Retribution.* Last week, after the
police had vacated her home, Jane had fallen apart. Sarah
had decided that it would be too anxiety-producing for Jane
to stay in the Westchester home. "You'll come back to the
hotel with us," Sarah had declared. "Mick, honey, call the
hotel and sort something out." So he had. They'd packed
the helicopter to the gills and returned to Manhattan with

Sarah's daughter, Lilly, and her aunt Jane in tow. The amount of luggage that was required for Sarah's aunt and one small child boggled the mind. On the LA side, turned out, Bob the intern was a cat person and was happily ensconced on the pullout sofa bed in Sarah's apartment so Charlie wouldn't have to acclimate to a new person *and* a new place.

For the first few days Jane had clearly been in shock. Mick didn't blame her. In the course of an afternoon, Jane not only had killed her husband of almost forty years but also learned he had murdered her best friend. Add to the mix the murder of her best friend's husband, the attempted murder of Sarah, and the possible murder of his secretary and lover for the last twenty-eight years . . . It was a lot to take in. Jane's elder son, Daniel, had flown in with his wife, Kendra, on Saturday. Stephan, the younger son, arrived on Monday, which had helped enormously. They had rallied around Jane, shored her up, and dealt with the funeral arrangements. Burial. No service. Just Jane, her sons, Sarah, and Mick. Jane had been quite adamant that Lilly not attend. So, Flora, Lilly's devoted nanny, took her to the Transit Museum, which was followed by a visit to A La Mode Shoppe for an ice cream sundae with all the fixings. After Phillip had been laid to rest, Jane seemed much better, as if a burden had been lifted from her shoulders. The color returned to her face, she wasn't weeping anymore, and Mick no longer had to keep a fat wad of clean tissues at the ready.

"The police felt it was an open-and-shut case of self-defense," Sarah said for the umpteenth time as she helped herself to another slice of oozy gooey burrata pizza. "You saved my life." Mick folded his third slice of pepperoni and bit into the tomatoey, cheesy, spicy goodness. *It's true. New York pizza is the best. The crust has just the right amount of chew and crisp, a texture thing.* He was glad Jane's offspring had declined to join them for pizza and had gone to the restaurant downstairs for dinner. *More tasty goodness for me.* Mick had gotten Jane's family tickets to the premiere, the after-party, and had arranged transportation, which gave them the freedom to come and go as they wished. Many people imagined these shindigs to be glamourous affairs, but generally it was just a lot of in-house schmoozing and boring as hell.

"I like pizza," Lilly chimed in. The kid sure packed a lot of food into her small little body. She had single-handedly devoured almost an entire margarita pizza.

"Last night," Jane continued. "As I was lying in bed, it suddenly crossed my mind that perhaps after Phillip had knocked you off, he was going to do away with me. Plant us both under that northern red oak tree."

"I'm sure he wouldn't have, Auntie Jane," Sarah said firmly, but Mick knew her well enough to know she wasn't so certain.

"I don't know about that." Jane shook her head. She thought about it for a moment and then shrugged, like it was of no more consequence than whether one preferred trout to bass. "By the way, I've decided I want a fresh start. I'm going to sell both the New York apartment and our home in Westchester."

"They do say that you shouldn't make any big life-changing decisions for the first six months after a death in the family," Sarah said, handing Lilly the final slice of margarita.

"In normal circumstances, yes. However, I think this"—Jane swirled her hands in the air—"requires an entirely different approach. Those places are permeated with him, with memories, his things, his temper tantrums. It's my turn now." Jane dabbed her mouth daintily with her napkin and then stood, shoulders back, her chin held high. "I'm not going to wait another day to begin my life anew. I am going to get dressed to the nines and go to your fancy premiere. And I intend to *enjoy* myself. What a novelty it will be to socialize without feeling Phillip's disapproving glare at my back, always kicking me under the table or jabbing his bony elbow into my ribs. I hated that. Never could relax. Always watching my words. As if he were the great arbitrator of what constituted appropriate conversation."

"He was a mean old man," Lilly said with a scowl, which was so ferocious it made everyone laugh.

The doorbell rang. "That will be Flora." Sarah was still chuckling as she rose, crossed the room, and opened the front door of the suite.

"Flora!" Lilly hopped out of her chair. She ran over to her nanny and tugged on her hand. "Come on in. We're having pizza!"

"I can see that," Flora replied, laughing affectionately down at Lilly's sauce-smeared face.

"We have plenty." Sarah waved her hand toward the dining table laden with pizza boxes. "Help yourself."

"Hi, Flora," Jane said, dabbing her napkin against her lips. "Thanks for taking the train in." She pushed away from the table. "Well, I'm off to get beautified for the big night. Wish me luck! After all that pizza, I hope I don't have difficulty squeezing into that glorious dress Sarah made me buy." Smiling happily, Jane blew Sarah and Lilly kisses, wiggled her fingers at Mick, and then disappeared into her bedroom.

"WHAT ARE YOU GRINNING ABOUT?" SARAH ASKED as she stepped out of the shower and wrapped herself in one of the hotel's big robes. He would need to purchase a couple of those robes to bring home, as the sight of Sarah in one conjured memories of the very first time they'd made love. The stitches in her hand had been removed that morning, and throughout her shower, she had kept up a running commentary about how wonderful it was to no longer have to wear the protective covering while bathing. How grateful she was that her abdomen was healing so nicely, and that she was finally able to withstand warmer water and what a blessing it was. And all the while his heart was full to overflowing listening to her happy chatter about all the good in her life, this woman, who had been to hell and back, talking about blessings. No wonder he loved her.

"What?" Sarah nudged him with her hip. "Are you laughing because I look goofy?"

"No." Sarah was wearing a shower cap to protect her new haircut for tonight, but that wasn't why he was grinning.

"You look too pleased with yourself," she murmured, wrapping her arms around his waist from behind, nuzzling his neck. "You've got to be up to some kind of mischief."

"I can't tell you." He turned from the mirror, where he'd been halfway through shaving.

"No secrets," she said, tugging on his towel, both of them remembering what had happened the last time she'd done that. However, things were different. They were getting ready to go to his premiere and couldn't be late. Lilly was sprawled on her belly in the next room playing a rousing game of old maid with Flora. "Tell me," Sarah demanded as imperious as a queen, which just made him burn for her even hotter.

"Later."

"No. I can't wait until later, when your eyes are dancing with such suppressed glee. I'll die of curiosity. And besides, what if you forget what you were thinking about?"

"All right," Mick said. "But I don't want to hear any complaints about this later. Shut your eyes." Sarah shut her eyes, a huge smile on her face, and Mick thought his heart would burst into a million pieces, he loved her that much. "Keep them closed until I tell you to open them." She nodded, and there was something of Lilly in her face as she stood there, her eyes shut, trusting him totally. Mick opened the bathroom drawer and removed the ring box from where he had hastily stuffed it when he heard Sarah's footsteps approaching the bathroom. Mashing the iconic Tiffany Blue shopping bag that held his other purchases as well. Earlier, when he had slammed the bathroom drawer shut, a tiny corner of blue got caught. He had quickly covered it with his knee. Once Sarah was in the shower, he had slid the drawer open a crack and crammed the telltale scrap of blue inside while Sarah's back was turned.

"I heard rustling," Sarah had said. And for the first time in his life, Mick knew what the joy and anticipation of Christmas felt like, and waves of gratitude welled over him and made his heart ache with joy and his eyes hot. He flipped the ring box open with his thumb as he lowered himself to one knee.

"Open your eyes," he said softly.

She opened her eyes. "Oh . . . oh . . . oh . . ." Sarah whispered softly, bouncing up and down, her hands to her mouth almost as if she were in prayer.

"Sarah Audrey Rainsford, you have lit up my world. What was once a palette of grays and beige now has every color of the rainbow and then some. I never knew what love was before you. I'd never known it was possible, and yet I find myself so very deeply in love with you. I love you more than breath itself. And I am hoping and praying that you will be willing to do me the great honor of accepting my hand in holy matrimony?"

The next thing Mick knew, Sarah was on her knees, too, her arms wrapped around his neck, her mouth on his, passionate and tender all at once. "Yes," she murmured, kissing his cheeks, the tip of his nose, his eyelids. "Yes. Yes. A million yeses. I love you so much, Mick, sometimes I think my heart is going to explode." And then her warm mouth found his again.

The bathroom door flung open. "Why are you guys crying and kneeling on the floor?" And there was Lilly standing in the doorway.

Sarah stretched out her arm, and Lilly pattered over and nestled into the hug. "We're crying because we are happy," Sarah said. "Mick has asked me to marry him, and I said yes."

"Does that mean you would be my daddy?" Lilly's buttercup face tilted back so she could see him.

Mick's gaze captured Sarah's, wanting so much, but taking his cue from her. Sarah smiled softly and gave a slight nod. Mick let out the breath he was holding. "I would be"—

his voice had gone gruff with emotion—"so honored for you to be my little girl."

"Good. I'd like that," Lilly said, as if life were that simple. And sometimes it was. Then she leaned her tiny body against the two of them and plopped her thumb into her mouth. And somehow, at that moment, kneeling on the wet bathroom floor, his arms around his new family, he felt like he had come full circle and it was the absolutely perfect place to have gotten engaged.

TWO HOURS LATER THE LIMO PULLED UP IN FRONT of the theater. The red carpet was rolled out, cameras were flashing as the stars posed for the paparazzi and the press. Farther down the line were the camera crews from the entertainment channels. "You ready?" Mick asked. Sarah nodded, her eyes warm with love. She looked sensational in a midnight-blue silk sheath dress she had purchased on a shopping trip with Lilly and Jane. It clung to her curves and accentuated her lean body and her endless legs. Her hair no longer looked like a lawn mower had rolled over her head while she was sleeping. The Soho hair salon had transformed it into a chic pixie cut with an edge. She was wearing the diamond opera necklace he'd purchased at Tiffany & Co. Sarah had tied it in a knot, which bumped gently between her breasts as the long, looped strand of diamonds swayed and sparkled. Mick's gaze traveled to the two rose-gold slender bangles and the delicate whisper-thin diamond one on her elegant left wrist. His gaze traveled farther past her healing hand, to the brilliant flawless 3.2 carat diamond on her ring finger, which seemed to float above the simple platinum band, twinkling and sparkling at him, promising family and happiness and forever. He had planned to set the stage for the proposal: music, rose petals, chocolates, and champagne . . . He shook his head and smiled. *The best-made plans laid low by a simple question.*

"How about you, Auntie Jane?" Sarah's voice pulled

Mick's attention back to the present. "Are you ready to face the madding crowd?"

Jane's beatific smile included both of them. "Let the games begin." The chauffeur got out, rounded the car, and opened the door. The second Mick exited, the cameras started flashing and the shouting began. "Mick!" "Mick Talford!" "Look over here!" He ignored them and helped first Jane and then Sarah, his wife-to-be, out of the limo. The two women slipped their hands through his crooked arms. He could feel the gentle weight of them resting against the black silk of his Tom Ford Shelton suit.

"Mick, my man!" His producer Paul rushed over, grabbed Mick's face, and standing on tiptoes, managed to lay a loud kiss on each cheek. The camera flashed.

"Again!" the photographers cried. "Look this way!"

"Don't even," Mick said to Peterson, who was starting to rise onto his tiptoes again. Peterson shrugged good-naturedly. "Paul, I'd like you to meet my fiancée, Sarah Rainsford, and her aunt, Jane Clarke."

"Harris," Jane said. "I've decided to reclaim my maiden name."

"Hello, ladies," Peterson said, sweeping into a Shake-spearian bow. "Paul Peterson at your service. You've snagged a good one." He gave Sarah a wink and a nudge. "Never thought I'd see Mick Talford, the bad boy of Hollywood, settling down. Speaking of . . ." He turned back to Mick. "You're *never* gonna believe my good fortune. I'm in the clear! The police got a confession out of some guy in New York. Thank God. I've been dealing with an absolute nightmare while you wiled the days away on a fuckin' vacation." He turned to Jane. "Excuse my French." His eyes widened as he took her in. "Hey, *Mick*ster! How come you get two beautiful ladies on your arm and I've got none?" He looped his arm through Jane's and gazed admiringly into her eyes. "Pure East Coast class, born and bred. That's what I'm missing in my life. Are you married, sweetheart?" Jane shook her head, her eyes twinkling. Her lip caught between her teeth as if she were holding back laughter.

Sarah was nestled next to Mick. He could feel the suppressed laughter shaking her slender frame. "Hmm . . . Don't think he's quite what Auntie Jane had in mind for her new beginning," Sarah murmured.

"And you're the perfect height, too!" Peterson continued happily. "I need an old broad. I'm so damned tired of chasing after women half my age and twice as tall as me. Always come home empty-handed, with blue balls and a crick in my neck." That comment was the tipping point that broke the dam, and Sarah and Jane burst into laughter. There was a frenzy of flashes from behind the area cordoned off with a red velvet rope.

After the laughter subsided, the four of them walked the red carpet together, and many posed photos were taken, both before the screening and at the after-party, while Jane's sons futilely attempted to shield their "delicate" mother from Peterson's avid attentions.

THE POUCH ARRIVED FROM THE STUDIO WHILE MICK and Sarah were lounging lazily in bed, enjoying breakfast in bed, buttery croissants with raspberry jam, hot coffee, and yogurt with fresh fruit and granola. Lilly was bouncing around the room describing in great detail every millisecond of the plot of *Frozen*. "Umm . . ." Mick said, only half listening as he slit open the pouch and pulled out the trades, clippings of reviews, and the overnight box office numbers and flipped through them, scanning the contents. *Retribution* was dominating, was more than double that of the closest competitor. If the momentum carried through the weekend, his movie would break box office opening-weekend records. *Not bad,* Mick thought, and for the first time ever he discovered he could enjoy the ride without worrying about when the inevitable wall would hit. *Why is that?* He glanced over at Sarah, who was listening to her daughter's recital with a contented smile on her face, and suddenly he knew why he had enjoyed last night so much. *Because it's not all you have.* Sarah loved him for the man

he was, warts and all. Lilly did, too. Neither of them had
seen his movies before they had found him worthy of their
love. He had a life outside of making films, a steady ballast
in the storm, and it made a world of difference. Mick was
gathering the clippings. His thoughts had already turned
to their plans for the day. Jane's son Daniel had called,
thanked Mick again for inviting them to *Retribution*,
and then asked to speak with Sarah. When Sarah had hung
up the phone, he knew she had gotten good news because
joy was radiating from every pore of her body. While de-
cluttering their parents' New York apartment so it could be
put on the market, Daniel and Stephan had discovered a
floor safe in their father's office, hidden under a rug beneath the desk. Inside were Sarah's files, her missing ID,
and labeled keys to the Rainsford family properties.

Sarah didn't even have to ask. She just looked at him
with glowing eyes, and he picked up the phone and pushed
their return flight to LA. So instead of heading to the airport, they would be tromping around Sarah's childhood
homes. Mick started to slide the clippings back into the
pouch when Sarah's hand alighted on his. "What's this?"
she asked, nestling close, peeking over his shoulder.

"It's a photo of Auntie Jane," Lilly piped up as she clam-
bered onto the bed.

"It certainly is," said Sarah, grinning, as she tucked her
daughter into the crook of her arm.

"And there you are, Mommy. You look so pretty. Daddy
does, too. But why did that funny-looking man squeeze into
your picture? Do you think he's a leprechaun in disguise?"
And suddenly Mick and Sarah were laughing again, because out of all of the photos the press could have used, the
photo that ended up gracing the entertainment pages was
Mick, Sarah, and Jane, their heads thrown back in hoots of
laughter, Peterson looking like a puzzled little gnome,
scratching the fringe of hair above his ear with a bemused
expression on his face.

"Anything is possible," Mick said, still chuckling. "I'm
living proof of that."

Lilly looked at him, her eyes widening. "You're magic?"

"No, sweetheart," he said, ruffling Lilly's hair affectionately as he smiled at Sarah over Lilly's head. "But I feel"—he paused, emotion, gratitude welling up—"like I've stepped into a fairy-tale world, complete with the family I didn't know I longed for. A life I didn't know to wish for. I am such a lucky bugger, and I promise never to take the blessing of you for granted."

ACKNOWLEDGMENTS

I want to start off by thanking my readers, my Cozy Tea Timers, and all the librarians and booksellers for your support. Thank you for taking a chance on me and my books, for putting my books in readers' hands, for writing reviews and sharing my offerings with other like-minded readers. I put my heart into my writing, and the kindness you have shown fills me with gratitude. Thank you.

One of the enormous blessings of recent years is the friendships I have been gifted with while writing in this genre that I've read for decades. And yes, I felt like I already knew these authors through their wonderful books long before I met them in person. Never in my wildest dreams would I have imagined these heroes of mine would become personal friends who would help guide and advise me through these new-to-me waters. My heartfelt love and thanks to Mary Bly/Eloisa James, Jayne Ann Krentz/Jayne Castle/Amanda Quick, Susan Elizabeth Phillips, Christina Dodd, Mariah Stewart, and Jill Shalvis.

Speaking of friendships, thank you, Cissy Hartley, Susan Simpson from Writerspace, and Nancy Berland at NBPR, for all that you do on my behalf, for the shared laughs and meals, and for helping blow up and deflate *all those air mattresses* at Book Lovers Con! All of us sweating like dogs as we stomped, rolled, and laughed our guts out trying to get the air out of those damned things! Thank you to Degan and Celeste as well.

To my brilliant editors Kerry Donovan and Cindy Hwang, thank you so much! *The Runaway Heiress* is so much better because of your insights and editorial questions and comments. I'd also like to thank the rest of the team at Jove/Penguin Random House, including Michelle Kasper and Mary Geren for catching the multitude of slipups that had snuck past me, and the design crew. A shout-out to Katie Anderson for her art direction and Jeff Miller for his design. They created such a gorgeous cover for *The Runaway Heiress* that it stopped my heart. And thank you to George Towne for the great interior design. I am grateful for the marketing and publicity expertise of Erin Galloway, Jin Yu, Jessica Brock, Stephanie Felty, and Fareeda Bullert, who sort out the battle plan to get eyes on my books. My thanks also to Linda Korn and Leeza Watstein at PRH Audio for creating the wonderful audio recording of my books for those who prefer to experience the worlds I create through sound.

Special thanks to my agents, Kim Witherspoon and Jessica Mileo at InkWell Management, for your encouragement and help with this manuscript. When Mick started rolling out on the page, I was a little surprised, to say the least. And how the heck were my readers going to be able to follow a heroine who had three different names? I sent you the first pages, wondering if I should toss this unruly pair in the garbage heap or keep going. Luckily, you both voted for the latter, with a few helpful comments and tweaks. You gave me confidence, shored me up, and I am so glad, because I really, really, really love this book!

And last but not least, my love and thanks to my husband, Don, and my family and lifelong friends who fill my heart and day-to-day life with thanksgiving and joy.

Thank you, all!

Much love,
Meg xo

Don't miss

SOLACE ISLAND

by Meg Tilly

Available now!
Continue reading for a preview.

1

MAGGIE HARRIS HAD HER CELL PHONE JAMMED against her right ear, a finger stuffed in her left, but still, Brett's voice was an indistinct murmur. "Sorry, honey. Could you please speak a little louder? It's kind of noisy in here."

That was an understatement. The club was packed with writhing, sweaty bodies undulating to the pounding pulse of the music, not to mention the shrieking laughter of her eight bridesmaids and assorted female family members and friends.

Maggie felt a tug on her arm. It was Carol Endercott from the office, who had been knocking back shooters since they had arrived an hour ago. Maggie didn't know her well, but the woman's husband had walked out on her and their kid after ten years of wedded bliss. Probably not the best person to invite to one's bachelorette party; however, Carol had overheard Maggie and Sarah making plans and Maggie hadn't had the heart not to include her.

"Magsters," Carol slurred, leaning close, stumbling

slightly. "Come on, girl, off za phone. It's pardy time!" She wore a big, sloppy smile, her mascara was smeared, and wisps of frizzy blond hair clung to her perspiring face. "Let's have fuuun!" she bellowed like an elephant in heat.

Maggie held up a finger. *One moment, Carol,* she mouthed. *It's Brett.*

"Ooooh," Carol said, throwing up her hands and tiptoeing backward, eyes wide, like a cartoon character removing herself from a bomb site. "The luuuvebirds. I bettah give you some privacy, seeing as how yer talkin' to za *fab*ulous Mr. Nolan!"

"Yes, well . . ." Maggie smiled at Carol. "Thanks. I think I'll just . . ." She tipped her head toward the bathrooms and started moving past Carol.

"Good idea!" Carol said, giving Maggie a crazy-hard nudge in the ribs and an attempt at a wink. "I'll tell the gang you're in za potski having phone sex, so they won't barge in at an inopportune moment," she bleated, and lurched off.

"Jeez," Maggie said, watching her leave. "I am very grateful not to have a drinking problem."

"Huh?"

"Nothing, Brett. Hang on a second," Maggie said. She started weaving her way through the crowd.

Once she was in the restroom, she heaved a sigh of relief. It was cooler in there, almost peaceful. She could still hear the thump and roar of the music, but it was muffled. "Thank goodness," she said. "You still there?"

"Yeah," Brett said, his voice mostly clear, just a little static.

"What time is it?"

"Uh . . . ten fifteen. Look, babe, I wanted to—"

"Ten fifteen! Oh my gosh, we've only been here an hour? I'm pooped already. How long do you think I need to stay? Don't want to be rude or anything. Everyone's come from so far away. But I gotta say, this going to clubs, drinking copious amounts of alcohol, the meat-market behavior typical of these places? It's not really me." Maggie laughed. "Well, you know that better than anyone, don't you? Honey, I am *so* glad we met."

"Yeah, well . . ."

"I can hardly wait until this is over. Maybe I can drop by after, if it's not too late, and snuggle in bed with you. Oh my goodness, my feet are sore," Maggie said, slipping off her heels, the polished concrete floor cool and soothing under her feet.

"That might be a problem."

"I know, right? I don't know what I'm going to do tomorrow! I don't know why I let my sister talk me into those strappy, sparkly heels to finish off my wedding ensemble. I should have stuck with my original idea and bought those glittery Doc Martens. Nobody cares what you're wearing underneath, and then I'd be comfort—"

"Margaret," Brett cut in. "I need you to stop talking for a minute. Can you do that?"

"What?" Maggie's breath caught in her chest. He'd used her formal name, and his voice sounded strange. "Are you all right? Is everything okay? You didn't get in an accident, did you?"

"No, I'm fine. I just want to—"

"Oh, thank goodness!" A wave of relief rushed through her. "How horrible would that be—you having to hobble up the aisle in your handsome tux on a pair of crutches."

"Can you shut up for a second? I've been trying to tell you something for the last five minutes, but you just keep jabbering on and on."

Wait. Did Brett just tell me to shut up?

"I've been doing a lot of soul-searching the last couple months," Brett said. "And I just . . . I can't do it."

Maggie's stomach lurched as her world, her happy-ever-after future, suddenly swerved off course. She felt both removed from her body and hyperaware of her surroundings, like she was an alien observing the events of her own life. The water dripping from the faucet, the beating of her heart, it all sounded loud, loud, loud. Her mouth tasted like chalk, throat constricted.

"Can't . . . You can't do what?" she asked, but she already knew the answer.

2

"ARE YOU SURE YOU'RE GOING TO BE OKAY?" ROSE-mund Harris asked. There were violet shadows under Maggie's mother's eyes, as if she, too, hadn't been able to sleep for the last three nights.

"I'm totally fine, Mom." Maggie managed a smile. She glanced at the departure display board. Good. Their flight to Tampa was on time. Another couple minutes and her parents would have no choice but to go through security.

Her sister, Eve, had taken the red-eye back to New York last night, and the plane's departure had been delayed twice. While they'd waited, Eve had managed to extract a promise that Maggie would go on vacation with her. Who knew what kind of concessions her parents would've wiggled out of her had their flight been delayed.

By some miracle Maggie had been able to maintain her composure while contacting the wedding guests, canceling what services she could and donating the rest. She still had to contact the store where she'd registered and arrange to return the enormous pile of gifts so credit cards could be refunded. However, first she needed to sort through the

presents so she could personalize the thank-you notes that
had to be written. There was too much to do. No way in hell
was she going to allow herself to fall apart now and start
bawling in the middle of the Phoenix Sky Harbor International Airport.

"I want to kill that son of a bitch," her dad said. Her dad
had always been even-tempered and slow to anger, but he
was angry now.

Maggie dragged her gaze from the departure board to
where her dad stood beside her mom. Bill Harris's large hands,
hardened by years of construction work, were clenched, and
worry had etched deeper grooves in the lines on his face.

"Dad," Maggie said, reaching out and patting his arm,
"really, it's all right." Her parents looked at least five years
older than they had a week ago, and for that alone, she
wanted to kill the bastard herself. "I'm just sorry you flew
all this way for nothing—"

"Nonsense," her dad said, his voice gruff.

"We're grateful we were here," Rosemund said, pulling
Maggie in for a hug. Her mom was small, a tiny bird of a
woman, but seriously strong for a woman of any age, let
alone one in her sixties. All those years pitching in on sites,
running wiring, lugging pipes, installing pot-lights, had
kept not just her mom but the whole family fit.

Maggie felt her dad's arms encircle the two of them. A
part of her longed to give herself over to the comfort of her
parents' support, but she couldn't. She didn't want to shat-
ter. "Not every occasion," her mom continued as if Maggie
weren't standing stiffly in her arms, "is going to be a happy
one. But it's the spending of time, the sharing of experi-
ences, that is the glue that bonds a family together."

The boarding announcement for the flight to Tampa
came over the loudspeaker just in time. Maggie blinked her
eyes hard and pulled away. "You gotta go," she said, her
voice cracking slightly. "You don't want to miss your flight."

There was a final hasty hug, and then her parents left,
turning to wave a few times before disappearing from sight.

3

"DON'T YOU THINK YOU ARE BEING A LITTLE UNREA-sonable?" Brett said, leaning forward and steepling his tanned, manicured fingers on the desk in front of him. *Their* desk. He was smiling that smile that used to make her melt. *Funny how two weeks of hell can change one's perceptions,* she mused. She'd always thought he blow-dried his "sun-streaked" blond hair a little too poofy, but she had never noticed before just how practiced his smile was.

Her sister had. "He's too slick," Eve had said when she'd first met him. "Too smooth. I don't trust him."

Maggie had waved her worries aside. "Are you kidding? He's perfect."

"Yes, and that's what worries me, because *no* one— Maggie, look at me—no one is perfect."

And now, standing in the Camelback East Village office that she and Brett had shared, she saw what Eve had seen all those years ago. Five years and four months of her life Maggie had wasted on this narcissistic, insensitive creep. *A frigging five-year engagement. Ha! That should have been a clue.*

"Just because I decided I didn't want to marry you doesn't mean I don't want to continue working with you. We're a great team. I'm the ideas man and you implement all the details. Take that derelict church, for instance. Turning it into a high-end condo development was a brilliant idea, if I do say so myself. Presales are moving extremely well. Yes, I know you're doing a lot of work, but we're going to make a shitload of money on this one. Comfort Homes is just starting to hit the big leagues. Seriously, sweetie, you're making a mountain out of a molehill."

"First," Maggie said, holding up her hand, palm thrust out like a traffic cop, "I am *not* your 'sweetie.' Second, even you, with your pin-sized brain, must know that calling off a wedding the night before it's supposed to occur would not, under any circumstances, be classified as a *molehill*!"

Brett opened his mouth to speak, but Maggie steamrollered right over him. "If you were having all these doubts, why did you insist on making it such a big event? I wanted something small and intimate, but no! You felt it was necessary to invite *three hundred and eighty-six* friends, family members, and business colleagues to *our* wedding! Some of them could ill afford to fly themselves out here and put themselves up in a hotel, but they did it because they wanted to show us their love and support. My mom and dad rebooked their world cruise vacation because they wanted to be here for our special day. Did that even cross your mind, how you inconvenienced so many people? Then you get cold feet, and you don't even have the balls to stand up like a man and let people know. What a jerk!"

"A guy's entitled to—"

"*You* are entitled to *nothing*. Not after leaving me to make excuses and explanations and to settle the accounts. Oh, by the way, did you and Kristal enjoy our honeymoon holiday?"

Brett blanched.

"Yes, I know all about that. Carol enlightened me. Amazing how loose the lips of everyone at the office got once the shit hit the fan. I gather your little fling has been